Mosquito Sands

By

Jef Huntsman

Belray Books, LLC

This book, and all characters contained herein are fiction. Any resemblance to actual people or real events is unintended. The places found in these pages are real with some adjustment to make them fit the story. Any liberties taken are those of the author.

DEDICATION

This novel is dedicated to two people, my father, JAMES KEITH HUNTSMAN, an alignment and brake mechanic with a short-lived boxing career in prize fighting, who loved to read the old mystery magazines. He was one of the beginning heart patients where the odds were against him. He once wrote a hilarious poem about his bosses in the auto repair business which set him up as the first author I ever knew. Thanks Dad, for teaching me perseverance and determination.

And to my son, KYLE, a boy who stood ten feet high when it comes to dealing with his illness as if it were no more than a friendly thought passing through his life. A true trooper. Son, my love never fades.

Also, by the author
Jef Huntsman

Heart Attack, Yak, Yak

Tattered Portrait

Jamaica Rush
(A Carson thriller)

Bald Cats and Deaf Elephants
(A book of poetry)

Heart Beats

ACKNOWLEDGMENTS

Thanks to all those writer friends in Utah and abroad that I have come to know so well. Big hugs for all your push, handshakes, back pats, criticism, faith, and patience with an old dog still learning new tricks.

As always, teary appreciation toward the sky to my dear mother who taught me the privilege of reading. And to God, who allowed me to have an abundant supply of the smile and laughter genes.

Carson's Cabin

Mosquito Sands

By

Jef Huntsman

Belray Books, LLC

1

Carson

Mosquitoes hung in speckled clouds as we searched the dry swamp for Harold Sim's body. April rain and crazy-warm temperatures had brought out the bloodsuckers early. I couldn't even imagine how thick they'd be by summer. I walked the banks of the Sevier River, slipping on mud and grasping for tamarack bushes. Other searchers spread out across the dry areas. One yelled when she found a Cuervo bottle; a short swallow remained.

This wasn't the type of search I usually did, but there were enough stories swirling around about my recent exploits that the local police had grabbed me to help find Harold. Most forces would discount a civilian recruit, but this town had so few officers any aid was welcome. They even brought me a fresh cup of coffee from the Maverick store in town. Fair enough pay for battling mosquitos and dung, intermixed with mud, while looking for a dead guy.

After twelve years of living in my remote cabin, I was still considered an outsider. Oh, the townspeople were friendly enough, all two thousand and eight of them. I got nods at the store but was rarely invited into town for home-cooked dinners. It suited me just fine.

We fanned out along Fayette Road on both sides of the Sevier River. The brush was thick, and the mud made movement slow. Rabbits and ducks fled in our wake. I watched as a garter snake writhed across still water, escaping our disruption. We came across several islands of dry sand pounded by hooves and littered with cow pies and the occasional weathered beer can. Dense tamarack surrounded the pockets of sand, tiny inlets running through them like a maze. I kept glancing at the sky, searching for circling buzzards—a sure sign of carrion.

Mosquito Sands

I edged around an abandoned salt lick and spotted a partial sleeve of a checkered shirt. Calling out to Heath, the town's only detective, I held up the ripped piece of cloth with a gloved hand. Gloves courtesy of the city.

"Yeah, that's Harold's," Heath said. "He has only two shirts, and I've seen him in both."

I noticed an overturned rock and a scuffle of footprints dug deep into the cracked clay ground. We both squatted down to see if they meant anything. My eyes followed a path through the bushes. It appeared there had been four large boots, the kind that could be used to make waffles. Matted bushes and broken branches prompted me and Heath to follow the trail through a thicket of brush. I could barely see ten feet ahead as I parted the twigs that rose a foot above my six-foot frame.

I entered a sandy, dry tributary from the river, then spotted the rest of the shirt. I rushed toward it, getting slapped in the face by the tamaracks. In a small ravine lay the body of old Harold. Dust caked his open lips. Blood had coagulated after running from a gash on his head, around his ear, and down his neck.

We had searched for about two hours; six hours had passed since Little Jim had confessed to killing him. The police told me Little Jim cried like a baby, blurting out nonsensical words about a fight down by some river. He was so drunk they had to wake him up four or more times to gather any semblance of what had happened. Little Jim and Harold were best of friends and spent most afternoons, into the evening hours, on bar stools in the Horseshoe Bar and Grill at the edge of Gunnison, Utah.

My cell rang. I grunted with irritation and slapped my pocket. *Why the hell did I bring my phone? I never do that.* I answered mostly to stop the ridiculous tune my girlfriend, Maria, had installed. "Highway to Hell" rang through the air as if summoning dark clouds. Heath raised his brow. My eyes panned over to the body.

"Yes," I answered curtly.

"Wow Carson, cut back on the caffeine, man." It was my friend Hub. "I'm at your house, and you're not here. I need your help, like days ago."

"I'm with the deputies searching for Harold. Actually, we just found him." I knelt closer to Harold's body. I could still smell the alcohol; it was as if he'd bathed in tequila. All his top teeth were missing, and I couldn't remember if that was the usual case for Harold. I didn't know him that well.

The deputy read my mind. "He had teeth, probably false."

"*Compadre*, you there?" asked Hub. "Why're you searching for Harold Sims? Have you checked the bars?"

"Let me call you back. This isn't a good time." I noticed Harold's left leg bent at an odd angle. Definitely broken. A dark spot of crimson stained the leg of his Wrangler jeans.

"But I have a missing little girl that needs your expertise. My spiritual teacher —"

"Hub, that sounds serious," I said, taking in a deep breath. "But I've got to go. Let me call you back." I pushed **End** and slipped the cell back into my pocket. I turned to the deputy. "When's the medical examiner going to be here?"

He gazed back at me as if I'd spoken a foreign language.

"Uhhh, let me call." He fumbled for his phone. "Doc Andrews from Richfield is the only one."

"He's at least an hour away," I said, more to myself than anyone.

Four more of the searchers came through the brush, stopped, and stared at Harold's dusty body. One put her fingers on his chest, looking for motion. Her face turned ashen as she lifted her hand and backed away. We waited, hoping to see his chest rise. It didn't.

I leaned closer and put my fingers on Harold's jugular, even though his stillness reeked of death. I felt a faint something. I shook my head. It was probably just the wind over the back of my hand. I grabbed his limp arm and shook it. Nothing.

Someone behind me said, "You shouldn't be doing that. Harold may be dead and drunk, but he's still one of us."

I ignored the comment, shook Harold again, and leaned in close to his mouth, listening for any sign of breath. Harold came to with a spasm and knocked his nose into my cheekbone.

"Harold," I said. Two more people came through the bushes.

He groaned and mumbled something. I put my ear closer to his mouth. "Where's my bottle?" he whined in a low voice.

Everyone clapped, and several patted him on the side. He growled. An officer backed them off in case there were any unknown injuries. I smiled at the thought of how Little Jim would react when he found out he hadn't murdered his best friend. Crazy drunks.

An ambulance arrived, and I headed on foot down Fayette River Road toward my cabin. It was only about five miles. I declined several rides, knowing the morning jog would clear my mind and stretch out some of the damage my second line of work had inflicted on my body. About halfway there, I noticed Hub's truck coming toward me. I eased over to the side of the gravel road by a neighbor's cow pasture and filled my lungs with the morning air.

Hub usually drove like a state employee on the clock, but this time his truck spit gravel and dirt as the vehicle slid to a stop. He stepped out, hair wild and eyes a touch crazy. His arms flailed in front of him as he closed the ten-foot gap between me and him. He left the truck door open.

"I've been trying to find you for an hour," he said. "Who would have thought you'd actually take your phone with you someplace? I headed up the mountain earlier in case you went for a morning run. Nothing. Maria about bit my head off when I called her." His breath was labored as he prattled on.

"What's this big problem you seem to have?" I asked. Hub is my best friend, a wacky shaman with the computer skills of a hacker.

"Juan Diego, the shaman spiritual teacher you met three years ago in Mexico. His daughter is missing." Hub sucked in air through his teeth. "It's been two days and the *federales* have found nothing. He remembered your skills and called me. I told him you'd be glad to help."

I closed my eyes and ground my teeth. "I told you I'm off for the summer. I promised Maria we'd go to California and visit her sister." I tented my fingers to my mouth. I wasn't feeling good about either option. "You know Maria."

"But you owe him."

"What?" My arms crossed my chest.

"Well," Hub backtracked, "I owe him, and you owe me. It works out the same. Maria will understand. Seronia is a lost little girl, Juan's only child."

He was right that Maria had a soft spot for kids, but I couldn't leave her hanging. She has little patience for people who change their promises. Especially since I'd cancelled the last three trips.

"Remember all that computer time I spent last month for you. Not to mention the spiritual acquisitions I obtained. Both helped you find that father."

"Yeah, I know, but . . ."

"And the help John Lennon gave us last year." His eyes pleaded. "Seronia is super-functional, but she's only seven and a nonverbal autistic. She needs our help."

Jef Huntsman

Throwing an autistic young girl in the mix was a clincher, and Hub knew it. I have a soft heart for physiological problems. They are the reason I have money. What started as a chart I developed for doctor's offices to help read psychological aberrations from physical symptoms had turned into an online guide for psychiatrists, physicians, nurses, and hospitals. To my complete shock it had gone worldwide.

Maria might understand. I hoped.

"Let me talk to Maria," I said. "I think I can make her appreciate the situation." I cringed at the thought of her voice responding to my plea. "I need to finish my walk and muster up the courage I'll need."

"I knew you wouldn't let me down." Hub came at me for a hug. "Oh, I booked our flight for tomorrow morning, out of Salt Lake International."

My ears heated. I raised my palms to Hub, warning him to step back, and I began jogging.

2

Seronia—Thirty Days Earlier

Like a dog shaking water from its fur, Seronia raised her arms in a ritualistic morning celebration. Her solid body cast away the demons of her mind. Silhouetted by the sun climbing over the distant mountain, her father, Juan Diego, rested against a tree peeled of its bark. A grin folded the fat of his cheeks. He stood and gazed at the countryside as Seronia's hum echoed into the cool air and vast view. A stream of fog highlighted the river below.

"Seronia, we are almost there. An hour."

She danced on the dirt as if fully ignoring him. He clomped down the hillside, and she followed, a smile pasted to her face. Seronia chirped in sheer happiness as pheasants darted from the bushes to her right in a clawed race to safety. Her soft hands quaked in glee.

The boy lay drenched in sweat. The sheets were too soaked to sponge any more from his fevered, frail torso. His mother, Carlita, forced water down his throat as his eyes rolled back with lost abandon. Juan Diego and his daughter, Seronia, had just arrived and were rushed to the back by two wide-eyed, eight-year-old, twin girls. The mother craned her neck; an expression of hope washed over her face for the first time in days as Seronia and Juan Diego entered the darkened room.

"Sunlight," Juan Diego roared as he began ripping the thin, worn blankets that covered the windows. Rakes of light pierced through the outside trees and brightened the room but did nothing to the horrid smell of sickness and tired old remedies.

Juan Diego was a *curando,* a shaman healer, known throughout central Mexico for his expertise in helping the afflicted. His rounded belly and tree-trunk-thick arms moved with grace and agility. His green eyes had layers to them like the stories and truths that hid deep behind them. His brows were thick, and his hair had rarely seen a comb, but he had that air of knowledge—perhaps even genius. He had trained many new upstarts, including Hubbard Tinning from *Los Estados Unitos*.

Seronia, Juan Diego's only child, was a natural healer with a flair for curing the creatures that resided around her village—a broken-winged hawk, a legless butterfly, even a red-collared lizard that had fallen into a can of gasoline. Her nonverbal autism gave her a shamanistic distance Juan Diego had never seen before. She had been his best student, inadvertently teaching him without speaking a word.

Juan Diego placed his hands over the boy's eyes as they swam for life in a misty glaze fighting toward the edge of consciousness. "Pando," he whispered.

"Will Pando be all right?" the mother asked in Spanish. The words seemed to rattle fear through her tight throat.

With the soft voice of a patient father, Juan Diego said, "Seronia, this boy needs help." He nodded to the boy's frail limbs and bundled knots of swollen skin where toes should have been. The boy gave a birdlike shriek when Juan Diego stroked his damp hair.

Seronia shuffled in short, measured steps to take her place next to the bed. Her neck was turned just slightly. Her eyes strained to the left, staring away from the boy and into a distance only she knew. A right hand crept from the long sleeve of her blue knitted sweater. Her fingers tapped the air as if playing an imaginary piano that drifted like clouds in the sky. Seronia's eyes never left her focused spot. Her right hand touched Pando's ankle and tapped in a fluid, rolling motion like ocean waves on jutted rocks. Her knuckles followed the rhythm.

Seronia's free fist pumped like a flag waving in a stormy wind, tirelessly inconsistent with the right. Her focus stayed off to the side, completely detached from her hands.

Juan Diego plucked arrowhead-shaped leaves from a leather satchel after dropping it from his shoulder. With meticulous care, Juan Diego shaped the tiny emerald leaves into a six-pointed star on the boy's forehead. He then rubbed Pando's jaw in circular motions. Juan Diego's lips moved, but nothing came out.

He turned to the mother. "I need something sweet, a wet cloth, and perked coffee grounds." His Spanish was slow and measured.

"I have only fresh grounds." She spoke quickly in a frantic tone that seemed laced with worry.

"Then boil some water and make some. Take your time. It will be all right."

Mosquito Sands

Carlita raced out after one long gaze at her son. Her eyes had the droopy, dark stare of a mother's heart.

"You are doing splendidly, Seronia," said Juan Diego.

Seronia hummed, the stucco walls of the room absorbing the sweet notes. Her gaze had not left the corner of the room. Her focus seemed to burn through the wall and out to infinity. Her movements never varied.

Carlita came back with a tray. A wet, red dishtowel lay folded on one side. A cup filled with blackish, steaming grounds and a plate with Mexican candy and a heap of sugar sat on the other. She raised the tray and scooted around Seronia.

Juan Diego lifted the dishtowel and folded it into a perfect, tight triangle, tucking in a wedge like the military do with a flag for a widow. He carefully placed it point down below Pando's hairline, making sure not to disturb the pattern of the leaves. From his leather satchel he retrieved a flat stone and a wooden mallet. He set the coffee grounds on the rock then pulled out a clear vial of brownish dust that looked a lot like common dirt. He spread the fine particles of dust on the grounds and began grinding them into the stone with the head of the pestle. Seronia kept up her part of the healing process. Her humming was repeatedly drawn out to her last puff of air, and the single note repeated was after a soft inhale.

The mother leaned against a far wall, the skin of her face tight. "What is that dust?" she asked.

"Shaman-blessed mushrooms."

He picked up globs of the coffee grounds and rolled it into balls in the palm of his hand. As if he were a dentist inserting cotton plugs, he placed the half-inch black orbs between Pando's gums and his lips. When eight of them were perfectly placed, Juan Diego stood back and checked different angles of the boy's mouth. The flesh around his mouth jutted out like rows of mountain ranges. Pando's blank face seemed oblivious to anything that was going on.

Suddenly Seronia began laughing between her sing-song mutterings. Her smile beamed. The movements of her hands became faster and faster thumping on Pando's legs until they were reddened. Her unruly hair drifted over her eyes in black streams. Her chest heaved with excitement. Juan Diego watched with a grin. Carlita's slackened jaw drooped, and her eyes widened.

Juan Diego often spoke fondly of a dream he had had many years earlier, just weeks before his daughter's second birthday as her gift of autism evolved and took away her ability to speak. In the dream, the slight coolness of a cloudy day and the billowy clouds burdened with moisture as high breezes pushed them toward the taller peaks pulled Juan Diego into a restful sleep on the worn seat of his chair at the front of his adobe house. The animals had been fed, and the winter wheat had been tended to. The hustle-bustle of the village was shadowed by the late-afternoon siesta. Seronia had been born three weeks earlier. Her rounded face filled with expressions of awareness and wonder. Her tiny hands grabbed at glistening dust as if it was the most fascinating thing on earth. Under Juan Diego's quivering eyelids, the image changed, and Seronia grew into an unsteady, walking toddler. Her voice, soft and sweet, rang with several words. A smile passed his lips as she peeked up at him and said, *"Papá."* The young shaman's heart swelled.

A faded image opened into colors and twisting wind. Bolts of lightning grew from the ground and shot like arrows into an infinite, blue sky. Juan Diego could see his only daughter in the distance. Her head swelled like a balloon filling with air. Her sweet acorn eyes stared at him as if trying to send a message. The lightning and wind ceased. The bands of color were transparent, hollow, seeming like angel wings surrounding his daughter. She had grown to school age. Seronia gazed to the right and up toward a distant sphere. She roared and walked closer to her father. Her sight never strayed from the glowing sphere. Black smoke streamed from her head, and she sat down cross-legged. Juan Diego said he could taste and smell a sweet fragrance like roses and sagebrush after a rain. He focused on the smell and woke with a jolt.

Later, he told his wife, Perdita, about the dream. She laughed and said, "To you, everything is a shamanistic experience."

"It was an omen, a destiny. All the symbols of a great journey were there. She is better than us. A deep-seeded shaman spirit without any constraints. I saw what I saw."

A cry came from inside. Perdita chuckled again. "I need to tend to the little shaman." She held her hand over her swollen breasts. "She'll need her strength for this gift to come." She teased Juan Diego, but she knew that with his powers he was probably right. She walked inside the house, shaking her head and wondering if she could handle a daughter filled with inner power.

Pando's chest raised in a steady rhythm. The room filled with

Mosquito Sands

Seronia's detached pleasure. Each mumbling note dribbled her now-breathy sounds on the air around the room.

Juan Diego stepped forward, lightly rubbed Seronia's back, and hummed with her. "Okay, Seronia," he said in easy-going Spanish. "You are beautiful. You have done well." He crossed his hands over his chest slightly below his thick neck.

After several more seconds, Seronia backed away and began flapping her arms in glee like a duck rising out of a lake. Carlita backed up so she would not be clipped by excited fingers spearing the air. Then Seronia sat down on the floor and stared at her hands as they opened and closed into tight fists.

With a knowledge kept deep within, Juan Diego pinched Pando's nose to stop any air flow. Pando writhed like a snake under a farmer's shovel blade. He began bucking. His mouth opened and filled with a long suck of oxygen. After a few dissipating heaves, Pando's lids opened. The cloudy film of his walnut-colored eyes was now clear. Blood mapped the white of his sclera. Juan Diego turned to Carlita. "He has the eyes of a bear, powerful and steady."

Over the next hour, Pando's ashen face returned to its normal oak tint. His breathing, though heavy, had a calmness to it, a constant rhythm.

Juan Diego signaled Carlita to follow him outside. Seronia stayed cross-legged on the floor, opening and closing her hands. She seemed oblivious to everything around her, but Juan Diego was sure she knew everything.

"He will begin talking in a day or two," said Juan Diego, "and the swelling in his toes will be down by week's end. I will visit him in the next few days and make sure all is okay."

"But you live so far away. Why don't you and Seronia stay at my cousin's house next door? They have extra beds." Carlita's face twisted with the worried expression of a mother. Her hands couldn't seem to find a place to settle.

"No. I will check on Pando from afar. It is the shaman way." He shifted his weight to the other side. His brow crinkled, and he nodded. "He will feel my presence. Don't worry. You know I have done this for many."

She seemed unsure, but her lips parted. "Yes," she whispered in a weak voice. A late spring breeze whistled through the rafters, and a barn owl took flight.

Jef Huntsman

Juan Diego sat cross-legged under a tree in the shade of its bulbous trunk. His meaty eyelids quivered in rapid blinks. He faced east, away from the game trail that led to his small house. A grin perched on his face. After a deep suck of high desert air, Juan Diego stood and eased his way back to the house.

From the crest of the hill, Seronia laughed and patted Toro, her gigantic pig, with loving care.

3

Carson

My long legs jarred against the forward seat. As the small jet landed across the rough terrain of Mexican soil, a sigh washed across Hub's face. He crossed himself, though I doubt he was ever Catholic. Noodles of heat rose from the desert surface. We were the only passengers left on the plane. The only passengers dumb enough to get dropped off at nowhere, Mexico. My boots clanged as we exited the rickety metal stairway onto the tarmac.

We headed toward the lone hanger where a prop-job lay tilted on its only wing. I couldn't see anyone around. My neck tightened while our jet raced off down the precarious runway as if chased by demons, gaining speed for takeoff. It was great to be off that plane, but where the crap were we? Hub's smile and easy gait did nothing to disperse the anxiety swirling around my gut. Perhaps he was just happy to be on the ground.

Hub explained that we were just outside an unmapped town, forty miles from Balleza, Mexico. Where the hell was his friend Andres, anyway? He was to take us farther into the desert, to the place where Juan Diego lived. I was relying on Hub's plan, which seemed a touch optimistic.

Sweat soaked my collar and chest as I pulled the baseball cap down closer to my brow. The heat invigorated Hub as he held out his arms, raised his face to the sun, and absorbed all that powerful solar energy, as he had put it. I was much less enthusiastic. Sweat dripped from my chin to my collared, white shirt that clung to me like a wet towel. The shade of a lean-to off the hanger dropped the temperature down ten degrees from today's one-hundred-plus. The place was silent and empty. I pulled out my jug of water and drank sparingly.

Three hours passed; Hub's solar glow had been replaced with darting eyes and a magazine fan. The sound of a rumbling engine finally came from our left. I put my fingers on my shoulder-strapped pistol in case the sound didn't signal the arrival of Andres.

A decked-out, black pickup flew over the hill toward us. Five big spotlights perched on top like glass buzzards. The grill smiled with chrome, light flickering off it like a chandelier. The truck slid to within feet of us, churning up a cloud of dust. Hub blurted out, "*¿Que paso mi amigo?*" They ran toward each other like two lost aunts at a family reunion.

"*Perfecto*, you just arrived." Andres said in broken English.

With a raise of my eyes, I wiped my brow on my shirttail and tossed my backpack in the back of his truck.

"You must be doing well." Hub gazed at the truck in admiration.

"You no here for long time," Andres said. "*Mi esposa*, Carmella, buy for me." He folded his arms proudly. "Her *padre* is *rico*, and he no like me, *pero*; he loves his princess."

"Ahhh, for a minute I thought you'd been taking work seriously."

"*Yo trabajo muy seriamente, pero* . . . just not too long. I working for her father now. He owns a . . . *como se dice* . . . sand and dirt business and make me under-foreman." Andres held out his palm and raised his eyes. "Who have thought peoples wanting buy rocks and sand."

Hub tilted his head toward me. Andres shook my hand as if pumping a dry well. We loaded up and took off. The truck had no top, and the air conditioner wasn't any match for desert heat. The way the truck jostled and swerved under Andres' inattention to the dirt road, I was glad to see a roll bar.

Hours later, the fragrance of beans and chilies cooking sliced through the dust as we pulled up to the adobe-and-straw house of Juan Diego. It was one of six houses—huts, really—I could see. Chicken scattered as the dust settled. Trees were sparse, but the garden glowed from obvious care. I eyed an older woman, ancient, sweeping dirt in front of the neighbor's home. Several cows swatted flies with their tails in a corral to the north. We hopped out.

As I edged around the pickup, Juan Diego came out in a large, brimmed, straw hat, dusty pants, and bare feet—his toes curled under like a bear. He quickly pulled Hub into his grasp. They both busted into schoolgirl laughter. When they finished hugging, Juan Diego's eyes met mine, and his smile barreled toward me. I braced for the same reception, but instead he raised his arms and pounded my chest lovingly with his fists. I gazed down. This old shaman with wise eyes was barely four-and-a-half feet tall with the body of Buddha and the hair of Brad Pitt.

"Moses, it is so good to see you again." Juan's English was better than that of an Oxford professor.

"Moses?" I asked. "No, I'm Carson." My brow furrowed, and I glanced at Hub.

"You have a great man in your Bible—Moses. No?" He grabbed my hands. "He parted the waters. You will do the same for my Seronia." He put the palm of his hand against the center of my chest. His eyes held an emptiness as he peered up at me. "I can feel your power and your goodness. I have little money, but I'll pay you in some way."

"Don't worry about that," I said. "I am in debt to Hub, and he is in debt to you. It all works out." I nodded toward his house. "Show me where you last saw your daughter."

He kept his hand on my chest for a few more uneasy seconds, then dropped his arm and walked to the side of his house. A saddened darkness had enveloped his face. I followed.

Juan Diego's arm made a wide sweep toward a shabby wooden pen. "She was tending to the *puerco* in that area. Her favorite, Toro, was sick that day, and she stayed with him in the shade of the trees." He pointed to a giant pig sleeping by himself in the distance. "Seronia's best friend. She had pulled a thorn from his swollen foot that day. I think he misses her too." Juan Diego's eyes searched the crest of the hill. His teeth clamped onto his bottom lip in thought.

"Any strangers around that day?" I asked.

"No, and it would be hard to hide in our scruffy paradise. It happened during the night. She begged me to let her sleep with Toro." Juan Diego gazed skyward. "I thought nothing of it. She spent many nights with her pet. Who wants to visit here?"

Hub came up and patted him on the back. "It's no one's fault."

"Let's stroll out of the sun." Juan Diego nodded to Andres, who headed for his truck. We followed him down a hard, clay path. Two trees that looked petrified guarded the outside of his humble home. Just when I think my cabin is far from civilization, I come across a scattered village that's not even a *part* of civilization.

A cell rang, then Andres spoke in quick but timid Spanish as he scratched at his eyebrow. Within a minute, Andres pocketed the phone and shook his head. "*Mi esposa* say her *padre* is searching for me. He hate when I'm around, and he hate when I not there. I must go." He stormed away in his wife's gift, the balloon-tired fancy truck. A plume of dust soon trailed the rutted road toward Balleza.

Cooking smells came from behind the house: tortillas, tomatoes, cilantro, peppers. Juan Diego slid a dusty blanket to one side, and we entered his front door. Beds lay on opposite sides of the house with a table in the middle. Two logs extended from the clay walls, supporting aged, grey-board shelves. Light from a window brightened a large rug that lay on the dirt floor. The house was unchanged since I had been there years ago with Hub—it was still simple and elegant. Juan Diego sat on the rug, cross-legged, and Hub and I did the same.

"That shelf holds some of Seronia's things." His arm flicked to the left. Sad eyes gazed down. "The rest is in the trunk at the foot of her bed. Search them if you need to."

I waited in thick silence until Hub nodded. I rose and walked to the foot of the single bed. It appeared to be mostly blankets piled on top of a two-by-five-foot box. The trunk held neatly folded clothes with an extra pair of well-worn shoes on top. My thoughts went to the meager amount of girl's things. In the city, she would have had haphazard closets, drawers filled with socks and notes and mementos, childhood toys, and pictures of rock stars plastering each wall. This sparse collection of belongings matched the semi-vacant village she lived in. The village and her autism.

I nodded my forehead at the two slivers of light streaming from the blanket door. "I know it's been some time, but could I look at the pig pen?" Juan sat staring at the single picture on the shelf. His eyes were glazed, glossy, and dark.

"I had a dream the night she disappeared." Juan Diego's gaze stayed riveted on the portrait. "My Seronia hung off a cliff as pebbles struck her in the face and shoulders. Her muscles were tense, and blood dripped from tiny openings on her forehead. There was a voice from above in a language unknown to me." Tears streamed across his pudgy, brown cheeks. His voice broke slightly.

"I awoke in a sweat," he continued. "Not truly awake, still in the dream. Night stars filled the sky as I ran up a plateau toward her. I could see her in the distance, but the distance lengthened with each step I took. She became smaller and smaller, then vanished." His body deflated, and his eyes shut tight. A curl of thick hair fell across his chubby cheeks.

His pain was contagious. I didn't know what to say. I walked out to examine the pen. Loss is such a formidable weapon against yourself.

Mosquito Sands

The pig relaxed in the shade of a scraggly bush. The smell of rotted vegetables, sagebrush, and unwashed beast assaulted me. I opened the gate and tiptoed in, hoping the docile animal would stay asleep. Barn grass crept around a tree in one corner. It was where Seronia had slept with her pig, but there was no sign that she had even been there. Nor was there any sign of a struggle—no ripped cloth, no specks of blood on the slats between the rails. Weeks had passed.

My foot slipped into a lone puddle of mud. I bent down for a closer inspection of the ground. One of Toro's eyes opened, his snout raised, and he made a grunt. "What happened here?" I asked, eyeballing him. His eyes had a devil's fire to them. I quick-stepped out the gate as Toro spun with the ease of a much more agile animal and raced toward me with a lot of noise and swagger. He rammed against the boards. Dust plumed between hardwood slats. I backed away.

"You don't want to play with Toro," said Juan Diego. "He'll take you down like his last meal."

My chest tightened. I thought about his thin daughter sleeping with this giant creature and wiped my brow.

Juan noticed my uneasiness and seemed to read my thoughts. "Seronia took care of Toro beginning with the time he was no bigger than a field rat. He thinks she is family. You are just brunch."

I walked around the dry grounds for a bit and searched for clues. Hub followed as if I knew where I was going. That's the problem with clues: they're not sitting on a pretty shelf. And they were not laying around in this dusty village weeks later. My eyes scanned a couple of clouds too thin to hold more than a drop of water between them.

"Her essential fragrance is gone," said Hub. "I can't even connect to a strand of her aura."

"Search deeper. Into the sounds of the pebbles and straw grass. The old tree by the pen—its bark speaks of her life—her leaning in the shade to watch Toro." Juan Diego's chest filled with air as his eyes closed. "She is still here. Alive. My compass says south, but her scent is thinning."

I nodded as if I understood any of that. With a long-defeated sigh, I said, more to myself, "I've found people with less to go on than this." My voice had no conviction.

"I'll do a deep travel," Hub said.

In Hub-speak, that meant he would dream, probably with the help of peyote or jimson weed. I had never understood Hub's spiritual shaman ways, but I'd found he usually came up with something—especially if he used his incredible hacking abilities. Was internet reception available here? Hub walked toward Juan Diego's house, and I hiked a beaten path to a small plateau overlooking the village.

I gazed over the tiny town. Roughshod homes of adobe and sticks poked up in even lines like gravesites on earth that prayed for rain. Three desert roads meandered out over the hills in the background as if they were snakes escaping in each direction. I could count the ramshackle houses without using all my fingers and toes. There were a few signs of life—hung laundry, smoke from cooking, and furrowed ground. I took in the familiar scent of heat on dry earth. It reminded me of my ranch and home and Maria's sweet smile, which appeared more than people thought.

Scrutinizing the ground, I tried to find some reason for Seronia's disappearance. She had only animal friends, didn't stray far from Juan Diego's home, and visitors would be noticed. Nothing came. I noticed a mud ball had stuck to the side of my shoe. I pried it off with a stick then focused on the town again. My brain clicked. I stared intently at the mud ball. It was black, the color of dark chocolate. My hand had picked it up even though my mind realized what it was. I held it up to my nose for confirmation—putrid human meat. My eyes watered, and my head jerked back. I tossed it back to the ground, thought a second, picked it back up, and hurried toward Juan Diego's home holding the ball at arm's length.

I knew of only one thing with that particular scent. My heart went out to Juan Diego, but he had to know.

I found Hub sitting cross-legged on a rock. A wide-brimmed hat angled down as his neck muscles stretched.

"Hub," I said. "I need your help."

He remained motionless in his bowed position.

"Hub!"

He looked up, his eyes struggling to focus. "You pulled me out. I was almost deep enough." His chest rose and fell in quick spurts. "You know never to disrupt a shaman on a journey."

"Yeah, sorry," I said, placating him without much conviction. "I need your help."

After a short discussion about what I found, Hub followed me over to Toro's pen. He opened the gate and in his mesmerizing voice, coaxed the giant animal out. The pig followed him up the path. Hub spoke to

Mosquito Sands

Toro as if the beast were a distressed friend.

I jumped over the fence and thoroughly searched the ground, focusing mainly on the mud puddle. I dug my hands deep into soft earth and whatever other ghastly refuse was in there. My thumb felt a sharp object, and I carefully lifted it from the miasma. Using spit and my shirt sleeve, I wiped it off enough to know it was a phalange, broken at the tip with enough cartilage to hold the joint between the two pieces. I set the partial toe on a rock outside the pen and searched again. After an hour of searching, I had found nothing but a few rocks and the toe bones. Hub was walking back, and Toro was none too pleased with my invading his pen. I backed up and balanced myself on a corner piling.

Hub coaxed the pig into the pen, stroking his massive head and whispering to the animal.

Juan Diego met Hub and me at the walkway. We all stopped just outside his house.

"That look, it is the face of bad news," said Juan Diego. His mouth hung open and one hand clutched his chest.

The words I needed to say clung like ashes in my mouth. I knew mother pigs ate their young at times, but the idea put a lump in my throat the size of a boot. I watched his eyes slide over to my hand. I slipped it behind my back. I was afraid that I may be holding the last remnants of his beloved daughter. My mouth opened, and nothing came out.

"No!" he said. His head shook in quick, short movements. "Not Toro. *Nunca*." The fatty tissue of his neck throbbed and twisted. "There is a holiness between Toro and Seronia. He would only protect her."

I knew he would never accept this. He'd been the one to let her sleep with the pig. He would forever think it was his fault. "I'm sorry," I said.

Hub eased around Juan Diego and stopped at my side. "Let me see it. If Juan says it couldn't happen, then it's impossible."

Hub knows nothing about human flesh. He hasn't seen the death I've seen. Slow and agonizing death. Quick, explosive death. And the death of the spirit. The death of war.

I knew it would have to be analyzed, but the most likely is the most probable. As I held the ball and toe out to him, I noticed several of the villagers standing around with puzzled looks.

"*Agua, por favor*," Hub said. His hand swiped the air. "I'm not touching that." He meant the muddied toe.

A lady in a white dress and turquoise shawl raced to her house.

Jef Huntsman

Minutes later, she came out with a bowl and a white cloth draped to one side. Hub met her halfway there and asked her to set the bowl on the ground. Hub genuflected and sat cross-legged with the bowl centered in front of him. He gently washed the clay from the black mass. As he did, a wad of Khaki fabric floated and opened at one side as it detached from the dead tissue. It was about a half-inch square.

"What was she wearing that night?" Hub asked Juan Diego.

Juan Diego rubbed his temples then gazed over at the pig pen. A full minute passed. Everyone stood silent. More had gathered, forming a circle of neighbors around the whole scene.

"A white blouse with embroidered flowers around the neck and a pair of blue cotton pants," he said. "She has only two outfits, and the other is folded on her bed."

All eyes went back to Hub. He picked up the tiny swatch of cloth and examined it then handed it to me. "It's heavy fabric, and the mixed colors are military or *policia*. More than likely pants."

I nodded in agreement. *Now all we need is to find someone with a missing toe and a torn pair of pants with a pig bite out of them*, I thought to myself.

Juan Diego howled in celebration. My lips curled upward in agreement, though I knew there are worse fates than death.

4

Carson

Morning light and heat woke me. I gazed around at the abandoned adobe brick *casa* where the desert wind had taken off most of the roof. Stretching, I pulled my knotted muscles out. My face grimaced. Time and floods had laid a floor of cracked clay—hard as cement, but not as comfortable. Before we'd left, Hub and I argued over what to bring. I was glad I triumphed over his idea of "the earth will provide." The earth would have given us one sleepless night without the camping pads. Hub snored in a soft, catlike purr. I nudged him with my foot.

We left the hut Juan Diego had set us up in for the night and followed a deer trail back to his house. The morning was calm and heating quickly. Juan Diego and Perdita fried up *chilaquiles rojos* with a sweet corn flavor and a spicy afterbite.

I noticed detailed, hand-drawn pictures nailed to a wall. "Juan Diego, those are interesting." I pointed. They reminded me of architectural renderings.

"That is Balleza, the town you're headed to. Seronia sees details others miss. We took a trip to Balleza several months back. When we returned, she drew these from memory." He turned away wiping a tear from his cheek.

I gazed closer. The streets formed a path, probably the one Seronia and her father had walked. Each building was drawn in detail, with signs, doors, and window displays. The cobblestone streets had rocks missing and litter in the gutters. A small dog crossed the street in an alley. I could tell by her perfect attention to detail which buildings had brick or wood facades. The pictures were like photographs in pencil. "These are amazing."

"She has talent and an amazing mind," Juan Diego said. "She has drawn every bush and tree on each hill around our village. She is a wonder." His eyes averted to the ground.

We filled our water jugs and packed up. We knew the easiest route was toward the south and figured most people, even kidnappers, would take the easy way.

My gut clenched upon finding out that Hub and I would travel most of the way on horseback with Juan Diego's cousin, Emelio. Emilio smiled, toothless, pointing to two horses tied to a fencepost. He seemed thrilled to have us help herd his sheep to another location on the way to Balleza.

Hub was excited. I wished we had left with Andres, but we hadn't developed any plan before he took off. The only sheep herding I'd ever done was shooing a couple of ewes out of my outhouse. Even though I live in a cabin on a twenty-two-acre ranch, I'm a city boy through and through—a fact I hide from my neighbors and fellow Fayetteites eight miles away. I don't outright lie about it; I just delete my history and deter conversations. The only people I share an abbreviated version of my background are my girlfriend, Maria, and my best friend, Hub.

Juan Diego broke my thoughts. "Big storm coming." He said. "You three need to pass over the *arroyo de muerto* before the sun centers."

I glanced at the clear blue sky and winked at Hub as I reluctantly swung my butt into the saddle. Bucket seats and a windshield would have been better.

"If he says it's going to rain buckets on a clear day in the desert, I listen," replied Hub. He and Emelio galloped up the trail.

I raised my eyes and gave the horse a gentle nudge with my heels. My beast stood still as marble. I slapped the side of my saddle horn. Nothing. I hated horses. Actually, it's a concealed fear. Horses trot anywhere but where I want them to go. I usually end up at a watering trough or rubbed into branches that knock on my butt. With a deep breath, I grabbed the reins tight and kicked the horse's ribs much harder than before. The horse shook its stone head, shot snot out of its nostrils, but it stood its ground. Then Juan Diego slapped the horse on its fanny and the rock turned into muscles raging with blood and spirit. I held on for dear life as bushes sped by in a blur.

Luckily, the horse knew its job and slowed to a trot when we reached the herd of sheep. It nudged them in when needed and flushed out the small lambs from behind sagebrush. My breathing eased. I had little control, but with my back straight I could've posed for a picture of a true sheepherder—minus my khaki shorts and T-shirt.

After a couple of miles, the wind howled, and black clouds rushed in from the west. Emelio yelled in Spanish so rapid it sounded as if each paragraph was only a word. He drew a circle in the air. We needed to bunch up the sheep. My horse crow hopped and disregarded my pull of its reins, but somehow, we forced the sheep into a tight circle. Hub calmed my horse so I could slip off its back. He knew of my previous misadventures with the thousand-pound animals. My eyes probably begged for help. I had no problem taking on three Taliban soldiers, but put a horse under me, and I can barely breathe.

The promised storm hit.

We huddled on the slope of a once-dry mountain under the only four trees in miles. My clothes were no better than a wet towel, but even slipping on the muddy slope in squishy shoes felt better than being on that horse. The rain pelted us for a lifetime, though my cell phone told me only fifteen minutes passed. The clouds raced away, and the noon sun sucked steam from the earth. With considerable coaching, I got back in the saddle again. The smell of wet wool and sagebrush reminded me of my ranch and pleasant times.

We followed the fluffy white mass across the muddy slope. It's ironic: sheep devastate the land with their nonstop grazing, picking at every blade of scrappy grass, and then they fertilize the barren ground behind them. The Bible's reference to humans as the Lord's sheep always baffled me. What a dumb, unthinking beast to be compared to. I can only assume it's proof of God's sarcastic humor.

An hour later, Emelio stopped, circled his arm around, and gazed at the land. Sheep vacuumed the ground. Beyond the white mass, thick brush and yellow grasses filled the hillside above a fertile valley. In the distance, I could see the smokestacks of a small city with large buildings that appeared permanent. Hub and I led the horses to a stream, tied them to a lone fence post, and unloaded the saddles onto the ground. After a brief exchange of *gracias* with Emelio, we headed on foot toward the city. Emelio would keep his sheep there for a week.

Balleza is a city in the state of Chihuahua full of streets and churches, pleasant markets, and cell phone reception. After hiking a mile and a half to the dirt road Emilio had pointed out, Hub called Andres. Forty minutes later, his decked-out truck arrived. I slapped at the mud drying on my clothes out of respect for his vehicle.

"Welcome to my city." Andres motioned with a thumb, directing us to throw our packs into the truck bed. I apologized for taking him from his work.

"My father-in-law hardly no cares if I'm there or not. He glares down his nose at me as if a roach passed across his desk." When Andres smiled, it was all teeth and sparkling eyes. "My friend, Perino, I take you to his car rental."

"Would he have a four-wheel drive?" I asked. "We might have to travel in rough terrain."

He pulled out onto the street. Soft mud flicked behind. *"¿Que?"*

"¿Como camión de tus para los montañas?" said Hub while mimicking steering a car.

"Ah, traccion en las cuatro ruedas." He laughed loud and slapped his chest. "Perhaps, *pero no*, Perino rents *viejo* cars." He chuckled to himself. "Like wine—only time makes them more bitter."

I peered at Hub. He flung his hands out in defeat. "He rents junk."

I simmered on that for a few minutes until we pulled down a lane to a farm. A house with a leaning barn behind it came into view. A well-tended garden took up what would have been the front yard. A lady in a housedress glanced up from the vegetable garden and pointed her hoe handle toward the barn. Andres waved. As we pulled up to the barn, I noticed two old Chevy Novas and the shell of a burned truck up on bricks. My irritation rose. Andres smiled as he stepped from his shiny new truck.

A thin, short man came out of the barn. He flung his wayward hair from his eyes and grinned. Time passed. I listened to Andres and Perino shoot bursts of Spanish, which I lost track of after *"hola amigo."* There seemed to be a lot of catching up to do. Hub and I swatted flies the size of hummingbirds and waited until all rounds were fired. Andres finally turned, walked over, and put his arm around our shoulders. *"Mis amigos Americanos."*

Perino came at us with bubbling chatter and the smile of someone who had lost many a bar fight. I smiled and nodded as if I understood a word he spoke. He spoke rapidly but with a friendliness that swelled like pride. He walked backward and clawed at the air for us to follow.

Inside the barn I was relieved to see two rows of clean, shiny vehicles, a few with plastic tarps over them. I counted eight lined up against two walls. Hertz had nothing over him except for an airport location. Hub glanced at me and grinned, his eyebrows bouncing up and down.

Mosquito Sands

I noticed a Nissan Sentra, a Hyundai Sonata, a couple of Fords, and a Volkswagen Beetle, all about five years old but showroom detailed. Perino pulled the tarp off one that I could tell by the shape was a truck. A fluorescent lime-green Ford F-150 lay underneath. I shook my head. He yanked the cover off another. I glanced at Hub and nodded as I eyed the 2013 or 2014 Jeep Cherokee. A few scratches along one side cinched the deal. I'd probably add to those.

"Does it run?" I asked.

Andres translated. Perino's mouth slackened. The tone of his voice said, "What a stupid question."

Perino jumped in the black Jeep, rifled through the glove box for a key, and within moments the vehicle purred to life. He shut it off after listening to a local station with his fingers beating on the dash to the music. Perino jumped out with a grin that could power New York for a month and tossed me the keys.

Hub leaned close to me. "Do you think he offers insurance?"

I lowered one eyebrow and shook my head.

"He should," Hub whispered. "Cause we're going to beat the hell out of that thing."

"*Cuánto dinero?*" I asked.

Perino held up two fingers. "*Veintiuno* American dollars *por semana.*"

I thought about that ridiculous amount: twenty-one dollars for a whole week. In the United States you couldn't rent a hand drill for that. "I'll give you a fifty. *Cincuenta.*" He didn't argue. Hub nodded and said, "No, a hundred. *Cien.*" Perino smiled and hugged us as if we'd hauled him from a sinking boat.

Hub slipped him four fifties saying, "Dos semanas."

"I take you to the right place?" Andres patted his chest.

"Never a doubt," I said.

Hub pulled the Cherokee out of the barn, and I hopped in. Andres parked his beast of a truck alongside. Andres seemed to know people, so I asked him if he could check on any other missing girls or boys in the area. He thought about it for a time. Finally, his eyes rose to the sky and he said, "*El suegro* is best for that." He twirled his finger in the air. "*El suegro sabes todos,*" he said with a disgruntled raise of eyebrows.

I peeked at Hub.

"His father-in-law thinks he knows everything."

I looked back at Andres. He nodded. With a roar of RPMs, Andres took off. We'd driven about a half a mile toward the hotel we'd picked out when we spotted Andres's black truck barreling our way. He passed us in a cloud of dust. I watched as his vehicle fish-tailed and headed back toward us, honking and waving. Hub pulled over and put the Jeep in park. Andres jumped down and headed our way, a smile glistening through the dust.

"*No mi recuerdo, el suegro* is having *fiesta grande* tonight. *Comida, cervesa, vino, todos los cosas.* You come. You ask him what you want. He likes to feel like a . . . How you say? Big man? I tell him you are private eyes. He loves Magnum. He may think I am *el payaso, pero* me inviting you two, *tener buena opinión de Andres.*"

"Magnum?" I asked.

"It's not Spanish. You know—Tom Selleck, the actor. He played in an old show, *Magnum P.I.*" Hub responded.

"What, who?" I questioned.

Hub peeked out to Andres. "Can you believe Carson's as smart as he is and never watches television? Doesn't even own one."

Andres gazed down his nose at me in disbelief. He shook his head then turned back to Hub. They spoke for a minute about directions.

I let it go. I wasn't about to explain to him that I wasn't a licensed investigator.

Back at the hotel, we shaved, showered, dropped mud-caked clothes off to a lady the owner told us washed laundry, and headed out to eat.

My assumption was that whoever had taken Seronia would pass through the nearest town, Balleza. But they could have headed the other way toward Semachic in the north. That was four times the distance. Seemed unlikely, although I've found some kidnappers do just the opposite of easy—some because they're incredibly smart, and others because their skulls house the activity of a watermelon. The most likely routes are usually the right answer. I explained this to Hub.

Hub's eyes widened, and he looked like an excited child. "I had a total manifestation while in the shower. I'm not sure why I waited to tell you, but this is so confirming." He began tapping his fork against his empty plate. "She passed through here. I first thought she was with two men, but my heart felt three. Finally, it occurred to me. One, the third one, was younger—maybe Seronia's age."

I grabbed the fork from Hub and laid it down at the side of his plate. The constant tapping was driving me crazy.

A slight pout formed as he stared at the fork. "They're heading west," he continued. "It was the pelting of water. The shower. I could see through a windshield the heavy drops of a cloudburst. Wipers on a constant beat. She had a puppy in her lap, curled tight. The glare of shop lights reflected off the window. The motor hummed as it passed through a city, and a faint whisper repeated *"got-a-pay."* Hub reached down for the fork. He caught my glare and rested his hand on the table, fingers drumming softly.

"Got-a- pay? Sounds like we're right on their tail," I said, a bit too sarcastically based on the way Hub tucked his chin. Cords of muscles tightened his face. I knew I should have kept my thoughts to myself. His damn shaman stuff irked me, but he always hit just outside the bullseye with enough scattered punches to lead us somewhere.

Hub stretched his neck. "I wonder if the voice was John Lennon again . . . but a different tempo. Rough. Could it have been . . .?" Hub clapped the flat of his hands several times like those wind-up toy monkeys with the cymbals. His grin widened, and he held out his pointer finger to me. "It was either Janice or Jerry. I'm sure of it."

We'd been through this before. He always thought his messages from the other world came from dead rock stars. I gave him a fake smile and nodded. So, Janice Joplin or Jerry Garcia had told him—"Got-a-pay."

Hub tilted his head, eyebrows raised, and said, "Got-a-pay. What's it mean?"

I shrugged my shoulders.

"You're the tracker. You understand these kinds of people." He sipped his coffee. "Think about it. It must stand for something. Who pays? What kind of pay? A ransom?" He stirred a glob of ketchup into a design on his plate. "Juan Diego couldn't pay anything."

I signaled the waitress for the check and thought about the hard facts. If Seronia was taken, there wasn't a scuffle unless you count a bite from the pig. Seronia had only one friend—that friend was accounted for and as surprised as everyone else. Juan Diego couldn't pay anything unless they wanted the healing magic of an old shaman, which in this area might be worth a great deal. But they would have taken him, not his daughter. Seronia had no verbal skills; was super smart; had the uncontrollable hand movements of most autistics; related mostly to her pig, Toro; and had never left the village for extended periods. She didn't seem like a great pick for an abduction, unless they came for someone else and took her by mistake.

Jef Huntsman

The bill lay on the table. When did that happen? Hub hummed softly and stared out the window as if trying to gain focus. I picked up the check. Hub noticed and yanked it from my hand.

"This trip's my treat."

5

Carson

Outside, the heat stifled even the birds from singing. We split up. Hub went to the police station. He seemed to have a way with the *federales* and all other government workers. I never understood it, but most would tell him things they withheld from their spouse. I strolled down two blocks to the newspaper office.

El Sol Periocico had a space barely wider than the door. Through the door's window, it looked more like an alley than an office. A lone bald man leaned back on the chair's rear legs and propped his feet on a short bookshelf. He was on the phone and skimming through a stack of papers that rested on his lap. As I entered, he eyed me and nodded. A swamp cooler in a far back window howled as if demons were escaping. I shut the door and waited for him to finish his phone call.

After a few more shuffles of paper, he clicked the phone off. He rubbed his chin and examined me. *"Americano,"* he stated without like or dislike. *"Habla Espanol?"*

"Muy mal, pero a veces, asi," I said in slow, deliberate words.

He set the papers on a shelf and swung his feet to the floor. The front legs of the chair landed with a thud, as he laughed. "You Americans." His voice had the high pitch to which Spanish changes when using English. "All that money you spend on schools, and all they teach is English. Like that's the only language in the world." He shook his head then raised his chin in pride. "My son who is twelve years old speaks Spanish, English, Portuguese, and is learning Japanese."

"That's impressive," I said.

"No, it's as it should be. Two things cause wars: religion and language. I'm not letting him leave the church." He crossed himself. "But he's going to be able to speak to a lot of different people, and he's going to know about different religions." He stood straighter, his eyes gazing at me over the top of wire glasses.

"I can't argue with you there." I held out my hand, "My name's Carson."

"Is that a first or last name?"

"Just Carson."

He thought about that for a few seconds. "Okay. I'm just Garcia."

I liked this guy. He had a way of putting down *Americanos* and embracing them at the same time. "Garcia, I'm searching for someone— a girl."

"Aren't we all," he said. "I found Angelina *viente-uno anos* ago. She gave me these wrinkles, but I love her more than life." He rubbed his face.

"No, not that kind of girl. Seronia is missing. Abducted, probably. I'm trying to help her get back home."

"Where's she from?"

"Northwest. A village called *Dedo Del Pia.*"

"Juan Diego's daughter?" His mouth opened then curled into his teeth as he held his chin. "I didn't know she was missing."

"You know her?"

"No, just Juan. Everyone knows Juan Diego. He's a legend around here." He looked as if he was in pain.

"Do you know if anyone else has been abducted in the area?" I asked.

Garcia walked over and sat in his chair. He clicked through his laptop without speaking. The noise of the cooler echoed through the narrow space. The cool air brought a chill to my bones, and I rubbed my arms. The howling air conditioner and the tapping of computer keys created their own silence. Minutes passed.

The tu-tu-tu of a printer made me turn. Paper poked out from the side and curled into a tray. I leaned over and glanced at it. The face of a young boy with hope in his eyes stared back at me. He was holding a soccer ball in his arm and you could see the field behind him. Another page began printing. Garcia rose, reached across the narrow aisle, and retrieved them. He handed them to me.

"These are the two I know about. Both from the *Valle de Zaragoza* to the west." His eyes were solemn, and he bit his lip for a second. "Missing the same day, just more than three weeks ago. Pederno Julio Alverez and Juan Lopez. The parents of both found their beds empty in the morning."

Mosquito Sands

The articles I held were in Spanish. I could make out a few words but couldn't tie them together. "Any signs of a break-in or any leads?" I asked.

Garcia shook his head. "Some of the locks here you could open with a toothpick." He read the pages while I waited. "One neighbor heard a muffled scream. She thought it might have been a cat."

We exchanged cell numbers with the promise to keep each other informed. I shut the door, and an unoiled moan followed me out. Hub had the Jeep, so I walked back to the hotel. I thought about the similarities: three kids, all around ten to thirteen years old, abducted at night, all in the lower part of Chihuahua, and no signs of a struggle except for a long cry that could have been a cat. Even with no more than these slim facts to go on, I felt they were related.

Hub arrived back at the hotel around four. The police had told him about the two I knew of and one other, a fourteen-year-old who had run away three times before. He had always returned home four to five days later. He'd been missing two weeks. His parents weren't overly worried.

The fiesta tonight was at six. We decided to get ready. I hoped that Andre's father-in-law would know more about the kidnappings. Andre said he was well connected to everyone.

6

Seronia

Seronia let out a short burst of childish laughter that echoed through the trees. Their home glowed backlit by the setting sun. A stream of smoke corkscrewed into the air from the aged, brick chimney. The smell of rice, cayenne, and broiled chicken crawled the hill toward them. Seronia flapped her arms and wiggled her shoulders in glee. The hooves of their barely manageable appaloosa, Bandito, clopped in quickened patter on the hard, clay trail. The sagebrush dusted in the horse's wake.

Juan Diego put his foot in the stirrup and dropped down off the saddle. The dry earth puffed in front of his horse corral; a lean-to surrounded by grey knurled posts that squared hardly large enough for two lengths of his appaloosa. He helped his daughter onto the ground. She slid from the saddle still flopping her arms around like newly discovered wings.

Seronia never actually ran, but she hurried to her best friend, Toro. Her jaw jutted forward, leading her feet almost by a stride. Toro the pig snorted with excitement. Seronia eased the gate open and plopped down in a patch of mud next to her pig. Her laugh filled the air. She patted him with the palm of her hand hard enough to put out a fire. Toro twisted his fat neck and made a gurgling sound through his wide nostrils. Saliva sprayed out as if from a burping shower nozzle.

With a closed-mouth chuckle, Juan Diego led Bandito inside the tiny horse corral. Perdita came around the side of the house, a spoon in one hand. With the other hand, she wiped her checkered apron and waved. Within seconds, Juan Diego and Perdita embraced, angling in to adjust for their well-fed bellies. He patted her lovingly on her behind. She looked over his shoulder and groaned as Seronia rolled with the pig on soaked earth.

After a sponge bath and dinner, Seronia grabbed her father's hand

and pulled him out to the yard and over to Toro's pen. She pointed to Toro, her chin nestled into her chest. She angled her head to the side and lifted one shoulder into her ear—her way of saying *please.*

Juan Diego let out a stream of held air. "You want to stay with Toro tonight? Yes."

"I can tell you missed him." He glanced back at the house with a weary look. "I'll make it right with Mama." He immediately grabbed his pitchfork and loaded hay into the pen.

She let out a screech and Juan Diego opened the latch and let her in.

Seronia had slept with her pet pig on *special* nights since She was two years old and Toro was a newborn. He was her best friend, and she spent most of her time with him. Coincidentally, her autism had developed just before Toro's birth. Perdita hated these *special* nights. She would shake her head in discomfort and try to understand the connection the two had. Toro would have been slaughtered years ago, but Juan Diego couldn't do that to his only daughter.

The lights went off in the adobe cottage. Seronia fell fast asleep on a mound of straw cuddled next to her friend. Juan Diego brought out a wool blanket and covered both of them against the cold desert night. A sliver of a moon cast blue light and shadows over the hills, arroyos, and sagebrush.

The moon was halfway across its path when the motor stopped on the mountain crest above the village.

Three figures exited an F-150 truck with the speedometer rolled over and rust-bearing teeth curled around the fenders. The silhouettes had long hair and were short in stature. One pulled out binoculars and scanned the village below. A pack of coyotes howled in the background.

The sights of the three focused on the two-room house, the sleeping horse, and the pig pen. After they assured themselves all were asleep, the three crept down the mountain hump. Two had stubby pistols in baggy pockets. The other had a knife with a six-inch blade tucked into a leather sheath and strapped to her belt. Between them, they carried rope, a pair of handcuffs stolen from a *federales* cruiser, a sock, and a tiny leather bag of blue dust. The dust was to be used as a last resort.

The leader—Trueno, named after thunder by their crazy queen, *Dama Seis Cielo*—led the way to the yard. The other two, Mari and Sandoza, fanned out around the house. Making less sound than a caterpillar feathering across a leaf, Trueno quietly opened the front door and padded across the hardened dirt floor on bare feet. Her eyes adjusted to the dark quickly, and she moved catlike as she searched the small home. She peered in at the two lumps under covers in the tiny bedroom. Trueno slipped back into the main room, searching. Her heart pounded at a quickened pace. It was a wonder no one could hear her in the room.

A puzzled scowl crossed her lips. She gazed at the two adult figures in the one bed then peered over to the small, empty bed. In frustration and with her temper mounting, she crept out of the house and closed the door as if it never opened. She stormed through the open gate. Her arms wrapped tightly to her chest as she sucked in full gulps of crisp air. Mari and Sandoza came to her side, their foreheads crinkled.

"Where the hell is she?" Trueno whispered in street Spanish through gritted teeth. "Did she go to a friend's house?"

The two other girls remained silent, with good reason.

Trueno bumped Sandoza with her shoulder. "Search the horse corral." Both girls took off in a quiet gait. While the others searched the corral, Trueno walked around the house, scanning the blue glaze of the darkened village. The moon shadows were long and unrevealing. As she circled to the front of the house again, she slapped her forehead. Her reptilian eyes scanned to the left. A lone tree with bare branches hovered over an aged timber pen.

A snort came from the pig pen. Trueno raced through bluish darkness toward the tree that rose above the ancient enclosure. With a catlike leap, her hands caught the top rail. She raised herself up on the second rung of the stall. A darkened smile filled her face. Sandoza and Mari came out of the shadows of the corral. The lone horse eyed them through a bushy forelock.

Twirling a finger, Trueno signaled the others to join her. She stepped down off the boards and met them fifteen feet away from the pig pen.

In a low voice, Trueno said, "She's in the pen with a gigantic pig. We'll have to get her out and away without waking the pig. That filthy beast could swallow a cow in one bite." Her eyes widened. She put her hand to her mouth in thought.

"Let's go get her," said Sandoza. She stepped up one rung on the pen.

"*Idiota.*" Trueno pointed to the ground at her feet. "*Aqui.*" Sandoza moved back, her head slightly bowed. "The animal's as big as a bull. And they eat anything."

Trueno dropped to her knees. With her long index finger, she drew out a plan, explaining as she marked the earth. When she was done, she erased the lines and crosses with the flat of both hands. She stood.

The three edged over to the pen's gate. Mari carefully unwound the rope that laced the gate shut. As if opening the gates of hell themselves, she inched the gate open. Her breath held deep in her lungs. The pig snorted. They all stood still as statues, holding their breath. The chirp of crickets seemed to explode from nowhere. A veiled cloud swung across the moon, darkening the ground like a warning. The pig rolled the folds of fat on its neck in a slight stretch then settled in comfort. The only sounds were the muffled snore of the pig and the chickens scratching the ground in the yard. With a signal from Trueno, Mari eased the gate open.

Mari's blood surged like a river that could be heard clear to the house. Finally, with a short inhalation, Trueno nodded to an anxious Sandoza. The two padded into the stall, bumping into each other on the uneven ground. Trueno bent down and carefully pulled the small portion of the blanket that was embedded between the hind legs and pink belly of the pig. Her breath held still as a corpse.

Seronia's hair cascaded down her shoulder and into the warm mud. Trueno positioned herself at Seronia's shoulders. Her hands hovered inches from the tucked arm as she waited for Sandoza to stand at Seronia's feet. Sandoza signaled to her after folding the blanket back to expose the dirt-crusted ankles and toes. The travel and bath had put Seronia into a deep sleep, which was rare for her. Trueno mouthed, *"Uno, dos, tres,"* and their fingers eased forward.

With speed, months of forced muscle training, and youthful agility, they grabbed Seronia by her feet and underarms. She weighed more than they thought, and they hustled to grab for better handholds. Seronia's eyes opened and a puzzled look crossed her face, then her mouth tightened, and she kicked her powerful legs. Sandoza fell onto the pig's solid hip. A loud grunt erupted, and the pig lifted its massive head. Devil eyes turned toward the intrusion. Trueno had hold of Seronia's underarms and began dragging her out of the pen. Sandoza had lost her grip on the girl's legs but followed as if chasing windblown paper.

Sandoza slipped sideways. She pushed herself up from the massive body. Her eyes met those of the pig. Adrenaline and fear surged through her body. She rolled to her knee and stood as her hands seized Seronia's kicking foot. Seronia screamed. The pig lurched forward like a demon barreling out of the earth. The pig's snout jolted, mouth open, and saliva flung to one side. Dark, marble eyes under pink folds of flesh burned into Sandoza's frightened eyes.

Trueno was part of the way out. Seronia began to let out a glass-shattering scream. Trueno, still pulling to escape the stall, stuffed the loose, flapping blanket into Seronia's wide-open mouth. The sound, like a long bird squawk, muffled into a hum. Sandoza's fingers pushed at Seronia's bare feet, inches from the gate posts.

The pig sunk its teeth into Sandoza's foot. Sandozo let go of Seronia; on two hands and one free leg, she tried feverishly to escape the beast. Teeth gripped her ankle. Sandoza cussed fiercely and kicked at the pig's snout. Toro lost his hold. Free from the pig's grip, Sandoza moved forward. Seronia was the furthest thing from her mind, but she watched her feet drag out the open gate. Sandoza drowned in sweat and anxiety. She had only a short distance to go.

Mari yelled to get out. Sandoza saw the gate begin to close. Her crushed foot wobbled with no control. She hung on to a post and hobbled toward the gate. As her fingers reached out and grabbed the boards, she felt her leg yanked back. The beast had her pained ankle in its powerful jaws. Sweat streamed down her face. With every cell in her body she tried to free herself. With arms stretched, she glanced back. The pig clamped deeper onto her ankle. A frightened guttural sound echoed from her lips. She dug in with her only foot on the ground and pulled with weakened arms. The pig bit into bone. Blood gushed through the pig's yellow teeth. She heard a snap.

Sandoza slid her leg forward to run as her body's momentum sent her onward. A burst of excruciating pain hit as her severed bone dug into the dusty clay earth. She fell midway through the gate curling up in unbearable agony. Blood oozed through the mud packed on her severed ankle.

Trueno watched in horror as the pig shook the bone and meat hanging from his mouth.

Mari reached down and yanked Sandoza away from the gate. With strength and agility she didn't know she had, she shut the gate, and jammed a thick stick between the gate and the ground. The pig rammed the gate. It inched open. Mari braced an angled board against the gate. The adrenaline surging through her bloodstream kept her focused. The pig snorted and rammed the gate again. The gate held, but Mari wasn't sure how long it would continue to do so.

Trueno hauled the blanket-wrapped Seronia away from the house.

Mosquito Sands

No lights had turned on. Seronia's hands were bound in the blanket, but her feet kicked Trueno like a wild mustang. Trueno glanced back at the tiny house to make sure the disturbance hadn't wakened anyone. There were still no lights or motion. An evil grin crossed her face.

The village lay quiet, a trim of sunrise graced the contour of the hills thirty miles away. Trueno limped toward the truck, her ankles sore from the constant bashing she had received from her prisoner. She struggled up the hill with her package and didn't look back to see if her companions were coming. Seronia's muffled screams and bucking kicks continued relentlessly. The cords of Trueno's arm and neck muscles stretched to their limit. The last of the night's coyote howls sang through a dawn breeze.

Mari helped Sandoza up the hill, keeping her torn leg elevated from the ground. She cradled her with both arms as they crept along the angled path. Tears rolled down Sandoza's cheeks. An agonized grimace masked her face. She was afraid to make any more noise than a low, never-ending moan. Her leg hung, bit off above the ankle; packed mud was the only thing slowing the stream of blood. Mari had placed a dusty stick in Sandoza's mouth, and her teeth clamped tight with pain. Both girls sucked in desperate gasps of air. Sleeping sage grouse stirred and darted from patches of brush in front of them.

Above Mari and Sandoza, Trueno clubbed Seronia with a rock to get her to slump into a mass she could control. Lifting her into the ancient truck bed, she wrapped duct tape around the limp body and blanket and used a box knife to cut a hole in the blanket where Seronia's mouth should be. A trickle of blood colored the threads of the grey tape and crawled down Seronia's chin.

Trueno drummed her fingers as she waited for Mari to carry a semi-conscious Sandoza over the hill. She didn't go back down to help. Mari's back curved from the hundred plus pounds of immobile flesh and bone. A thin trail of Sandoza's blood dripped into the dry earth and was immediately swallowed up. Her head lolled to one side, and Mari strained to keep her upright. She tripped, and they both dropped to the ground with a thud. They stayed in a lump, still as a headstone.

7

Carson

We arrived at a large ranch surrounded by desert palms and thick brush. The sun would not dip below the horizon for a few more hours. Cars were everywhere. We parked about a block away, next to a dry riverbed. The humidity glued my collar to my neck as we walked. I used my fingers to shake the collar like wind on a clothesline. It didn't help.

The lift of chatter and music grew as we approached. A young girl with a smile made for welcoming handed us two *cervezas*. I nodded, and we strolled in further. A four-piece band played their version of nineties rock-and-roll from the far corner. Lights laced the trees, and an aroma of grilled meat and corn wafted through the large, flowery bushes. The buffet lay in the center—the busiest spot on the expansive grounds. Andres stood off to one side, his arm draped over a handsome lady with long, curled hair. He prattled with two other couples. His free arm was animated like a mime. We headed his way.

Andre's eyes caught mine; he turned in mid-sentence and broke from the group. He grabbed both of us by our arms and steered us toward his group. "*Mis amigos Americanos*," Andres blurted with pride, "Hubbard Tinning and Carson, the real Magnum P.I."

Before I could explain that I wasn't a private investigator, they surrounded me and patted me on the back, uncomfortably fondling me like a new puppy. Rapid, inquisitive Spanish blared at me. I glowered at Hub to get me out of this friendly torture. Hub raised his hands in surrender and chuckled. This Magnum guy must have been some kind of hero. I nodded and smiled graciously as if I understood. Andres grabbed me by the arm as he explained something to the group. I followed with relief. Hub disappeared further into the party.

Several men stood in front of what looked to be a gazebo with thousands of lights. They were in white linen suits, all with the posture of importance, speaking in loud, short bursts. It had the air of an outdoor business meeting—money discussed with power at the helm.

Andres tapped on the larger of the four men's shoulders. The man gave a furtive glare at Andres then kept talking as if Andres were no more than a light breeze.

"*Señor* Mancera," Andres interrupted. *"Este es el Americano te dije sobre."*

The big man turned. A toothy grin appeared below a well-trained mustache. His eyes glistened as he stared at me. A downward curl of his lip told me he was puzzled. He stared at my blonde hair, then dropped his eyes, scanning my stature the same way a cowboy checks an auction horse. Uncomfortable again, I wondered if the party was such a good idea.

To hell with it. I held out my hand to shake. I waited. He grabbed it with both hands, pulled me forward, and gave me a hug.

Finally, *Señor* Mancera stood back with one hand on my shoulder. *"El P.I."* He turned to his friends. *"El P.I. de los Estados Unidos."* They welcomed me into their group. Andres shadowed behind, his face long.

I reached back and pulled him toward me. "This is my friend, Andres."

Even the father-in-law approved of him for that moment. Andres glowed.

"Pardon my manners," *Señor* Mancera said, "I forget you Americans know only one language."

Another hit on the stupid Americans. I tried to redeem my failing. *"Yo hablo espanol, pero no estan bueno como todos ustedes hablan inglés."* It's always good to pay someone a compliment about their English in a foreign land. My birth language is muddled in complexity. My hat goes off to the world teachers and governments that understand it.

"I am Eduardo Mancera." He patted his chest. With a gesture of his head he introduced the group. "Enrique, the Mayor of Balleza, Felipe, Ernesto, and Tomás, my business associates." Eduardo turned, searched, then pointed out an aristocratic lady in a lavender-and-salmon, striped dress who was holding court with other ladies in the distance. He put his hands to his heart. "The love of my life and the pain in my ass." His group all laughed. "I assume Adelina says the same of me."

After a lull, Eduardo asked, "You are an American P.I.?" The group gathered expectantly around me.

"I'm not a P.I.," I said. "I'm just looking for a missing girl for a friend."

Eduardo held his hands out as if to catch a ball. "Ahhh, undercover. I understand." He winked at me, and his friends nodded.

"No, I'm—"

"He's looking for Juan Diego's daughter," Andres cut in. "He has questions for all of you."

More agreeable nods. They seemed to relish the idea of being questioned by an American P.I., even one who wasn't a P.I. The silence persisted a bit too long for me. I assumed if they knew I was just a psychologist rancher without animals who sometimes tracks people down, I would be viewed as a quack. I decided to go with the façade.

"Do any of you know of any children who have disappeared in the area?" I asked *Señor* Mancera to explain my question in Spanish to Felipe. At that, they all came alive, all talking at once. The mayor told me about the two I knew of from the newspaper office and several others. I assumed half were runaways and the others were possibilities. I also found out about two missing cows and an eighty-seven-year-old butcher who had disappeared a year ago without a trace.

They all wanted to know about Hawaii. I couldn't understand their excitement for a place I'd stopped at for only a few days when I was in the U.S. Marines. Exasperated, I explained Fort Sumpter in Oahu—the plain buildings, airstrip, and a touch about a briefing I'd had. They couldn't believe that I'd never gone to the beach or that I didn't know any ladies in swimsuits.

Eduardo Mancera leaned in close to my side. "Do you need a pistol? The laws are very strict on bringing guns into my country."

I had wondered about weapons if we got into a tight situation. "Yes." He seemed pleased. He grabbed my arm and escorted me away from his friends.

His house was a delight, airy with tall windows and spacious uncluttered floors of bamboo. Walls of sea blue and banana yellow framed a wide hallway with an oak door at the end. He took out a ring of keys and fumbled through them. With a glint in his eye, he found the right one and opened the deadbolt. With a flick of a finger on the light switch, metal objects sparkled to life. He led the way.

My mouth dropped open. A wall of swords and knives from ancient dynasties and Mayan civilizations were displayed in symmetry as though at a museum. To my left were the instruments of bullfighting—a cape, several lances, a row of *banderillas* (barbed sticks), swords, and a glittering costume of a matador. I turned to watch *Señor* Mancera opening one of the rows of drawers just below a glass display section of ancient rifles and one 90mm M20 bazooka from the Korean war.

Mancera reached into the drawer and pulled out a 9mm Makarov. "What do you think about this one?"

I shifted my weight to my left. "The Russians make a good pistol, but I've never liked the grip. What else do you have?"

He stood back. I peeked into the drawer. Rows of pistols and revolvers slept like dead soldiers on black velvet. He had an impressive collection, all angled with the grip down and the barrel up. I glanced back at him. His neck raised straight, chest out, a proud peacock who loved to show off his special room.

"Any of these you don't want to sell or loan?"

"They are in the other drawers. I'll show those later, so you can know what you missed." His finger touched the corner of the open drawer. "These are for firing."

I reached in and lifted out a Beretta 92f. The weight balanced perfectly. I felt the gun oil caress my palm as I lifted it up and slid the hammer back. "Bullets?"

"Of course, 9mm ammunition is like stray cats. They're everywhere."

We spent another hour in his weapon room while he showed me his other drawers. The pride never left his face.

When we returned, the party bustled. More people had arrived. The singing— off key and drunkenly loud—caused me to scrunch my face. I usually loved the soft melody of Spanish music, but this was somewhere between rusted doors and cats in heat. They were better with their old top forty.

I excused myself from *Señor* Mancera and headed toward the bar, where I had spotted Hub talking to a woman. She had short, thick hair and the conversational ease of a diplomat. I asked for red wine, and I motioned Hub to meet me with a shift of my head. After a few minutes, Hub joined me by a gurgling fountain, ten feet from the bar. I watched two uniformed police officers wander the crowd.

"You ready?" I asked.

He cocked his head as if I was crazy.

"I've learned about all I'm going to here." I waited a beat. "And I'm tired." The gun was scraping an old wound in my backside—and no matter how well you conceal, someone will notice. I didn't need the questions.

He looked back at the lady to whom he'd been talking. "Olivia there has had a light experience—three, to be exact. She's enchanting and mysterious. I've got to find out more." He reached into his pocket and handed me the Jeep keys. "You run along. I'll find my way home later." His brows rose up and down.

I wasn't sure what a light experience was, but I'd heard him mention it before. Something shamanistic, I presumed. I said goodbye to Andres and spent another hour trying to pry myself gracefully away from *Señor* Mancera, who wanted to talk about Magnum P.I. episodes and Hawaiian nights.

At the hotel, I stuffed the Beretta deep into my backpack after dropping it in a sock. The overkill of a hundred rounds of ammo went into hiding places on the truck; I stuffed a handful into the backpack. After bunching up pillows, I read a few pages from *Leaves of Grass* by Walt Whitman and fell asleep.

I blasted awake as the door splintered to the whirr of bullets singing through.

Carson

The first bullet hit the desert landscape picture above my head. More followed at an even keel to my left. I rolled to my right. Instinct. No thought. The second pass was lower. The pillow that my head had laid on seconds before burst and feathers danced softly to the floor.

I yelled to Hub. No answer. Seconds passed. Adrenaline seared through my veins. I thought about the Beretta buried in my pack on the other side of the bed, and I lizard-crawled toward Hub's bed. Bullets whizzed overhead. My eyes scanned the door, hoping I could make it before the shooters burst in. My mind spun as I reached the other side of the bed. I reached up on Hub's bed. He wasn't there. My hands passed over wet sheets. Animal logic told me not to raise my head. My heart pounded, and I sucked in deep breaths through gritted teeth. I heard the snap of a reload.

My eyes caught the shape of my pack under a table that separated the two beds. The lamp on top was shattered, and I could make out the cracked-egg shape of the base. In survival mode, I yanked my mattress from my bed and shielded myself with frustrated hope. With my other hand, I turned the bag upside down and dumped my clothes out on the feathered floor. The full magazine dropped out of one sock as I retrieved the 9mm from the other. With speed ingrained from unstable bases in foreign countries, I clicked the magazine in, racked the slide, flipped the safety with my thumb, and cocked the hammer.

I hadn't heard any shots in a long row of seconds. The air was filled with the smell of gunpowder, old motel, and the dry taste of gypsum from bullets cutting through plaster walls. I heard a motor idling; the slam of two doors, one right after the other; and gravel shooting from spinning tires. Then the quiet settled in, as unnerving as the machine gun swath.

Jef Huntsman

I lifted my eyes above the mattress and peered. Floating feathers waltzed to the floor. I waited sixty seconds more to make sure there was only one vehicle. "Hub!" I cried with a crackling, dry voice. I crab-walked over to the broken window and peered through the shades. All I saw was a peaceful night; one dog barked in the far distance. I caught the reflection of several room lights stretched out on long rectangles across the empty gravel of the parking lot.

I clicked on lights and raced over to the other bed, hoping to find Hub alive. On the floor lay old carpet and lightly settled feathers across shards of window glass. My eyes veered to the bed. Hub's six-pack of *Pacifico* was a pile of cut tin. The remains soaked the mattress in a bubbly froth. Where was Hub?

I remembered the party last night—the pretty, round-faced girl that Hub was talking to. I hoped he was with her. My pulse raced. But what if he wasn't?

I called his cell, no answer. I thought about whoever had tried to execute us, and I wondered if they were outside staking the place to make sure we were dead. A sideways peek through the curtains told me no—unless they were hidden in the trees in the vacant lot across from the hotel, but I doubted it. They had fired so many bullets in two passes that they must have thought the job was done.

Now I had to find out who sent them. It had to have come from the party—of that much I was sure. We had asked too many questions. Even an eavesdropping bartender could have picked up his cell and made a call to the right people. I thought about that. It gave me about a hundred and thirty suspects, if I didn't count the spouses and boyfriends any of them might have talked to later.

My phone rang the same annoying tune, "Highway to Hell." I really needed to figure out how to change that. I found my cell on the floor and glanced at the caller. It was Maria.

"Good almost morning," she said. "I haven't been able to sleep and figured this was a perfect time to catch you."

I pulled the phone back and glanced at the time. "It's 4:15 in the a.m., but I'm up." Sweat cooled on my face as a soft wind lifted the tattered drapes.

"You're an hour ahead, and I had a late night with a couple of drunk teens." I heard coffee percolating. "I thought I'd call before I collapse. So, any sign of Seronia?"

Maria works as a teacher/therapist/mother to a bunch of youth whose parents can't control them, so they send them out west to her live-in school. The kids learn math, English, how to ride a horse. They do community service and cook.

I lifted my mattress back up on the bed and sat. "I think we're getting close." I glanced around the room at the broken glass and feathers.

"Mmmmm hummm," Maria hummed. "So, you've pissed people off and you've only been there two days."

"Pretty much." I didn't have to say more; Maria always understood.

"You be careful. That's a whole different country, with different rules. I don't want you shot at by the third day."

I chuckled wryly.

Silence filled the line. I heard her let out a puff of air. "You've been shot at." It was not a question.

"I think some locals and I had a miscommunication."

"Bullshit!"

I shared a sanitized version of the morning's visitors and told her about the party and all the guests. I added in the horse ride to ease her tension.

She snorted. "You rode a live horse?" After a few seconds, her voice lowered. "Be really careful. I know you can handle yourself, but you still owe me a vacation. Oh, Harold Sims told me he'd call you."

"Don't worry, you'll get your vacation. I'm just poking a hornet's nest with a long stick." I stood and peered through the broken window again. "Tell Harold he already thanked me. You didn't give him my number, did you?"

"I'll let you go." She ignored my question. "Love you."

"Same here," I answered.

She made that noise with her lips she makes when she's annoyed with me. "You love . . . you too?"

"Nooo. You know what I mean."

I heard the phone click off. That didn't go well.

I took a hard gaze out the window, careful not to slit my neck on glass shards protruding like stalactites out of the sides of the frame. Nothing looked out of place. I'd spent enough time searching hillsides and jungles to know when an enemy was near. It was an internal thing beyond sight—intuition, maybe? They were gone.

I sat on the edge of the bed. For the first time, I noticed my boxers, ripped on one side and blood spotted. The sight brought on the biting pain that should have been there minutes before. Adrenaline is a drug that shields your mind from agony. It turns everything to fight or flight. I eased several glass fragments from my shoulder, a tiny one from my butt, and another embedded in my left knee.

With my 9mm on the toilet tank, I let the shower clean my wounds. When the crimson rivulets on my legs turned clear, I toweled off, then ripped the thinning hotel towel into strips to seal my wounds. No way to wrap my rump, so I blotted toilet paper onto it like I would a shaving cut. Maria would laugh at my explanation of a shaving cut on my ass. A thin smile crossed my face.

My mind was hyper aware of each noise from outside. I pulled long pants over my scraped knees, slipped my pistol into the crevice of my back, and donned a clean shirt, ready to head out. To where, I wasn't sure.

Window glass spread like tiny sparklers across the floor and bed. Poles of light shot through holes in the door A haphazard frayed line cut the wall, exposing plaster, wire, and two-by-fours. What was once a lamp lay like a decomposing rooster on the floor. My gut gave a twist.

Soft footsteps paced outside my room. My breathing stopped. I grabbed the gun and thumbed the safety. The steps halted at the door. There were two of them. By the heaviness on the gravel, I knew they were either male or large women, but the cadence sounded more masculine. They shifted to one side of the door, flickering the light coming through. One tapped knuckles on the jamb. I stepped to the right and crouched by the hinges. Seconds passed. A key fumbled at the lock. I listened as it lurched in and turned the tumblers. I heard whispering in Spanish but couldn't make out any words. The door swung open in front of me. I dropped on my cut shoulder, my body angled, the Beretta barrel facing the opening with both hands in a tight grip.

The night clerk saw me and raised his hands. His terracotta face turned ashen—mouth agape, eyes pleading.

"Who's with you?" I yelled.

Without taking his bulging eyes off me, he signaled with his fingers. A large-headed lady with just-got-up hair peeked around the corner of the door. Tears rolled down her puffy cheeks.

They were no threat. I stood, tucked the gun into my pants, and apologized.

The night clerk dropped his hands, his breath rasping between clenched teeth. The lady rattled something in Spanish about hiding after the gunfire. *"Llamó a la policia hace diez minutos,"* she said.

The last part I worried about. An *Americano* possessing a gun in Mexico is a serious offense. I hurried back in, grabbed my backpack, slipped the sock over the gun, and pressed it under some clothes in the bag. I raced past them and tossed the backpack behind the passenger seat and folded down the rear seat. The clerk and the lady were frozen as winter tombs but watched my every move. I walked over to them with a smile pasted on my face.

"No pistola." I waved my hands horizontally as if pressing out sheets on a bed. *"No pistola,"* I repeated. They understood. I reached in my wallet. I had only six hundred dollars and some change. Pulling it out, I pressed the whole wad into the clerk's hands. A smile brightened his lightened face. I knew that wouldn't cover the damage, but I'd send more as soon as possible.

The man responded, *"No pistola, intiendo."* The color returned to his face just as two police cars pulled up. Dust swirled and rocks crunched under braking tires.

9

Seronia

The vehicle sputtered and coughed, breaking the hushed dawn. The whine of the starter motor screeched like a cat in heat. Trueno's grip on the steering wheel tightened. Cords in her neck pulled her skin into taut pleats. Finally, exhaust puffed out the back and the truck started just as the first sign of lantern light poked out from one house and the sun shot long ribbons through the dirty windshield. A light turned on in another house, then another. She dropped the truck into gear, and the wheels spun plumes of dry earth. On a sunlit hill, a gunshot fired.

Trueno cowered her chin to the steering wheel, expecting a bullet to zing by. Her hands clamped around the wheel, knuckles as white as sun-bleached antlers. Her neck twisted into the direction of the boom to see a deer pounce over a fence and bound into a stand of scrub oak on the opposite mountain. *A hunter.* Relief poured through her body. A full inhale. Her foot pressed down harder on the gas pedal.

Mari had curled into a ball, pretending sleep in the seat next to Trueno. The distant gunshot hadn't stirred her. Blood-soaked hands were wedged between her breasts. She shivered with erratic gasps of air. Her long, black hair caked into the dried blood on her neck.

Trueno had sworn in a sizzling mantra at the ground several minutes before as she headed back down the path to help Mari and Sandoza. She thought about leaving them and taking all the credit for capturing the crazy girl. They were as still as death lying in rabbit brush on the side of the path, mouths open, sucking air into taxed lungs, eyelids drooped. Trueno kicked both in the ribs.

"Rapidamente burros." The globe-size whites of their eyes reflected the moonlight as Mari groaned and Sandoza squeaked. Trueno ordered Mari to get up, yanking her by her long, muddied hair. Mari's hair tightened, lifting her scalp like hundreds of puppet strings.

Mosquito Sands

Mari quickly lifted herself with a groan. Blood drizzled from a wound on her cheek. "I'm moving, asshole." She slapped at Trueno's fist. Trueno released her hair but narrowed her eyes into Mari's.

Mari had never had the guts to smack her before and felt a glint of bravado that faded with the tight knot growing in her insides. Trueno wouldn't forget.

They dragged Sandoza up the hill, working both sides with their arms wrapped around her back. She began a high-pitched whine, but Trueno stuffed a rag in her mouth. It was amazing they hadn't wakened the whole village. They both glanced back. A few houses were lit; corkscrewed smoke curled from some of the chimneys.

Muscles ached as Trueno and Mari lugged Sandoza further towards the truck. Sandoza's uninjured foot furrowed the ground behind them. Her other half leg dangled, lifeless. Sandoza had passed out from pain.

The two heaved Sandoza up into the bed of the truck next to a cocooned Seronia, who became a hornet's nest trying to break the binds. Trueno took a heel to her cheek and smacked the heaving bundle that was Seronia. The drug she'd injected earlier hadn't worked very long. Spitting expletives, Trueno stormed to the cab, fumbled behind the seat, and came up with a tin and a rag. She ran to the other side of the truck, slamming into Mari who stood dumbfounded by the tailgate. She poured ether onto the rag and stood on the wheel well. Like a cat chasing a rolling ball, Trueno struggled to grab Seronia.

"Mari, hold that bitch."

Mari just stared at the cab with her lips parted.

Trueno finally found Seronia's mouth. Seronia twisted her face in convulsions. She yanked one rag out and shoved another in. Seronia tried to spit it out and chew through it, but the rag stayed, and she was soon flaccid and still.

Mari headed to the cab, rubbing her scalp. She closed the door and slumped in the seat.

Trueno took a few seconds to wrap Sandoza's partial leg with a sweater she found behind the truck seat. What was left after the pig's bite was nothing more than loose meat and a splintered bone covered with crimson mud and caked dust—the only thing that kept her from bleeding to death.

The two-track rolled down one mound and up another as the truck maneuvered through sagebrush and scraggly oak. *"Estupido campesinos pobre,"* said Trueno.

In a faint voice Mari spoke into her clasped hands, chin down, eyes shut, "My family is poor."

"You have no family. We are your family. Lady Six Sky is the mother of all." Her voice raised. "She has the power of the Gods. She chose you." Trueno shook her head in disgust. "Those people couldn't even put food on the table."

Mari never moved. A tremble soared through her body.

Seronia awakened from a drug-induced sleep around 11 a.m. Within seconds, she was screaming through the rag that was stuffed into her mouth. The truck was miles away on a back road that paralleled the main paved road. Seronia's brain was on fire. In a claustrophobic rage, she had torn one arm out from her bonds and clawed at the tape holding her other wrist to her side.

Partially free of her restraints, she turned into a wild boar. She rolled into the wheel well then pinged herself back into the limp body next to her. A couple of fingers broke through at her neck. Then a hand. Seronia yanked the rag from her mouth with such ferocity that she reopened her cut lip, which spouted like a tiny sprinkler. Drops smeared across her face. She kicked at the tailgate. Its fragile, ancient metal bowed with each blast. Her taped wrist finally came free, shredded by fingernails and anxiety. She had dug deep into her own skin to get the tape off her wrists.

In autistic panic and anxiety, Seronia edged up onto her knees. Eyes like blazing suns, she stood, twirled, and fell half-wrapped like an Egyptian mummy. Her tied feet caught around the limp arm of Sandoza. A screech that could stop the earth wailed toward the sunbeams flickering through high wisps of clouds.

Trueno and Mari craned their necks. They both began yelling at their prisoner through the glass as Seronia inched up against the cab's back window. In panicked madness, she screamed with such ferocity it seemed as if it would crack the window. The two in the cab were stunned. The truck hit a mud track on one side, causing it to shift and bounce. Seronia flew into the air. Her bare feet caught the lid of the bed, and with a flip, she tumbled over the tailgate. Her voice came out hollow and eerie like a beginning bugler. Her body rolled across the roadside and tumbled into a patch of spreading sagebrush.

The sagebrush eased Seronia's collision with the hard ground. The rough bark of the bushes scraped her arms and legs. A thin cut across her forehead oozed blood onto her closed eye. Dirt settled. Her eyes sputtered open. She glanced at her cuts and bruises but felt no pain. Seronia had never felt pain the way most do. At one time she had a compound fracture on her forearm, and she never cried; in fact, she barely noticed that something was wrong.

Seronia sat up. She focused on the truck, which was two hundred yards down the trail and off to the left. She inhaled softly. Seconds later, her hands began to strum her calves. A beat held deep within her skull— a beat only an autistic understands.

Down the mountain, Trueno had one hand on the wheel as she focused on Seronia rolling through the bushes. The truck barreled forward. She twisted back around. It had taken Trueno a full fifteen seconds to respond. She now faced the road, but it had disappeared. Her eyes wide and her mouth open, they sailed over rocks and brush. Sandoza pin-balled in the truck bed.

The truck's undercarriage scraped the spreading branches of small junipers and sage. Trueno's foot begun to push the brake pedal. The truck barreled over a ribbon of rocks, throwing Trueno's knee into the old metal dash. A stab of pain burst up her leg and sickened her stomach. The truck's front end jumped over a dug-out game trail, and the front bumper barreled into a solid tree trunk, curling it as if it were nothing more than tin. A crunch of metal sounded as the truck bed raised and dropped with a thud.

Spider cracks formed in the shape of two footballs on the windshield. One head barely jammed back into her seat; the other head took out the dome light and dropped. Both girls were out cold. Tiny streams of crimson fanned out across their foreheads. Their necks went flaccid as their bodies finished the reverberating bounce.

Mari's head rested in the hollow behind the seat. Her breaths were shallow. Blood dripped down onto rusted tools and crumbled clothes. Her torso folded over the seat like a discarded coat. Mari's face lightened to the color of coffee with too much cream. A white bone poked through her left arm. Blood pooled on the headrest from a slow, viscous drip.

Sandoza was a bloody heap in the back of the pickup. Her faint breath came in spurts between clenched teeth. Her muscles loose. It appeared she may never fog a mirror again.

The bridge of Trueno's nose rested on the steering wheel. Crimson dripped steadily onto the discolored floor. Her oily hair spilled over her curled back. Her arms were limp at her sides, resting on the torn seat cover. Her eyelids were loose. Below the surface, blood spiders trailed around her bruised cheeks. The motor ran in gasped shudders. Steam sizzled from a bent radiator. Two crows landed on busted branches of the tree. They peered to the side. The motor died. A short breeze whispered through the lifeless cab. An eerie quiet shadowed over the scene.

10

Carson

The police station sat in the center of town, a new building, the pride of taxpayers' funds. After hours, *Señor* Mancera and a highly decorated officer entered the windowless room in which I was held. It was the cleanest interrogation room I'd ever seen. The room smelled of new paint and waxed floors. If I had a Facebook account, I might have taken a selfie.

The policeman introduced himself as *el jefe de policia Mexicano, Señor* Cartel. The police chief straightened his short, pudgy stature and swept his hand through thick hair as if in front of a mirror. I was released shortly after. The chief apologized to me for the unfortunate incident involving a famous American tourist. His posture and deep stare said otherwise, but he kept that from *Señor* Mancera. Perhaps this Magnum P.I. thing was working out for me after all.

Hub was waiting outside, his arm draped over the thirtyish woman from the night before. They leaned against what I assumed was her car. As I headed toward them, *Señor* Mancera told me again that we would be guests at his house. The hotel had checked us out—no surprise there—but our Jeep was still waiting to be picked up.

"I need coffee and breakfast," I said to Hub. As I turned, an agonizing pain shot from my shoulder down my back and arm.

"I knew that."

"Is this one of your shaman things again?"

"No. I just knew you hadn't eaten." He nodded for me to get in the back seat of a white sedan with pink seat covers. "Olivia's parents own the best restaurant in town. And the coffee," he exaggerated a sigh, "is from Mexican Altura coffee beans." His flat palm went to his chest. Olivia's smile radiated.

Jef Huntsman

The unwelcome visit from the shooters had given me a voracious appetite, and the breakfast tasted incredible. I described my crazy night but declined Hub's offer, accompanied by a naughty lift of his brow, to tell me about his.

Hub explained that he had had the two Jeep tires replaced by the garage that morning. They dropped the Jeep off at the restaurant while we were finishing breakfast. I hurried over to the Jeep and glanced in the back. The tension in my muscles loosened when I noticed my pack wasn't disturbed. Olivia took off in her car to go to work. With my body skating on an edge of lingering adrenaline and exhaustion, I had Hub drive us to the home of *Señor* Manceras.

Hub nodded at the motel as he ground across the gravel parking lot. "Did you even ask for a different room?"

"Funny."

A few puffy clouds pushed north, and the sun pushed the temperature up. As we approached the house, *Señor* Mancera waved. He sat behind a table of fruit and sweetbreads, a tall glass raised high in a greeting. He stood as we neared the table. Glistening white teeth smiled behind acorn skin. I held out my hand to shake his, and he wrapped his arms around me with the grip of a bear.

As we sat, he offered limeade and food with a sway of his powerful hands.

"I just wanted to thank you for your hospitality," I said. "We will be taking off in about an hour, but thanks for your invitation to stay here."

His smile faded, and his eyes rounded. He patted my hand on the table. "No, no, no. My friends are traveling from El Tule to meet you, the private investigator." He shook his head; his lips tightened.

"Didn't we meet your friends?" I paused as he grinned. "And I'm not a—"

"He would be happy to meet your friends," Hub broke in. "When will they be here?"

Señor Mancera's spotlight smile returned. He leaned back and crossed his arms. "They'll arrive in about an hour."

Hub glanced at my disapproving face. "Perfect." He poured a drink for both of us.

"*Perdóname*, I need to make a few business calls." *Señor* Mancera reached in his shirt pocket, retrieved a thin cell, turned, and strolled away.

I knew staying was the nice thing to do, but I was antsy after getting shot at, and I wanted to try to catch up to the gunmen. I realized that might be difficult after this much time had passed.

I rose, nodded to Hub, and strolled toward a trail leading over a wooden bridge between a pond with cattails. At the crest of the bridge, I watched the water spurt over the rocks below and thought about the morning.

I recalled the click of the gun and closed my eyes. My fingers rolled the two 9mm casings that I had picked up from the cement porch around in my pocket. My eyes opened. The weapons were Heckler and Koch MP-5s or one of their derivatives. They had a distinctive spitting sound, like an old man coughing with mucus. They would be perfect. The weapon is compact, portable, and fires about six hundred rounds per minute—which would be about right for the two passes both guns made. And they fire 9mm ammunition. I sucked in the country air, realizing how lucky I had been.

I glanced around the yard. It was well maintained but still had a natural growth look to it. About forty feet from me and under the canopy of a loaded lime tree, Hub had his back on the ground and his legs raised in a *Z* formation. It was a yoga position I'd seen him use before.

My eyes moved back to the river. A memory from years ago entered my mind. There was a slight sound difference, like a raise in pitch as bullets buzzed over my head like a hive of rabid bees. It had happened before—in Iraq. I had yanked two Marines through a blasted hole. The Taliban had peered through the cloudy hole seconds later with guns drawn. We'd run parallel to a hill as they fired upwards, bellies to the ground. When bullets are that close, you feel them pass.

It had been the same that morning. There had been a definite angle. The motel shooters had fired from a height of about four feet, give or take a few inches. They'd been kneeling, or short, or firing from the waist—which only happens in movies. What the heck did all this mean? I hadn't a clue.

Horns honked. I turned. Four cars arrived in procession. *Señor* Mancera walked out to greet them. Excited faces popped above the roof of each of the cars. Quick prattle raised in volume. The host pointed in my direction.

"Crap!"

Seventeen enthusiastic grins headed my way with *Señor* Mancera at the helm. I stepped quickly from the bridge and thought about sprinting for the Cherokee. Hub was standing now, hands on his knees and laughing. The group surrounded me, all talking at once. I became lightheaded but stood my ground. Who the hell is this Magnum P.I.? I had never known throat-clamping fear in the Marines, but these groupies sucked the air from my soul. I peered over the group at Hub for help.

Hub yelled something in Spanish and rolled his arms vertically as if signaling an airplane into the gate. *Señor* Mancera helped guide his "friends." Soon a line formed directly in front of me. I clamped my fists at my side and prayed for the solitude of my ranch.

The first one in line, a round, eager man, shoved a paper at me. I gazed at it. It was blank. I looked over at Hub. He pretended to write on his palm as I've done many times asking a waitress for the check. *Señor* Mancera handed me a pen. I hid my exasperation with the insides of my lips pressed tightly against my front teeth.

An hour and a half later, after listening to *Señor* Mancera interpret each one's story about a certain episode or a made-up abduction, signing autographs in someone else's name as Hub suggested, and feigning a smile that made my lips numb, the group disappeared with a reverse show of their entrance.

Hub thanked *Señor* Mancera. I think I growled.

I decided to pick up full insurance on the Cherokee before we left. Hub thought this prudent. He kidded that perhaps we should upgrade our health plan and pick out a plot, but his mouth tightened, and his forehead creased with the transparent thought he might actually need it.

We stopped at Olivia's work. Hub promised her he would be back to take her on a real date when this was over. She looked hopeful, but I could tell she was not convinced when her fists landed on her hips, elbows out. We drove through town.

"I had a vision," said Hub, "well, more of an auditory signal during a camel pose. Yoga really opens me up to the dimensions. I know I keep pushing this, but you should really try this out."

"Um hum."

"You know I'm a master instructor. I could help you with the basics."

"I exercise my way," I countered. "You exercise your way."

"I get it," Hub said. "But running up mountains and mending fences is purely physical. You need something that helps with your inner spirit, your being. It would center you."

We'd had this discussion many times before. I think it helped Hub to just talk. He wasn't the silent introvert that I prided myself on being.

Mosquito Sands

"So, what about this vision?"

"Oh, yeah, my mind bounces like a rabbit. Stimulus from there, and there, and there." He pointed in all directions while steering with his knees. "So much comes in, I need to release it, or my dam might burst. But Carson, you know this head, skull, cranium—can take in tons. I'm just not sure where the bursting point is."

"The vision?"

"Yes, the auditory signal." He pointed straight ahead. "South. We should head south."

"We are heading south," I said. "We decided that yesterday."

"Yes, but I had verification."

I rolled down the window, laid my head in my bent elbow, and let the numbing rush of air be the only sound I heard.

Forty-five minutes later, I sat upright. An older Cadillac in the rear-view mirror had followed at the same distance for almost an hour. The distinctive pink color reminded me of the Mary Kay vehicles leased to top-performing sales agents. This one had a crinkled fender on the right side and dark, tinted windows. The grill was missing a few bars. I doubted Mary Kay owned this car.

Ten miles later, the Caddy was still there, and a black truck had pulled behind it from a dirt side road. Soon the truck passed the Caddy. As it maneuvered to overtake our Jeep, I reached in my pack and retrieved the loaded Beretta, dropping the sock to the floor behind me. The truck pulled along our side and stayed seconds too long. Hub whistled with eyes straight on the road. The windows were tinted. Two passengers. I was in motion as the window rolled down. Metal glinted.

"Down!" I yelled.

11

Carson

My left hand grabbed the steering wheel. I arched up over the console, my foot kicking Hub's out of the way as I jammed on the brake. Bullets pinged a wiper blade. More glazed across the hood. My right hand lifted the pistol. Hub instinctively ducked his body down at an angle. Our Jeep slid over to the shoulder. The black truck sped by with muzzle flashes firing at the cornfield on my right. They were horrible shots.

I glanced at our rear-view mirror to see the pink Cadillac creeping up on our tail. A figure leaned out the window from a rear seat. The barrel of a rifle pointed in our direction. I hit the brake again, and the Caddy rammed our rear end. I watched the rifle do a slow circle in the air and hit the gravel behind the pink car.

I pushed the gas pedal down to the floor and tightened my left grip on the steering wheel. Hub was balled up in his seat, eyes wide as full moons. We swerved and pulled out onto the road, careening toward the black truck. The driver of the truck tried to block our way. I feigned a right swerve then cut to the left with the gas to the floor. Our front end rumbled. The black truck hit a rut in the shoulder and swerved to pull out. We passed, barely nicking the pickup's rear fender. A second later we were side by side. I saw only a driver. I aimed the Beretta with my arm outstretched and watched the road with my peripheral vision. I shot a hole in the side window, and the black truck curled into a fence post. Barbed wire and posts yanked into the cornfield. In the rear-view mirror, I watched the truck as it dropped into a deep irrigation ditch, rear tires still spinning.

I nudged Hub. "You need to drive by yourself but keep low." I humped my leg back over the console. Biting agony surged from the wounds on my butt and knee

Hub mumbled something. The Jeep slowed.

Mosquito Sands

I nudged him again. "Hit it! We're going to be okay. Do this!"

He unfolded himself, grabbed the wheel from me, and slipped his foot back onto the pedal. The Jeep surged forward, giving my neck a whiplash.

The pink Cadillac was still on our tail but keeping its distance. I wondered if the people in it had any other weapons. I reached out the window and fired a shot at the driver. Without aiming, I hit the center of the windshield. That would never happen again. The Caddy slowed and followed at a safer distance.

"They're giving up. Right?" Hub asked.

"They may be calling for reinforcements." I reached into the overturned Styrofoam cooler and pulled out a bottle of water. It tasted wonderful in my dry mouth.

Hub's brow creased. "Who *are* these people? We need to get away."

"No. We need to capture one. We need answers."

"You realize they're shooting at us. Guns, man. Bullets. My inner spirit wants me to stay alive. We need to run. Fast."

"Slow down a bit; let me see how they react."

"Slow down?"

"You'd rather I repeat what happened before?" I started to lift my foot.

"My ankle is still killing me," Hub said, complaining as he slowed to about forty-five. I watched as the people in the pink Caddy tossed a crimson-spattered body out the passenger door. The Caddy began to creep up then pulled back to a safe distance. I knew they had called for help. We had to make our move, and fast. I slid over closer to Hub, my eyes still on the Cadillac. With the sun hitting right, I could see that three people were still in the car. They seemed to be crouched down; I could see only the tops of their heads.

A sudden cramp caused my foot to lift.

"HEYYY!" Hub slapped my leg. "I'll drive!"

My eyes steadied as the Cadillac became a smaller, fuzzy dot. "Sorry." I rubbed my ankle and settled my butt down on the seat. The Cherokee began to slow. "Keep the speed up to about sixty," I said.

"Fast, slow, make up your mind, I say we scoot on out of here." Hub's voice sounded strained.

"We need speed just as they round the corner. It'll give us a few extra car lengths."

"Really, Carson, the metatarsals fracture like chalk. I think I lost my arch. Major bad voodoo, man." Hub's eyes scanned the rear-view mirror and widened. "Crap, these guys never give up. I'm picking up solid, solar flare-ups from their front seat." Hub's breaths came in large gulps. "They're nuts."

"I have a plan." I turned back to the tail. The pink dot grew. "Okay, cut off the road at an angle. Now!"

The Cherokee lurched to the left, crossing to the other side. I turned forward. The front tires were airborne for a few seconds then thudded off the raised shoulder. The truck shook as we rumbled over uneven ground, shot through an opening in the fence, and headed deep into the short, un-watered cornstalks. Pheasants darted. The brakes squealed, and dust loomed from behind as the Jeep came to a sudden stop. Cornstalks braced all sides.

With my pistol in one hand and ammo in my pocket, I rolled out the door. "Jump out and hide behind the front. Leave the car running and remember that the motor is your bulletproof vest. Keep it between you and them." I knew Hub would overthink this, but I heard the door click and him drop on the ground.

"And don't let them see you. They may assume we were shot and bled out."

I stormed through the corn in an arc, away and then back toward the road in a crab walk. The corn was only three feet high where I crouched; it was so sparsely planted that it seemed like an afterthought. I heard the pink Caddy crumble the gravel to my left. The car eased up and then stopped. I heard mumbling in Spanish, but nothing distinct. A door opened. Then another. I figured the driver would stay in the car. Nope. Metal clicked and a scrape rang as the driver got out on the far side of the car.

I lay down still on my belly, listening. I stayed behind the only thick patch of corn where a ravine held muddy water. Four feet moved with soft crunches like tennis shoes on loose rocks. The driver stayed behind the car, nervously shuffling his feet. I heard padding down the soft incline just before the corn. Hesitant steps. They were following the Cherokee tracks, which meant they were walking away from me. Perfect.

I lifted my head above the young sprouts. The driver wore a baseball cap turned backward, a T-shirt, and green camo pants. Long hair drifted down a thin back. He held the gun straight out, aimed at the horizon over the top of the car, elbows locked in a two-hand hold. He was the perfect target. I glanced back, hoping Hub had high-tailed it into the far trees instead of following my suggestion. I wasn't sure I could get to them before they snuck up on the Jeep. I took in a long silent breath. My hand felt hot on the grip of my pistol.

I had about a minute, maybe two. On hands and knees, I scuffled further around to the back of the pink Caddy. Birds squawked in the trees on the other side of the road. I peeked around the back fender. The young driver was maybe four-foot-six. His feet planted triangularly, his focus and weapon were on the distant corn.

In three swift steps, I was behind him. He turned, mouth open, swinging the gun toward my face. I grabbed and twisted the barrel. There was a sharp snap as his index finger bent backwards. The gun released. He was about to yell as I clubbed him in the forehead with his own gun. He staggered and leaned on the Caddy. My left hand covered his mouth. Teeth clawed at my palm without breaking skin. I kicked behind his knee, and he folded on hands and knees. With my free hand spread like alligator jaws, I squeezed his carotid. Arms flailed, eyes rolled back. In desperation, his hands beat into my body but without any force. I held his neck for a few more seconds, long enough to make him pass out but not kill him. His body became rubber; the back of his skull clunked to the ground.

I took one more glance at the face. That's when I noticed. The short guy's skin was filthy but with a soft texture revealing he had never shaved. Two metal earrings glistened from his ears. There was a fullness to his lips. It couldn't be—but then again, why not? I patted his chest with the back of my hand. Firm breasts. It was a young girl. Maybe sixteen. I gasped, paralyzed for a few seconds. I had been shot at by too-young soldiers in overseas wars, but you never get used to it. My mind swirled, then I shook the realization off.

I quickly checked the vehicle through the window. No noticeable weapons. I glanced from the hole in the windshield to the blood splatter on the front seat. My chest tugged for a few seconds at the thought of the fourth passenger. Was that one a juvenile, too? And a girl? I shook it off. Didn't mean they weren't deadly. People get shot by teenage gangbangers all the time. Still, the thought didn't settle well.

I didn't have time to tie up the young girl on the ground, but I figured she would be out for at least fifteen minutes. I scuttled around the pink Caddy toward the other two. They were following the two lines of broken cornstalks where the Jeep had barreled through the field. Each one swept their pistol as if spraying a yard for dandelions. The Jeep was about sixty yards from me with the motor droning at idle. The two were halfway there. They swaggered like men, but I wasn't convinced they were men after discovering the first one was a girl. Regardless of gender, one thing I knew: they were deadly.

My feet hurried silently toward them over soft earth and broken vegetation. As I caught up to them, I patterned my stride after the one directly in front of me. With my longer legs, my steps closed the gap. He was about two steps behind the other one; a short cigarette dangled from his lips. As I silently tracked within two steps of them, I could smell their feral sweat.

With one stride between us, the smoker began turning. The barrel of his gun circled. Seconds passed. His mouth opened. His eyes tightened, and the cords of his neck pulled in as he noticed my leg raising. Before he had time to warn the other one or raise his gun, my boot heel cracked his teeth and jaw. Cigarette and blood flung to the side. The force was enough to slam his brain around inside his skull before a word left his mouth. A knockout. Brown eyes rolled back into his wide forehead. His body twisted. I was spinning toward the other one as the smoker dropped. His arms dangled at his side until the sound of his body meeting the earth thudded in a clump.

I kicked his gun further away.

The taller one turned and yelled "Cabrón!" in a high-pitched scream. Definitely a girl. She aimed her revolver with both hands. I knew this was it, but my sorry-ass life didn't flash before me. I accepted my fate, even though I had pulled Mancera's Beretta from my waist. I heard the click and thought of Maria's soft lips. I lifted my gun as my mind waited for the impact. Cremation. That's what I wanted. Ashes spread across the ranch. A few friends sipping my best wines. Cremation.

A hollow click broke the air. There was no bullet in her chamber. Just as she realized it, I shot her in the leg. She flinched with pain as she pulled the trigger again. The sound of a .22 caliber buzzed past, inches from my right ear. Her animalistic growl turned to a moan. I sidestepped to her left and slapped away the gun she was loosely holding in her hands. The .22 pistol sailed yards into the thick corn. She dropped to her butt and started gently rubbing her leg where an amoeba shape blackened her pants as her heart pumped fluid out of a hidden hole.

Then an otherworldly scream sent feeding birds into flight. I grabbed her and hauled her back down the two tire tracks. Her nails dug into my forearm. A car on the road slowed, the passengers glanced over, and the car sped away. I pushed her on the ground next to the smoker. Her arms came at me like lawnmower blades. I thought for a full second, then decked her with an open-handed pop to the cheekbone. She lost focus and tumbled to the ground. I slipped her pistol into my back pocket; it was a small Remington Air Lite revolver that weighed about as much as a thin paperback. At close range, it could have been deadly.

Suddenly Hub came bounding out of the cornfield. I handed the Remington to Hub. He pointed it at the girls, his hands unsteady and quivering. I had taken him to target practice before, but he'd never been in such a situation.

"Hub, you're going to have to watch these two girls. Okay?"

A hesitant nod. "Girls?"

I quickly yanked both their army-type boots off, slid the leather laces out, and tied their hands together behind them, back to back. The smoker was female too, or at least something close to it. I knew immediately the one I shot was a girl by the octave and timbre of her voice.

"Keep your eyes on them—one move, you shoot." I headed back to the pink Cadillac, hoping the first one would still be out cold. I knew Hub wouldn't shoot them, but *they* didn't know that.

I held the Beretta in both hands and eased around the front fender. Nothing. There was just a slight smear of gravel and earth where her body had been. I dropped to my belly and checked under the car. Nothing. I quickly glanced into the car. Gone. She didn't have her gun, but she could probably run like the wind through the cornfield and disappear.

"Hub." I scanned the crop for anything odd. "The short one's missing."

"I saw her get up by the car and head across the street," Hub whisper yelled.

I turned and focused on the other side of the road. A small strip of crop about seventy feet in stopped at the edge of a forest. I couldn't see farther than ten feet into the thick trees. I hoped she might be crouched down in the corn. It was a newer crop, thick but only about two feet tall. With a boost from the Caddy bumper, I hopped up on the hood and then up to the roof. The metal creased with a moan from my weight. My eyes concentrated on the lime-green stalks. There was an area to my left where the irrigation missed, and a long strip a couple of yards wide yielded only yellow, dry growth between robust plants. I scanned the field. In my periphery, a quick jerk of something black moved. My neck craned to the spot.

I eased off the car. "All is quiet. You think she made it to the trees?" I asked Hub. I crinkled my forehead slightly.

"I'll back up the Jeep." He said.

One of the girls on the ground began squirming and screeching all sorts of Hispanic profanity. I recognized two of the swear words from high school; the rest just *sounded* like cussing. Bloody spit flew from her lips with each word, her eyes flaming.

"Hub, try not to run them over," I said. "And keep the gun on them."

The two spun their heads in my direction. Fear and loathing swept across their faces. The expletives began again. Color drained from the wounded girl, her chin trembled, and she grabbed her leg in moaning pain.

I leveled the gun sight on one of the girls. She stopped mid-stream; her face shook in anger. After another short burst, I could see that her hands were cut and bleeding from struggling with the bindings. She gave me a defiant glare. The wounded girl's eyes widened with fear; bloody handprints reddened her filthy yellow T-shirt. I was sure the bullet went through by the stain on her pants.

I jumped down and checked the bootlaces. They were secure.

With a twist and a roar from a crazed lanky white guy, I ran back to the car, across the road, and into the corn on the other side, hopefully throwing fear into the missing driver. My speed and bulk crashed through the corn like a rhino, the gun arched in front of me. I headed for the area where I'd seen the black object. I caught a glimpse of it scooting on all fours toward the dry spot in the corn.

With my angle on slippery mud, my feet went left and my body right as shoes caught in irrigation furrows. My face planted in the muck. The gun pressed into the soft earth. I lifted and tried to wipe mud from my eyes with my sleeve. The mud smeared, giving me limited vision. I focused on the object. The black mass reversed course. My eyes followed as it darted across the un-watered area. As my feet grabbed on dry ground, I lifted my drenched revolver, pointed, aimed at movement in the corn, and my finger tightened against the trigger. I blinked several times to gain vision as swampy water ran down my face.

I caught the tail end of a black badger as it scurried into the tall stalks. I fell again, my shoes caked with viscous mud. My finger loosened on the trigger as my shoulder hit and slid across shriveled crop.

Mosquito Sands

The gun bounced from my hand. My face scraped the dirt as the gun did a loop and dropped a couple of feet from me. I gasped for fresh air as I caught a flicker of something overhead. Ten scenarios passed in seconds. I rolled toward the shiny, glistening object coming down at me. My chest rammed into the tibia bones of the little killer. Her machete dropped into the wet earth and stopped short of my belly. I kept the roll going and the machete lifted then flung into the air; her frame buckled backward.

She was a biter, too. I got a knee up and drove it into her chest. Teeth snarled at my leg. My heel kneed into her throat. Her mouth closed with a clack, and she let out a short gurgle as the pressure clamped oxygen off. Meanness turned to fright. Eyes bulged, and frantic hands beat into the side of my body. The motion slowed. Eyelids drifted down, and she went slack. I waited a few more seconds to make sure she'd remain unconscious for a bit. I raised on my fingertips and released the pressure. I slid off. Her breathing came in short bursts like shivers, then her chest lifted and lowered slowly. Her limbs lay limp.

I retrieved my gun and tucked it into the back of my pants. The search for the machete took longer, but I finally found it and tossed it high and into the trees. I walked back to the short girl and gently slapped her face until her eyelids opened. Her pupils were rolled back. The shadow of a single cloud shaded us for an instant. Then brightness. A minute later she came to and began a frantic pull for precious air. Her memory started to come back but couldn't keep up with reality.

I eased her up and hauled her over to where the other young women were. I tied her up the same as I had the others, and I tossed her boots into the corn. The Cherokee idled. Hub sat at the wheel, one hand outstretched with the Remington semi-limp as he gazed in a trance at his lap. I asked him how he was; he nodded but didn't raise his head. I watched his shoulders rise with deep breaths.

As far as the girls were concerned, the smoker was still glaring with defiance. Her companion looked scared, holding tight to her bloody leg. Shorty lay sedate with a scowl on her bespattered face.

Hub looked up as I reached in the Cherokee to get some bottled water. A smirk crossed his face.

"Love the earthy makeup, *amigo*," Hub said.

I turned my head and poured the water across my face. Hub tossed me a dirty T-shirt to dry off.

I ripped a clean rag off one of my favorite shirts to tie around the wounded girl's leg. Her face scrunched and tears flowed as I checked the entry and exit wounds. The wounds had been mostly cauterized by the heat of the bullet, and she had kept pressure on it, as I had instructed her. Though her wounds looked like hell, I was fairly sure the bullet hadn't injured anything major. I had seen a loose bottle of rum in the back of the Caddy, so I retrieved it and poured the leftover inch or so onto the hole in her leg. She screamed and writhed on the dirt. I held her and tried to keep the dirt away from the wound while bandaging her up the best I could. She'd be okay until she made it to a hospital, where I was sure she wouldn't venture in.

I found the Cadillac keys in my pants pocket, walked back, and started the gas guzzler. It purred with the rumble of a big engine. I ran it down the road about a quarter of a mile. Leveraging both speed and the weight of the car, I barreled it deep into the haphazard rows of corn until it stuck in a culvert. I wiped anything I had touched to smudge the fingerprints and hiked back to the Cherokee.

When I arrived, Hub was giving life advice to the three girls. One spit, one stared, and one listened with disinterest. He made me wait until he gave them a shaman blessing that involved kicking up dust and some hand clapping. They seemed annoyed.

12

Seronia

Seronia peered in through a shattered window. She liked the sparkles of glass on the floorboards. A few dangling threads on her nightclothes were all that remained of the blanket. Grey duct tape hung like Post-it notes from her clothes. Excitement soared through her body in quivers and yelps. The constant sound of her tongue clicking accompanied the last bursts of steam from under the crunched hood. She knew what to do.

Juan Diego had trained her well. She cared little for people, but she loved the ritualistic healings of a shaman. She took to it like breathing air or blinking; to her, it was a duty. During her training, she never seemed to be aware. She stared at a spot on the ground, constantly hummed, flapped her arms like clothes hung in a windstorm, and watched her father with side glances. But she knew every herb and chant her father used. There was a transcendental passing of her true purpose that she absorbed without the use of speech or sight. She just knew.

In a distracted trance, she glanced back at the lump in the truck bed. With agility and strength, Seronia leaped up next to it. Drips from scrapes and scratches formed a roadmap of red on her legs and arms, but her wounds didn't seem to affect her. Seronia knelt beside Sandoza, who was heaped in a corner like a discarded rag doll. Her chin folded into her chest. Abrasions on her face had blossomed in dark nebulas. Seronia touched the wrapped leg as if petting a new puppy. Then both her palms rested on Sandoza's forehead. Seronia's eyes closed in concentration. A giggle echoed from her lips.

Her head bobbed and turned. She hopped out. Without understandable purpose or speed, she moved toward a stand of trees about fifty yards away. The echo of Seronia's hums through the hills delighted her. Offset chortles punctuated her rhythmic purr.

Her hands played in the air as if she was pulling on kite strings. Her giggling sang to the beat of her hike. Grasses and bushes that looked like scattered twigs, more dead than alive, circled under each tree. A few flowers blossomed at the outskirts and rose from the dry grass. She picked certain plants, dug around their roots, then pulled at the base as her father had shown her.

Seronia used a flat rock to make a bowl of bark and scraped into it the sap of some Mexican valerian, an herb thought to disinfect external wounds. She set her cache down then created a pouch with the shirttail of her long T-shirt; into the pouch she tossed bits and pieces of things she found, her eyes always in a mesmerized gaze away from whatever she found. At one point, she bent down, keeping her sight straight ahead as she dug and scooped a plant into the front of her T-shirt.

Without any apparent sign of discovery, she walked lazily above the grove of trees to a jutted rock formation. At the base of the rock, she knelt and eyed peripherally a single plant out of a group of three. She used a forked stick to dig around the root of one of the plants, still seemingly disinterested in her quest. She carefully pulled out a whole jimson weed, keeping the thick root intact.

A forced laugh, neither happy nor sad, bellowed at the truck. Seronia gazed at her prize in the pouch of her torn shirt. Her lip bled, cuts and scratches covered all her exposed skin, two small bones of her right foot were slightly fractured, and the toes on the same side had begun to swell, but she seemed not to notice any of it. She had little knowledge of pain. It was one of the connections that autism seemed to separate.

Something had caught her eye. She traversed the side of the hill in a skip, careful not to lose the things she had gathered. Seronia stopped at a stand of Chinese elm and rain-fed grasses. As if searching for perfection, her free hand caressed each leaflet, checking for size and texture. With a whistle, she carefully snapped specific leaves off their stem and dropped them into the bundle in her shirt. She giggled and nodded her head after picking the perfect amount.

Seronia crow-hopped down the hill toward the disheveled truck that sat crushed into the tree, lifeless as a tomb.

13

Carson

An endless, straight shot of pounded rock road passed under the truck as we headed south. Gravel pinging against the wheel wells didn't drown out the hysteria of anger and fear coming from the back seat. Bare feet pounded against the plastic-paneled doors. I had stuck knotted shirt sleeves into their mouths to quiet them down, but they spit those out. Their craziness grew louder and more nasal. The girl I'd nicknamed "Smoker" because of her yellowed fingers cried nonstop; the other girls kept insults flying. They were a tag team: first shorty, then the smoker, then the tall one, then all three, and then they started all over again. It was like a bad opera.

"You sure about this?" asked Hub.

"Yeah, we're almost there. Advertising signs are starting to appear, which means another town is up ahead." With a pump of my hand, I signaled for him to slow down. The trees were thicker on our right. I could tell a snaking river fed them along its banks.

"Pull down this dirt road," I said. We had passed a sign that proclaimed, *ciudad El Vergel catorce kilometros.* An arrow pointed down a pressed gravel path through the trees. Hub pulled in and drove to the edge of the trees. I opened the hatch and let the three wiggle their way out. Unsure, they came tumbling out. I kept my distance. I didn't want a quick knee to the groin, and I was pretty sure that's exactly what they'd love to do.

I questioned them; their eyes said they understood English, but their lips held tight. I tried another tack by having Hub help with the Spanish. Two faces drilled defiance into me. Their sweat formed rivulets of washed filth down their necks like tree roots. The injured one wept into a foul, oversized golf shirt. I pointed to the river and began pushing them in that direction.

Hub looked astonished. "You're not going to drown them?"

I narrowed my eyes at Hub. The girls understood.

The crier went first. The other two snarled at her but knew they were helpless. They had no idea actual drowning wasn't an option I would use.

Between wheezing sobs, one told me they were part of a group called the *Madres de fuego* (mothers of fire). Teenage mothers? Her English came out hard, stumbling on her tongue, but she was semi-fluent. I assumed the other two spoke English as well, though they would never let on.

I made the other two sit on the ground and steered the crier to a clearing downstream. I led her with my Berretta pointed in her direction. Hub stayed at my left; at his side was the gun I had confiscated from the girls. The crier told us they were instructed to find the two Americans and scare them.

I lifted her chin and wiped her grimy face with a cloth. Her wet cheeks and eyes came clean, revealing a soft, slightly round face. "Scare us or kill us?" I asked. Her head began to drop, but I held it up with two fingers. "Your orders were to kill us, weren't they?"

Her frightened dark eyes glanced over to the other two. I leaned closer, my eyes level with hers. She gave a quick nod.

"Why?" I asked.

After a long hesitation, she said, "You look for the *Mapa Chica*."

I cocked my head toward Hub.

"*Map girl* or *girl of maps*," said Hub.

My forehead creased in puzzlement.

"*Seronia. Recuerdas lo* . . . Sorry, I love this culture, this language. Once I get started it absorbs me," said Hub. "I believe in one of my past lives I was a South American shaman. A great healer. I have had several dream-talks from the person I once was. Juan Diego agrees. I have a spiritual ancestral linage to the earth and the people here. And there's some significance about hovering wings beating faster, and—"

"Hubbard!" I said, cutting him off. He stood still as a statue, mouth open, as I asked, "*Seronia Recuerdas*?"

His lips sucked tight and his forehead creased. "Remember what Juan Diego mentioned about taking her to town?" he asked.

"Yes, she drew every city block from memory. Maps." I turned back to the crying girl. She had stopped blubbering. "Do you know where . . . *De donde el Mapa Chica?*"

The other two began threatening her in fits of Spanish. Their faces reddened with rage, though their eyes held a slight tinge of fear. I knew I had to even the battlefield or they'd kill the crier as soon as they got loose. I hurried over to the other two and grabbed the short smoker. She clawed at me like a feral beast. I slapped her head with the back of my fist. Maybe too hard. Her head lurched. Hair spread like vulture wings. Her eyes rolled up from the force of her brain smacking the back of her skull. A short, dry heave spasmed. I watched as her corneas clouded. The other one clucked Spanish cuss words as her thin chicken neck tightened. I raised my hand at an angle. She slid back a few inches in a quiet pose of hate.

I hated doing this. I had to keep reminding myself that these young girls were trying to kill me and Hub. They had little conscience. Or did they? Maybe it was more a fear of something or someone?

I grabbed the tall one and eased her over to the water's edge. She winced with pain from the gunshot wound to her leg. The current ran swift, bending reeds even in the shallows. Her eyes bulged, and she braced her feet, digging them deep into the wet soil. I held her by her crossed arms, which were still bound behind her, and eased her slowly closer to the swift current for effect. People tend to have more fear of the possibility of something happening than when it actually happens—and I used that against her. I pushed, released, and pushed her again. Her horrid scream penetrated the countryside and into the forest beyond. She tried to back pedal in a frantic push of deep mud and lime-green grass. She was ready.

"Where is Seronia?" I kept pressure on her elbows from behind, trying to cause significant pain without fracturing anything. "*¿De donde es la chica Seronia? ¿Mapa chica?* Who has her?"

She was hysterical. She shouted and pled for release.

"Tell me, and I'll let you go," I whispered into her ear.

She bucked and snorted for a long time and then gave in. "She's with *Dama Sexto Cielo.*"

"Where?" I tightened my grip on her elbows.

"I am still a *rata*. I'm not allowed into the main palace."

The short one began chanting, *"Perra perra, perra. Estupido!"*

That one I knew—*stupid bitch*. I moved the tall one back and rebound her legs. With as much craziness as I could muster, I grabbed the smoker, who seemed to be the leader, and hauled her over to a grove of trees by the river. We disappeared from the sight of the others as I shoved her down into wet grass and onto the elbows of raised roots. The muscles in her face tightened, her teeth ground together, and she filled with fire. I raised my revolver and pressed the barrel into the hair of her skull.

She went silent, stretching her buzzard neck back as far as possible. Her mouth opened to say something, but nothing came. Spittle eased down her filthy chin. I knew she wouldn't talk. There was a stoic fear in this girl, and it wasn't the fear of me. I waited. When enough time had passed, I slid her up and hauled her back to the group.

I peeked at Hub and said, "She told me everything. Let's go find this *Señora Sexto Cielo.*"

The other two looked at each other, wondering what shorty had said. She feverishly shook her head no. The other two didn't believe her. That would keep them all alive and silent for some time.

I used the leather bootlace to make sure they were well bound to each other by the wrists, back to back. I used the belt loops on their pants to secure their hips together. They spastically stood up with my help. Now they could move with their backs to each other like a six-legged creature—a cockroach.

Hub crinkled his nose and kept shaking his head to let me know he didn't approve. We jumped into the Cherokee. The motor grabbed as I put it in gear.

"You sure about this?" Hub asked.

"What? Leaving them tied up like that or letting them go?" I asked. I glanced at the Jeep's new bullet holes and closed the driver's door. *Perino's not going to like that. Insurance covers dents. I wonder about target practice.*

"Carson, they're so mad at each other. Tied like that, it'll take them hours to get back. What if a vehicle picks them up?"

"With the traffic on this back road, they'd be more likely to find an ice cream cone before a ride. But if they do, so what?" I chuckled then felt a slight touch of regret for their predicament. My mind envisioned the three all trying to lead each other as they spun and spun. Glancing over at Hub, I knew he didn't see the humor. "It's fine if they get picked up. I want them to let the people in charge know we're coming. The leaders will be both irritated at them and crazy mad at us. People with heightened emotions make mistakes."

I glanced at Hub. "I didn't kill them."

"You love this stuff. Don't ya?" Hub shook his head but gave a toothy grin.

Mosquito Sands

I thought about that. "It's more the good ending. That gives me purpose and a touch of humanity as nothing else can. Or, as Maria says, 'My focus does things.'" I drove back to the main road.

Hub rolled his window down, lifting and dipping his hand like a soaring bird on the stream of air. "What about when it doesn't end so well?"

"Even in the worst of outcomes, there is always some good." We had left the cornfields and began to see small huts. They were occupied by the loners who live on the fringe of cities without being bothered by street maintenance and building permits.

Hub nodded. His flat hand still sailed on the rush of wind.

Twenty-five minutes later, we came to a road sign: *Guadalupe dos kilometros*.

Hub brought his hand back into the truck and slapped my leg. "See. See. I was right." He was all motion and energy. "This is the place. We were led here by the powers." Hub thumped his chest. "You can feel the current. Voltage sailing on invisible wind and building as we close the gap."

"What?" Hub was the one person that could leave me feeling idiotic. He saw things I never would—or would never *want* to. I took in a deep breath. *Here comes a Hubism*, I thought.

"Seronia is here. She has to be." He stared at his hand. "You see those sparks. My fingers are like terminals, light flashes between each digit. Shamanistic light show." He held his fingers in front of my face. I watched five fingers play an imaginary piano—no flashes.

"Hey, I'm driving here." I lightly batted his hand away from my face.

"This is the Janice/Jerry thing, though I'm inclined to think it's Joplin. That low rumble of the voice, deep home blues." He was still staring at his hands, turning them as if they were the beam of a lighthouse.

"And?"

He swiveled from his hip to face me. His hand dropped into his lap. "Got-a-pay—Guadalupe? It was there all along and we missed it."

I swept my palm over my head. "You lost me."

"We're almost to Guadalupe. Her surreal voice. The dream. I mistook it for got-a-pay. She led us right to Seronia." He laughed, still staring at his fingertips. "Guad-a-lupe."

"Not to burst your psychic bubble, but they're close, not that similar."

"You wait. She'll be here," he said with certainty.

I let it go. There was a chance he could be right. The fringe of Guadalupe started out as fruit stands, which led to paved streets, and finally the signs of commerce—smog and an overabundance of Catholic churches.

Using his I-Pad, Hub found a place to stay. We circled narrow back streets to find it. The small motel was plain on the outside, and nothing changed as we entered. Clean and well used, it boasted a small kitchen to the left of the double bed and everything in seventies decor. Perfect. Hub took *seis,* and I laid out my things in *cinco*. The owner and his wife were all smiles and nods. They spoke no English but treated us like royalty as Hub slipped American dollars into their hands.

Opening the drapes brought needed sunlight into my room, which was dimly lit by two forty-watt bulbs. I took a shower and checked for signs of infection in any of the glass cuts I'd received. Filth circled the drain in a tan puddle. Showered, shaved, and teeth brushed, I called Maria.

"I was just about to call you," came her sweet voice. "I've even considered missing you, but the thought faded."

I took in a long breath of air. Maria's voice and quick sarcasm ran a peaceful, soft brush through my body. "After today . . . a day like today, I realize how much I miss our morning coffee and our nightly conversations."

"Those were conversations?" Her spitfire laugh rolled through the phone. "I love our conversations. I could use one now. When're you coming back?"

"It could be a while, or it could be tomorrow. You know how these things go. We have a name and a lot of Mexico to look through. Hub's shaman powers tell him Seronia is in Guadalupe."

"Another dead rock star talking to him, or was it one of his travel dreams?"

"You sound strongly skeptical," I said.

"Duh."

A mangy cat jumped up on the outside window ledge and cocked its head. "How are things there?"

"That's why I was going to call." Her voice gained cadence. "Harold Sims is coming to help you. He wants to pay you back for finding him half-dead by the river."

Mosquito Sands

"What?"

"I assumed you knew." She paused. "Hub has been sending him updates on your travels. He was on his way as of yesterday—booked a flight to somewhere in central Mexico. He says he knows the area."

My fists tightened, followed by a twist in my stomach. "You didn't talk him out of it?"

"I'm just the messenger, Carson." She said my name like she was kicking it down the hall.

"Sorry." I eyeballed the cat. It raised its back and took off. "I'm going to kill Hub. I can't babysit a drunk down here."

"More good news. Little Jim's coming with him."

"What the . . . Maria, I've got to go. I hope Hub's asleep so I can wake him."

"Carson," she cautioned.

"I'll call you back. I promise."

14

Carson

I banged on Hub's door. I heard shuffling, then the radio quieted. The clomping of heavy shoes approached. I was mad enough to deck my best friend. The door opened an inch, caught on the latch, closed, then reopened.

"Hey, buddy!" Harold Sims stormed at me, arms reached out. He clamped me so tight, I could feel his breath in my ear. I pried him away, my hands on his ample belly. I sucked in air through gritted teeth. He moved closer, reaching for another hug. I grabbed him by the shoulders and held him at arms' length. I felt his hands on my waist. This was too touchy-feely for me. I gently backed up, holding my palms out in a stay-there gesture.

"Harold. What are you doing here?" Heat crept into my ears. "How did you find us?"

"Lucky break. We've been in Guadalupe for a day now. Hub called us an hour ago."

Every muscle in my body tightened. I wanted to kill Hub.

Harold's smile radiated. "I'm here to help you find this *Señora* Sara-e-on-e-a."

"Seronia. Look, Harold, I appreciate the gesture, but you need to get back to Gunnison. I have this covered."

His shoulders slumped. "But I owe ya. You saved my life."

"You can buy me a beer when I get back." I forced a smile.

"Carson, I could have died out there in the mud. Buzzards yanking at my flesh. I haven't had a drink since." His chin raised. "I know this country. I was a doctor down here for twenty-two years. I still have friends."

"You're . . . a medical doctor?"

"Yes. A good one." Harold folded his arms in front of him and straightened his back.

Mosquito Sands

"No offense, but what happened?" I was half believing him and half wondering why I should believe him. I had known him for years. At least in the acquaintance sort of way. I had heard that unless he was passed out, there was always a bottle in his hand. No one ever mentioned him holding a scalpel. That was definitely a bad idea.

His chin dropped to his chest. "I lost four patients in a week and couldn't figure out what it was that killed them. One was *Señorita* Natalia, the love of my life." Tears curled around his puffy cheeks. "No one else died." His lips quivered a bit. "I never found a clue as to what caused those deaths. But I did find Cuervo and her sister Bacardi, and I just disappeared." His eyes searched the ground.

"Harold, I'm truly sorry about all that, but this is dangerous. See the sights, find old friends, and head home." I lifted his chin. "We will be okay."

He wiped his eyes. "I know this area from Durango to Jalisco, and I've even been to Guatemala a few times. I can help."

I grabbed his shoulder, turned him around, and steered him into Hub's room. As I walked in after Harold, I spotted Little Jim on an orange couch, a half-empty bottle between his legs. I looked at Harold with all the disgust I could muster.

"I said *I* wasn't drinking. Didn't say anything about Little Jim."

"Where's Hub?"

"Right here."

I turned. Hub held a tiny, white hand towel in front of his privates, his wet hair dripping onto the ancient tile floor. "That showers got two temperatures—cold and colder. Not sure why there's two taps. And this towel—not sure whether I should dry myself or scrub the dishes." He noticed my posture and the scowl I shot in his direction. "Harold and Little Jim are here. Harold knows this part of the country. Figured we could use his help."

"Uh huh." I turned and walked back to my motel room. Then changed my mind and kept on walking. Forty-plus minutes later, I found myself in front of a café and *la panaderia*. After a strong cup of coffee, I wiped the sugar off my lips from the *conchas* I'd inhaled and leaned back in my chair.

Slipping the cell from my pocket, I called Maria.

"How are Harold and Little Jim?" she answered.

I groaned.

"What's that saying about making lemonade?"

I thought for a few seconds. "You're saying you want me to squeeze the liquid out of them and then discard the two in a garbage can?"

"Well, I was thinking something a touch more civilized. I assume you took a steaming noggin' walk far from the three of them."

"You know me too well." I heard road sounds coming from her end. "I'm having coffee and *pan dulce*. That seems to have helped. Tell me about your day."

"My day's inconsequential. Driving into Gunnison, warm sun on my face. Larue's lost her key again, so I'm off to the hardware store. The milk in your fridge had a foul smell, so I tossed it. I hope you don't mind. I could retrieve it and keep it for you until you return."

I waited for her to say more. Her voice was always soothing, a hint of Spanish tickling each word. I drew the silence in with a slow inhale.

"Yo también te quiero." Maria said.

"I didn't say anything."

"You didn't have to. So, what are you going to do with Thing One and Thing Two?"

"That's why I called you." A mangy dog stretched his neck over my knee, resting his chin as he eyed the crumbs on my plate.

"Smart of you. They're going to follow you no matter what. If they think they can help, let 'em. Or at least use them in a way that's useful to you and keeps them out of trouble. I really think Harold can help. Little Jim's just there for Harold and *cerveza*. Keep that in mind."

"Did you know Harold had a medical degree?" I asked.

"Por supuesto. He talks about it all the time. I just hope he doesn't have to use his rusty skills on you."

"Trust me, Harold's not playing doctor with this body." I tilted the plate over the edge of the table. The dog's tongue wiped everything off in one sweep. He wandered away.

"He needs to feel as if he's paid you back for saving his life. See if he can help then send them home."

"I'd rather reverse that order. Just that would help." I stood, tossed a few American dollars on the table, and took one more swig of coffee.

"Your voice has calmed. You take care. I'm pulling up to the hardware store."

"You sure you don't need me to come home for something?"

"Yes, *mi amor*, but it can wait. Find Seronia."

15

Seronia

Seronia kneeled on her haunches, letting her cache of roots, leaves, and flowers tumble out onto a level spot where the careening truck had scraped away all vegetation. She set down her curl of bark that contained the mixed concoction, viscous as honey. As she had been instructed by Juan Diego, she gathered rocks of various sizes. With the precision of a surgeon, she placed five larger stones equidistant in a circle. Using the same care, she set stones just slightly smaller than the first on each side of the larger stones, humming as if speaking to the bees that darted above her. This went on until the stones made a circle around the plants in descending and ascending order from each of the five larger stones like a symmetrical roller-coaster. After a few nudges here and there to get the circle to her satisfaction, she stood. The few bees above her head rose with her as if soldiers on well-trained maneuvers.

She sniffed the air, arms helicoptering, and proceeded to her patients.

She pulled one of Sandoza's eyelids open. Seronia stared at Sandoza's vacant, clouded iris from two inches away. She leaned closer as if trying to meld their two eyes together. Seronia laid the girl's head back down on the truck bed and skipped over to the cab of the truck. She peered in.

Trueno was out cold. The bridge of her nose still rested on the steering wheel. The blood from her nostrils oozed black and coagulated across her open lips. Mari was draped over the top of the seat. Between long periods of silence, a breath periodically whistled like the dive of an airplane.

Seronia reached over Trueno's shoulders into the space behind the seat. Trueno was still as a cadaver. Seronia lifted out a milk jug full of water, three blouses, and a coat and set them on the ground. She reached over again and retrieved a partially empty Coke can and a plastic bottle of motor oil; she shook the bottle. It contained only half an inch of oil. The sun was high overhead and sweat dripped from her hair and neck. Veil-like clouds fizzled above the hills to the east. Seronia finger-combed her hair and wiped her brow with the sleeve of her T-shirt. The heat wasn't bothering her, but the sweat dripping into her eyes drove her batty.

Seronia went back to her circle of remedies and picked out a jimson root. With a piece of glass that she'd pulled from the windshield, she scraped at the tuber. Tiny flakes fell onto the top of the soda can. When she had the right amount, Seronia pushed the scrapings into the pop top with the side of her thumb. Her giggles quaked the can so hard she almost dropped it. She poured water from the milk jug into the can, placed her palm over the hole, and shook the can. Satisfied, she set it down on the ground in the center of the circle. With an air of innocence, she skipped around the circle making a chattering noise like a chipmunk. The bees darted in and out as they followed her wave of circles. Minutes later, Seronia slowed and stopped.

Carrying the bottle of shaved jimson root, cola, and water, she slow-skipped back to the truck, being careful not to spill a drop. She lifted up Sandoza's head by her hair and tilted her neck. Sandoza lay limp and ashen, emptied by the enormity of her pain and the loss of blood. Seronia blew into Sandoza's nose. Sandoza's mouth opened involuntarily; her breath was so weak it had no sound. Seronia leaned her back and poured some of the liquid down her throat. Sandoza remained flaccid as though nothing was happening; her normal gag response was absent.

Seronia set her down, and Sandoza's head lolled to one side. Boneless. Lifeless. Seronia then lifted Sandoza's leg that had been chewed by the pig. She patted around the dried mud that caked the wound and had stopped the flow of blood. Dust scattered into the light breeze. Sandoza's tibia protruded out of her calf, making her leg look like a hot dog on a stick.

It was obvious that the mud was the only thing that had stopped the bleeding. Most of the rags Trueno had wrapped around the wound had come off in the crash. Coagulated blood solidified the mud, though a drizzle of red dripped to the truck bed and vaporized on the thick dust that had settled from the crash. Seronia set the injured leg down and covered any seepage with dust. She then picked up her Coke can mixture and walked around to the passenger side.

Mosquito Sands

Mari had awoken and yanked herself from her precarious position over the back seat. She was now turned facing forward, her neck lobbed to one side. Her body curled like a question mark on the seat. One open eye stared at Seronia, who peered back at her through the open window.

"¿Está aqui para matarme?" Mari's weak voice quivered with fear.

Seronia understood. She took Mari's hand and rubbed calming circles around the knuckles. Seronia knew that Mari wouldn't die.

"¿Ayuadame?" Mari asked in a shaky voice barely more than a whisper. Her brow furrowed.

Seronia nodded, indicating that she was there to help.

Mari's left leg was numb, and something trickled down over her ankle.

Seronia smiled without looking into Mari's eyes. Because of her autism, she never looked into anyone's eyes—eye contact caused too much stress. Seronia stepped back and yanked on the door. After three tries, it gave and opened with a grinding sound of metal on metal. Seronia fell backward onto a stand of rabbit brush. It took her a few minutes to figure out what happened. She rolled to one side and lifted herself up. A new scrape on her arm was white, dotted in red.

Mari followed Seronia with both eyes. She gritted her teeth. Red trickled over her ankle. Seconds later, Mari's shoulders slumped.

Seronia found the Coke can; it was a little more than half full. Cupping Mari's chin, she urged her to drink from the cup. Mari clamped her mouth shut and shook furiously. She spotted the bees circling Seronia's head, and her mouth opened in fear as she pointed up at them. Seronia paid no attention to the bees but tilted the can so the liquid flowed down Mari's throat. Mari's eyes widened in surprise as she gagged. Seronia lifted the cup and shook it gently to see if Mari had taken enough. She nodded as if satisfied that it was the perfect amount. Setting the can down on the ground by her side, she gazed over her patient.

Mari watched anxiously as Seronia lifted and checked each part of her body, stopping only at scrapes and cuts.

Mari's chin dropped to her chest; she looked ashamed. Without lifting her head, she began speaking. "I was alone in Tonala waiting for my friends at the bus stop. We were all going to Lidea's birthday." Mari flinched as Seronia cleaned a scrape on her elbow. The cool mountain breeze soothed her, and she lowered her head again, talking to no one in particular. Her words seemed more of a verbal memory, something she had kept hidden for months.

"I didn't want to go with my parents. I thought I was too old to arrive with momma and daddy." Mari sniffled. "Stupid."

"Three girls approached me, smiling. I smiled back, but their clothes were so out of it—khaki pants and white T-shirts. I thought it was their school uniform. They seemed nice and said they'd wait with me until my friends arrived. I remember their soft voices."

Seronia applied wet leaves to a slash on Mari's shoulder. Mari paid no attention.

Mari's chin trembled against her chest. "A blue truck swerved toward us, spraying water from the gutter on my new dress. I jumped back. The girls grabbed me. Their voices threw out razor-sharp insults. I was thrown into the back of the truck—a panel truck like the one our bakery uses."

Tears ran down her cheeks and dripped off her chin. "There were other girls, not just the three; there were four more with frightened faces and tied hands. The truck reeked of urine and girl sweat. They shoved me further in. One punched me in the face while the other bound my hands."

Seronia finished and stood up. Her eyes still averted to one side. Mari glanced up and began hysterically bawling. Seronia walked away.

Mari slowly talked into her hands. "I should have arrived with my papa."

Trueno began to wake up, making tiny groans and lifting her face from the steering wheel. Her eyes blinked rapidly as if she was trying to rid them of dust. She rubbed the sockets with crusty red knuckles. Her head leaned on the truck's window frame.

Seronia peeked at Trueno and knew instinctively that her vision was impaired. Maybe she was blind.

Seronia went back to the circle where her remedies were. After holding several leaves up to the sunlight, she selected four large and two small emerald-green leaves. She returned to Mari.

Mari's head wound was the worst. It spider-webbed out; thin, red streams of blood etched squiggly lines down her face.

Seronia licked the largest leaf; with her palm, she pressed it gently over the main head wound where Mari had hit the windshield. Seronia held her palm against the leaf for several seconds while her lips moved as if saying a silent prayer. She released and clapped her hands, a pretty grin on her face.

Mari's eyes softened. A thankful tear broke from the corner of her eye.

Trueno stared at what she thought was Seronia but heard a young girl's happy giggle. On instinct, Trueno reached for her pistol on the seat, not knowing it had bounced out of the truck as they went over the embankment. Her hand frantically searched the seat. Nothing. She crammed her elbows to her belly and sank her head into both hands. Her body shook in despair.

Seronia worked on Mari as if they were alone. She placed various-sized leaves on Mari as she had placed the first one; Mari became a patchwork of green and brown. Mari accepted whatever Seronia was doing to her. When Seronia touched Mari's left side, Mari let out a squeal—a sure sign to Seronia that Mari had broken a rib. She remembered when a boy in the valley fell from a tree and landed on the wood stack. It took weeks for the bones to heal, and he made that same screeching sound when Juan Diego touched it.

Satisfied, Seronia stepped back, picked up the Coke can, walked back to her stash, crumpled a few flower petals into the can, and poured in more water. She shook the contents and skipped to the driver's side where Trueno sat. She patted Trueno on the shoulder and lifted the Coke can to Trueno's lips. In her semi-stupor, Trueno gulped it down. Her lips immediately puckered, and she batted the can from her lips. The can clanged empty to the ground. Trueno's tongue darted in and out. She spat with distaste.

"Are you poisoning me?" she screamed. Punctuating a blast of Spanish obscenity, she kept spitting as if she could expunge the liquid from her throat. Saliva peppered the cracked windshield and dash. Her feet pounded the floorboard.

Seronia giggled and tried to tap Trueno on the shoulder. Trueno whacked her hand away. Seronia chuckled and skipped back to her circle of stones.

Mari raised her eyes.

Trueno blinked repeatedly as if trying to focus her eyes. Her black hair stuck to the sweat of her forehead, and her face scrunched into reddened folds of skin, bitter and odious. Sunlight filtered through the back window of the cab and highlighted her anxiety.

Trueno spat, screaming *"Mierda, mierda, mierda!"* into the mountain air. Her cheeks puffed, her neck muscles tightened. Worn, she laid her head back against the top of the seat and appeared to be deep in thought.

Seronia returned to the truck. Her smile radiated, even though Trueno glared in the other direction.

Hearing a rustle near the open door, Trueno swiveled her head to check out the source of the sound. *"Que es—"*

Before Trueno could finish the question, Seronia shoved mint-green leaves into her mouth and held her jaw shut.

Trueno struggled, slapping at Seronia's hands. Her head banged in every direction, but Seronia was strong and knew what she was doing. Trueno sucked air in through her nose, sounding like the whinny of a horse. Seronia let go of her jaw. Using her tongue and teeth, Trueno tried to spit out the leaves, but Seronia yanked Trueno's head back with her hair and poured water into her half-open mouth. Trueno gagged. Seronia shoved her jaw closed again. Trueno's eyes popped, her face reddened, and her hands beat at Seronia's arms. Finally, she swallowed.

Seronia backed away. She knew she would have to wait for the medicine to take effect.

Trueno barrel-rolled from the truck cab and landed on all fours in the desert soil. In her fuzzy blindness, her hands clawed at the ground for a stick or rock she could use to kill Seronia. All she felt were pebbles, dirt, and sagebrush. *"Perraaaaa . . . Perraaaaaa . . . Perraaaaahhhh!"* she cussed at Seronia. Her neck strained like a wolf calling the pack.

16

Carson

The aroma of cheap tequila and empty Pacifico cans crept from the back seat as Little Jim snored and Harold, who was stoically staying sober, talked nonstop. Stories of mountain climbing, studies at the University of Texas, how to pick the best avocado, and the realization that love is a parting gesture. I turned up the radio. Guitar and accordion music filled the Cherokee. A treble voice resonated about his broken *corazon* (heart). Guadalupe was alive with shops opening and the scurry of workers preparing for the day. I took in a calming breath.

"Do you mind if I turn this down?" asked Hub. "I can't hear Harold."

My cheeks puffed with a fake grin. I listened as one sound faded and another persisted. Harold rambled on.

We were heading to the studio of an artist friend of Harold's. He supposedly knew everything about people in the area. "He's a perpetual gossip who hangs out more dirty laundry than any of the neighbor ladies," Harold had told me.

At the end of a long, narrow road we came to what appeared to be a closed restaurant. An old Harley leaned against a ramble of boards on an unsteady porch. The lime-green front door displayed the cracks of age. *Tres Pelicanos* adorned the warped sign in coral and yellow letters above the entrance. Little Jim belched and fell back to sleep. The rest of us hopped from the bullet-riddled Cherokee.

Harold pointed. "That's Pedro's motorcycle." His red cheeks dimpled as a wide smile spread across his face. "I can't believe he still has the beast."

A blond man with the muscles of a buffalo stormed out. The flimsy door slammed against the bright-yellow facade. "Doctor! It's about time you show up. Late as usual. It's been so long since you put that cast on my leg, I'm not sure I can even sue you for malpractice."

"Pedro, *amigo,* leg looks sturdy to me," said Harold.

"I'm getting a second opinion." Pedro bounded down off the wood porch and bear-hugged his old friend.

Pedro was six-foot-three, barrel-chested, with curly, blond bangs that swept across his eyebrows. A Nordic god with African ancestry. He grasped my hand like he was chopping wood and shook it vigorously.

"Pedro?" I questioned.

"Paul, actually," he stated. "Paul Johanssen. Originally from Chicago, but that was another life."

He invited us in. I glanced back at the Jeep. Little Jim was still sleeping, mouth open, neck curled over the back of his seat.

The old restaurant kitchen overlooked a long bar and booths under mud-dusted windows; it reminded me of an unused movie set. The thirty-two-inch flat screen sat lonely on a Formica table in the opposite corner. A red rug covering the center of a worn oak floor billowed dust as I stepped on it.

"This is my front room, dining room, and entertainment room." Pedro's hands rolled in circles. He turned and pointed to the front door. "The porch is my meditation suite." He laughed then spun on his heels. "And through these doors is my gallery and art studio."

We followed.

As I entered, the smell of paint, turpentine, and varnish stung my nose. The room was an add-on to the original restaurant. More like a barn than a room. I gazed up at a rounded ceiling of corrugated steel hung with cables and pulleys mounted from two beams at a forty-five-degree angle from the roof. Some cables held sheets of plywood. Others dangled like thin, long icicles from the pulleys. I followed Pedro through a slit in a clear plastic wall that separated the half circle into two rooms.

I stopped in my tracks. A nude, six-foot woman stared back at me. As I slowly shifted, a row of semi-nude women and men came into view. Some were sitting on tables or chairs, others stood posed and grinning by palm-lined beaches or vintage cars. It was disturbing—as surreal as if I'd entered a world of giant, tacky calendars. Pedro's art consisted of giant posters, like *Playboy* centerfolds, glued to full or half sheets of plywood with coats jef polyurethane reflecting halogen lights off the nudes.

I glanced at Hub. He shrugged his shoulders.

"Well?" asked Pedro.

I grimaced. "You have a consistent theme, even though it's a bit distasteful and alarming. You sell these?"

"All over the world, my friend." His face beamed as he nodded. "It's abhorrent, I know. But this cheap art . . ." Pedro pointed at a twenty-something male with his palms clasped around a golf club, eyes focused, as if looking off into the distance. His golf bag hid one leg and his groin. "I get $1,700 a pop for that."

I shook my head in disbelief.

"The best thing is that this building's paid for, I have zero debt, and I net on the upper edge of $300K per year." His cheeks rose into a devilish grin. "In Chicago, I'd probably be driving one of those street sweepers alongside my old man and making forty grand a year."

"Fair enough. Can we go back into the restaurant to talk?" I asked.

Filing quietly out of the studio, we moved back through the plastic slit, out the swinging door, and into a dusty booth in the front. Pedro came out from the back. He opened a fridge, grabbed a six-pack of beer, and wetted a towel at the sink. With big arms flexed, he wiped off the top. We held elbows high until he set the beer on the worn Formica surface. He slid a chair over to where we were and sat with its back to his round chest. We all grabbed a Corona. Well, except Harold.

Harold began. "We're looking for a person called Six Sky or *Sexto Cielo*. The only thing we know is that she runs a group of young *matóns*, hoodlums. We've heard she may be in this area."

Pedro took a draw on his beer. "She's a rumor. At least, I don't know anyone who's ever seen her. There's talk she's a princess or a queen of the Mayans who rose from the dead."

We turned as the door crashed open.

In stumbled Little Jim. He walked into a chair, swiveled his neck, and noticed us. "There you are. Left me bakin' in the sun." His eyes were half closed. Everyone watched as he stiff-legged it over to us. He put his hand on Hub's shoulder. His lids popped open and he reached out to snatch a beer off the table. "Don't mind if I do. Don't mind at all." He guzzled the beer.

I turned back to Pedro. "You know anything about the gang? Some 'followers' tried to put bullet holes in us."

"In Mexico, there's lots of *pandillas*. Different names, different places. They all steal, buy guns from the States, frighten the locals, think they're bad asses. Same as in L. A. or any city in the U. S. of A. I stay away from those areas and those types. A guy like me, living in a run-down restaurant? They think I'm just another old, lost hippie surviving on scraps and smoking my retirement away." He turned to Hub. "Tried to put a hole in you?"

"Lucky for us, they weren't very good shots," said Hub. "And Carson's and my karma certainly helped."

"Any more beer?" asked Little Jim.

Pedro nodded at the cooler behind the bar. "You might try Saint Augustine's Church over on *Camino Viejo,*"

"Is Father Ortiz still there?" asked Harold.

"Holy shit!" bellowed Little Jim. "You got more beer in here than a Maverick station."

"No, he died maybe eight years ago." Pedro glanced suspiciously at Little Jim. "But that's the biggest church in town, and the priests hear about everything."

We all stood and thanked Pedro from Chicago for his help. Harold and Pedro hugged then nodded at each other.

As I got into the Cherokee, I glanced around, jumped out, and stormed through the restaurant door.

Little Jim looked up from the table where he was sitting. "You mind if I just stay here?"

"No! You're coming with us," I noticed relief on Pedro's face. I grabbed Little Jim by the arm and lifted him up.

Little Jim turned to Pedro. "Mind if we take this beer for the road? It's mighty hot."

"Sure, it's yours." Pedro walked us to the door and mouthed, "Thanks."

Following Harold's directions, we headed for the church.

After a bit of zigzagging, we pulled up in front of a large stone church with an ornate carved door. We followed Harold around the side of the building. A narrow path weaved between furrowed ground. Beans, peppers, and squash hung from thick, verdant vines. Just past a stone statue of the Virgin Mary cuddling baby Jesus stood a solitary eight-foot door with a bell pull to the side. Harold pulled the chain, and the bell chimed. We waited.

A young, bearded priest answered. He peered skeptically at the four white guys who hadn't visited a church in a lifetime. A thin smile raised his cheeks.

"*Hola, señors.*" It was more of a question than a greeting.

Harold explained in rapid Spanish who we were and that he was a good friend of Father Ortiz. Harold's ease with the language showed in his familiar tone.

The priest invited us in with hands steepled at his chest. We walked down a narrow stone hallway; the only light peered from holes above our head the size of bread loaves. He led us to a room with a thick timber table and high-backed chairs.

Harold interpreted for us. It seemed his friend Father Ortiz passed away seven years ago. Condolences were exchanged. This man was Father Comedor, Father Ortiz's replacement. The priest was stocky with broad, prominent Aztec features. A three-inch pigtail crawled down his thick neck.

"¿Conoces a Sexto Cielo?" asked Harold.

Father Comedor's face slackened. He seemed shocked by the question and his mouth hung open for several seconds. His eyes focused on a blemish marring the table. *"No la conozco,"* he finally said in a weak voice. He shook his head, still staring downward.

"Sí lo haces. Por favor díganos." Harold's voice was stern but friendly.

I could tell the Father knew who Six Sky was, but fear made him hesitant. Minutes passed in silence. Father Comedor's eyes turned to me then Harold.

"Ella es una mala mujer." He paused and licked his lips. *"Magia malvada."*

Hub interjected. "She's a bad woman. Evil magic."

Father Comedor hesitantly answered my questions through Harold and Hub for an hour. His fingers twisted together in an impatient dance, and he talked into them. Harold thanked him, and we were ushered out the same door through which we came. The priest's neck muscles relaxed as he hurried us past the garden.

"I understood some, but tell us what's up?" I asked.

"Blood sugar," replied Harold, "Let's find a café. Do we have any water in the truck? I'm getting dizzy."

Knowing this had much to do with his sobriety, I grabbed a warm water from the trunk and some Mexican candy from my backpack. He thanked me. We drove about three blocks to La Paloma restaurant. I picked a seat outside near the traffic and far away from other guests. The white-dressed waitress looked annoyed at having to walk clear over to us. I ordered *cervezas* and turned to Harold for his order. He mumbled as he ordered nothing but coffee. Little Jim added a tequila on the rocks for himself. The young waitress slapped the menus down with limited hospitality.

With anxious looks, we leaned in and waited for Harold. His hands were shaking.

"Lady Six Sky is a woman about thirty or maybe a touch younger," he began. "Scares the willies out of Father Comedor, as you could see. She has hundreds of followers, perhaps thousands, and her troops pick up more kidnapped 'volunteers' whenever she sees fit. There is an unwritten rule that her followers—she calls them her 'tribe'—never take anyone from Guadalupe, and he thinks a couple of other cities as well. Here, they can join of their own free will but not be forced."

"Are there many who join?" I asked.

"Father Comedor said too many," Hub answered. "He seemed worried by that."

Harold continued, "The group is trained and deadly. They are forcibly taught in the *templo de la vida y muerto*—temple of life and death—to follow and obey her and her shamans."

"Shamans are supposed to do good," said Hub. "They are the key to helping and enlightenment." He paused, "Did they say *¿Brujo o curandero*? Native healer or witch doctor?"

"Obviously, there are different interpretations," I interjected.

"But it's wrong. It could create a slash in the universe. An apocalypse in the dimensions. It goes against all the teachings."

"What about the bloodletting and sacrifices made by the ancient Mayan shamans?"

"That all changed with better knowledge." Hub leaned across the table and peered into my face.

"Or not," I said.

The waitress came back with our drinks and took our orders for lunch. She also left us with warm tortillas and a bowl of refried beans. I think we'd all waited too long to eat. I tore off a piece of tortilla, dipped it in the hot beans, and shoved it into my mouth. All that mixed-in lard tasted incredible.

We ripped and dipped, the only sounds coming from the street and our chomping. The tortillas were gone. The Pacifico bottles lay empty when the waitress brought our food. The conversation could wait.

The smell of meat, beans, exhaust, street litter, and lime trees sifted through our nostrils. Weaving motorbikes honked as we settled back in our chairs, satiated and content. We hadn't spoken during our lunch—a man-indulgence thing. We all waited for Harold to slop the last swirl

Mosquito Sands

from his plate with a tortilla.

Pushing my plate away, I cocked my head and asked, "Well?"

Harold held up a finger and wiped sauce from his chin. "Father Comedor does not want his name mentioned. He fears for the safety of his congregation and his church. In his words, 'Anticipation of retaliation builds fences and takes the tongue.'"

"So, we shouldn't expect anyone to voluntarily help us. Story of my life." I tapped my knuckles on the table.

The waitress picked up the dishes. I ordered three more Pacificos and a coffee refill for Harold. The waitress nodded and left.

"He hears rumors. *Señora Sexto Cielo* is only spoken of behind locked doors. The legend is that she uses dark magic to control the weather, snakes, panthers, rodents, and the moon. From the sweat on the priest's brow, I think he believes it. She has a fleet of girls ranging in age from fourteen to twenty. She commands a much smaller portion of boys about the same age. The boys are slaves with no status. The talk is that they are used mostly for procreation and are kept in cells." The waitress returned with the beers. She set two in front of Little Jim. He smiled.

Harold waited until she was gone before continuing, "They say she's descended from a Mayan queen who ruled centuries ago. No one has seen her. And get this, Lady Six Sky can turn into a black mist and rip out hearts with three fingers."

"Which three?" asked Little Jim.

We all glared at him.

"Yeah, which three fingers? Or does she only have three?" He rested his chin on his forefinger and thumb as if deep in thought. "It could matter." He nodded to himself. "I saw a movie once—"

"Was there anything else?" I asked Harold.

"Wait," said Hub. "What about this movie?"

I shook my head and turned back to Harold.

"Just other tales," Harold said. "She can throw fire. Not sure what that means. And read minds."

"Usually when there's fear there's exaggeration," I interjected. "Anything else that might help?"

He nodded like a schoolboy holding something back. "She has property all over southern Mexico and a ranch just outside Guadalupe. Father Comedor says he thinks it's vacant now."

We definitely needed to check out the ranch. I assumed she picks up youth because they're malleable, but I wasn't sure why she chose Seronia, an autistic living in the middle of nowhere. Maybe it was just a fluke? They did abduct several youths from the area. But if what Father Comedor said was true, she was much younger than the usual "volunteer." I remembered that look of defiance on the short driver from the pink Caddy. It was laced with total fright.

"Did you ask the priest if he would ask around and let us know?"

Harold smiled. "Of course. That's when he froze up and scooted us out of the church. I'll never forget that look of terror in his eyes."

17

Seronia

On the passenger side of the truck, Seronia helped Mari out through the door with a gentle pull. Mari's face seemed to flatten as every muscle in her head and neck stretched. Seronia grabbed her from behind, lifted, and duck-walked her over to a tree shading a soft patch of green barn grass. Little squeaks and gasps erupted as Seronia set Mari down. Seronia smiled as she watched a distant object, that perhaps, only she could see. Mari laid on her back in the shade and stared at Seronia with disbelief.

Seronia left Mari and jumped back into the truck with Sandoza. With her nose almost touching Sandoza's greyish cheek, Seronia listened as she repeatedly bit her bottom lip. She sniffed at her eyes. She pried her mouth open and tapped on her neck. Seronia pulled at Sandoza's bloodied shirt. Sandoza remained limp as her hair. *Dead?* Seronia stood and leapt to the ground.

Trueno had crawled a few feet on flat hands and knees. She bellowed in a mad cry, arms searching the air in front of her. Tears flowed from her tightly closed eyes. She grabbed at her pockets for her cell phone. Nothing.

Seronia searched through the herbs, leaves, and roots within her rock circle. The more frustrated she became, the faster her hands pedaled at her sides. Seconds later, her hand flew up even with her chest, and she let out a half-giggle. She scooted up the hill with determination, hands still flapping in the air. She stopped about twenty yards from the truck and jutted to her left. Walking along a game trail, she stopped and searched the hillside at different points. Finally, she knelt at the side of a small mountain ball cactus. With a nearby piece of slate, she chipped at the side of the plant until she removed a wedge and dropped it to the ground. With thumb and forefinger, she picked it up by one thorn. With her other hand she grasped the lime-green wet center and held it up to the light.

She hurried back to Sandoza. With a flick of her wrist, she jabbed the needles into the flesh of Sandoza's inside wrist. There was an almost unnoticeable twitch. Seronia flapped her hands in happiness. The cactus chunk flew to a corner of the truck bed. With new purpose, she hopped out and began working. She gathered a few things from her stash in the circle, a rag from the cab, the water jug, and a few termites she found in a hollowed log.

Mari slept in the shade of the tree while Trueno swore, threw dust into the air, and kept blinking her eyes in an effort to focus her vision.

For several hours, Seronia worked on Sandoza. She cleaned the chewed leg, plugged a main artery with a stick no bigger than a toothpick applied mud, wrapped it all in leaves and tree sap, tied ripped fabric around the wound, and patted Sandoza's face with a wet shirtsleeve. Sandoza, still in a comatose state, hadn't responded to anything. Her breathing was as narrow as a mosquito.

Seronia had also tried to help Trueno, who batted her away with a maniacal laugh. The jimson weed had taken effect hours ago, and both Trueno and Mari were lost in its inebriating and hallucinogenic effects. Pain and reality were of no consequence. They slept and smiled at dreams only they knew.

Seronia, who had been nursing her three kidnappers for hours, was drenched in sweat. The sun barely peeked over the western hills, casting an orange and purple hue on the thin clouds. After covering Sandoza with the ripped blanket Seronia had been wrapped in, Seronia laid on a bed of wheat grass and fell asleep.

The effects of the jimson weed on Trueno seemed to have worn off; she awakened with a scream. Her eyes batted crazily as if searching for vision. The truck was in front of her, and she fumbled her way up into the cab. Her hands fondled the seat and the steering wheel. She swept her fingers across the dash to the glovebox. She slapped the front until her finger landed on the button. The glovebox opened. She peered inside as if she could see. Her fingers shuffled through maps and papers, searching for a gun or cell. A goose egg at her hairline had grown and turned a horrid shade of purple and orange; hardened blood streaked her skin and clothes.

Trueno sat back in frustration. She felt her pockets and under the seat. She cut the back of her hand on something sharp on the floor.

Mosquito Sands

Annoyed, she tightly clasped the cut. Dried blood marbled her face, and she wouldn't let Seronia clean her off. Dark was seeping over the truck as the shadows lengthened. She peeked out the passenger window and squinted. A slight snore wafted over to the truck.

Seronia and Mari had fallen asleep under the spiked branches of a Russian olive tree.

Trueno slipped from the truck and again searched the ground by the door. After twenty minutes, she found her cell by the front tire, which now curved into the stout trunk. She fumbled for the on button. Her fingers pressed it into a cupped hand. Though she couldn't make out any details, Trueno's eyes caught the soft, green glow of the phone as it waited for service. On her knees, sitting on her heels, back straight, she prepared to punch in the number with her thumbs. The light from the cell collapsed. In anger, she jammed her finger into the on button. Nothing. She tried again. Dead. She smashed it into the crumpled hood of the truck.

A chirping laugh bubbled from fifteen feet away. Trueno turned and tried to focus. Her shoulders slumped as she heard Seronia standing a few yards away, her voice happy as a lotto winner.

Who has taken charge? Trueno silently wondered. Could Seronia be the prisoner? Or were Trueno, Mari, and Sandoza the prisoners?

Trueno started toward the laughter. Her head smacked into a tree branch, opening a scar on her head. She huddled unsteadily on hands and knees. The giggling echoed behind her.

Suddenly the laughing stopped. Seronia reached back and picked up the cell, which had landed in a bush. She walked over and handed the phone to Trueno. Trueno shook the kindness from her head. Cords in her throat tightened into protruding bands. With her lips bolted to her teeth, she finally let out a whoosh of defeated air and sat back on her butt. She pocketed the cell in case she could somehow recharge the battery later.

Seronia ripped the bottom of her large T-shirt and used it to blot the streaming blood from Trueno's head. Trueno cowered but let Seronia tend to her.

When Seronia was done with Trueno, she headed back to Sandoza in the truck bed. She wetted a cloth and wiped Sandoza's face with the precision of a watchmaker. Sandoza's breath was faint, but her chest raised and lowered slightly. Semi-conscious, her lips quivered as chills rolled through her body. Seronia lifted Sandoza's arm. It dropped as though it had no bone.

Jef Huntsman

A new day began. All was silent except for the occasional chirping of birds and the mountain breeze that fluttered leaves far overhead. The sun had been up for hours but was hidden behind black clouds. Mari muttered in her endless sleep. She had awakened a few times in the last sixteen hours, raised her head, peeked through slits of eyes, then fallen back to sleep. Trueno had finally fallen exhausted onto the truck seat after blindly seeking her charger and finding the truck battery crushed and dripping acid into soft dirt. Sandoza was still comatose in the truck bed, closer to death than life.

Seronia had awakened early. She hummed a tune her mother sang to her as a baby. It was her favorite of the three songs she knew. The other two both had to do with birthdays: *Las Mañanitas*, the song she listened to in the early mornings of each of the village children's birthdays; and a lovely, fun song that cheered the children on as they swung at a homemade *piñata*. Seronia whistled, delighted with her day. She knew how happy her father would be with her healing abilities. A hidden pride blossomed though she wasn't sure about it. The words *curandero chamán* echoed in her head. A smile filled her face as she danced and flitted her hands above her head.

A jut of light flared, then a crackle boomed in the distance. Seronia paid no attention. She danced and trilled and danced. A whoosh of wind lifted her hair as it streamed behind her. The sky darkened, and a two-legged lightning bolt temporarily lit the sky. The darkness returned with the sound of an explosion several hilltops away. Soft drops tickled Seronia's face. She arched her neck and held out her tongue for more. Drop after drop, she caught the cool rain on her tongue.

Another flash lit the sky, this time closer. The rumbling was felt as much as heard, and then the rain pelleted down in a sudden fury.

Seronia ran to Sandoza and covered her face with the blanket. Mari had awakened and seen Seronia in the truck bed. She headed for the cab, fumbled under the seat until she came up with a crumpled sheet of clear plastic, and took it to Seronia. The two covered Sandoza with the plastic tarp, setting rocks around the edges to keep the gale of wind from blowing it away. When they were done, Mari pried Seronia away. Seronia wanted to stay with her patient, but Mari took her by the hand and led her into the cab that rested under the big tree. Then Mari pushed Trueno over. Trueno grumbled and slapped back, swearing at her *compadre*. Trueno finally complied, though she grimaced and growled.

Mosquito Sands

The three in the cab waited and watched. Lightning struck closer, and the sound between lightning strikes was faster. Soon rivulets snaked through the countryside around them. Mud buckled up on the sides of newly formed streams as rainwater drenched the desert hills. Lightning strobed all around them as Trueno shivered and spit expletives into her clenched hands.

Under the tarp, Sandoza lay oblivious as buckets of rain seeped through the rusted metal of the truck bed.

Empty stomachs churned. Cups of water were the only relief from heads that spun and ached for solid food. On the morning of the third day, the sun lifted over the mountains. Steam danced on tip toes. The dread black of puddles glistened and sparked in the morning light. Soon, branches and leaves would lift from the bright energy, their final drips hitting the tiny ponds below.

Trueno was cuddled up to Seronia, her head in the curl of her prisoner's neck. Mari leaned from the other side, her head asleep on Seronia's lap. Their breathing was slow and gentle. They looked like teens at a sleepover.

Seronia was the first to awaken. As her head cleared, she panicked. Her neck twisted back and forth. Her arms were trapped under the other girls. Her hands shook. The autism roared to life, and with volcanic eruption her arms raised and shoved her two companions into the opposite doors. The tight quarters had were too much for a girl who had never liked being hugged or caressed.

Trueno and Mari shook sleep from their minds for a brief second. Mari's head was shoved into the door as a panicked Seronia reached for the handle, and they both spilled out into a bog of mud and uprooted weeds. Seronia landed on Mari and pressed her deep into a puddle. Seronia then took off running, spraying spurts of brown water behind her feet.

Seronia did not stop running until she reached the crest of the hill. Her hands rapidly patted the sides of her legs. She sucked in deep breaths of moist, warm air; her chest heaved as she tried to calm herself.

Mari lifted her head. Chunks of clumped, wet soil ran down her hair and dripped into the puddle below. Trueno swore into the morning air. Eyes big as baseballs, she screamed at Seronia up the hill. Seronia was too far away to hear. Mari's mouth opened, and she took in a defeated breath. A soggy desert flower with only one pedal left crested her head.

Mari lifted herself and sat back in the truck. Muddy water dripped from her hands and knees.

Once calm, Seronia knew she needed food. Her hands still padded at her sides but with less force. She had watched Juan Diego forage plants and berries as they traveled from village to village in his work as "the" *Curando Chamán.* Her mind had stored everything he had shown her. She could not form words, but she knew things few others could fathom.

Seronia gazed around at the wet, semi-barren desert mountain. The relentless rain had driven all the animals in their burrows and kept them there. Nothing chirped from the trees. Birds rested and dried their feathers on the edges of nests that were pooled with water. Plants drooped like defeated soldiers in swampy ground. Finally, something caught Seronia's attention. She sloshed up one hill, down a ravine, across a storm-birthed spring, and up another, higher hill. At the top of the hill was a plateau, a mile long and half that wide. It was covered in various cacti. She smiled and giggled.

Seronia hiked over to a grove of prickly pear cacti that were loaded with pods. Some of the pods had been knocked to the ground from the storm. She began filling her damp, muddy shirt with the egg-shaped fruit. Seronia popped a few into her mouth. The sweet taste rolled across her tongue and down her throat. Sighs of joy sprung from her lips.

With her shirt bulging, she carried the food down to the others. As she came back over the second hill, she heard tires spinning in the mud. Seronia stopped at a tree about a third of the way back to the truck. She could see two vehicles, black Explorers, like the one she'd drawn in front of the barber shop in Balleza. Seronia loved the way the moonlight reflected off the hood.

The SUVs slid, spraying water and mud behind their massive tires. The front one stopped on thick sagebrush as the hill leveled.

18

Carson

I dropped off Harold, Little Jim, and Hub at the motel, explaining that I needed stealth. Hub argued, but I left alone anyway. I needed to check out this ranch without the fanfare and visibility of the whole troop. Hub retrieved his computer from the trunk and said he'd do some internet recon. A dent on his laptop had scratched to bare metal, marking the spot where a stray bullet hit. He booted it up. The laptop worked but wiggled in one spot on the screen. Hub seemed okay with it.

I had hazy directions, a full tank of gas, and the Beretta. The Cherokee had enough dust and mud on it to be a camouflage vehicle. I pulled out, and the three men waved like kindergarten kids whose mothers had just dropped them off for the first time.

Five miles out of town a well-used dirt road angled off through a field of baled hay. A long-abandoned sign lay face down in the sagebrush. The priest had mentioned that the small sign would say *Fernandez Inc.*, the name of the original owners who had left twenty years ago for America. The place had been abandoned since. I hefted the sign. All that was left was a sprinkling of paint, but I could make out *Fernandez*.

Feathered dust left a plume behind me as I headed between two rolling hills. The ranch would be more than four more miles at the edge of sparse mountains. I watched the odometer, slowing at three miles in. From there I crept off the road, plowed through sagebrush and yellow grass, and climbed a large hill. It was impossible not to churn up dust, but a northern wind helped dissipate my truck's upheaval.

Nearing the top of the hill, I stopped and got out of the Jeep. Sliding my Berretta into the front of my pants, I proceeded on foot. Sharp, black rocks jutted out along the deer trail I followed. At the top, an abandoned ranch house came into view. Six corrugated steel, half-round buildings dotted the forgotten pasture below. A few wooden outbuildings and a fenced corral stood behind the house. Several old trucks buried up to the wheel wells in hardened mud and thin grass hinted at what once was a working ranch. Well-used paths snaked between each steel building. Rows of sunken rocks lined each path.

I saw all those things, but I *didn't* see people and vehicles. Nor did I see horses or cattle. The place looked recently used but vacant, as if the family who lived there would be returning any time from a day run to the city.

I sat on that knoll for several hours waiting for some sign of life. Finally, a doe jumped the fence below and tore across the compound, free as a bird. As it gracefully bounced across the land in front of one of the steel buildings, I watched the ground explode. A bloody spray of animal parts rose from the parched earth. Gravity dropped them gracefully back to earth like rice at a wedding.

Then silence.

Mice and rats scurried from their holes. The ground was mined. The poor doe had made a deadly step in the wrong place. My heart pounded. Someone didn't want visitors. I wondered how many more mines there might be. Using binoculars, I eyed the ground and the buildings. The puff of dust was still settling.

No one ran out from any of the buildings. Nothing else stirred. I wondered if I should be here. Seronia probably wasn't here, I reasoned, but if anyone *was* here, he or she might know something.

I walked back to the Jeep and took it down the incline to the road. My heart pounded against my chest as I drove down the road toward the ranch. I assumed the mines would be only around the buildings, but I knew I could be wrong. My eyes scanned the dirt path ahead for any telltale signs of mines. A surprise explosion wasn't the way I wanted to go. But I had to find out why someone would mine an area where no one lived. *Something* had to be there.

I needed to talk to Hub. I tried my cell, no bars. The sun kicked little dust devils across the valley below. I patted my pistol and kept driving toward the cluster of buildings.

Arriving at the gate, a stillness flowed through me. I stopped, got out, and checked my surroundings. I hopped back in the car after a ten-minute surveillance. The Jeep eased forward until it was facing the exit. Shutting off the motor, pocketing the keys, and stepping out, I headed for what looked like the main building.

I followed days-old tire tracks as best as I could. My lungs felt too loud. My eyes scanned the area for other hidden mines. They could have been ancient World War II mines that, due to the Ottawa Treaty, were banned from being produced or stockpiled in most of the world. I didn't know about the regulations in Mexico. The explosion might also have come from an IED that someone had built right in this compound from plans on the internet. Either way, I was taking no chances.

As I neared the main building, I noticed several dozen holes. Someone had removed many of the mines. Maybe someone was waiting at another compound to shred a human to parts. These devices had no boundaries. They could kill an innocent child or a soldier in the blink of an eye. My mouth tightened as I thought about the people who would use indiscriminatory warfare.

The tire tracks I was following ended in a curve ten feet from the building. On hands and knees, I crawled to the front, where a garage door was tightly shut and padlocked. My fingers rolled gently across the earth, searching. My eyes strained, unblinking. I could taste dust and anxiety with each breath from my open mouth. A slight raise in the earth caught my fingertip. I stopped. My lungs froze. My hand backed slowly away. I leaned in. Something was there. I eyed the curve of a dome. I carefully blew the dirt over the dome, and metal twinkled in the dimming sunlight. I was four feet from the roll-down door. A barred window was sixteen feet from the door to my right. I snaked around the mostly hidden dome of death. A burst of wind came up from behind me, kicking my heart into overtime. In windy stillness, I took deep breaths to slow my pulse. Two more knee crawls, and I was at the massive door. *A tank or a semi could drive through this*, I thought.

Grabbing a nearby rock, I pounded the rusty lock until my fingers bled. It held. I stepped out from the inset of the door and gazed toward the window. I worried about crawling along the edge. Would they be stupid enough to put mines so close to the building? They could tear a hole in the metal. Not likely, but I didn't understand these people yet. And there was one four feet from the main door. I paused. I picked up a handful of rocks that lined a path in the direction of the next building. Standing behind the inset of the garage door, I rolled the rocks toward the window. By the sixth rock, I felt safe.

The wind picked up. Debris rolled across the compound in an eerie roar. I had just started my trek to the window when I noticed a slight glint. I turned around to where I'd crawled. The top of the mine showed through. I edged closer to read an inscription. It had two letters—VW. I laughed. The damn "mine" was a Volkswagen hubcap.

I headed to the window in a better mood but still cautious. Through the bars and heavy plexiglass was an office—complete with a desk, filing cabinet, scattered papers, and a completely erased white board. A dead mouse lay on the dusty desk. Something in the corner glistened. My breath caught for a second. An eighteen-inch spider web netted three walls. Judging from the dust, the mouse, and the spider web, it didn't look as if anyone had been there for some time. I pounded on the window, but the glass was at least an inch thick and sandwiched in a heavy, metal frame.

I went back to the door and retraced my footsteps out about fifteen feet. Laying on the ground was a metal post like those farmers use to string barbed wire. After checking the ground, I moved toward it. I noticed a slight hump in the ground. A buried IED lay to its left. I moved around, grabbed the post with two fingers, and slid it toward me. A groundhog poked her head out of a hole two feet from the IED. I turned and quickly stepped back the way I'd come. The groundhog disappeared. *At least the mines are probably cutting down the rodent population*, I thought.

Back at the door, I pried the lock with the post. Then I tried banging it in long, forceful swings. The rusty lock finally snapped open. Revolver in hand, I carefully opened the door. It creaked. I kept my body hidden behind the building. With a quick rush and roll to the ground, I held the Beretta in two hands, arms outstretched. The only sound was an empty echo.

With mines outside, I had to be doubly careful inside. Empty wooden crates the size of fridges were stacked everywhere. I eased around the wall toward the room into which I had peered. Bricks formed a space for the room, though there wasn't an entrance. It appeared there never was a door—just a room with an interior door that had been bricked in. A false room? The only window into the place revealed an office that had been abandoned—or maybe never used. Interesting.

I heard a noise and caught a blur of motion across as I swung around. The silence spoke loudly. Another mirage? A rodent? I didn't think so. I ventured closer to the noise, keeping partially covered by the open crates that filled the space in a haphazard maze. I heard a faint slide of shoes. My breathing stopped. My gun swung in an arc. My eyes were wide open. I felt my heart pound within my chest.

I heard the bullet whiz by before the bang of the shell. I dropped to

Mosquito Sands

the floor, face first, then rolled behind another crate. Drips of blood spotted the cement floor. More shots slammed into the wooden box behind which I had previously hidden. Pine shards splintered around me. I tried to detect where the bullet came from. Everything appeared intact until my hand felt warm, crimson fluid below my nose. Shit—a nosebleed from my fall at a time like this! I pinched the bridge of my nose with one hand and sighted the nine-millimeter in the direction from which the shots came. I held my breath as I listened to a hollow quiet. My eyes searched.

I spotted one of them. A short gun barrel stuck out from a hole in a crate. There was another two-inch hole about a palm's length above the first one. There was a flicker of movement. They had the gun pointed to my left. I took aim, pulled the trigger slowly, and within a millisecond the sound of dead weight dropped inside the box. The gun fell with it. I moved quickly three crates over, my pistol leading the way. I recalled the tried-and-true rule: never stay in the same place too long when bullets are flying. A dusty rag lay on the ground. I ripped it into two strips and stuffed the vile cloth into my nostrils. I waited.

Still no sound. It was a waiting game. First one to move loses. Ears, eyes, taste focused. Twenty minutes passed. Then I heard it: a quiet shave of shoe on paper about ten yards to my left. I hunched down and circled to my right. Each step eased down as if I was stepping on hot coals. My breath paced in rhythm with my movement. I stopped two feet away from the crate. An accidental thump pierced the silence from the far side of the building.

Neck extended, I took one short step and peered into the the open eye of my victim. The other eye had exploded from the nine-millimeter. No exit wounds. Instant death. I retrieved the gun by her curled knee. She was probably nineteen. Such a waste.

What is this all about? How many more young girls had been made for this kind of life, for combat?

I reloaded both guns. Hers was a twenty-two pistol—deadly, but not at a distance. I tucked hers into my pants pocket and crept further in. A plaster wall came up on my right. Somewhere there must be a door. My ears picked up the sound of feet running over concrete floor. I shot just above the sound. The movement stopped. She (or possibly, but not likely, he) waited as I crept silently on the balls of my feet. Two crates away I paused.

Long black hair and devil eyes came at me with a knife as big as a sword. I shifted before the blade swiped through the skin and bone of my neck. Her motion followed through, and the knife plunged into a wooden crate, cutting it like butter. I twisted and raised my leg as she went past. My foot hammered into her spine with enough force to disable anyone. The sound of lungs deflating, and an airless scream of pain shot through the warehouse. I kicked her hand. The knife released. With speed, I grabbed the handle and tossed it on top of a crate. I pressed the barrel of my gun into the back of her head. She tried to hold still, but her body shook. I swiftly scanned the part of the room I could see. The only sound was her gasping air. I turned her over.

"How many more?"

Her eyes widened.

"¿Cuántos más?"

She shook her head. Her face trembled.

I pressed the gun into her forehead. *"¿Cuántos más . . . gente aqui?"*

One finger rose in shaky movements. She pointed toward the wall.

It took me a few moments to translate English into Spanish. I needed Hub, but I was glad he wasn't here. He develops silly anxiety when guns start firing. He freezes. *"¿Hay más gente con pistolas?"*

Worried eyes scanned the Beretta's barrel. She was thinking. Either her fear was subsiding, or she was weighing options.

I clicked the hammer back.

She nodded affirmatively. Sweat dripped along her hairline. I used a plastic tie that I'd picked up from the hardware store in Guadalupe to clamp her wrists and ankles together—it was so much easier than using shoelaces. I tore her sleeve off and crammed it in her unwilling mouth. Her face shuddered as she gasped for air through flared nostrils. My face held steady above, watching hers. Blood dripped from my nose onto her cheek and painted a thin line down her jaw. I put the gun to her head and put my index finger to my lips. She quieted.

Snaking through empty crates I found the door. Sweat dripped from my brow. It must have been a hundred-plus in there. I pressed the wad of cloth further into my nostril. The knob turned. I eased it open, keeping my Beretta ready and my body shielded by the wall. I knew bullets could penetrate a wall or pine box, but it felt safer. No sound. I did a quick peek. Nothing. I eased around the door frame.

19

Carson

The room carried echoes well. Each step sounded back to me. Skylights lighted the room in dusty daylight. Tables followed the perimeter like docks at an empty marina. Pegboard and a smattering of hooks filled the cinderblock walls. Mice scuttered across the floor in darts and dashes. The cement floor had been swept, though not recently. I eased in. It reminded me of a vacant stage: a few props, hollow with leftover importance, and not a single living person.

I thought about going back to the strapped girl and asking more questions. What was here? Where is everyone? Why are you still here? I had hundreds more, but I kept advancing. It intrigued me. I glanced back to the door through which I had escaped. A twelve-foot statue perched above the door on a metal buttress. It looked ancient—like an actual relic. The statue was a Mayan god—the body of a snake and the face of a flat-browed man with a pronounced nose and thick hair that extended to the heavens. He held a row of axes in one hand. A large tear dripped from his eye. It was magnificent.

A brushing sound pulled me from the statue. I swung around to find a snake weaving across the cement and stone floor. I smiled, thinking about Hub. He would have seen this as a sign, something arriving from the myth. He knows volumes of information about the Mayan culture. I vowed that when I got back, I would ask him about the statue.

I ventured farther into the eerie warehouse. Three-quarters of the way I noticed two large metal grates in the far corners. Stepping more quickly, I headed toward the one on my right. With trepidation, I peered over the edge into total darkness. I shined the light from my phone down into a bottomless pit. Searching further, a metal ladder descended into the blackness. Musky air rose from the hole. I tried to heft up the grate. It lifted about an eighth of an inch before my back wanted to crack in half. It dropped with a soft clang.

I noticed a twelve-foot-long irrigation pipe attached vertically to the wall. I walked over to it. A slit ran down the hidden side and a latch held the two halves together. I unsnapped the latch to find a thin, long, metal pipe with a screwdriver welded to one end. It must do something. I went back to the grate and laid down on my stomach. I used my cell light to search. Satisfied, I crawled to another spot and searched some more. Nothing stood out that the pipe might fit into, and it wasn't strong enough to use as a lever.

In frustration, I ran back to where I'd left the tied-up girl. I eased silently forward. She wasn't there. I slid the 9mm out from my waist and followed drips and the swipe of blood in a path around the crates. My feet were like air on the hard cement. Down a second row of crates I heard a scraping to my right. The wadded cloth that I'd stuffed in her mouth lay wet on the floor. About six feet away, a scarred leg poked out of a crate, muscles tensed. I stealthily moved forward, my breathing slowed until I was getting barely enough air to keep me conscious.

I could hear her work feverishly, panting and scraping. I gripped my gun with both hands. I came closer and leaned forward. Her breath stopped. Her eyes locked on mine. She dropped her hands and swung both feet at my groin. I turned my legs to an angle. Her force caught me hard on the hip bone. The force popped me back a few inches. I swiveled in a swift motion. My foot cranked sideways and landed on her chest just above her breasts. I quickly slid it forward and put pressure on her throat. Her eyes bulged. Her tied feet flipped frantically as would a reeled-in fish on a boat deck. I applied more pressure, and her legs slowly retreated.

Staring hard at her, I asked, "You want this boot to crush your pretty neck?"

Eyes like moons gazed up. She shook her head in short, quick motions. Her face relaxed slightly in a pleading way.

I spotted the jutting nail from the crate that she had used to cut through her binds. I released my foot and lifted her arms. The plastic tie had marks across it, but she had not succeeded in cutting it all the way through. That would have taken a full hour or more. I released her, and she dropped to the ground.

I knew she understood English when she wanted to. "How do I get the grate open?"

"Grate?" her accent squeezed the word out.

Mosquito Sands

I motioned by raising my forearms from the elbow, palms up. "Open to below? What's your name?"

Her eyes darted. "Edita."

I picked her up by the armpit and dragged her behind me through the door into the open room. Her voice squealed, though weakly. Her feet scampered; they were tied, and she was trying to stay upright. I pulled her over to the right corner of the building, let her drop, took a step forward, and lifted the metal rod.

"Edita, how does this work?"

Her head dropped, and she peered at the ground.

I moved closer, the rod held firmly upright. I knew I wouldn't hurt her any more than she already was, but she didn't know that. I tapped her bent knee with my foot.

Edita peeked at me with frightened eyes. Her head nodded to the left.

I picked her up and walked in that direction.

"There," she said. Another nod.

I couldn't see a hole or anything where the rod might insert. I stuffed the 9mm back into my pants and raised my hands up. "What?"

She looked at the plastic binding her.

I slipped out my knife and cut her hands free. She glanced at her legs. I shook my head. With gentlemanly assistance, I walked her over to the wall. On a cement seam between bricks, her finger disappeared into solid concrete. Edita pulled her finger out and turned. A cranking noise came from the other corner and the grate lifted by two rainbow-shaped iron braces.

"What the hell?" I said. I walked back to the wall and felt around where her finger disappeared. I found a soft spot. With a press of my finger a rubber slot opened, and my finger slipped into the concrete. I could feel a button on the inside. I pulled my finger out and marked the spot with my knife blade.

"*¿Déjame ir?* You let Edita go?" she pleaded.

I thought about that for a few seconds. If I let her go, she might close the grate down on me or get a message to someone. I could imagine a bus load of guns coming after me—or a hundred other bad things.

"I will make sure you get safely out. Maybe to your family, but not yet."

Her mouth loosened in regret. "I give you *la puerta, no?*"

I ignored her. "What's down there?"

She sucked her lips in and glared at the floor.

"Edita, you tell me, and I'll get you out of here and let you live."

She took her time about the decision. Twice she glanced up at me. She must be weighing my honesty verses my betrayal. *"Gente,"* she said.

"How many?"

She shrugged. *"Treinta o quarenta."*

"Thirty or forty?" I softly touched her shoulder for reassurance. "With guns?"

"Tal vez cinco."

"Only five?"

"Si."

"Who are the ones without guns?" I asked.

"Prisioneros de los dioses."

"Prisoners of what?"

She thought for a second. "The gods."

"Prisoners of the gods?"

"Si."

"Anyone else?"

"Trabajadores."

"Workers?"

"Si."

I think she was telling me the truth. Could I trust Edita? Her façade of innocence masked her taught personality. No choice. Prisoners, workers, and about five guards. Her and the other girl must have been guards for the main floor. My thoughts about the dead girl with so much life ahead churned my stomach. Sweat dripped from my brow.

I grasped Edita's wrist and moved her over to the lifted grate door. I pulled out two plastic ties and bound her wrists with one. I used the other tie to attach her to the grate. Pushing her into a sitting position, I pulled out my only granola bar, opened it, and slipped it into her bound hands. From my pack I pulled out a water, took a long swig, and set half down for her. That was reassurance that I'd be back to help her. She pursed her lips, face tightening around high cheekbones. She wasn't sure about me.

I checked my ammo, tucked the gun away, and headed down the ladder of the big square hole. *Is this smart?* kept rolling around in my head. The window light shone a yellowish-grey tinge into the hole. Metal prongs ran in grooves along two sides; I wondered what they were for. They appeared antique and useless. It reminded me of a mine shaft I

Mosquito Sands

was once stuck in for three days in Iraq. My breath became shallow; my blood was pumping like a freight train.

I gazed up. The square beam of light didn't penetrate this far down. Above, I could discern the outline of Edita, dark and hazy. Her hands clung to the grate. I dangled my foot until I hit the next bar, counting on consistent spacing between the rungs as I climbed farther down into deep darkness. The ladder seemed sturdy, but anything could happen in this black hole. I shined my cell light down. Bricks lined the walls, some poking out, others chipped away by time. A section below looked empty—the darkness inky without form. I slipped the phone back and lowered into the foreboding gloom. The odor of thick oil and mold constantly crept through my nostrils.

Fifteen feet later, I stopped. Warm wind funneled around me. I couldn't see my feet or the bar they perched on. A rough opening appeared in the far wall. A pinhole of yellow light throbbed in the distance. I swung my cell light around. There were timber braces supporting the entrance and what appeared to be roots creeping around them and onto the brick walls. The opening raised up ten feet and almost the width of the shaft. I could make out ruts on the floor as if trucks had passed through and dropped into the blackness. There must be another entrance. It was too far for me to jump. I clicked off the light and proceeded down.

Rung after rung, I descended into the unknown. I peered up. The shaft opening was now the size of a slice of bread, indistinct around the edges. My legs and arms were exhausted. Sweat seeped from my every pore, my shirt soaked and clingy. I hung on to one rung trying to rest and regain my strength. The shaft seemed endless. I reached into my pocket and pulled out some pesos. My hand released them into the abyss. No clinking sound came back. Soft mud? The alternative weighted my shoulders. I wiped the sweat that poured from my hair into my eyes, but it merely smeared from my soaked shirt sleeve. A thought struck me. What if there was no end, and I turned back? Do I have the strength to pull myself all the way up? Had my battle with the two girls above drained me?

After a few minutes of respite, I continued down. On the third step, I couldn't find my footing. My foot dangled in empty space. I kicked further down. Nothing. Easing into a crouch, I swung my foot into the void. I ran my fingers along the ladder's supports. One sat angled and crunched. The other side was more intact. I ran my boot down its length as far as I could, but it dropped off into the dark shaft. I glanced back up at the dot of light way above. A stream of air sifted through clenched teeth. I pulled out my cell and peered down the shaft. The one good bracing extended as far as I could see. A rung loomed into sight. It sat four or five feet down, and I made out more treads below.

I took a final glance at the speck of light above me. With my foot snaked around the side vertical rail, I eased my body down. Muscles tensed. Tendons extended to their limits. The brace seemed sturdy, but . . . I lowered myself farther, my arms tender and aching, pain shooting upward. The tendons in my neck tensed to a breaking point.

I felt a softening assurance as one toe touched a rung, and I drew comfort from its sturdiness. The arch of my foot curled around the bar. I eased down the upright bracing. Another step, and relief swelled through heavy perspiration. Four more rungs and I stopped. The shaft's cool, musty breeze felt good for the first time. I paused several minutes before advancing.

Two more steps down, I heard a growl followed by something clicking not far below. There was a shift of gears. I could hear the gigantic chain creeping and struggling along the struts to either side. A door shut. It belonged to a car not far below.

I grabbed the phone from my pocket and flipped on the flashlight again. I couldn't see more than eight feet down. The ladder began to rattle as the giant chain tightened. A brick above me came loose and toppled inches from my head. It landed with a hard, metallic sound. Dust peppered my hair and shoulders. The taste of ground stone filled my mouth. Through squinted eyes, I saw the floor rising below me where there was nothing before. The ladder shuddered, and I dropped my cell. It landed with a clang. Its light drew closer and closer. There was a space of about five inches between the edge and the ladder. Inevitably, it crept up the brick cistern.

An elevator?

My timing had to be perfect, or the approaching steel floor would crush me. It crawled closer. Slow and steady. Five feet . . . Four feet . . . Three feet . . . I leapt and landed on a cross beam, tripped, and dropped to all fours, my cell inches from my face. I seized it and searched my surroundings. Several bricks from the shaft's sides lay scattered across the metal. It seemed to be the top of a freight elevator. Ancient, yet mechanically sound. The chains on the sides lifted it by latching onto heavy metal prongs welded to the reinforced sides. It worked like the mechanism that pulled San Francisco trolley cars up steep inclines. I clicked off my cell to preserve the dimming light.

I couldn't see inside the elevator, but I heard mumblings. The cadence had the singsong of the Romance languages. Spanish. Someone was inside. I was afraid to use the light now in case they spotted it through tiny cracks. I groped the surface. To the left, my hands clutched an inset handle. With further inspection, I followed the edge of a hatch and hinges on one side.

The elevator rose, and I wondered if we would reach the top. They would find Edita handcuffed to the opening. Then what? I needed a plan.

The lift came to a halt.

A door cranked open, rolling back on itself with a repetitive rattle. I waited, adrenaline surging through my veins.

I could see over the top of the elevator. Vehicle lights brightly illuminated a large cavern with railroad ties along the sides. It was the opening I'd seen earlier. A motor started. The lights crept along the cavern walls, revealing a series of timbers and chicken wire holding back rocky earth. A few minutes later, a truck pulled into sight. It was one of those three-wheeled trucks I'd seen all over Italy with a fiberglass shell and a few tools hanging out the back window. I heard a door open to the right. A small figure in a stain-blotted white T-shirt got out and pulled a lever attached to an eight-by-eight post. There was a grinding noise, and I watched the massive chain move laboriously, lowering the elevator back down the shaft. I flattened myself as much as possible to avoid being seen. Disappearing lights drove down the dark tunnel.

I lay still with my ear to the hatch. No voices, just the eerie catch and shift of the chain as it lowered me into the abyss. Dark minutes passed. I lost bracing as the elevator banged to a hard stop. The force slammed my cheek into the cold metal. Brick dust settled on my back. I lifted my head and gazed around. That smell of grease and earth clung to my nose and mouth. Everything lay pitch black and soundless.

I worked without sight. With my knife, I pried the hatch open slightly. Cold air whooshed through the opening. I curled around and stuck my head down. Shadowed, ambient light from far off provided scant illumination. No one was there. I raised the lid fully and slipped my legs down the opening. I hesitated. Without sight of a floor, even though I knew it was there, something made me wonder if I'd hit bottom. My feet dangled into nothingness. Then I let go. Calm washed through my chest as I hit a timber floor and rolled. I felt my way to the elevator door and stepped out into another cave. My eyes adjusted to the new darkness, taking in dark, formless shapes. An eerie wash of light caught on streams of metal supports and hanging roots.

20

Seronia

One tall girl got out with something in her hand. Her boots sunk in the mud. Her face shot a foul, downturned mouth at the ground. She held a box the size of a shoe in front of her. A constant beep sounded. At one point the speed of the beep increased. She signaled to the other vehicle and pointed in the direction of the crashed pickup. Four more people exited from the two vehicles. After some discussion, they walked up the hill with the beeping machine leading the way.

Seronia watched. Her hands tired of holding the weight of pods in her shirt, but she dared not move. Something was wrong. She felt it. She moved behind a thicket of scrub oak and waited.

Seronia spied down the other side of the hill. She could make out Mari as she moved in the back of the pickup. Mari lifted Sandoza up and cuddled into her. A shrieking bellow rang through the hills as Mari clutched the girl to her bosom. Trueno bent around and poked her head through the open window with a tight face, her hands clutching at her eye sockets.

Sandoza had shifted during the storm. Her back had slid off the backpack she rested on, and her face had landed in the puddle of pooling water. She drowned without ever regaining consciousness.

Trueno kicked the door open and got out of the truck. Her sight was blurry but getting better. Her hands followed the pickup fender. She stopped in front of the wailing Mari; she reached out and patted Mari on the back. Mari peeked over the rim of the truck bed. Her cheeks glossed from tears. Trueno showed caring for a few minutes, then remembered her sight and swore through gritted teeth.

Seronia turned and saw the five girls now listening to Mari's cries. They started moving faster. It would be only a matter of minutes before they found the crashed truck and the survivors. Seronia kneeled and let the cactus fruit roll out of her shirt to the ground. She picked up one and ate it. She was still hungry. She was a young girl who trusted everyone and had never had reason not to. Still, her shaman side told her something wasn't right. She peered through the leaves as the five girls rounded the corner and spotted Trueno and Mari.

With guns drawn, they hurried to the truck, young faces tightened and ready for battle. They spread out and converged in a half-circle formation. A round-faced girl with dark eyes slipped on loose mud, leaned forward, and caught her balance. Her foot was caught in the twisted stems of a sagebrush, and she tumbled. A hollow boom sounded from her rifle as her face planted in a puddle.

Trueno turned. She spotted the dim outlines of four approaching figures. "Who's there?" Her chest tightened. She blinked several times, trying to focus.

Mari wiped tears from her eyes, startled by the gunfire. The fifth girl lifted from the muck. Her rifle pointed in the air as she used it to hoist herself up from her knees.

"Katalina!" Mari screamed. "Katalina, you found us!"

Katalina swiped her face with her wet sleeve and stood up straight. "Mari!" she moved toward her old friend.

Mari jumped from the pickup, forgetting about Sandoza in the moment, and ran to Katalina. They embraced and bounced up and down like schoolgirls. The others approached with stern grimaces and stiff legs.

"How did you find us?" asked Mari as she moved out of the embrace. She and Katalina held each other by the shoulders and exchanged fond grins.

Mari and Katalina were both kidnapped from the Ste. Chaprel, a school in Los Mochis City on the gulf. They had hated each other at school, but they found they needed each other in the heat and humidity on Lady Six Sky's farm. That was more than three years ago. Through their obedience, Mari and Katalina moved up in rank until they became Mayan soldiers.

"All compound vehicles are fitted with transmitters," Katalina said matter-of-factly. "I didn't know you were one of the ones we were searching for."

The leader cleared her throat. "I'm Luciana." She stated as if they should know her name and quiver at the thought.

Mari and Katalina turned. All eyes were on them. The others glared with raised eyebrows. In the ranks, affection was frowned upon.

Mosquito Sands

Realizing their error, the two girls quickly let go of each other. Smiles faded and were replaced by the accepted scowl. The others uncrossed their arms and moved forward.

"My eyes have been cursed," said Trueno.

Luciana ignored her. She was short with shoulders like those of a man and a flattened nose that was wider than her mouth. "Have you captured the map girl?"

"She's the one who saved us," said Mari.

"Crap, she blinded me," said Trueno. "Look." She pulled down on the skin of her cheeks and widened her bloodshot eyes. "And her pet killed Sandoza. She and that pig are Satan."

Mari's face tightened. "She healed Sandoza, and she had nothing to do with your eyes." She pointed at Trueno and raised her voice. "You . . .you drove us into the tree."

"Shit." Trueno's face reddened, and she stormed towards Mari, her fists clenched.

A gun barrel stopped her, knocking the air from her lungs.

"We don't care about you two. Where's the girl?"

Still hidden in the stand of trees, Seronia was eating the fruit she had collected. She was also feeding a rock squirrel that had been attracted by the smell of food. The squirrel waited for the next tidbit that Seronia bit off and held up to the tiny mouth. Seronia caused no fear in the tiny creature, nor in any other. That was one of her gifts. Her innocence was felt by all creatures. She patted the squirrel on the head and placed another morsel into his mouth.

"She took off to look for food. She gave us medicine," Mari said.

Luciana lifted her chin toward the truck. "And her?"

"She drowned during the rain." Mari's voice quivered. "She was lucky to have made it this far. She lost her foot and a lot of blood."

"Which way did the girl go?" asked Luciana. "She had better not have escaped."

The others nodded.

Mari pointed up the hill. "I lost sight of her at the top of that second hill."

"How long ago?"

"Hour, maybe more."

Luciana sucked her cheek in against her teeth. She glared hard at Mari then toward Trueno. "You with the bad eyes, stay here." She nodded at Mari. "You show us where."

Mari wanted to complain about all the bruises on her body, the fact that it hurt to stand, the fact that she hadn't eaten in twenty-four hours or longer, but she turned and hiked up the muddy hill.

"Quintana, you stay here in case she comes back. We'll both signal with three shots if we find her." Luciana jammed a finger into Quintana's face. "Understand?"

A bushy-browed girl with a dirty pink bandana walked over to the open tailgate, glanced with an uncaring expression at Sandoza, and sat down. Sandoza's blank eyes stared into oblivion.

Trueno waited until the main group was out of earshot before asking, "You got any food?"

Quintana reached in her pocket and pulled out a mango. She took a healthy bite then handed it to Trueno. Trueno wolfed it down.

The journey up the hill was steep and slippery. They wore sneakers with little traction. Their knees were caked with mud from falling. They clung to bushes that came out by their roots and mumbled expletives under heavy breath.

It took them three times longer than it had Seronia, but they finally made it to the plateau. Luciana followed water-filled footprints to a group of cacti covered with red bulbs. Batches of the pods were missing. Another trail of footprints headed north then circled back to the mud-churned soil where they previously climbed. Little curls of steam rose as the sun heated the flat land of the plateau.

"She headed back down," Luciana said as if no one else had figured that out. "Fan out and keep your eyes open." She turned to Mari, who hung her head from exhaustion, "You think she might have taken off or gotten lost?"

Mari barely raised her head. "I've watched this girl. Even after we kidnapped her, drugged her, taped her up in a blanket, and she fell out of the truck, she still wanted to help us. Seronia could have easily escaped, but she came back to where we were in the crashed truck. She would try to get the food back to us."

"Then why haven't we seen her?"

"When you girls arrived, you might have scared her. Though I don't see much fear in her." Mari crinkled her brow. "She's probably watching us right now."

They all glanced around.

Mari peeked at the cacti. Her stomach grumbled. "Do you mind if I grab a couple of those red balls?"

"Go for it. They're probably poison, and I won't have to worry about hauling you out of here."

Mari grabbed four.

"You're an idiot," said Luciana. The others laughed.

They headed back down the hill, stopping every ten feet or so to check the surroundings. They tried to walk on the brush, but several ended up slipping and sliding on their butts. Soon they were at the ravine where Seronia passed. They rested for a bit then headed up the other side. At the top, they looked over all the hills in the distance. Nothing. Halfway down they heard giggling.

Luciana held up her hand, motioning the others to remain still. She eased down, trying to be silent. The trail gave way, and she slipped like an out-of-control skier, sliding ten feet ahead. She caught herself by wrapping her arms around the branch of a lone tree. Her feet stumbled, then she righted herself. Her gun swung from her curled finger through the trigger guard. As her eyes lifted, she caught a glimpse of Seronia's black hair; the girl was rocking back and forth, muttering a low, rhythmic sound.

With the pistol now gripped in both hands, Luciana eased forward on stable, rocky ground. She watched Seronia for a few seconds but couldn't figure out what she was doing.

"Hold it right there," Luciana growled.

Seronia kept swaying and didn't turn around.

Mari had moved within five feet of Luciana. "She's autistic, you know."

Luciana swung in Mari's direction, gun pointed. "What? She can't hear?"

"She hears, but the message doesn't always get through," Mari explained. "She doesn't respond well to humans."

Luciana used the gun to motion up the hill. "Like you. I told you to stay put."

Mari's eyes stayed on the leader. "Let me go down there. I think she'll come with me."

After thoughtful silence, the gun motioned for Mari to proceed.

Mari eased down by Seronia's side. She noticed the squirrel in Seronia's lap feeding from her fingertips. Seronia petted the rodent with her free hand.

"Seronia, will you come with me?" asked Mari in a gentle tone.

Jef Huntsman

With a light chuckle, Seronia twisted her neck to look at Mari. Mari held out her hand. Seronia rolled forward and stood; the squirrel nestled into her hand. With Mari at her side, Seronia eased out of the brush and down the hill. The others followed.

When they reached the truck, Luciana told two of the girls from the second vehicle to haul Sandoza's body a mile away before burying her.

Mari's eyes widened, but she didn't say anything.

They followed Luciana to the other vehicles. Mari walked by Seronia, who kept stroking the calm squirrel. Mari, Seronia, Trueno, and one of the soldiers were told to get into the first vehicle with Luciana. Two of the girls carried Sandoza's body to the other vehicle; the other soldier followed.

Luciana shook her head as Mari helped Seronia in. "That varmint doesn't go with."

"But he calms Seronia," said Mari.

Luciana pitched forward, swiped the squirrel from Seronia's grip, tossed it to the ground, and fired a bullet into the poor creature's skull.

Seronia's mouth slackened for a brief second, then she let out a horrifying squeal. Without warning, she lunged at the killer's throat and backed her against the truck. Her neck being crushed by this wild, mad child, Luciana's pistol tumbled from her grip. She gagged and tried to speak, but nothing came out. Her legs began to go limp. Her face whitened. Seronia kept up an unremitting scream that echoed down the mountain. Birds took flight from nearby trees.

A thud from a rifle butt stopped the screaming. Seronia dropped as if she didn't have a bone in her body, smacking into the wet, brown earth. Her eyes rolled up to her brow, then closed.

Mari ran over to Seronia and rubbed her face with both hands.

Trueno stepped from the vehicle, smirked, and said, "She deserved that."

Luciana coughed and spit, grasping the sides of her neck as if she had to hold it up. She dropped to her knees. Her eyes flamed as she stared at Seronia, limp on the ground. In a rough, weak voice, she muttered, "I hope you killed the bitch, so I don't have to."

21

Carson

I edged farther out from the open elevator box. A dim light glowed through what appeared to be a window on the cave wall. Music whispered in the distance, far away. I eased toward the window. My hand touched the grip of my gun, then slid down to the handle of my knife. There was comfort in both.

It took forever to reach the window. My feet stumbled silently on uneven ground, unsure through the dimly lit cavern. My stomach twisted in knots as I listened to my shallow breath. The window had no glass, just an opening with a wooden frame against rock. I peered in. For a split second, the delicious smell of strong coffee gave me a longing for calmer, gentler times.

Someone sat in a chair; the back of the chair was higher than the person's head. A girl faced in the other direction. She puzzled over a flat rock on an unsteady table. In addition to the rock, the table bore a lamp, a couple of books, and a plate with a green and yellow substance congealed to it. The girl wore a white wife-beater with camouflage pants. A waterfall of black hair streamed out from beneath her ball cap, cascading over her long neck. Smooth skin rolled across high cheekbones. She leaned over the table in obvious concentration.

I looked around and caught sight of wires running parallel to the ceiling of timbers and chicken wire in the main tunnel. It reminded me of an old mine I'd searched in the military. I wondered if that's what it was. About thirty yards down the earthen passage, I spotted lights coming equidistant from each other on one side. The quiet was broken only by the faint music I'd heard earlier and the hum of an electric vehicle. I glanced back through the window. Nothing had changed. The vehicle stopped, did a U-turn, and headed the other way.

Kneeling, I crawled beneath the window and stood up again. There was a closed door with lamplight filtering in around the frame. There was no lock on the door. I weighed barging in and questioning the busy ball cap on the other side but decided it might cause more alarm than needed. Invisible, I slouched along the dark cavern wall toward the next lit window in the other room.

I approached the second window, my breath shallow. Three young women laughed at something said in Spanish. They dressed the same as ball cap and seemed to be in a break room of some kind. A fridge, a metal table with eight chairs, and a wall-mounted rack of rifles filled the room. No pictures or other decoration hung on the dirt-and-chicken-wire wall. One of the girls reached into the fridge and pulled out a *Jarritos* yellow-green soda.

All the girls had holsters with pistols attached to their belts and a woven strap across the backs for extra bullets. The bullets looked small—probably a .22 caliber. The girls' faces were hard but still had the smiles and cheeks of adolescence. I crouched down again and crawled forward.

The puttering of a small engine sounded in the distance. It was heading my way. My head swiveled. I needed to find somewhere to hide. I saw something across the way that might work. I braved another glance through the window. The girls were oblivious. On hands and knees, I bolted across the tunnel for an alcove back fifteen feet and across the way. I prayed they kept up their jovial banter and didn't look out their window and that the approaching vehicle took its time. With luck, I made it to the recess. There was a door at the back of it with no indication of light on the other side. I quickly opened it and ducked inside. I pressed my ear to the door and hid in the shadows.

The vehicle passed. I felt for a switch then decided against it. Using the light of my cell phone, my eyes scanned the space. It seemed to be a broad tunnel that angled to my left. I moved forward into the unknown, my steps hesitant but steady. Twenty feet in, I heard distant whimpering. It was the exhausted whine of an animal too long in a trap—the voice of something wanting to die. I was assaulted by an ungodly smell that reminded me of a building in Afghanistan thick with death.

I crept in about twenty yards and noticed an outstretched arm on the tunnel's soil floor. A lifeless palm lay open. I hurried closer. The arm was attached to a blood-speckled shoulder that was splayed at an odd angle. Then I saw the face, eyes wide in a death stare. A boy peered back, the features of an early teen. Bruises marked his face and back. I bit hard on my lower lip as my mind envisioned parents calling his name and a schoolyard of friends playing soccer.

His arm stuck out from the cage that was his final resting place. The smell assailed my nose. Cockroaches scattered. I didn't think he'd been dead for more than a day. He still lay in flaccid rigor, his skin purple on one side. I shined my light around the cage. It was the size of a small bedroom. Another body curled like a fetus in the corner. He was about the same age and covered in dirt. An empty tin pan lay on the earthen floor between them.

I checked for an entrance. A barred door about four feet high was to my left. A rusty lock kept the captives in. I glanced around the tunnel and found a shovel leaning on the opposite wall. With two hard swings of the shovel, the lock broke and fell to the ground. I hustled over to the curled-up boy to check for any signs of life. No pulse, and stiff as the dead can be. A millipede crawled out his open mouth. Sorrow filled my heart. My mind screamed inside, echoing through my skull. These boys were younger than any soldiers I'd seen. The smell of death seeped into my bones. *What the hell's going on here?* my brain yelled in silence. This was not just another day.

"Seronia," I whispered. My throat tightened. My pulse raced in anger and fear for her.

Then I remembered the whimpering. It hadn't come from these two. I stormed out of the cage and followed my light deeper into the tunnel. My cell power was fading. Only a sliver of white showed on the battery icon. I shined it up on the ceiling. More wires. I followed them until one dropped down and ended in a switch. It was the old type with a single button that pushed in to turn the power on. With a press of my thumb, dim lights flickered and came to life. I shut the power down on my cell. This probably wasn't a good idea. But without light, I couldn't go any farther. The thought of not making it out sent a chill through me.

The tunnel seemed to stretch into infinity. The whimpering stopped when the lights went on. My feet followed a worn path in the center. I pulled out my Berretta in case one of the soldier girls was out there. Fifteen feet later, I spotted another cage. This one ran longer and circled a corner in the shape of a horseshoe. With fingers grasping the bars, I searched its dark interior. Nothing.

I rounded the corner to find dozens of staring eyes and shadowed forms huddled in the dark recesses of the cell. I approached the bars. The faces were hollow and gaunt, withdrawn into themselves. They had lost all identity and any spark of humanity. Their mouths gaped open as they watched me. Some were boys, but most appeared to be girls.

A boy stepped forward from the shadows. His clothes were in shambles and clung to him like molting snakeskin; his dark face was peppered with dirt. A slow, breathless, *"¿Qué haces aquí?"* issued from cracked lips. His feeble arms held on to the bars for support.

The sight of him stopped me cold. The boy's deep-set eyes penetrated my heart. I had a hard time breathing. Finally, I patted my chest and said, *"Amigo. Yo soy amigo Americano."*

Blank stares gazed back at me. It was as if there was no comprehension. They probably thought I was the next horrible thing to happen to them. I held up a finger, turned, and ran back for the shovel. Within a few minutes, I returned. Some had moved forward, clinging to the rusted bars. I noticed they were skinny but not starving. I signaled with my hand to move away from the wire-and-steel gate. They didn't understand. *"Vamos a puerto!"* I yelled.

More puzzled stares. I wish I'd listened more to Mrs. Vallencia in my high school Spanish class. It took forever for me to even try to communicate. I patted the gun in the back of my pants and signaled with both hands waving frantically.

The tinny voice of the first boy said, *"Retrocedar . . . retrocedar."*

They drifted away from the locked gate without ambition or purpose. They were like sheep clamoring into the crevices of dirt and stone.

This lock was newer. I took a hard swipe at it. It bounced but remained solid. I reeled back for a long swing when I heard voices and the clickety-clack of burdened wheels. Someone was coming toward us. I scuttled back into the far shadows.

There were two voices. I couldn't understand the Spanish well enough to decipher what they said, but there was no alarm in their tone. I waited and wondered about the lights.

The wheels stopped just short of me. Two of the three girls I'd seen earlier swaggered up to the bars. The captured children cowered against the back wall. Quick Spanish commands echoed through the tunnel. The chubbier of the two girls kicked dirt between the bars.

"Malditos hombres débiles y chicas feas," she said in disgust— *damn weak men and ugly girls*. The other laughed, stepped back, and pulled a wooden cart a few feet closer to the bars. She reached in and began tossing stacks of tortillas into the cell.

The chubby one took her keys and began to open the gate. A boy of about seventeen slid forward a few inches. She swiped her gun from her

Mosquito Sands

holster in one quick motion and aimed at his head. He froze. With no more concern than tossing a rock at a tin can, she shot him. A black dot on his forehead leaked crimson. The gunshot echoed through the canyon walls. His body crumbled to the side, eyes wide and unbelieving.

My neck heated. I gripped the shovel tight with both hands, raised it in the air, and ran forward. Metal slammed into skull. Her gun dropped, and her body slackened as it jellied to the ground. Eyes of wonder set on mine. Her face bounced and puffed the dirt. Her chubby cheeks bagged like loose jowls. Out cold.

I swirled around. I raised the shovel, red slithering down the wooden handle like crimson snakes. The other girl stood in shock. Face blank. Mouth agape. Her hands held a stack of tortillas. Her eyes focused on her partner. I stepped past the cart. Her neck turned as she dropped the tortillas to the ground. I watched her eyes raise to me in amazement. As the seconds passed, her jaw slackened, and her eyes focused to a deep fear. She looked up at the shovel blade. Her shoulders curled, and she began to duck down.

Her gun was still planted in her holster, and her hand was shifting toward it. With a twist of weight for momentum, my right foot caught her ankle, and she twirled feet first into the air. In seconds I was on top of her with the shovel handle pressed into her neck. Tears began flowing around the sides of her caramel face. Her lids shut tight, waiting for the inevitable.

With pressure still on her throat, I reached back, removed her gun from its holster and tossed it toward a pillar on the earth wall. She trembled. I gazed up to see the row of young faces pressed to the bars with blank eagerness to watch her death.

I lifted the shovel and tossed it by her gun. I smelled the acid, pungent odor of urine. I sat on her legs; my hands rummaged her pants for other weapons. A folded knife and a tin of Kodiak tobacco chew were all I could find. I rolled off her, pulling her upright as I stood. She was still trembling. Her legs barely held her up, and I braced her against the bars. Finally, her eyes opened.

"Habla Ingles?" I asked.

She shook her head.

A voice behind the bars said, "You going to kill her?"

I raised my head. A boy about ten years of age pressed his head between the bars. He wore ratty clothes; his black hair was matted with soil above round eyes and cracked lips.

"No," I replied.

"Why not?"

The others remained silent. Faces that had lost human desire waited as if something else horrid could happen. It would be just another day.

"I need her. We need her to get us out."

I reached in my pocket, grabbed the remaining plastic tie, and hitched her wrists together. She stared at the boys behind the bars and the open gate. Her rounded shoulders pressed around a wooden post. She panted in rapid sucks of breath. Her body bucked with bull force into my arm that was trying to hold her still, and I slammed her into a piling. The impact knocked the air out of her lungs, and she began heaving and gasping. I pressed her into the back wall. I grabbed her hair and turned her face toward me. "Never do that again." I said. She didn't understand the language but knew the tone well. Her shoulders drooped. She bowed her head in surrender.

I nodded toward the gate. The boy who had been talking to me moved carefully to it then stood at the entrance. He seemed to be the healthiest of the group, though that wasn't saying much. I pointed to a spot by me. He walked around the guard's body, spat, then proceeded. I patted him on a scrawny shoulder.

"Ask her how many guards there are."

He rattled off Spanish for some time. I could tell he added insults and commentary.

The guard peered up at me. I tapped my gun. She answered. This went on for a few minutes.

My last question was about Seronia, the main reason I was here. I held Seronia's picture to her face, shaking it. She thought about it and shook her head. I walked over, picked up her gun from the place where I'd tossed it, then opened the gate fully. "¡Vamanos!" I said. I grabbed the guard by the arm and walked deeper into the tunnel. The rest followed. Some helped others as we moved forward. I turned to the young boy now by my side and asked, "What's your name?"

"Paulo Martinez," he answered, giving me an awkward smile.

I had him search the dead guard for weapons. He was thorough, throwing nonessential items he found onto the clay floor. Paulo found a small pocketknife and eyed it with pride. He scored a pack of cigarettes and dropped it into his pocket.

"Okay, Paulo, I'm Carson. Let's find out if there's truth to what this piece of shit told us." I grabbed my prisoner's arm and lifted her up.

Mosquito Sands

Thirty feet later, I spotted a metal gate with boards attached to it. The boards hid whatever was behind it. The young guard shook her head violently and tried to pull away. I pressed my fingers into her muscles enough to bruise her arm. The sight of her young face filled me with disgust and sympathy at the same time. She kept trying to pull away. I shoved her to the ground and handed Paulo her weapon. "You watch her."

He grinned with an evil upturn of his cheeks. She sat still on the ground with one arm bracing herself upright. Others spat on her as they strolled by. I shot the lock with my pistol. A kick of my heel sent the lock flying into a beam. I figured anyone hearing the gunshot would figure it was another prisoner death, and I was mad enough to take on the whole group of guards if I had to. What I had found was nothing less than deplorable.

Anger raced through my chest to my clenched fists. The guard's eyes caught mine. Sweat and quiet tears glistened her cheeks in the dull light. She could tell what I was thinking even though I tried to suppress the savage retaliation deep within me.

Not sure what was behind the boarded gate, I waited for someone to come out. My gun was aimed at the opening. Nothing happened. I stood to the side and eased the door open with my fingertips. The hinges were nailed on leather straps that made a ripping sound as the door swung wide.

The room was pitch black. I followed the wires that entered from a corner of the door in and down the wall, my fingers catching on jutted rocks. I came to a box and pressed the button. Two lights flickered to life. I moved in, signaling the others with the palm of my hand to stay put. Three stairs dropped down to a stone floor. A gigantic altar of carved stone sat in the center of the room. The top of the altar was scooped like ice cream spooned from a new bucket. The walls were laid with ancient bricks—some with detailed Mayan glyphs in evenly spaced panels. I moved in closer. Chiseled stone plates with large-nosed faces wearing fanciful headdresses had been placed around the room. Some of the plates were simply circles and lines. None of it made sense to me. To my left on a jut of stone sat three metal-and-bone pieces like tiny spears and an eaten-away, rusted axe blade. The pieces appeared authentic and looked like they were a thousand years old, but I'd need Hub to verify. I took several pictures with my phone.

I noticed the smoothly concaved stone of the surface and the slightly rounded edges of the altar. It was the size of a lawyer's desk. I had no idea what the chiseled glyphs meant, but they were impressive and well preserved. Perhaps that was what was in the first room I came to. The guard from the main tunnel seemed to be studying a rock on a table. At the far end of the altar, a dried black paint crept down to the stone floor. I traced the dry thick liquid down to a crescent-shaped bowl with a one-inch hole in the center. A cold breeze crawled up my spine. As if repelled, I bounced backward. The black liquid was old blood. Old—but not ancient.

My lungs stalled as I stood motionless. Every tendon in my body cramped tightly as if chased by haunting demons. I ran for the entrance, noticing three yellowed skulls watching from above the door. They were angled as if peering at the stone altar. I slammed the door shut, put my hands on my knees, and took in deep breaths. I have seen things that still bring nightmares to my nights. This was going to be another one. Who are these people? *What* are these people?

I have seen horrible places and witnessed the complex cruelty of man. This was more—it reeked of unearthly deeds and evil darkness. How much exposure has Seronia had to this? Her autism, which made her disinterested in true friendship, had probably saved her. If, that is, she was still alive.

With my hands still on my knees, I continued to take in deep breaths to calm myself. The prisoners and the guard waited in silence. I glared at the guard. My hands tightened as I thought about her neck. I shook that off.

I heard a weak voice.

"*Señor* Carson? Are you okay?" It was Paulo. He stood next to me, his hand on mine. His other hand pointed the pistol at the chubby guard.

I took a gulp of the dark cavern air and stood upright. My fingers grabbed the guard's hair. I stood her up, the black strands tight in my grip. "Where are the *chicas*?"

She struggled to keep her balance. Her dark, crying eyes stared into mine. A single finger lifted and pointed farther down the tunnel. With a firm push, I made her lead me.

Not far along the tunnel stood another cage with a gate. I gazed in at three young girls, probably pre-teens, sitting at a table with guava and bananas in the center. They looked at me in fear. I searched faces for any sign of Seronia. I turned to Paulo and the guard.

"What are they in here for?"

Mosquito Sands

The guard shook her head.

Paulo handed me the Beretta and walked over to the cage. "Why are you held captive?" he asked in Spanish.

They stared for a minute. *"Queremos ir los casa,"* said the youngest, who had slash marks down her arms.

Paulo peeked at me to see if I understood. I shrugged. "They were taken from their houses," said Paulo. "They are new captives."

I noticed they all had slash marks in different places; the marks looked like they had been caused by being beaten with a belt or a stick. We learned the girls had been kidnapped just two weeks earlier and were being held there until they cooperated. It must be the first stop; if they refused to join, they would be put in the other cell. I asked with whom they needed to cooperate; they didn't know. The flimsy lock popped off the door of the cage with several swift smacks of a rock. The sound echoed through the cave. Paulo raced in and grabbed the fruit in his arms. The girls startled and ran to a corner, cuddling each other. *They must feed the new girls much better*, I thought. It's an old tactic to brainwash prisoners. I had seen it used in countries around the world. Treat the prisoners as friends until they believe they are.

I told Paulo what to say. He told them I wouldn't hurt them. They kept still. He explained that I would help them escape. He said I would return them to their families. The girls whimpered and pressed themselves into the black crevices of the cavern. Then I had Paulo ask them about Seronia, and I held her picture up where they could see it. I wasn't sure if they looked. They didn't answer.

In a fit of frustrated madness, I leaped between the captives and grabbed the guard. I lifted her up by her jaw against a chicken-wire-and-dirt wall. My thumbs locked at her neck. I could feel my own sweat wash down my back. "Seronia! Where the hell is Seronia!"

She gagged, and her hands grabbed for my shoulders. Her boots flung out at my shins, and I pressed harder. Just as her eyes began to roll back, she pointed to her lips.

I lowered her until her feet touched the ground and then relaxed my grip on her throat. She sucked in air like a sharp wind. I slapped her—not hard, just enough to awaken her. Her eyes opened to slits.

I reached into my pocket and took out the picture again. "Seronia?" I caught a slight nod and waited. My one hand held her upright against the wall. I waved the picture at her.

She spoke in slow, deliberate Spanish. She sounded as if her tongue was knotted.

"She remembers a girl that couldn't talk," interpreted Paulo. "The girl's hands shook at her sides. She was only here one day and was taken to the farm."

My excitement grew. Seronia hadn't talked since she was two. The uncontrolled shake of the hands at her sides sounded like a description of autism. "What farm?" I asked.

The guard shook her head and dropped her chin. Tears began flowing.

"She just says *the farm*."

"*¿De donde?*" I asked.

She stood silent for twenty seconds or so then blurted something as if not quite sure. "Jalisco."

"*¿Que ciudad?*" Paulo asked as he waved the small knife at her. A moment later, he turned to me. "The farm might be by *El Copomo*."

"*El Copomo*?" I asked.

"It's in the state of Jalisco by the beach. *Mucho toristas*."

"How do we get there?" I asked.

Paulo interpreted, and I waited. "She's never been there," he said.

I knew that was probably the best clue I was going to get from her, but I had one more thing to try. I was exhausted, though feeling elated with this news.

I turned back to the girls in the now-lockless cage. The sharp smell of urine had overpowered the mustiness of the cave. They seemed terrified. It took a minute for me to realize it was me they were terrified of. I nodded at Paulo with a look of desperation, and he began talking to the girl prisoners.

After minutes of coaching, they came carefully to the open gate. I turned and asked the guard if there were any more prisoners. She shook her head. I wasn't sure if I trusted her. I walked away from the three girls and the guard as if I didn't care if they followed. The group moved with me. The new girls fell in line behind the others.

We arrived at the second cell, and I realized I was famished. I grabbed a tortilla and some cold beans from a bucket on the cart. I ate for fuel, not pleasure. Some of the other young teens did the same. The guard had fallen behind so I ran back to her, grabbed her by the tie on her wrists, and pulled her into the cell. I took the handle off the pot of beans and twisted the wire handle around the plastic tie and a cell bar. She would stay there until someone found her. I signaled for the others.

Mosquito Sands

We walked to where I'd entered. A spigot came out of a pipe at a ninety-degree angle. When I turned it, grayish water trickled out at a rate barely more than a drip. I slurped some down and moved to the door. I held my finger to my lips to instruct everyone to be quiet. Paulo repeated my motion. I wasn't sure I

needed to keep them silent. Except for Paulo and the smaller boy, no one had said a word. I pushed the light off. Darkness enveloped

us.

22

Carson

I peeked around the edge of the door. The tunnel was creepy and silent, except for an electric hum. The lights from the windows caused an unearthly glow. All we had to do was make it to the elevator. With a signal to the others, I raced across to the other side of the tunnel. The others followed in pairs and somewhat more slowly. My heart galloped.

Their slow pace made me anxious. I moved down the wall to allow a single-file escape. They followed at a turtle's pace. Fear oozed from their tight lips and hollow eyes. The radio from down the tunnel echoed soft Spanish music off the walls. We had only one window to duck under, and it was fifteen feet ahead. The door was open. I glanced in. The same young girl was at the table, elbows out, face down. Asleep? The stone tablet was under her right cheek. I thought about closing the wooden door but realized the hinges probably hadn't been oiled in years.

With a press on Paulo's head, I directed him to move swiftly. His hand motioned for the others to follow. The longest minute passed as each one walked silently past the open door and the light of the window. The three newest captives were last. The middle one stopped to look in the door; I pushed on her shoulder to press her ahead. The sleeper stirred and turned with eyes closed to face the door. I scuttled past the window then hurried to the front of the line.

My cell was dead, so we had no light. In the dark crevices of the tunnel's ceiling I detected dead bulbs hanging down off old wire. I realized there must be limited power, probably from a far-off generator since I didn't see power lines when I approached the building.

I thought I could find the elevator easily enough. Maybe.

A few more feet, and I heard a noise. I turned as each of the captives melted into the dark recesses of the wall. The stone sleeper came out the door, lit a cigarette, and leaned against the window frame. A cloud of tobacco smoke blew from her mouth. The group remained still. I could see the frightened faces of the ones nearest me. The others probably had the same expressions of terror. Minutes passed.

One of the girls to my left loosened a rock with her back against the wall. It dropped onto her heel, and she let out a mousy squeal. The smoker turned. Her neck strained as her eyes probed the shadows around us. She took a couple of steps, squinting into the tunnel. I feared she might hear the roar of our hearts pounding, blood surging.

Finally, she shrugged her shoulders and turned away. I watched as she flung the hot tip of the cigarette to the ground and stomped it out. The sleeper returned to her cave.

"You sure there are no other prisoners?" I whispered to Paulo.

He shrugged.

I exhaled and leaned against the tunnel wall. I could feel the group watch me with frightened eyes. It was best to get these people out of here. If I went after any more, I might compromise all of us. And there might not be anyone else here. Edita, the guard I had tied to the grate, said there were only five guards down here. That alone would limit the number of prisoners. I had seen only three guards and a girl studying the Mayan glyphs. Oh, and the two driving the truck out of the elevator and the other two in their three-wheeled vehicle. That made eight. Some could be the workers she talked about. I felt sure Edita lied about the number. I'm not surprised. She seemed as afraid of them as she was of me.

I pushed away from the wall and signaled with a crank of my arm for all to follow. We snaked our way back towards where I'd entered. With Paulo's help I moved them in quick succession. The cave became darker and musky. I proceeded in careful steps, my hands feeling the wall of wire, earth, and timbers. I caught my fingers on sharp nails as I inched the group along. I could feel the blood seeping down my palm.

I couldn't see it, but I knew each of these teens were holding on to one another's hands and clothing as we etched further into the unknown blackness. These poor, young souls had been put through a hell I could only imagine. Ripped from their youth. Taken from the safety of home, school, and playgrounds. I clenched the hand of the girl behind me, giving her as much comfort as she did me.

I could hear the shuffle of rats clamoring on the other side of the tunnel. Their yellow eyes made a ghostly glow in the darkness. Sounds of my group clinging closer to the wall and stepping up the pace filled my ears.

Jef Huntsman

A tiny, red glimmer shone from the ceiling. My heart raced. I plowed further. The wall pulled away from me. I tripped forward, pulling part of the human string with me. My mind was muddy for an instant. Then I realized this was the elevator inlet. I hadn't noticed the tiny red light before. I let go of the hand I was holding and marched into the darkness, my hands swinging wildly in front of me.

My feet tripped on the metal ledge of the elevator. In a frantic search, I felt the walls of our safe passage for a switch or control of some type. I recalled a lever at about waist height. Was that to my right or left? Rubbing the wall in long arcs, I advanced. Within seconds, my fingers stubbed on a protrusion—the lever.

I moved blindly back to the young group. Hands grabbed at me, my face, my shirt, my arms. I held tight to a couple of hands and pulled them into the inky cutout. "Paulo?" I whispered.

"Si."

"Tell them, *mano a mano* and follow me." Like yarn, I wove them tightly into the metal box. It was large enough for a small car but somewhat tight for my group. I raced back out and skimmed the wall with frantic swings of my arms. Finally, I found the outside lever attached to a post. With muscle and determination, I broke the outside handle off so no one could follow. My body fell backward onto the ground. I righted myself quickly and headed into the elevator. My hand was on the inside lever as the last youth entered. I pressed the lever and a growling began above us.

Headlights lit up the tunnel in front of us—at first faint, then growing nearer. The metal box squeaked and ground, but nothing moved. I knew the adrenalin of fear surged through all our veins. A clanking began, and the elevator jumped an inch. The light brightened. We surged another couple of inches. Did we weigh too much? I pulled out my gun. A brilliant flash of white and a vehicle passed by. Faces under camouflage hats peered as we huddled together in the glow of the red light. The elevator began shaking violently. I heard brakes squeal and a motor rev up. The floor rose in jerky succession. Rear lights backed up, their glow sinking my heart. Some of the girls began screaming. I watched the back of the truck come to a stop. With my knife, I knocked out the red bulb above us.

The chain caught, and we lifted slowly. Halfway up the opening one could almost hear the stampeding pulse of heart valves. On my hands and knees, I saw two guards reaching for weapons. My Berretta tight in my hands, I fired into the knee of one guard. The other one jumped behind the vehicle. I fired another warning shot just as the gap closed and the elevator headed up the bricked walls. We lifted with the elevator's patience. My breath caught in sharp gasps as I stood back up. I couldn't see the smiles on my group's faces, but I felt them.

I knew this wasn't over. We had to pass the other tunnel where I'd watched the truck disappear. I kept my gun out and waited.

The wind of the other tunnel cooled us as we approached. The elevator lifted and growled. The tunnel was dark. We could only hope it would stay that way. A long minute passed, and the secondary exit fell at our feet. The slowness of the elevator kept our spirits bleak but hopeful.

A wash of light came over us as we lifted into another unknown. I smiled as we reached the top. With exuberance the group exited the elevator. The guard, Edita, glared at me, but without much behind it. Her bleeding wrists strained at the metal grate.

Several of the captive girls ran over and kicked Edita and yanked at her hair. Others rushed to the scene with expressions of vengeance on their faces. I hustled over, pulled the girls away, and made them back off. Her clothes were ripped, and her face was battered and blotchy. An exchange of words—none of which I understood—heightened and echoed off the blank walls. With my hands out and my voice hushed, I kept repeating, "Calm." Like firecrackers finally finding the end of stray fuses, the noise bubbled to a hush. We stood in silence for a moment, though I could tell they wanted to beat Edita to a pulp.

"Paulo, tell them to save their energy." I wasn't sure if it was the daylight or just the single guard that got them all riled, but I knew it had to stop.

Through Paulo, I explained they had to wait for me. I pointed at the door on the far side of the building and told them they should wait there. The idea of mines outside took a little longer for them to grasp. With nods of their heads, they finally scurried away.

I walked over to Edita with my knife drawn. She convulsed into a whimpering ball. Her hands yanked at her binds, her wrists slashed and bleeding from the strain. It took time for me to pacify her. She watched the knife as I held it above her. "Do you want to go home?" I asked.

Her face softened. She struggled with the concept. I could see the fear of leaving sweep across her face. The fright of retaliation. I'm sure the acts she had seen Six Sky's leaders perform sent chills down her spine. From what I had experienced in my past, I could fully relate to her wavering.

"Me matarán," she said.

"Yes, they could kill you." I said.

"Esta vivo o otro vivo?"

I touched her shoulder. She didn't cringe. "We have to go. What do you want?"

Her head shook in despair

I took one last look at her bloody and beaten face. Crimson seeped from the edge of the wrapped bullet wound I'd given her before. I turned and walked away. I couldn't fulfill the promise if she didn't want it.

Thirty feet away a tiny voice asked, *"Por favor?"* The air was still for a moment. "I go."

I hurried back, cut her binds, and grabbed her hand. She reluctantly followed as I dragged her through the warehouse. I glanced up as I approached the door. The others were not happy. If it wasn't that I'd just saved their lives, they would have ripped her to shreds.

I turned around. "She goes with us. She has a home too." I stood watching for a minute while Paulo repeated my words in Spanish. Eyes searched each other. Then nods of okay. I mentally counted my new group. Twenty-three including Edita. I thought about the Cherokee. My breath whistled as I let everything out of my lungs.

I kept Edita next to me as we reached the warmth of daylight. I explained that everyone needed to follow my footsteps exactly to avoid any mines. I knew there was another exit somewhere that the guards were rushing to—if they were not already out—and we had to be quick. Hopefully it would be only a small group from the elevator tunnel. My eyes scoped the landscape then I moved out.

My group bounced like bunnies following my previous path, and we made it back to the Cherokee without incident. The clouds were darkening above the eastern hills. I peeked at the five-passenger vehicle and back to the group. *How's this supposed to work?* Puzzled faces surrounded the jeep. I couldn't make two trips. The guards would be here soon—maybe more of Six Sky's girls had been called from somewhere else. I thought about the buses I'd traveled on in Bangladesh and got an idea. "Load everyone up!" I shouted to Paulo.

He gazed at me as if I was crazy.

The inside of the Jeep was stuffed; arms and legs were everywhere. Several jumped from the hood to the roof of the Cherokee. Others stood precariously on the thin strip that ran below the doors with fingertips on the luggage rack. Some stood with wobbly feet on the back bumper. There were so many sitting on the hood that I could barely see between their shoulders through the windshield to the road. After minutes of finding the ignition and adjusting legs to change the gears, we moved forward. Gunshots sounded in the distance. I pressed deeper into the gas pedal. The girl with her legs on my lap and her body resting on the ledge of the open window bounced and kneed me in the chin. They held on for dear life as I followed the ruts of the road.

I heard more rifles firing. My vision was limited to a crack of light between bodies in my front and snapshots of country in the rear-view mirror. I saw the speedometer reach forty and could taste the dust swirling from the upheaval. More shots fired, but I assumed they were too far away. I couldn't have reached my Barretta if I had wanted to. Running was the only escape. The ride was rough, the suspension pressed to the limit. A bullet zinged past us on my left about two feet from the truck. Someone on the roof groaned as another bullet hit muscle.

I pressed as hard on the gas as I dared with my bus load of passengers clinging to an unbalanced vehicle on an uneven path. I heard thunder from behind. I noticed the road became darker. We hit a rut, and I watched as hands grabbed each other to stay on. Right then the tone of the road made a clawing hum. We had hit pavement. I swerved to head us in the direction of Guadalupe. At a ninety-degree angle and between arm and hip, I spied the three-wheeled, tiny trucks bounding over the same road. They didn't have enough power to catch us. A volley of rifle shots came nowhere near us. The guards stopped at the main road.

A cheering roar came from the roof. I think I let out a whoop too. One could feel the excitement in the air. The rain raced in a curtain over the hills to our left, about five miles out. The air cooled. I slowed with the feeling of safety.

My thoughts jumped to the four girls that had tried to kill Hub and me days earlier. I began to wonder if Six Sky would send more young women soldiers from the city in our direction. Or would it be someone else under her reign? Surely, she had her own problems to solve without anyone calling her. If the priest was right, she had thousands of followers—voluntary and involuntary. My stomach churned. The truck with the billowing, captive refugees cheered on. The storm followed.

23

Seronia

Brakes squealed. The two filthy Explorers rested at the bottom of a winding dirt road. The sun cast a goldish glaze over the fanned mound of tailings. On the hill above, a rusted metal door, big enough for a semi to roll through, stood shut with two puck-shaped locks through latches. Luciana slipped her phone from her pocket and punched in several digits. They waited, motors running. She rattled off Spanish in her gravelly voice. After speaking, she rubbed her sore, scratched throat and grimaced at a sedated Seronia. They had kept Seronia calm with a sporadic flow of nitrous oxide stolen from a dental clinic months ago.

The door rolled up and a tiny, three-wheeled truck drove out. The truck bed was about the size of a bathtub. Two fifteen-year-old girls stepped out. Their black hair was covered with white dust. They lifted their breathing masks, and one signaled to drive the Explorers up.

The gravel road zig-zagged up the shaded north side of the hill. They stopped on the flat table of the tailings. Luciana nodded to her young female soldiers to get Seronia out. Mari stepped out of the cab with slow, cautious movements. The others drug Seronia from the seat after Trueno slipped the mask off. Trueno seemed to enjoy being the one on the dial of the nitrous.

The three soldiers dropped Seronia into the bed of the small truck. Seronia's head clunked on the metal frame. Luciano laughed with indifference.

Mari wiped her eyes as the tiny truck U-turned back through the door. They watched as the door rolled shut.

The truck putted with dim headlights through a sparsely lit tunnel. Seronia lay flaccid, her body bouncing with every bump.

The tunnel traveled into the mountain for a mile then forked. They took the left fork. Within twenty minutes, a row of caged mine lights spotted the walls every fifty feet. They stopped at an office embedded

Mosquito Sands

into one of the walls. The room had a window, a table, a chair, an old fridge that rattled, a crusted basin with a single faucet, and a long counter made from doors laid flat on sawhorses. The girl inside came out and talked to the two in the truck. They all laughed. She handed them a ring of keys, and they took off down a corridor.

The truck stopped again, and the two girls lifted Seronia out. She was groggy, eyes barely open. Her arms dropped to her sides. They carried her through an open door. A flashlight was the only illumination. They sucked in air as they came to a wall of bars and dropped her onto the dusty floor. One of them used keys to unlock a gate and came back to pick Seronia up. They dragged her through the gate with her heels furrowing the ground. She laid flat on her back as they locked the gate and walked away. A single bulb lighted the barred cage.

24

Carson

Hub's jaw scraped the ground as I drove into the gravel parking lot of the motel. After a few seconds of puzzlement, he beamed. The girls unloaded. All the boys but Paulo held on a touch longer to the safety of the Cherokee. The springs on the Jeep sighed as it lifted from the tires. I jumped out and slammed the door. Edita stood in my shadow and watched the others. Dirty faces smiled, probably for the first time in weeks or months.

"Hub, I need you to call Father Comedor and ask for his help," I said. "We need a hidden place to stay and someone to organize getting these kids home."

I spotted Harold and Little Jim stroll out from Hub's room. They both appeared sober. "Can you boys rustle up some food? Just the basics. And I'll need first aid stuff. Bandages, antiseptic, Tylenol, cotton swabs. Never mind—Harold, you know what's needed."

Hub put his cell to his cheek, and within a few minutes he had a place just a few blocks from the motel where the released captives could spend some time without anyone knowing. I had planned on them going to Father Comedor's church, but he said that wouldn't work. Lady Six Sky would know within minutes. Hub jotted down the address and explained to everyone where we were going and who would help them.

I promised again to get them to their families. Hub acted as my translator. The understanding quieted all of them down. I had Hub text Harold where we'd be going, and I signaled to reload. Most crowded back into and onto the Jeep. A group of about eight walked with Hub to the site, which was a few blocks away. I think one ride of too many sardines in a can was enough for them.

Reloading was a feat. The truck sighed and wheels flattened again as we took off to safety.

Within a couple of minutes, we arrived. The building was an

Mosquito Sands

obsolete church where few windows remained unbroken. A wooded area encroached on the building from all sides. The steps, once a welcoming entrance, stilled as mossy boards and weeds sent their tendrils tying it to the earth. A stone fountain had been used for campfires; the ground around the once flowing sight was littered with beer bottles and paper. A metal cross on the roof pointed straight to the sky as a sign that some things don't change.

The teens squeezed themselves out of the Cherokee. Wide eyes of wonder and unsure safety scanned the façade. I wasn't sure if it would even keep the rain out. Hub arrived twenty minutes later with his group. The sound of a whining dog rang through the trees, then Father Comedor entered on a small motorcycle. He parked and stood. He smiled and spun his hands in a welcoming way. The girls instantly trusted the priest and gathered around him. He spoke in the kind tone of a loving parent. They responded. I had Hub tell them that I was going to go back for Harold and the groceries, and I'd be right back. Expressions of insecurity crossed their faces, but they were soon lost in the good priest's words.

Father Comedor seemed to have lost his fear of Lady Six Sky after watching the faces of the kidnapped girls and boys. Shoulders back and chin high, he wandered through the group with a smile that lit up their world.

When I returned, all were inside the abandoned church. The front steps were not disturbed, so I figured I'd look for another entrance. Harold, Little Jim, and I found an overgrown stone pathway that led to the back. A door, though old, seemed sturdy. We entered and caught the chatter of anxious voices. They were all talking at once. Father Comedor held his hands to his ears and shouted *"Silencio!"* over the roar. They were too excited to stop.

Father Comedor turned to me. *"Los pies, por favor."*

Harold leaned over my shoulder. "He wants you to feed them."

I didn't see a stove, so I began handing over bags of fruit and fresh-baked tortillas. Everyone helped.

"Father Comedor," I asked. "Is there a *cochina?"*

"Puerco?" His brow furrowed.

I thought for a minute. *"Cocina?* Kitchen?"

He laughed. *"No, no cocina pero voy a tener que cocinas las comidas en San Agustín."*

I peered at Hub.

"He'll have food cooked at Saint Augustin's and brought here."

Jef Huntsman

A clap of thunder struck nearby. The captives shrieked. The rain began pelting the flimsy roof and coming in through broken windows. I was surprised: the roof held most of the rain out, and the little that entered the windows was more of a mist than a downpour. We all stayed in the center of the room, listened to the rain tapping against the building, and ate everything that didn't have to be cooked.

Harold walked around applying bandages and ointment to cuts. He whispered to me, "Most of their injuries were psychological." He winked.

"As much as I'd like to, I can't help with that at this time." My chest tightened. "I have to find Juan Diego's daughter, Seronia. That is my first obligation."

Harold gave an understanding nod. "Father Comedor will have someone."

Father Comedor tapped me on the shoulder. I turned.

I tried to remember what it says on those yellow mop buckets. Oh yeah. *"Peligro aqui?"*

"No, no problema," Father Comedor said. *"Seguro aqui."*

I felt secure that they'd be safe there. I was beginning to feel proud of my Spanish until Hub said something to me in Spanish. My brow furrowed. My pride vanished.

I needed more ammo. I made sure Little Jim was sober and sent him to retrieve more 9mm shells.

When the rain subsided to a patter, I helped Father Comedor hand out blankets that four of his lady parishioners had brought. Paulo made lists of the names of each captive and the cities where they came from. He handed the list to the priest, and I glanced over his shoulder at the paper. Paulo mentioned that some were from as far away as two hundred miles. The captives formed into tiny groups except for Edita, the guard, who kept to herself. Her eyes always followed me to make sure I wouldn't leave her alone with this group. It was understandable, even though she was in the same predicament as the others.

The twelve kidnapped girls were in better spirits than the ten boys. After questioning them, I'd found out the newest arrivals were fed better, had lights on part of the time, were kept in a cleaner cage, and had an actual bathroom. Both groups were frightened to death of the evil guards. Some began shaking as they talked about the despicable treatment. They pointed at Edita, whose arm cramped back as if to throw a rock at anyone who came near. Others could do no more than curl up

Mosquito Sands

and cry.

The night air buzzed with frightened murmurs and endless whimpering. Hub and I tried to calm everyone as best we could. Soothing voices can only help so much when nightmares storm through the mind. The night dragged on without much sleep. Every burst of wind or scrape of tree branch sent the group into a murmuring panic. A single Coleman lantern lent a mystical illusion of ghostly shadows over the endless night. The vacant church held little safety after what the children had been through. We had no idea if Lady Six Sky's people would find us. A lot of prayers were offered.

I spent some time with Edita, the young guard no one liked. She told me of a large apple farm that she lived on ten miles from Balleza and how an old shaman, Juan Diego, cured her brother of a spider bite that blackened his leg. She didn't know Juan Diego had a daughter, but she did remember he'd taught her to suck the sweetness from a yellow flower. Was it fate or coincidence? My spirits lifted.

The room became still as the boys and girls fell to sleep, one by one. Harold tended to Edita's leg wound, cleaning and rewrapping it. I covered her with a blanket and told her I would be close by. Harold, Hub, and I used wadded-up clothing for a pillow, and each of us found a slice of filthy floor to sleep on. Little Jim, who surprisingly had been an enormous help with everyone, had fallen asleep hours earlier after telling stories to the kids.

The singsong of birds awakened me. The sun was crawling through the tree limbs on its morning journey. Father Comedor had disappeared sometime during the night. I stretched, feeling the tightness of muscles and old wounds creak and extend. Some of the group shifted but stayed asleep. The only person awake was Hub, who sat cross-legged on a box in what I assumed was some primary yoga position.

I knew better than to disturb Hub while he meditated. I strolled out the back door and took in the scent of decay and forest. They mixed well. A primal need for coffee made me check my pocket for car keys. Crap—I'd given them to Harold. I turned to go back to retrieve them when I heard a vehicle from behind. I saw a van drive up and park near the Jeep Cherokee. By reflex, my hand went to the back of my pants where the gun should have been. All I grabbed was cloth. I remembered it was in the glove box. My mind scoured over things to do in the situation, my eyes locked on the van. It stopped with a shudder. Out stepped Father Comedor followed by three smiling ladies in white housedresses. My chest inflated with the freshness of friendly air.

They began pulling out flat tins of food. I could smell the tortillas, salsa, and eggs. But most of all I detected the strong scent of black Mexican coffee. As I came closer, I noticed the wonderful aroma moving toward me. A beautiful plump lady passed by with a tray of *chilaquiles,* an incredible dish with cut corn tortillas, poblano and jalapeno peppers, chili sauce, and eggs. She smiled. Two more heaping trays and two more glorious smiles headed into the ancient church.

Father Comedor asked for my help. In the back of the van was a two-foot-high cylinder with a spigot. He filled paper cups with black, fragrant coffee and set them on top of a stack of trays. I reached in and grabbed one.

He peeked over the top of his glasses at me. *"Lleve la bandeja a neustros huépedes."* His head cocked towards the door.

I think he told me to quit being selfish and take these in to the others, but he could have been telling me to enjoy my cup of coffee. I settled on the first translation.

I entered the old church. The smells had awakened everyone who had been sleeping on the floor. Little Jim had passed me to retrieve another pot of coffee. Hub and Harold served up the *chilaquiles* on tiny paper plates. I served coffee, making sure no one took mine. When the tray was empty, I downed my coffee, burning my throat in the process, and walked out to help with more. Harold and I picked up a case of plastic water bottles each and headed back in. The priest said something to me as he passed by. I think he blessed me with sainthood, but his tone was a bit off.

After we all ate, I had Hub explain to the priest about Edita and ask him to make sure she was taken care of without any problems from the others. I also had Hub explain to everyone how Edita had given me the information to find them and help them escape. I needed to leave, and I didn't want anything to happen to any of them. Hub asked about Seronia. No one recognized the name or the girl in the picture.

Paulo had found several places where the Mayan Queen could be. After much questioning, Harold told me that two of the girls said Lady Six Sky could change from a serpent to a panther in the blink of an eye. With help from Hub, Paulo, and Harold, we asked the group questions throughout the morning, and I was able to piece together enough information about Six Sky to give me a few places to check.

Harold and Little Jim stayed to attend to the young girls and boys.

Mosquito Sands

Getting them back to their homes was a priority. Hub and I took off in the Cherokee after a blessing from the Father. We thanked him for all his help, and this time he seemed relieved and fulfilled instead of afraid.

25

Carson

We had about a thirteen-hour trip ahead of us, and I was hopeful about Seronia. Several of the girls had mentioned El Copomo, a city of palm trees, beach, paradise, and hopefully Lady Six Skies farm. We thought that would be our best bet.

According to what the devil girls in the pink Cadillac had told us, Six Sky was using Seronia for her ability to see places and draw the whole scene from different angles. I wondered why Six Sky couldn't just take cell phone pictures. She wanted an aerial view and no possibility of drones being spotted. According to Juan Diego, Seronia could draw an aerial view without making an aerial pass. Seemed just wacky enough to be true.

With rain and dirt streaking the Cherokee, we filled the tank and took off down the road. The rear-view mirror hung like meat on a hook waving and banging in the wind. Someone must have kicked it when I hauled the caravan of teens from the aged mine. I ripped it off and tossed it in the back seat.

"Do you think insurance will cover that too?" asked Hub, laughing.

"I'm still curious about the bullet holes," I replied.

Highway 24 would take us to the coast, and a long drive down Highway 150 would lead us into the Mexican state of Nayarit, where El Capoma lay. And hopefully, it would lead us to Seronia. Hub and I probably should have flown, but I didn't want to rent another vehicle or wait hours for an available flight. We were going to end up buying this Jeep from Perino, the car rental guy, by the time we were finished with it. But the Cherokee still ran well, even if she looked more like scrap metal every day.

"Think of all this antiquing as camouflage," I joked.

Hub said, "Yeah, we really blend in with the bullet holes, paint scraped off, one dented fender, suspension totaled, and two white-breads looking for young Mexican girls."

I nodded. My hands tightened on the steering wheel.

We traded off every four hours. I found that I slept much better with the comfort of road noise and Hub's babbling than back at the church. I had missed a lot of sleep over the last couple of days. These four-hour holidays felt great.

When I drove, my mind centered on the girls and boys who had been kidnapped from their homes. I had learned most of their names and where they were from by the time we left. Their tears pulled at me as they told of parents and sisters they had missed so much. Harold and Hub were patient with them and me as they helped translate. I had received so many hugs and had been embraced by so many teary, happy eyes this morning it would last a lifetime.

That's why I do what I do. I don't really need the money—which was lucky, since this one was a freebie anyway. Finding someone lost is a pleasure above all. The reuniting of friends and family is maybe a half-step below. I wished those kids from the tunnel thousands of new days filled with sunshine, skateboards, laughter, and friends.

Seronia, we're on our way, I thought and bit my lip.

Hours and hours passed. Roads quivered in the heat. My neck and muscles were tight as a sail in a tsunami.

We were getting closer to the Pacific. The smell and the change of vegetation was the first sign. I was driving. The horrible internet signal gave us glimpses of La Cruz just ahead. There we would buy a new cooler, some fruit, drinks, and a carafe of coffee. We would also stop at a *Torta* stand. I had been craving a Mexican sandwich all afternoon. My stomach had made more noise than the pressed gravel road.

A sun-worn man sat by his cart as I pulled over to the side of the road. I stretched and enjoyed the warm sun on my back. While Hub talked to the old vendor, I twisted my torso every which way and managed twenty-five squats on the side of the road. I received a few odd looks from the villagers. I assume most thought *Americano loco*. They weren't too far off.

Fruit drinks, a filling *torta*, roadside calisthenics, and we were off. The next city we would pass through of any importance was Mazatlan. The old vendor said it was about two hours away. That would put us in Mazatlan about 4:30 in the afternoon. That meant we might arrive in El Capomo a bit before midnight. Tomorrow morning, we'd head out to find Seronia.

"Have you ever wish you didn't have to sleep?" asked Hub.

"No, I feel lousy when I miss sleep. Don't you?" I replied.

"What I mean is—what if the body could maintain energy levels without any rest? Imagine if it rejuvenated itself, kind of like geothermal hot spots that keep water rising and bubbling from deep inside the earth." He grabbed his chin between his thumb and forefinger and closed his eyes.

"You know I'm not good with 'what-if' questions. They're meaningless unless you do something to make them happen. And I don't think you're going to invent spontaneous endless energy." I swerved around a porcupine in the road. "Coffee is the best answer."

"Yes, but even if you continuously guzzle coffee, the effects wear off after a while, and you fall asleep. I'm thinking something different," said Hub.

"That reminds me, I need to call Maria." I changed the subject.

"Perfect, let's get her opinion." He grabbed my phone from the console and began punching in her number.

"I doubt this is anything she'd want to talk to you about. It's an impossible quest."

"It may not be probable, but it could be possible."

I listened to the phone ring on the speaker while Hub whistled. I heard Maria pick up. She answered in a "Yes," which I knew meant she was busy and hadn't seen who was calling.

"What if you didn't ever have to rest?" asked Hub.

"Who the hell . . ." I heard her fumble with the phone.

"Maria, this is Hub. How would you like to never have to sleep again?"

She let out a stream of air from her lips with a garbled Spanish cuss word so loud that Hub held the cell farther from his ear. "Look, crazy; I'm in the middle of a government form that some overpaid bunch of Neanderthals wrote to piss me off. The due date is today." Maria began spitting out furious Spanish words that neither of us could understand. Seconds later, she stopped. "Where's Carson?" It came out more of a threat than a question.

Hub jammed the cell into my chest. I watched the road with one eye and flipped off the speaker with the other. "Maria?"

A pause. "You okay?" Anxiety tempered her voice.

I knew where this was going. "Peachy."

"Why the hell did you have Crazy call me with some new Hubism?

Mosquito Sands

He's the one who's not going to sleep when he finds out what I'm going to do to him."

I had a hall pass. "He didn't ask, and I only told him that **I** needed to call you." I shook my head at Hub, who acted oblivious, but wasn't. He busily bit his lip. "It sounds like you're in the middle of something. Why don't you buzz me when you're finished?"

"No, let's talk," she said. "Have you gotten the . . . What do you call them? . . . Your kids?" She paused. "Your kids, like you're taking them on a church picnic. Are they safe?"

"I only called them *my kids* once." The air inside the truck had heated up. I rolled down my window a few inches. "I think they're safe. Father Comedor, a few of the church ladies, Harold, and even Little Jim are finding their families or friends. They talked to five of the parents before I left, and they were on their way to get them. I'm not sure about the long-term trauma, but for now, they should be all right."

"Their situation makes me realize my stupid government papers are not that big of a deal. Sorry. Where you at?"

"We're about thirty minutes from Mazatlan headed toward another tourist city called El Capomo." I hit the brakes as a skunk and her brood of two took their time crossing the road. Someone pulled behind me and honked. "We're hoping Seronia is close by."

"The thought of that poor little girl stolen like that."

"Yeah. I know. I'll call you if I find anything further."

"I'd better get back before I lose funding from these assholes," she said. "Call me when you arrive."

"It'll be about midnight."

"I'll be up. Love ya, bye."

We were on the outskirts of Mazatlan. Signs dotted our path. I began wondering about Lady Six Sky. So far, no one I had talked to had ever seen her. Her mystique itself generated fear. The unknown combined with expanding rumors and gave rise to superstition and beliefs based on the dread of some foreboding evil. Even if she were only four feet tall, frightened people would see her as seven feet. She had become mysterious and supernatural—all the things that boil up terror.

"I have internet!" Hub boomed. He frantically punched on the tiny keyboard of his cell. A wide smile filled his face like a surprise birthday party. His feet kicked the floor.

I laughed, enjoying his antics and happiness. Ten minutes of silence passed. Hub's excitement erupted again.

Jef Huntsman

"You won't believe this!" he shouted. "Lady Six Sky was a real person. A Mayan warrior queen. She was known as Lady Wac Kan Ahau, Lady Six Sky, and she was one feisty leader. She was one of only three female Mayan rulers. Let me read this to you.

"Lady Six Sky was born in the Mayan city of Dos Pilos into a ruling family dynasty. Dos Pilos is now Petén, Guatemala. At a young age, she was selected over her older brother to be sent to the failing city of Naranjo. She formed a strong military and cleaned the capital from its shambles. Hieroglyphics depict her trampling captives in the manner of any warrior king. She was stern but understanding. She reigned from AD 682 to 741."

Hub let out a low whistle. "Lady Wac Kan Ahau was a powerhouse. Probably one of the first women leaders in a male-dominated world." Hub pounded the dash like a drum.

"I'm not so sure about her new reincarnation," I interjected.

"True." Hub tapped his phone. "The ancient one had the alpha male relentlessness and the female brains and compassion. It doesn't say, but she must have been a powerful shaman, too. Man, to live in that age."

"Yeah, that would be something," my voice resonated sarcasm.

"I'm going to have to do a mind travel and meet this great ruler—the warrior queen."

"Let's work on finding the new Six Sky now and hope she has Seronia." I peeked over at Hub. He gave a "mmm hmm" sound as he continued with his research.

Hub's fist shot to the roof as if throwing a spear. "The new Six Sky has a Facebook page." His eyes caught mine and lit up like a carnival. "Nine thousand four hundred and twenty-one followers

She's like a celebrity."

26

Seronia

Seronia awakened, mouth dry; her head spun like a carousel. Disoriented, panic surged from stomach to throat. She rolled to her side and puked yellow liquid. The porous sand absorbed it. She lay her head down and passed out.

Hours lapsed. She awakened again. Goosebumps speckled her skin. With her inability to feel pain and discomfort, she recognized only the darkness and her growing irritation. Her fingers spanned and ran along the black, earthen floor. Sandstone rose up on one side from a fine sugary dirt on the ground. She heard shuffling in the distance that had a slight echo to it like a horse moving in its stall. She listened until it ceased.

Except for the normal demons, Seronia's head cleared. An emptiness pitted her stomach, and she rubbed her tummy. She searched above her, her hands grasping at nothing. She stood and walked forward until one palm hit a bar. She grasped it. Her eyes were adjusting to the blackness, and she could make out the flutter of distant lights.

Her nostrils flared, and her hands tightened around the bars. She bellowed an awful sound, like an injured tiger. The roar bounced off the walls as she kept it up, barely slowing for air. Minutes passed. She finally quieted but stomped her feet as if trying to crush the earth.

"*¿Quien va alla?*" rang through the tunnel. "*¿Estás bien?*"
She stilled.
"*¿Estás bien?*"
Seronia's bushy eyebrows raised. Her breathing stopped.
"Ahhhhhhhhh," shouted Seronia. She tapped her shoulder as she always did when she needed something.
"*¿Necesitas ayuda?*"
The Spanish voice thrilled her. It sounded considerate and genuine.

She nodded her head, mouth curled open. Yes, she needed help. "Ahhhhhhhhhhhhhhhhhh!" she screamed in joy.

Lights came on. Her eyes blinked, and she jumped back. It was only a single yellow glow. She craned her neck to see down the tunnel. The metal bars rattled as she pressed them back and forth in her fists. Another light came on, faint, but still there—far down the cave. Pillars and chicken wire lined the earthen walls. She gazed around. Her hands rubbed along fence wire and bars. The room had been cut into the clay and sandstone in roughshod fashion. A few items of clothing and some empty tins littered the ground.

She heard hard boots approaching on the dirt floor. Two young girls with their hair tied back in knots came around a corner to her right. The voice she had heard before came from her left. The girls snickered until their eyes caught hers. Their backs straightened, and their lips became thin lines.

One carried a basket. She approached Seronia. Without a word, she kneeled and set the basket in front of her as the taller one gripped a holstered gun with her right hand. The kneeling girl folded the gray cloth from the basket top and began lifting things out. First, she nervously slid a cola can through the bars as her eyes held Seronia in view. Two hard-boiled eggs, tortillas, a generous scoop of beans, and an orange were arranged on a plate. She slid the plate under a gap in the bars and quickly yanked her hand out.

Seronia waited for them to unlock the gate. She squirmed and kept her eyes on the girls. She whimpered. The kneeling girl smiled and pulled the last item out of the basket. She stood and handed a folded blanket through the vertical bars to Seronia.

Seronia puzzled over this for a few seconds then batted the blanket to the floor. Her fists tightened around the bars, and she began rocking back and forth, shaking the bars with all her strength. Her face reddened. Her mouth opened wide, and she screamed a never-ending scream.

The two girls jumped. The taller one unsnapped her holster; the other's hands quivered at her sides. Seronia's scream got louder. The two girls glanced at each other, sweat rolling off their brows; they turned and ran down the tunnel. Moments later, a door slammed shut, but the noise it made was muffled under Seronia's wail.

Seronia became hoarse. She gulped oxygen and dropped to her knees. The cola can tipped and rolled against the bottom bar of the cage. Seronia tucked her knees to her chest, tapped her fingers against her

Mosquito Sands

legs, and dropped her head in despair. An upset hum trembled through her lips in a ceaseless mutter. Her fingers played an imaginary piano on her mud-crusted pants. It all continued for hours.

Finally, Seronia made a sideways glance at the cola can. Cola was her favorite. Her dad bought it for her when they went to Belleza for supplies. She used to sit in front of the store, listen to the hustle of the traffic, and sip cola while her dad bought groceries. As if she were stealing it, she grabbed the can and huddled around it while she opened it and took a long, refreshing sip. Cola always brought on a mischievous grin.

Hunger calmed her. She slid the plate closer, ripped off a chunk of tortilla, and dipped it in the congealed mass of beans. Her mouth opened before she even raised the food from the plate. She ate everything.

She lifted her chin and eyed the locked gate. Puckering her lips, she kicked the gate again and again. The padlock danced in metallic rhythm but wouldn't open, though the gate frame had bent outward.

She pounded on the gate for hours, screamed until her voice gave out, and ripped her clothes to threads until the two girls came back. They had three others with them. Seronia began shaking the gate with her hands. The girls arched around her cell like cats hugging a wall and proceeded down the tunnel. The hands of two of the girls were bound with thin nylon rope. The other three pushed them along while their shoulders curled, and their eyes peered sneakily with bowed heads. A shine of tears glossed their cheeks. Seronia pounded away at the bars, her ripped clothes hanging on her like waving flags.

Seronia stopped for a minute and listened. She heard the clatter of metal and angered voices in the distance. Soon, the three girls came back. They slowed as they approached her cell. Her eyes shot daggers at them. They tried to look away as they began to pass her. A catlike noise screeched from Seronia as her palms repeatedly smacked the main bars. The three hurried by. The one who had given Seronia the food glanced back; her teeth tight. She acted as if she wanted to say something then turned and hurried out of sight.

Seronia seldom cried. Normally, she stayed at the extremes of happy or mad. There in that cage, a single tear rolled from her tightly shut eyes. The veins in her hands bulged as she gripped the bars.

Hours passed. She had been in the cage for more than twenty-four hours. Her hands were raw and bloody.

More food was brought. Seronia grasped the cola and slugged it down. She picked up the tortillas and flung them through the bars. Seronia was smaller than all of them but fear never left their faces.

"Ahhhhhhhhhhhhhzzzzz!" Seronia screamed.

The three backed up. The taller one dialed her cell phone and mumbled something into it. Shortly after, two girls in their early twenties arrived. They wore camo pants with green T-shirts and black cowboy boots. With their sleeves rolled up, fit muscle cords twisted in the dim light. One had a red choke collar on her neck. The other wore a blue-and-white scarf that dangled from her arm. They didn't seem to care about all the racket Seronia made by screeching and pounding the gate with her hands and feet. The others stood back.

Red Collar opened her palm, and the tall girl handed her a set of keys. She eyed them and slipped one into the padlock. Seronia didn't release her grip on the gate but stood still as the lock was lifted. With a powerful push, Seronia jammed the gate into the face of Red Collar. The surprise shoved her off balance, and she fell onto the dirt floor on her back.

Scarf Girl wheeled around past Red Collar and grabbed Seronia's arm as she attempted to escape. Scarf Girl used Seronia's momentum to pull her forward, swing her in a half-circle, and shove a foot into Seronia's stomach. Air belched out, and Seronia lost her balance, falling to the floor. In a split second, Scarf Girl dropped her knee into Seronia's back and yanked her arms behind her. She whipped plastic cuffs from her back pocket and tied Seronia up within seconds.

Red Collar stood. A bar had cut a deep gouge in her cheek. Her jaw hardened, and she surged toward Seronia. Seronia pulled her foot back to get some force in her kick. Scarf Girl grabbed her foot and twisted her off balance.

Scarf Girl glared at her partner. "Lady Six Sky needs this one unharmed," she blurted as she spit.

Red Collar shook her head, stood, and scowled.

The two older girls hauled Seronia out kicking and screaming, while the others followed.

Seronia was taken into an elevator in one of the tiny trucks. Thirty feet up the elevator stopped, a door opened, and Red Collar drove out while Scarf Girl held Seronia down. They came to a wide-open area with hundreds of timber beams and a row of wooden rooms on one side that looked like a motel. They maneuvered between beams and pulled in front of a bluish door. They helped Seronia up and led her through the door, careful to avoid her swinging feet that were wildly kicking. Her screams echoed off the walls.

Inside, a young girl sat at a counter gazing at a computer screen. Several pictures of Mayan pyramids decorated one wall. A nine-foot statue of a priestess in a long, flowing robe stood watching with panther eyes. The girl behind the counter nodded her head at a door on her right. Red Collar opened it, and everyone went in. Seronia was still fighting them. They walked down an empty hallway with peeling paint and turned left into a bathroom. It contained several sinks, three soiled toilets that sat in the open, and a row of showers with a cement gutter that flowed to a large pipe in the floor by the far wall.

Red Collar turned on the tap for the center shower. Scarf girl began yanking off Seronia's shredded clothing. Seronia calmed as she stood there naked and watched the spray of water hit the cement floor. She loved showers. Juan Diego had set up a shower for her fashioned from a five-gallon bucket with a spigot attached to a plastic bottle with holes in the bottom. It was filled with rain, so she seldom got to enjoy wonderful showers at her desert home. But when she did it was blissful.

Without any urging or fight, she stepped under the shower head and let the water wash days of dirt from her long hair. Scarf Girl handed her a bar of soap, and Seronia laughed as she lathered herself in soap suds. The icy water would take most people's breath away, but not hers. She ignored her guards, who both raised their eyes with relieved grins.

Two hours later the bar of soap was a sliver. Her guards rested on the floor listening to the flow of water and Seronia's tiny giggles.

Red Collar shook her head with obvious boredom. "How much longer?"

"She's almost out of soap," said Scarf Girl. "Our job is to make sure she makes it down south and to keep her as happy as possible. The happy has happened."

Red Collar blew out a long draw of air and slumped. Her chin rested in her palm.

Seronia ran out of soap, but that didn't end the shower. Finally, Scarf Girl strolled to the outer room and found the main water valve. The shower dwindled and dripped. Seronia stood with wrinkled skin staring at the shower head. Scarf Girl handed her a towel. She put it over her shoulders like a cape. Scarf Girl took another towel and began drying her off.

Jef Huntsman

Clothes were folded on an empty stool. Dressed in a pullover purple dress with a banana-yellow belt and plastic sandals, Seronia placidly followed the two guards back to the small truck.

The electric motor hummed. Seronia stretched her neck, laughed in short snorts, and let her hair fly behind her.

Things would change.

27

Carson

I woke up after jumping from the top of a racing Humvee. Smoke and flickers of flame shot from the hood that was bent back like a tin can. Toothless Taliban with hair percolating in the wind turned and chased me. A ghostlike spirit followed like a lion on a leash across the hot desert. They were gaining on me.

I was soaked in sweat, my pulse thumping. I sat up. The sheets had been balled up and thrown into a corner. It took a minute to shake the dream away. Or *was* it a dream? The room was quiet and bleak, the first spears of sunlight shooting through the curtains. The ceramic tile chilled my feet as I wandered over to the open bathroom door. A splash of cold water on my face wiped the Humvee chase from my mind.

I hadn't had post-traumatic stress in years. As I gazed at my drawn-out face and deep-set eyes, I wondered what had tripped that brain switch.

The silence broke as Hub made sounds like a wounded warthog storming through a jungle in the bed next to mine. The cracked screen of my cell said five-forty. When did I break that? Hub let out another nasal blast. I shook him. "Get up. We need to find Seronia." I took a quick shower then checked on Hub again.

His head pressed deeper into the pillow. I went downstairs and across the pavement to the office. A pot of coffee bubbled on a table against the far wall. *Pan dulce* sat in rows on a tray next to the coffee pot. A handwritten sign said *Café 10 pesos*. A bowl with change sat nearby. I poured two coffees, wrapped a napkin around the sweet rolls, and dropped four American dollars into the bowl—a generous fifty-two pesos. The man behind the counter smiled as I headed back to the room.

I held a cup of coffee under Hub's nose, and he sputtered awake.

Forty-five minutes later, after wolfing down huevos rancheros and thick chorizo, we headed out of the lazy beach town of El Capomo.

Jef Huntsman

Tourists with chicken legs and oversized t-shirts strolled busily through the shops. I took one last look at the serenity of the ocean before turning toward the mountains. Lady Six Sky's farm was only eight miles out of town.

The motel clerk's eyes had widened and his mouth had clamped shut when Hub first asked about *Dama Cielo Sexto*. Twenty dollars loosened his tongue. He said the townspeople called the farm, *Diablo Verde*, the green devil. No residents that he knew of worked there, and no one left the farm except a few truck drivers and a small crew. He said people from the town wouldn't go anywhere near the farm. "*Mal magia,*" he kept repeating.

Fifteen minutes later we were pulled over by the Mexican police in a white sedan with a light centered on the roof. I sucked my cheeks in. "What now?"

Hub's brow raised.

I leaned back and watched from my rear-view mirror. The driver got out, centered his hat on his head, and opened the back door. A turkey-shaped man with a round body and small head stepped out. He was barely five feet tall, a head shorter than the driver. He wore a tan uniform and a thin loosened tie around the folds of his neck. The two chatted for a minute while the round man kept his eye on our Cherokee. They parted. The driver, his hand on his holster, went to the passenger side while the round man walked toward my side.

I sat up straighter. The top of the round man's chin barely cleared the bottom of my open window. He eyeballed me, then Hub.

"*¿Americanos?*" he asked in a tinny voice.

I nodded.

"*¿Hablo español?*"

I held up my hand, shaking it with my thumb slightly lower than my index. "*Un poco. Pero mi amigo habla español.*"

He puffed what might have been his chest out. "I speak Americano." His lips bubbled out. "Where are you going?"

I smiled a full hundred-watt smile. "We're looking for a friend's daughter." I wasn't sure how much to tell him. He stood with an air of self-importance.

He crossed his arms over his belly and leaned into the door. "I'm the *comisario de policía* of El Copomo. You Americano police?"

"No, no. We're just doing a favor for a friend." I watched. Police commissioner, huh? His badge said *Jaime Zapata*. His stiff uniform tightened around his ample middle and boasted scores of thin, colored ribbons and emblems. I wondered how many of those medals he had given himself.

His eyes narrowed. "I noticed a lot of holes in the side of your car." Lines creviced around his eyes as he narrowed them. His fingers rubbed his shaved chin in careful movements.

"Yes. Pedro was about to finish the body work before we borrowed it. He drilled holes to pull out the dents." I'm not sure where that came from. Even I didn't believe it. Hub's bottom lip raised, and he nodded as if he agreed.

"The holes suck in. never seen a drill do that." He stepped back to get a better look.

"Well, that's what Pedro told us. Actually, I know nothing about auto body work."

"Pedro?" He cocked his head. "So, what's two Americanos doing way down here in Mexico looking for a girl?"

Hub leaned down and met the police chief's eyes. "Do you know anything about *Dama Seis Cielo*? We hear she may have Seronia."

I kicked Hub's ankle and burned through him with my eyes. He gave me an innocent look and a nod that said, *I'll handle it*. Trusting fool. I kicked him again.

The police chief pulled at his ample chin. "*Dama Seis Cielo*? I don't think I've heard of her. Is she supposed to be a local girl?" He paused. "Crazy name."

"She has a farm out in the mountains near here," Hub said.

My ears were flaming.

"Lots of farms out here," the policeman said, rolling his hand back. "Do you have an address?"

"No, we're hoping to ask some other farmers out here," I blurted before Hub had a chance. "I'm curious. Were we speeding? I thought I was driving all right."

"No, we just thought you might be lost. We're here to help tourists. But I guess you're not tourists." He peered at Hub and waited for him to say more.

"We're probably in the wrong area, or maybe someone was pulling our leg."

"Pulling your leg?"

"Sorry. Someone was joking with us and gave us the wrong information."

"*Si.*" He nodded.

We needed to get away from Commissioner Zapata's interrogation. "Can we call you if we need any help?"

He wiped his brow with the palm of his hand. "Yes. At the police station. Someone will get hold of me." He took a step to the side, then moved back. "Where'd you say Pedro is from?"

"Oh, he's clear up in Chihuahua. He rented us his truck."

The police chief nodded to his deputy, and they walked back to their car. I noticed the chief taking note of the license plate. He'd know who Pedro was before they got back to the station house.

I started the car and turned to Hub as the police car pulled away. "You trusted him?"

"Well, I . . ."

"All those shaman abilities, and you trusted him?"

Hub reached down and rubbed his ankle.

The area turned out to be mountain jungle. Hub drove past the turnoff we'd heard about as I peered down the dirt lane. I spotted a guard sitting on a semi-hidden chair about fifty yards in. Hub found a break in the vegetation about a quarter mile past the entrance. We pulled deep into the trees until jungle hid the Cherokee. With a couple of guns, a backpack containing food and water, and a thermos of coffee, we headed on foot to a point inside the entrance. Birds fluttered at our approach through the thick growth. That wasn't good.

We came out of the bushes about fifteen feet from the guard. I signaled for Hub to hide. The guard was facing away from us, leaning into a tree trunk. Long black hair waterfalled down from a green cap. Her thin neck was bent slightly forward and to the side. She seemed to be sleeping. Probably waiting for motor blare from trucks entering and leaving.

I pulled back into the brush, and we moved parallel to the road about fifteen feet in. Scattering birds and branches broken by cows or wildlife became commonplace. Perhaps we were on a game trail. In the quick growth it was hard to tell.

A half mile further, we came to a clearing. Maintenance sheds and several bunkers formed a line like an old western ghost town. A tractor crawled down the center street, and two girls were replacing clay tiles on a section of roof. Other than that, the place seemed empty. The rest were probably all working the farm in the distance. We kept just inside a line

Mosquito Sands

of trees carved on a hillside.

Around the building, we gazed down at fertile crops of corn and wheat. A thresher was cutting long rows of corn and tossing the stalks into an old semitruck. Irrigation water followed furrows through the acres of wheat. As we moved closer to the hilltop, we saw cattle that looked like ants on a mound. I pulled out my binoculars. A few people on horses were funneling about forty or fifty head of cattle through a gate.

Then we noticed a small village of huts on a slight hill to the south. In the center were three pyramids laid out in a triangular pattern. One appeared twice as big as the others. There seemed to be a short, rock wall in a circle around the whole group. The forest came to a pinnacle of green just above the open space surrounding the pyramids. I pointed in that direction to Hub. We ducked back into the forest and made our way down the slope.

When we arrived, I asked Hub to wait. I figured it was easier to not see one person than two—my Marine training seeping through. Hub agreed, though he was fascinated by the pyramids and it took some persuasion. With no one around, I high tailed it down the incline. I reached a ravine where another hill began, and the pyramids rested. An eerie quiet surrounded the area. Spiritual. At the stone wall, I could hear the faint sound of cattle bellowing as they were herded. They didn't seem to like the idea. The noise gave me cover.

As I came closer to one of the smaller pyramids, I noticed they were made of wood, stone, and earth. The first one stood about twenty-five feet tall. An entrance tunneled into it from the second step up. I glanced in and saw only darkness. The rectangular tunnel had the same large wood pillars and chicken wire as the mine outside Guadalupe City where I helped the children escape. A tile and flat stone path in a zig-zag pattern flowed into the blackness. With caution, I searched the first twenty feet with my cell light. The path veered to the right.

I backed out and proceeded to the larger pyramid. On top, a pole shot from the apex into the air. The pyramid lay closest to the edge overlooking the cattle fences a football field away. Its cave entrance sat directly in front of me. Not a soul was sin sight. I signaled Hub to follow me. He rushed down the hill, disappeared in the ravine, and popped back up over the rock wall. Within seconds, he stood next to me. His face beamed as he caught his breath.

"Power," he said. "Do you feel the power? Well, and the death too.

Jef Huntsman

This place is kicking my neurons like the Fourth of July." A smile grew on his face, and his palms pounded his chest. "You feel it? I'm absorbing energy through every pore."

"I feel anxiety." I exhaled a drawn-out puff of air. "Any luck we may have had is thinning. Let's glance around and head back into the cover of the trees."

Hub's lips curled in childish disappointment.

We stepped up to the larger pyramid. The line of a repressed smile and wide eyes told me Hub hadn't entirely lost his enthusiasm. The dark entrance was up four giant stone steps. I put my finger to my lips, and we climbed up to the tunnel.

My cell said eleven-thirty. I hoped they didn't have lunch break at the pyramids. With deep breaths, we entered the tunnel. Streaks of wet moss lined the ceiling and walls. This one was narrower, maybe three feet wide, and only five feet high. We had to duck to walk inside. My light cast an eerie glow on the walls. The tunnel had been overlaid in a blue tile on the walls and tan stone on the base. Thirty feet in we came to a circular cutout. A round post triple the diameter of a telephone pole and much taller rose up into a cone formed by square oak pillars. The square wood beams were painted in reds and greens, forming newly painted Mayan glyphs. The glyphs ran vertical as high as the light allowed. Hub snapped pictures of them as he wandered, mouth hanging open, around the center post. There was a hollow uneasiness to this place.

"There has been some bad magic in here," whispered Hub. "You can almost hear the dead screaming."

"I'm not sure this leads us any closer to Seronia, but I've been in Afghan prisons that didn't crush my chest like this place. We need to leave." A brush of hot air swept past me.

"You feel that, too." Hub took one last picture. "Finally, you have some sense of otherworldly dimensions." He sniffed the air. "You can smell the evil. That is something Juan Diego has told me about, but I've never had the experience. He said you lose a slice of your soul when you come to a place like this, and it's gone forever."

"No, I just—"

"You felt it, Carson," he said, cutting me off. "I know you felt it even if you didn't smell it."

"Let's go." I took one last look. It was then I noticed the floor. The rock tiles were blotched in large black spots. Some of it peeled and curled at the edges. I knew without looking closer that the discolor beneath our feet was dried blood. I grabbed Hub by the arm, turned, and headed for the distant light.

We ran. We should have checked first before we stuck our heads out of the tunnel, but I needed fresh air and sun on my shoulders. The place had given me an uneasy feeling. I startled for a moment when I realized we were in the open. Luckily this unfathomable religious place lay vacant. Nothing but us and the ghosts. We stormed past the smaller pyramid. I stopped at the stone wall for a second, glanced around, and slipped over it. From just outside the wall, I noticed something I hadn't seen before.

To the south of the cattle ranch in a grove of trees sat buildings. They were more like tiny huts or cabins forming circles. The huts were big enough for maybe two people. There were also buildings like barracks forming circles around what appeared to be a giant fire pit in the center. I counted five circles, including the larger one with the barracks. Farther away, on a cleared ridge above the huts, I caught a glimpse of a larger building surrounded by forest. With a steepled roof, it appeared to be an ornate house. A stone path walked through the trees in a serpentine trail. It overlooked the huts.

"There's Six Sky city," said Hub. "You think the house is hers?"

With a nod of my head, we ran down to the ravine and up into the tree cover. We caught our breath, bending over, our hands on our rubbery knees.

Hub peered down at the three pyramids we had just left. "That's a temple of death. Isn't it?"

"Looks like Six Sky is trying to recreate the past. The question is, who are they sacrificing? You said the original Six Sky was known as the warrior queen. Who is the new queen at war with?"

"She's bad voodoo. Probably at war with everyone who doesn't follow her religious path." Hub glared off into the distance.

"If she's here, she's at the big house. You okay to go find her? You could sit this part out and wait at the car."

"No way—Seronia, all these young captured teens. An evil shaman queen with her own pyramids. I'm in." Hub patted me on the chest. "You'll need my shaman insight, anyway."

We stood peering through the jungle at the large house. Through the windows I saw a couple of golden-robed women in their mid-twenties.

They each wore a large feather ornament like a necklace around their necks that flared down over womanly chests. These were the oldest girls we'd seen so far.

I took out my binoculars from the backpack and scoped the area. Everyone who lived in the huts must be out working. Twisting around to a better spot, I watched the house. Low-cut grass separated the house from the jungle by about thirty feet. We'd have to cross that without being seen. I handed the binoculars to Hub, who had pulled two bottles of water, beef jerky, and some kind of sponge bread from my backpack. We ate and took turns spying on the house. Windows without drapes made it easy to see what was going on inside.

Hub's free hand became animated. He shook an outstretched finger at the house. "She's there." His voice was filled with excitement. I tried to grab the binoculars from him. With a bat of his hand, he signaled for me to wait.

I leaned forward next to him. I could see a couple of people but couldn't make out faces.

"It's Seronia," Hub stated. "They've cut her hair a bit, but those innocent eyes are still there."

He handed me the binoculars. My heart jumped against my chest. He was right. Seronia was sitting at a table by herself. She looked happy as she took a pencil from a box and began drawing lines on a sheet of paper. She was wearing a sleeveless turquoise dress. Just minutes ago, the room was empty.

"This is the time," I told Hub. "Everyone's in the fields or with the cattle. There are only a couple of fancy-dressed guards, and I don't see guns on them. They might have rifles in the house, though." My adrenaline slammed through my body like a shock wave. I left the pack and scooted down at an angled incline to the back of the house.

Hub was on my tail. I handed him one of my guns. He hesitantly took it. I knew he could shoot, even though he doesn't like to. He gazed at the gun like it was a stick of lit dynamite, pulled in a deep breath, and stuffed it in the back of his pants. We headed through thick trees and swaying brush.

"Wait. Is the safety on?" He pulled the gun back out.

"There's no safety."

Hub's eyes widened. "What?"

"When I loaded it, I made sure there wasn't a bullet in the chamber." I turned and scuttled through the trees. Hub followed.

Mosquito Sands

I saw it before I could stop my downward momentum: a camera mounted in a tree. Shit! I nodded at it to Hub. He saw it too late. One more step, and I slid forward. In my periphery, I caught the red flick of a laser through green leaves. An alarm went off. It sounded like an air raid siren from WWII. The volume stabbed my ears, and my face cringed at the pitch. I fell into the open space.

On autopilot, I headed for the side door of the house. As I reached for the knob, my ears deafened as the sound of gunshots broke through. I had no idea where Hub was. The door was locked. I stepped back and kicked with all my weight at the doorknob. It cranked to the side but didn't break. I went for another kick. To my left, a shotgun was aimed at my torso. I couldn't stop my forward momentum. I watched the shooter's serious eyes. A gun went off, and the shooter's knee shattered in a red burst. She fell to the ground as the gun sent pellets into a side window.

I turned my head from the flying shards and saw Hub standing behind me holding the gun in both hands. He jumped over the top of me and booted the shotgun away from the young girl's reach. She writhed in pain, screeching in lumbered agony.

The alarm never stopped. I rose from bent knees. In the distance a mob of girls were running to the house. About twenty of them were closing in, and another fifty were farther back. Girls in Indiana Jones' hats with rifles were yelling at the ones who stood stunned. Rifles were handed out from an old panel truck. Girls from the farm carried hoes and rakes as weapons. We had little time. I shot a hole in the door and punched a bigger opening with my foot.

We entered. The place was white, neat, and clean. An unused fireplace with flowers on the mantle centered the far side. I raced through a door to the corner room where I saw Seronia. The room was there. She was not. Colored pencils were scattered across the floor. The paper had an outline of a small city block with what appeared to be a fountain in the center. It branched out like the spokes of a wheel. Some buildings were taking a rough form. I heard Hub in another room. My feet rushed to him calling me. He was peering out the window, and I saw what he saw. A black van was headed down the main road, a tail of dust behind it.

My spirits sank for a second when my eyes spotted the rampaging herd of young girls streaming our way. They were maybe thirty yards out. Without saying anything, we raced to the door and up into the trees.

Jef Huntsman

Shots were fired at us as we entered the camouflage of jungle. We ran the same path that brought us here. I snatched up the backpack from the ground as we passed. Like a stampede of buffalo, I heard the madness of the group storming the forest right behind us.

This was one of those times I was so glad I run most mornings. Hub seemed beyond winded as we grabbed brush on our clumsy climb up the slope. It wasn't that steep until you had to race up it. My lungs were beginning to burn. Rifle shots fired haphazardly around us. I realized they could accidentally shoot us. I turned and fired off the full magazine. The jungle was suddenly quiet for a second. Hub frantically sucked air, not realizing until then that he'd been holding it in, and I felt my heart pound my chest.

A bullet sang over my head.

The brush thickened, and it was hard to find my bearings. The brightness of the sun flickered through the leaves. We raced into a clearing. Using my hand, I let Hub know we needed to head southward across the hill. We needed to distance ourselves from the girls who were coming right behind us. I glimpsed the chrome of the black vehicle as it raced in front of a stream of dust over the distant hills.

Seronia was gone. My lips tightened against my teeth as frustration boiled deep in my gut. Within minutes, I heard the twigs breaking, winded breathing, and birds escaping as the females advanced on our right, coming straight up the hill. The jungle gave them as much adversity as it did us. They were slave farmers and cattle feeders. Their forced chase had the voracity of a mob, not the stealth of soldiers. They were unorganized and lacked meaningful drive. Even the few guards seemed untrained.

We were getting ahead of them, even though we knew we were completely outnumbered. We needed to be careful, but most of them had lost our trail and were headed away from us. We figured they would fan out somewhere and we hoped bad luck wouldn't put them in our path. I stopped. Hub was gasping for air. He wrapped his arms around his chest and rocked back and forth. I gave him thirty seconds to slow his breathing, then we pushed on.

We slipped across the mountainside to our left, leaving the mob searching toward the main road. I heard the crash of untrained feet as they barged farther up the hill. It seemed we had escaped them.

Then branches snapped just eight feet or so below us. I pushed Hub into the brush and followed. Seconds later, a round-faced girl of about sixteen barged through the jungle with her rifle barrel waving in front of her. Though she was the hunter, she displayed the scared fierceness of cornered prey. We were hidden in the thickness of leaves and broken cobwebs.

She sucked in gasps of air. She muttered something under her breath, her neck twisted as if wondering how she had ended up alone. Her panicked eyes focused on the forest behind her. I could hear others farther behind. Sweat dripped from her tangled, coal-black hair. I could smell the fear. She proceeded forward.

With a quick slip of my foot into her path, she stumbled. Her rifle flew from her loose grasp and clanged against a tree. She face-planted into enormous leaves and earth with an audible thud. The young girl began to rise as if doing a pushup, eyes wide as grapefruits. I grabbed her elbow and flipped her over. I rolled firmly on top of her. With mouth open, eyes searching for escape, she tried to twist to the side. The power of my knees on her wrists was too great. She turned and tried to bite my arm, her chomping jaws just out of range. She bucked from her hips. My weight held her down.

"Don't hurt her," said Hub.

I rolled my eyes. "Grab her gun. It's by those roots."

It was then I noticed too much silence. A bad sign.

Out of nowhere, two older teenage girls—one with bushy eyebrows, one tall—headed toward me with kitchen knives. Hub stood behind the knotted roots of a fig tree, lifting a fallen branch the diameter of a baseball bat. The branch swung over my head, and I felt a whoosh of air. It slammed the tall girl firmly in the shoulder. Her knife dropped, and she tumbled back into the other one. Bushy Brow's foot tangled on a tree root. She fell with a scream, and her knife stabbed the taller one's leg. They rolled back in a heap of loose, black hair and tangled legs. Hub moved sideways in two full strides and planted himself above them with his pistol aimed in one hand and the tree limb ready to strike in the other. His body shook from adrenaline.

"Don't hurt her," I said, chuckling.

"What the hell have you gotten me into, Carson?" he asked. He had lost the humble, quiet face of the eternal shaman. Sweat circled his shirt below his neck and underarms. He panted like an out-of-shape runner. "And I need to pee. This can't get any worse."

As I sat on my captive, I turned to Hub, whose kind eyes were trying to look mean as he stared down at the two girls. "Gotten you into? I swear *you* asked *me* to come down here."

"But we're fighting kids with pimples and training bras."

"We've got to move. These so-called kids have automatic weapons and uncaring trigger fingers." My eyed danced around us in sputtered glimpses. I lifted the round-faced girl that I was sitting on. "Grab the bushy-browed girl. The tall one is wounded, and she can't run." I could hear feet crunch on leaves in the distance. A group of young soldiers were getting closer.

"What?"

"Keep it down. We need to talk to them, and we can't talk here." I headed south. The round-faced girl growled and tried to yank away. I pulled harder, and she unwillingly followed.

The tall girl let out a scream. I stopped and turned. With the round-faced girl in tow, I took two strides back and pressed my boot against the tall girl's throat with enough force to slowly drop her to sleep. *"Silencio."* Her eyes bulged. She flailed beneath my leg for a few seconds. Her eyes drooped, her rubbery arms dropped to her sides, her body limp. My Marine training is to kill; luckily, I learned from a master judoka, Tan Em, to just decapacitate. I hardly used that skill until now. These girls were as dangerous as they come, but most didn't deserve to die.

I lifted my boot, and after a full minute she awakened. I cocked my head and listened for sounds in the forest. There was some movement in the distance, but nothing worrisome. The group I heard from before had turned to the south, away from us. They either didn't hear the scream or their fear turned them away from the sound. The tall girl stared at me through slits of eyes. I saw the hatred in her tight face and bony knuckles. I considered putting her under for a longer time while we made a run for it.

"Wait, I've got something," Hub said.

From his pack he pulled out a couple of crunched flowers. They looked like tiny yellow footballs with a brown spot in the middle. He motioned for me to back off. He gently smoothed back the tall girl's hair. She seemed to relax to his touch. With his other hand he softly stuffed the leaves and part of the bud of the flower in her mouth. Her hands smacked his chest. His head nodded softly. In a whisper, he repeated a Spanish mantra of some sort. She listened and allowed him to crumble pieces into her mouth. Hub massaged her jaw in circles with his kind hands. The other two gazed over his shoulder. After a minute, he told the tall girl to spit out the chewed remains of the flower. He nodded, patted her hand, and stood.

"She'll be quiet for an hour or two," he stated. He started to walk away, then turned back.

Hub kneeled, ripped off his sleeve, and wrapped it around the taller girl's knife wound. Blood seeped across the back of her leg. "Hold it tight," he told her. Bushy Brows tried to escape from beneath the taller one's torso. Blood stained her peasant dress.

"*¿Oue?*" she barely whispered.

"*Manténgalo apretado,*" Hub pointed to the wound and motioned to apply pressure with the palm of her hand. Her mouth hung loose as if the muscles were detached.

The tall one gazed at him in puzzlement. Her forehead crinkled in the center. She grasped the cloth he tied around her leg. Bushy Brows peeked up at Hub. Hub smiled and held out his hand. The girl grabbed it, and he lifted her up.

"*No, les haremos daño aninguno de los dos,*" he said. "We won't hurt any of you," he repeated with a lift of his brow.

Bushy Brows followed him as if they were on a first date. Handling my captive, on the other hand, was like taming a wild horse. She screamed, and I slapped her across the mouth, just enough to get her attention. She glared at Hub as if he lied to her. I gripped her wrist and hauled her through the jungle. Hub said something in Spanish to her, and her arm muscles relaxed. She let me lead her. I didn't ask what Hub said.

I glanced back. The tall girl's eyes centered on Hub until we disappeared into the lush growth. Her jaw slackened as she tried to say something. Nothing came out. Her tongue lapped at the roof of her mouth.

Hub stopped and walked back. I watched and heard him say, "We'll be back to help you home." Hub held his index finger to his lips. She relaxed against a tall palm. I knew she could make it back to her group if they didn't find her first, but I had a feeling she would wait until we were far away. Hub's ways seemed to bring out the best in mankind.

I realized Hub had saved my life twice that day. News headlines flashed across my mind: *The hero of the lost and abducted saved by a wacky, peyote-traveling shaman.* My mortality no longer felt as rock-solid as it once had. I chuckled to myself. All three gazed at me in fearful wonder. I forged ahead.

Jef Huntsman

The two girls chattered in quick Spanish. Way too fast for me to understand.

I pulled out my knife and made a motion of slitting my throat. My tongue hung lopsided from my mouth. The two glanced at Hub and grew silent.

"Did you have to scare them half to death?" asked Hub.

"Didn't you just club a young girl in the head?"

Hub's bottom lip puffed out. I'd never seen him pout before. Both of us seemed a touch edgy from everything that had happened at the farm—and from losing Seronia.

"What did you give that girl with the hurt leg? She calmed and seemed to lose her voice."

"*Spilanthez Acmella.*"

I rolled my hands in front of me, urging him to tell me more.

"Bullseye. That's the name of the flower. It numbs the throat. They use it for toothache—like in Anbesol. It's also an aphrodisiac. I found a whole garden of it at the edge of the pyramids before we set the alarms off."

"And you used it to numb her throat, or as an aphrodisiac?"

Hub smiled.

We heard the shuffle of feet, hushed chatter, and swishing branches as more girls from the compound moved away from us searching across other directions, repelled like two positive ends of magnets.

Hub grinned. "It's a shaman thing."

"A luck thing." I grinned back. "Ask the girls about Seronia and Lady Six Sky. They may have info."

Within a few minutes he had the whole scoop. I would have had to tie them to a tree and threaten them at knifepoint, but Hub just used his poetic voice and manner, and they told him everything. Maybe I needed to listen to him more. Like the scorpion, it's just my nature.

Between the two, we found that *Mapa Chica*, Seronia, had probably been taken to Teuchitlán, Jalisco, a town about twenty-six miles west of Guadalajara, Mexico, and 150 miles from where we were. Bushy Brow had worked as the house cleaner for Seronia's top guard. I could tell by her eyes that she knew more than she would say. Six Sky's tentacles spanned all over Mexico and into Honduras. She may be bigger than even they thought.

The girls were hesitant, but with Hub's soft urging they told him that *Dama Sexto Cielo* would be in Teuchitlán—her base, a place of spirits and power. The queen had many shamans who ruled the other spots. Hub explained that *Dama Sexto Cielo* would be waiting for *Mapa Chica*. Seronia was supposed to leave the next day, but our arrival had changed that.

We learned that Seronia had spent weeks with *Pantera Emplumada* "feathered panther." I assumed a self-given name. She had traveled along the Pacific coast between Playa Los Conchos and Lo de Marcos, almost the same route we had taken to get here. All the girls knew was that *Mapa Chica* was on an important mission. No one was allowed to talk to her or *Pantera Emplumada,* the high-ranking *brujo,* witch doctor. A *curandero,* shaman healer stayed at the house with Seronia when she wasn't traveling with *Pantera Emplumada* and tended to her outbursts and tantrums. Two high-ranking guards were also always at the house. Not counting Seronia, the other four were the oldest women at the huge ranch—they were almost thirty. Even the eight captains that set up work schedules and administered discipline were in their early twenties.

Bushy Brows repeated a rumor that Mapa Chica was a powerful *curando*. Hub replied that Juan Diego, her father, was a noted shaman who had taught her.

We stopped, and I shared my bottled water with everyone. The young girls were at ease with Hub's questions. They seemed to wait for his approval. Hub asked them their names. The round-faced girl that I'd tackled was Aja, and the bushy-browed girl called herself Cataleya. Aja clung to Hub like a lost child. Cataleya hunched over with a pained face as if waiting for the strike of a belt to her back.

A warm breeze rolled up the hill and across our shoulders. There was a strange comfort in that. I wanted it to last. It wouldn't.

28

Carson

The rustle of heavy branches and the bubbling of the chasing mob disappeared. Even the birds barely stirred. In the dense brush and trees, I couldn't tell exactly where we were, but I'm used to that. We had traveled miles. My own internal compass had guided me out of worse situations than this, and Hub had pretty good insight himself. I downed one last gulp of water and proceeded.

Hub held out his hands; the two young girls each grabbed one and followed him into the jungle. They felt a security, his security I couldn't understand. Perhaps they needed a surrogate parent—an adult, someone who watched after them. Hub was it. In time, he would know everything about their home, parents, brothers and sisters, hometown, school, and, more than likely, even their favorite color. Hub had always been big on knowing the colors people enjoy. He says it gives him insight into their happy soul. I assumed it might also give him insight to their sad soul, but I kept that to myself. His kindness is a better interrogator than any of those supposed professionals in Afghanistan. No screaming, no torture—just loving smiles all around. I wondered if Hub could have broken the Taliban into emotional tears. Probably not.

We found the main road—more accurately, we stumbled across it. I knew we had strayed miles south in a roundabout arc to this point. We had to be a mile or so from the Cherokee. The thought of Six Sky's people finding it in the thick jungle tightened my throat. I dismissed the thought. We wouldn't have that bad of luck.

I kept us on the gravel, ready to pounce into the jungle at the first sound of approach. There were two. The first that passed by us as we hunkered in the brush turned out to be an old man hunting. He carried a rifle on one shoulder and two rabbits with their feet strung across his left shoulder. The second, a group of about fifteen young girls in t-shirts and khaki pants, carried weapons and searched the edge of the road for us.

Mosquito Sands

We moved deeper in.

I glared at the two girls with us and touched my tight lips. Mouths tightened to their skulls. They glanced at Hub, and he motioned for them to crouch down. They obeyed him with beaming smiles, looking like star-struck teens.

The search team seemed to be more interested in getting back than in finding us. They barely glanced our way. Hub pointed out they were missing dinner. I'm not sure how he knew; maybe he was just joking. My "mile or so" turned out to be five, but we found the Cherokee untouched.

Darkness settled into quietness on the pebbled road. I had worried that they may have found our Jeep, but we had hidden it well with palm fronds and thick branches. No one had touched it.

Hub asked the girls if they wanted to go with us and find their parents or stay here. I glared at Hub to let him know there was no choice. We would send them home. The two looked unsure as they searched the ground. They had been without hope for so long that *home* and *parents* were merely words. Cataleya twisted her foot into the broken branches that we'd pulled from the truck. She peeked up with wide eyes and nodded yes. Aja smiled and headed for the battered rear door of the Cherokee. She stared at the bullet holes and cocked her head to the side with pursed lips. She glanced back at Hub. He shrugged. She jumped in with her friend.

We were off. The sky flared an orange veil as the sun dropped into the trees. No one followed, though they would be on alert in Teuchitlán.

I pulled into a hotel in Ixtlán del Rio at eight-fifteen. The night was black, and the few streetlights did little to abate the darkness. A red *vacante* sign glowed like a devil's welcome. Hub procured two rooms, each with a single bed and a couch bed. He helped the two girls get organized in their room while I drove half a mile to locate some grub. The restaurant was closing, but between my pathetic Spanish and the owner's excellent English, I managed to get some reheated cheese enchiladas, a large plastic container of menudo, two cold cervezas, and two *soda de manzana.*

We sat on the floor of the girls' room and had dinner. They thanked Hub for the food and eyeballed me like I was curdled milk. Hub and I finished, and we left with my unopened beer.

I stopped Hub on the dirt path to our motel room. "You don't think they'll run back to the farm or call someone, do you?"

"They are more afraid of them than us, but the idea of going home after almost a year at the farm will keep them on our side."

"I hope so." I entered our motel room.

"I'm going to watch the sky for a moment," said Hub.

I nodded.

With the beer in one hand and soap in the other, I took an almost-warm shower. My skin tingled after sweating in the Mayan queen's pyramid and being chased by a hundred teens through damp jungle. I didn't want my shower to end, but my body was too tired to stay upright much longer. Toweled off, I turn down the sheets on the main bed. Hub came in as I slipped under the covers.

"You don't want the fold-out?" he asked with a smile.

"Relax; it'll be like sleeping on a comfy ironing board."

He laughed at something going through his mind. "We are like the Beatles."

A stream of air whistled through my clenched teeth, "Hub, I'm tired."

"We were chased by hundreds of teenagers, just like the Beatles," he explained.

"They were chased out of admiration and affection. I'm pretty sure none of their followers had guns and pitchforks."

"You make us sound like Frankenstein." He sat on the couch. "I like the Beatle image much better."

I sat up. "To change the subject, I know you think you've adopted children. Remember, though, they were coming after us with guns a few hours ago."

"Actually, one had a knife."

I raised my eyebrows.

"Yeah, I know, I know. But they are so sweet now," Hub said.

I combed my wet hair with my fingers. A horrid thought struck me: *Those girls are more afraid of them than us.* "You need to go over there and stay with them." I blurted. "They trust you. We need to be sure they won't take off to warn Six Sky. Our luck can't last forever."

"Why not you?"

I laughed.

"I get it. You'd probably end up with a plastic doorstop jammed in your heart." He nodded. "You need to be more of a people person. You are a nice guy. You just don't let many know that."

"Thanks for the psychoanalysis. Now, grab your blanket and stay with the girls."

"There are only two beds."

"The floor, Hub." I pointed to the door.

"All right. Let me take a shower first. Have you called Maria?"

"In the morning." I pulled the covers up and heard the shower as my head hit the stiff pillow. The thought of the two girls slipping away gave me pause. I dropped to sleep.

29

Carson

Hub opened the door to his room in response to my knocks, his stiff hair piled up like a teepee. I glanced to make sure the girls had stayed. The tension in my muscles drained when I saw them.

"We'll buy you breakfast and then get you on your way back home," Hub told the girls as he stood with eyes hazy from a bad night's sleep. With a pained glare at me, he rubbed his shoulder. Cataleya and Aja rolled over with the covers covering the back of their heads.

"Now!" I said.

I listened as a teenage groan sounded long and exasperated. Silence. I cleared my throat with a rumble.

"*¿Que?*" Cataleya stretched and rose from the couch.

"Explain it," I told Hub. The hinges creaked as I shut the door. Within minutes my things were in the truck. I'd filled the tank, grabbed some coffee, and sat on a stone wall waiting for them. The girls came out of the room with the clothes I had picked up that morning. Their hair, wet and shiny, glistened in the morning sun. They looked like they were walking off the steps of a church after Sunday services instead of the hollow-eyed, gun-toting, knife-slashing girls that tracked us through the jungle yesterday. I smiled and received a pleasant upturn of lips and deep dimples in return. Hub dropped off the keys, and we headed into downtown Ixtlán del Rio.

We found a red building with a row of white pillars that held a small café and two tiny retail stores. The waitress eyeballed us with distrust as Hub and I bought breakfast for two young schoolgirls. It was an uncomfortable, fast breakfast. The waitress thought better of us when Hub asked directions to the best church.

Two nuns were overjoyed to help anyone who escaped from *Dama Cielo Sexto.* Four girls from their church congregation had been taken seven months earlier. The parents of one went after them but hadn't been

Mosquito Sands

seen since. They all crossed themselves. They promised to get Cataleya and Aja back to their cities. We thanked them. Hub gave the girls some money. They cried and hugged us both. Only two days earlier they had been ready to kill us and had hated me.

Outside, Hub tossed me the keys. "You're driving. I need some shuteye after sleeping on rough carpet seeping with hantavirus." His head tilted back. "Stop at an *abogado*, I'm going to sue your ass for partnership belittlement and something about work conditions."

I nodded with a smile. "After this morning, I'm not sure the girls would have run away. But it was necessary to keep watch." The Cherokee engine turned over, and I backed out. "You were incredible with the girls. They fully trusted you."

Hub laid his seat back as far as it would go. He crunched up a jacket for a pillow. "Flattery isn't going to work."

"I'm just saying."

"Goodnight." Hub's voice streamed low and faded.

A shaman with an attitude. I headed out onto highway 15D. The road was busy with semi-trailers and ancient dump trucks. The few cars on the road had drivers with the same anxious grip as I had on the steering wheel. We crept along at a steady fifty mph. As I watched the scenery roll by, I thought about the change in Cataleya and Aja. They had been in a hellhole society for months, treated no better than the cattle they tended. Within a day, most of that brainwashing had worn down to a trickle. I wondered how many more could change that quickly. They were young and malleable, but there's still the PTSD. Things would hit them later. The mind holds on to trauma like that for years, sometimes forever.

We were almost to Teuchitlán. Hub bolted upright and hit his head on the sun visor. He wiped drool from his cheek. Eyes wide as a barn owl, he blurted, "I watched Lady Wac Kan Ahaw. She swirled above me like a herd of giant, rabid, colorful bats." Hub stopped and gazed skyward. "Is it a herd? Maybe a flock? Anyway, her face was tender and soft with the features of an angel, but her eyes were downturned, coal black. Instead of being white, the sclera was silver like mercury, with that same liquid, moving surface. So much beauty and evil in one package."

Hub's chest heaved as he sucked in shallow breaths. His face grew pale.

"Don't talk. Sit back and breathe slowly," I said. He clamped his hands together, leaned forward, and rested his forehead on the dash. Minutes passed, and the gasping sounds ceased.

"She's watching us," he said. "She has powers way above mine. And those piercing eyes. Don Juan was trying to back her off with a spear. That spear turned to dust in his hands. I couldn't move a muscle."

I rubbed the back of my neck and stifled a laugh. "It was a dream," I told him.

He glared up at me. "Yes, but my dreams come true and mean something."

"I admit, you have a fifty-fifty chance of your visions being right." I chuckled. "Roll of the dice."

I've never given much credence to his shamanism. His abilities kind of scare me in a way, but I've found he is right more often than not. But eyes that turn spears to dust? That was just a dream. I had plenty of them. I played along. "So, what does it mean?"

"Not sure yet. I'm trying to figure out the feathers."

"The feathers?"

"They kept shooting out from behind her head. Like a constant source of arrows. The feathers were alternating browns and reds. The plumage had power, and she was the source." Hub lifted his head up again. "Give me time. I'll figure this out."

"Well, we're almost there." I said. "Maybe we'll find her all decked out like a turkey."

"Or she'll find us." His teeth bit into his bottom lip. "Cataleya said Six Sky goes to Los Guachimontones, the archeological site, several nights a week. She heard they had ceremonies there. Only the most favored were allowed to go. Maybe we should check there."

"Later. Let's find her compound."

On the road that weaved its way down the mountain fingers I saw glimpses of the town about seven miles away. Below the peak, we found the turnoff Cataleya had described, with three posts bound together on both sides of a two-track road. Animal skulls were nailed on the outside of the poles. Most of the skulls were those of coyotes and deer. I wondered if they were meant to scare or make people laugh. My head shook, and I let out a noise that sounded like a repulsed chuckle.

"Reminds me of totem poles in that cheap budget movie," Hub said. "What was that old western where the cavalry rides in to the Sioux nation half-starved and frozen?"

I had no idea what he was talking about. All westerns have the cavalry or cowboys riding into an Indian village. "How far in did she say the compound was?"

"I think Henry Fonda rode a white appaloosa."

"Hub. Let's concentrate on the problem at hand."

"Oh, yeah, sure." He ripped open a bag of pork rinds and reached in, popping one after another in his mouth and crunching. "These things are awful, but they're so addictive."

"I told you to skip the pork rinds at the store."

"But the cute *señorita* behind the counter said they were her best seller."

"Seronia. Remember Seronia." I creased my brow and glared at him.

"Sorry. I think Six Sky has fogged my brain. Every time I try to concentrate, it's like a black cloud rolls through. She must have incredible powers. Way beyond mine. Of course, evil is easier to project than good." Hub squinted and nodded as if agreeing with himself.

"How far in did Cataleya say?"

"She said they had spotters about two miles in," said Hub.

I peeked at the gauges. "We've driven about half a mile. Keep your eyes peeled for any area where there is an overlook. To be safe, we'll park the Jeep in another mile."

"What about cameras and motion detectors? She may be old school with the Mayan stuff, but she seemed technologically up to date at the ranch house at El Copomo."

I kept both hands on the steering wheel as it pulled left and right in the ruts. My eyes scanned the terrain. We were in a small meadow between thick trees, driving sideways across bumps of mountain tentacles. The road seemed to be barely used. I reasoned that they must have another egress and ingress.

Out of nowhere, Hub slapped my arm with the back of his hand. "Into the trees!"

"What?" I glanced at him. He strained his neck and searched the path ahead.

"Pull over." He pointed. "Under that hazelnut tree."

A squirrel scuttled for cover as I cranked the wheel. "What's up?" My eyes scanned the jungle terrain. I couldn't see far because of the thick vegetation.

"I'm getting that falcon alarm. Like those sparrows back home when they see the falcon's shadow slipping across the earth."

I pulled under the limbs of the giant tree. Dry, small branches scraped the top of the Cherokee. I twisted the key, and the jeep shut down.

Seconds later, we heard the hum of a tiny motor—the same sound as in the deserts of Iraq. A drone. We were still as it passed overhead and arced to the south away from us. We strained our necks, craning sideways to stare through green, burred nuts and thin leaves above the windshield.

Hub pounded his chest. "I'm getting my shaman back."

"Six Sky has developed the Mayan culture with today's weapons." I reached back and grabbed my small backpack. "We need to leave the truck here and do surveillance on foot." I made sure we had water, binoculars, and a few packaged snacks. My hand patted the pistol that had been pressing deep into my tailbone. "Grab your gun."

Hub was hesitant but reached in the glove box and retrieved the .22 Smith and Wesson air-lite. The .22 caliber wasn't much of a weapon unless you were shooting someone in a closet, but it made a show, which is sometimes all that's needed. He shoved a bottle of water into the left pocket of his cargo pants and slipped the pistol into the other.

My eyebrows lifted in approval. "The bullets are in there too. Check the load. Remember, the air-lite doesn't have a safety."

We headed out. The sun flickered through the trees as we made our way to the edge of the two-track road. Within twenty minutes we stood on a bare knoll and looked down on a rolling blanket of green that stretched for miles. A lake spread out like a silver leg of lamb on one side of the city of Teuchitián. On the crest of the mountain lay the conical pyramids of Los Guachimontones that Hub had read about. They looked as if they were made from green felt stairs. I could make out one of the ancient ball courts to the side. The forty thousand people who lived here between 1000 BC and 200 AD were a highly complex, organized society. They were not Mayans, but they evolved with some of the same ideologies and knowledge.

Two hundred yards from where we stood, we could see the tops of structures in the trees below. I'm not a religious man, but I still spent a few minutes and prayed that Seronia was down there and alive. I couldn't imagine what she'd been through with this self-proclaimed Mayan leader, Lady Six Sky. The descent wasn't steep, maybe fifteen degrees.

Hub's neck raised. "She's there. She's troubled and misunderstood, but she's there."

Mosquito Sands

I hope so, I thought.

I turned to Hub. "At this point, we should see what's what first and then make a plan. We need to be careful. We can't lose her like the last time."

"Remember the house—laser lights, cameras, and things we probably missed," said Hub.

"Exactly."

30

Seronia

The metal door whined open. Daylight streamed in. At the sight of Luciana, Seronia shrilled and bounced herself out of the tiny vehicle. She bolted across the gravel road and bound up the mountainside on her right.

Luciana's jaw unhinged; she pushed herself away from the black Explorer and spat a cigarette from her pursed lips. She yelled at the others, who lounged on a bench in the shade. Mari shoved her hand over her grinning mouth. The two other girls snapped to attention, trying to figure out what Luciana was bellowing about now.

The truck in which Trueno had been put had left the day before to another of Lady Six Sky's compounds. Hopefully a doctor there could treat Trueno.

Luciana pointed up the hill with a finger. *"Ir a buscarla!"*

The young girls raced up the hill after Seronia. Mari half-heartedly ran behind the rest.

The girls from the truck yammered into a yellow walkie-talkie in voices laced with panic. Luciana was at their heels, screaming orders and kicking the ground.

Seronia giggled and sped around the edge of the hill. With country-girl lungs and muscles, she easily outdistanced them. Her laughter rained down over the crumbled rocks from the mine. Seronia stopped at the top of a rock and flapped her arms as a light breeze billowed her purple dress. Something glinted to her left. She stopped laughing. She knelt and picked up a split geode that sparkled in hues of rust and white. She kneaded the rock in her hands, an expression of fascination filling her face. Sighing deeply with eyes closed, Seronia pricked her fingers on the rough surface. She had left the outside world.

Teenage girls surrounded her from all sides. They crept closer. Seronia could feel their presence but could care less. The rock held her in a solitude of calm.

The girls rushed her and grabbed her by the arms and legs in roughshod fashion. They lifted Seronia like a heavy log up to their shoulders and hauled her down the slope. Seronia fumbled, almost losing her rock, then captured it. She relaxed and let the girls carry her toward Luciana, who stood with reddened face.

When they arrived at the base of the hill, Luciana tried to grab the rock from Seronia's grip.

"No!" yelled Mari.

Luciana turned. The nostrils of her wide nose flared, her lips scrunched.

"The rock seems to calm her," said Mari. "She would be easier to take to Six Sky if we let her keep it—and remember, she's not to be harmed."

Luciana glared at Mari. Quiet descended like a dark cloud. "Take her to the truck."

Mari's breath released.

31

Carson

The forest thinned as we made our way closer to Six Sky's compound. Forest animals scurried in the brush and around rocks as we proceeded. The wind rustled the leaves of the dark canopy we eased through. The rodents were not ones to worry about. The panthers, snakes, and other predators came out at night. I figured we would need to scope it out and then return just before dawn to help Seronia escape. Otherwise, we'd have crazy, brainwashed girls coming after us while we battled the carnivores in the forest. Suddenly Afghanistan was looking better.

"What animals?" asked Hub.

"I didn't say anything." My forehead creased, and I peeked at Hub. Apparently, he could now read minds? "Let's cut to the right here so we'll come out at about the center of the complex."

We came to a chain link fence with Cortina razor wire strung across the top. A hum sang through the air. The trees had been thinned around the fence. I moved to the side, searching for somewhere to enter. Ten feet in, I saw a grayish snake charred on the wire. She must have been moving through the trees when she got zapped. I pointed it out to Hub with my index finger then pressed the same digit to my lips. He shook his head, understanding. I touched my knife blade to the wire fence. Sparks ignited. The knife dropped to the ground as bits of offshoot current crossed the wooden handle and grounded on my fingers.

We searched the perimeter until we found a burrow that had been made by a large rat or groundhog. It was overgrown with a creeping vine and grass. I used my knife to cut the vine tentacles and yanked out handfuls of grass by the roots. Hub furrowed it out further with a dead tree branch a little bigger than the handle of a garden shovel. An hour later, we had a ravine hollowed out under the electric fence. Using two thick branches, I wedged the bottom of the fence up. It curled like the front of a toboggan. There was enough room to get a small sumo wrestler through in case we needed that.

Hub slipped under first; I followed. We camouflaged our entrance with a dead branch and a couple of bushes we yanked out. I took a long gaze at the area before we moved on. I wanted to make sure we could find it later. An underwater spring guzzled to our left and ran over pebbles down the slope. I pulled a sock out of my backpack and flung it over a branch five yards away.

We headed south through thick, green vines and trees.

An arrow zipped by my ear, snapping into the high roots of a fig tree. With my arm around Hub, I pulled us into a thick growth of elephant ears. The tall plants molded us in the camouflage of their giant leaves. Another arrow whizzed overhead and thudded into something solid on our left. Hub rolled deeper into the leaves as I motioned him to hide.

I knew where the arrows were coming from by their trajectory, so I circled around to a spot where I might catch the archer. I inhaled and exhaled as quietly as the snake that passed over my boot. I leaned forward and listened. A whisper in Spanish told another to move to the right, which was closer to where I huddled. I slipped my gun into my belt and pulled out the long knife.

The person coming my way was lightweight but careless about making noise. She rolled forward like a tank. I waited. A girl who looked about fifteen years old with arrow drawn walked within a foot of me. She wore camo pants and a regular white t-shirt. The thick foliage hid me. I slipped my knife back into its sheath. I waited until she passed then reached behind and pulled back on her foot, lifting her as I did. Her bow and arrow slipped from her grasp. She planted face first on the ground, her forehead hitting a fallen log. I slipped up next to her. She was out cold with a trickle of blood seeping from a gash at her hairline.

"Carina . . . Carina." A hushed, lilting voice came from the opposite direction.

I turned and headed toward the voice. I raised up just behind a tree with a clump of dirt clutched in my hand. I chucked the dirt clod to my left, turned swiftly, and glanced around the right of the trunk. A lanky girl with a ponytail let go of a taut string, and the point of the arrow sailed toward the noise. She nocked another arrow. I rushed her, slamming into her with all my weight. It was like hitting a sheet on a clothesline. Our bodies tumbled forward farther than I expected, and my foot caught on an upturned root. I tripped. Her momentum drove her about three yards farther into the jungle.

I unhitched my foot and raced forward to find her legs hidden in the brush. I yanked her out by her tennis shoes. She jabbed a tiny knife at me with both hands. The blade was short; it would barely make it through my skin. I swatted her wrists; her knife flew into the leaves, copy-paper-sized leaves.

She wrapped her hands around herself and began shivering. The whites of her eyes grew, and tears streamed down the sides of her face.

"It's okay," I said. *"No te haré daño."*

A noise startled me. I turned to see Hub's smile. He had his arm around the other girl—Carina, I assumed. A line of blood divided her face as it dripped off her thin, humped nose.

I started to stand, and the girl on the ground tried to kick me in my groin. I twisted, and her heel glazed off my thigh. I grabbed her by the collar and lifted. With her face close to mine, I growled, "I said, *no te haré daño.*"

Hub patted the back of my hand until I loosened my grip and finally let go. He talked to both the girls in his soft, Hubism way. They looked relieved as I backed up a few yards. I sat on a decaying log and waited.

It always amazed me how well Hub's soft words of kindness could reach down inside people and get them to open up. His body language, his gentle whisperings, and his true gift for empathy was beyond me. I once told him he could talk a soldier on the battlefield out of his weapon.

After an hour, Hub had discovered all sorts of information about Lady Six Sky and her compound. She had ceremonies almost daily, sometimes at night but other times in the early mornings. It was mandatory for all to join the proceedings unless it was harvest time, and then her farm workers knelt in the fields and faced the grand pyramid. Most of the girls here were afraid of the guards and scared to death of Six Sky's magic.

The compound was set up in sections of work. These girls knew only about the farm and the cattle ranch, but they heard there were other areas. To stray from one's area meant punishment or death. They had seen many girls beaten and some boys with faces battered beyond recognition. The soldiers drove them through the compound in carts where new workers were strapped to a metal rail that ran down the center. Good workers got advancement and better food.

Something moved under my rear. I sprung up and bounced to one

Mosquito Sands

side of the mound. A rat as chubby as a cantaloupe and with a long snout eyed me, shook its whiskers, and scampered into the brush.

The girls laughed.

I shushed them. Hub smiled and asked a few more questions.

These two girls had been taken from their schoolyard as they waited alone on the sidelines while their classmates played soccer. They had been here four months. They were forced to work the corn fields on most days now, but today they had to fill in on guard duty because of a special training.

With Hub's urging, we took Carina and her schoolmate back to where we entered. Hub gave the girls money for food and a bus and pointed them to two peaks in the terrain to follow on the way out. I lifted the fence up with a hefty stick, and the girls slipped through to freedom.

Would they curl back around and tell Six Sky's people? I wondered. My breath caught for a second at the thought. I had my doubts, but Hub was able to read people pretty well. Apprehensive, I raised my brow at Hub. He gave me a thumbs up.

Once we got back to where we found the young archers, I chopped a trail through the thick brush with my Morakniv ESEE-6. The blade had a black starburst on it from the electrified fence, and my fingers still tingled. We stepped over elbows of above-ground roots. My eyes scanned for snakes as we soft-footed toward the compound. Fresh air filled our nostrils with the tangy odor of rot and new growth. The hint of campfire smoke sifted through the trees just ahead. The forest ended abruptly, and we stood camouflaged in leaves. I was glad I wore khaki pants and a dark green golf shirt. Hub had dressed in clothes the color of dirty tan like a forest ranger. We hadn't talked about blending into the scenery. Sometimes things just work out.

Inside the perimeter, cut trees and cleared bushes gave way to yellow field grass. Thirty feet in, rectangular buildings curled, leaving an egg shape inside. In the center, raised up about forty feet, a pyramid rested firmly on the ground. It wasn't like the rounded ones at Los Guachimotones that we'd seen from above. This was more Mayan, square with steps up to the pinnacle. It was built of earth, wood, and faded amber stones. At this angle, I couldn't see any opening, but the side facing us had stairs that protruded from the base to give easier access to the top. The peak of the pyramid flattened with enough room for three to five people to stand. A thick post rose from the cap about ten feet like a thick antenna.

Jef Huntsman

Girls in white blouses and tan pants busied themselves with chores, wandering in and out of the buildings. A group of younger girls sat on wooden benches at the end of the egg-shaped arena. Two ladies who looked about twenty seemed to be teaching them. One teacher held up a mask while the other pointed to various parts of it. The masks were a cross between animals and large-nosed humans.

In the distance, a fire burned a ravine, turning green growth to black ash. Two farmhands leaned on shovels as the smoke rose.

Hub leaned close to me. "I couldn't have dreamed anything this cool."

"They're prisoners," I whispered.

"Oh . . . yeah. But it looks so surreal and pleasant there, like a real-life history lesson."

I glanced at Hub and raised my brows.

Color caught my eye. Three females in bright turquoise skirts and puffy, purple tops came around one corner of the pyramid. Their hair was piled high with rows of feathers stuck above their ears. Conch necklaces swooped down over their breasts, dangling to their navel. They seemed to be walking to a slow musical beat. Each carried a thin, wooden tube in front of her with arms outstretched from her elbows. *Ceremonial*, I thought.

The classes dispersed, and the workers began lining up around the perimeter.

I heard the soft patter of a drum and a two-note wail of something like a flute. Out stepped an outlandishly dressed lady with perfect posture, staring straight ahead. Her hand grasped a spear that raised above her six-foot height. Red and gold bracelets bunched at her ankles and wrists. A two-toned, diamond-checked skirt was held tight to her hips by a tasseled belt of blues, oranges, and lime green. She had a thirtyish face with pleasant features and a sculpted, prominent nose. Behind, her head feathers fanned out in three rows. I couldn't envision how they were attached. The feathers seemed to float behind her. Conch shells adorned her neck. A Cleopatra-like halter top molded around her breasts; her bare midriff showed down to her navel.

Every female in the open court bowed down on one knee. Girls streamed out from the barracks and followed the others in the position of honor.

"Lady Six Sky?" both Hub and I whispered at the same time.

I was in awe. Her presence exuded grace, power, and respect. She

Mosquito Sands

strolled forward, a surreal intelligence in an otherworldly costume. More than thirty black cats roamed the courtyard. I wondered if they were symbolic of the Mayan panther god. The cats sniffed the ground in front of them as if searching for something.

"Where did the cats come from?" I asked.

"Out of that square hole in the pyramid." Hub pointed to the right.

"Was that there before?"

"No. I watched it open before she rounded the far corner. I think someone put food on the ground before she arrived. The cats have done this before."

Older women—*older* being late teens to early twenties—came out of the buildings after all the other girls. They were herding the others into the courtyard. Most of them were in t-shirts and khaki shorts. By now there were hundreds lining the parade of Lady Six Sky along a grassy path that curved around to the back of the pyramid. The young girls wore solemn faces and kneeled on one knee. Though their heads were bowed, they peeked toward the ceremonial lady. I noticed several physically shook from their shoulders to their feet, making it difficult for them to keep their balance.

Thirty steps behind the ornate leader, from the same point of entrance, a short man appeared in a blue robe with yellow lightning bolts shooting out from the collar. His large, bald head bounced to the same cadence as Lady Six Sky. A gold, braided rope tied around his ample belly with tassels at the tied end; the tassels swung as he walked. He wore white silk pants that barely showed between the hem of his robe and his leather sandals. He had the look of overfed royalty—a petite mouth between puffy cheeks on a smooth face of dark, stained leather. His head was erect, but his eyes darted from side to side.

A tree branch poked deep into my neck, but I couldn't take my eyes off the proceedings. I scanned the crowd for Seronia. I pulled out my binoculars. A few of the girls in the crowd bore a resemblance to her, and I held my gaze. No, she wasn't there. I turned to Hub. He shook his head.

This was a show of power. I wondered how often the parade happened. Was this a special event, and what might it signify? Carina, the girl we let go, had told us about ceremonies. We should have asked for more detail.

The black cats wandered between all the kneeling girls. Three-quarters of the way around the egg-shaped path, Lady Six Sky stopped.

Jef Huntsman

She grasped her spear in both hands at an angle across her body. The girls around her noticeably leaned back. Sweat glistened from their hairline. Lady Six Sky pointed her long spear at a frightened girl who looked about fourteen. She flicked the spear upward in front of the trembling young abductee. Two of the older girls stepped forward and lifted the girl up by her armpits. The poor thing went limp, and the older one tried to hold her up. Her toes furrowed the ground, then she was released. Her elbows hit the sparse grass. The queen nodded, and the older girls let go. The little girl dropped in a curled heap at Six Sky's Feet. The leader lifted her spear in one hand to the clouds.

I hoped for lightning. Nothing but blue sky and bright sun.

The young girls around the area began digging through the thin grass, grabbing handfuls of dirt and tossing it onto the fainted lump of a child. Six Sky moved away. Within minutes the young body was covered in an inch of fine dust and blades of grass.

Lady Six Sky held her long spear in two hands over the girl and muttered something. She tapped her on the shoulders with the shiny spear blade. She lifted her weapon and stepped back with a nod to the two tall girls. The tall girls grabbed the young one under her arms and lifted her back and to the side. With regal posture, Lady Six Sky turned and walked away.

"A ceremony," whispered Hub. "I think she's come of age or something."

"If that was it, she didn't seem happy about it," I said between my teeth.

The queen's procession rounded the edge of the pyramid and disappeared one by one. The bald man was the last to leave. I'd gotten a better look at him. He was in his late fifties or early sixties and walked with a slight favor to one leg. His eyes reminded me of two small lumps of coal.

The mass of girls dispensed from the area, except two. A thin girl with rounded shoulders tried to help the one that lay crying. Caked with dirt and slightly revived, she peeked up. Her eyes were half shut. The thin girl gave her a loving hug. A lady came from behind and struck the thin girl with a two-foot stick. She let go and held her cheek with a grimace. The girl that Six Sky bestowed some ceremony on dropped to all fours, her neck limp; she stared at the grassy earth. With a sour glare from the older lady, the thin girl walked away.

Hub and I peered at each other. Hub patted his chest and blew air

Mosquito Sands

from his *O*-shaped lips. I nodded in agreement. Through the thick brush, we watched the fainting girl slowly stand and hazily move to one of the buildings. Dust and blades of grass still caked her hair and back.

An older girl in an ocean-blue blouse drove up the hill on an ATV with four giant cages mounted on trailers hooked behind. Dust billowed in the air. A group of younger girls picked up the wandering black cats and put them in the wooden cages.

The birds chirped and paid us no mind. A coatimundi ran across the field in front of us. The girls went about whatever duties they were doing. A loud blast caught me by surprise. I turned. The
explosion sent dirt into the sky and the ground rumbled.

32

Carson

Another blast rumbled through the trees. I jerked my head southward as the smell of bananas and dust filled the air, the defining trace of nitroglycerine-soaked sawdust igniting. Dynamite. With fearful curiosity, I stormed into the jungle toward the sound. I could feel Hub directly behind. We headed in the direction of the two blasts. Birds scattered from the trees into safer areas. Branches slashed at my face as I ran. I raised my hands in front to thwart the thin limbs and leaves from battering my face. With my brisk gait, I tripped over a hidden stone and tumbled down an unseen sharp incline. My back slid down a ravine of wet leaves and fertile mud. Hub followed close behind as we rolled twenty feet like balls speeding down a chute. My arm caught an elbow of banyan root. The force shot pain through my body as momentum and 190 pounds stopped abruptly. I yelped. Hub barreled over my face, His arms flaying at my chest. His fingers caught a grip on my belt, and his chest swung into my knees. I reached with my free arm and hugged the thick root.

We hung where the ravine emptied over a thirty-foot drop-off partially obscured by a tangle of branches and leaves. Below rocks and splintered logs piled below as refuse from the mine.

Another blast came from below and south of where we hung. I grabbed for a better handhold.

Hub groaned without looking up. He slipped slightly. His face was buried between my knees.

"There's a sturdy vine to your left about ten o'clock. Can you reach it?" I asked.

His hands pulled at my pants. His arms stretched parallel. Water dripped onto the top of my head from somewhere above. We swung closer to the mossy rock wall. One arm inched with the other; pain dug deep into the tense cords of my biceps.

Mosquito Sands

My pants slid down, scraping at the skin of my hips. My belt buckle burned onto my stomach. I sucked in air and pushed out my stomach. My teeth bit into my lip.

My pants slipped several inches. Hub's feet searched for ground where there wasn't any. I tightened my grip around the root and curled my legs upward. My pants dropped further as if they were buttered and finally stopped with a jolt at my knees.

Hub screamed.

"Hub!" I couldn't let my best friend fall to his death. I curled my legs, feeling his weight stretch my torso. I held on; if I lost him, I knew he couldn't survive the fall.

With my legs bent up, the tip of my boot hit something solid. I eased my foot around the curled surface of a branch. My other boot lifted and searched for the same precarious hold. My toes slipped up and over. The ever-so-slight relief on my arms let me take in a deep breath.

"Hub!" I bellowed. "Ease one hand at a time and grab around my calf."

"Okay."

I felt the panic in his voice.

"You can do this. There's a branch to your left by your foot."

"My arms. I'm not sure."

"You got this, *amigo*." Every muscle and tendon seemed to be ready to snap. I wasn't sure how much more my body could take. Hub's grip loosened for a split second, and his arm hooked around my curled leg. "Hold tight. I'll swing you to it." I chuckled. "When this is all over, remember *you* were the one who pulled my pants down."

"Shit, shit, shit," said Hub.

His fingers slipped sideways and gripped. Pressure pulled on my bent legs. He inched his way to my boot. The tendon on the top of my feet shot sparks of agony as I gripped the limb with all my might. With a sway of my hips, Hub swung and caught something solid. My pain subsided as Hub found the branch below. He grasped the limb. My feet clawed around and raised up.

"Holy crap, man." He let out a happy howl.

"I'm still stuck here," I pleaded.

"Oh, yeah. I got ya."

I grabbed hold of the trees and came to safety, peering down at a slight angle. I sucked in a deep breath and let it out.

Hub reached out, grabbed my belly, and pulled my legs in. My body angled over the cliff. Without the extra weight, my arms gained some strength. With one foot on the limb below and Hub holding on to my middle, I sloth-crawled into the base of the tree where the root was attached.

From the side of the trough it was like a maze of ladder steps and branch handholds that took us back up to the embankment at the top. I sat next to Hub. Breathing like spent marathoners, we waited, eyeing each other in disbelief. As I caught ribbons of light through the trees, something burned my nostrils. I turned, holding back spasms in my throat. My stomach churned.

To our left, encased in trees and vines, sat the blackened stones of an ancient Mayan ruin. It was mostly covered in curled vines, but recent chopping had kept the entrance open. A path to the opening showed new growth from the fertile ground. I heard a gurgling of water that sprouted to the side of the rock ruin edged in lime-green moss. The beginnings of the stream were hidden in the underbrush above.

My nostrils burned. "Where is that smell coming from?" I knew the smell from my Afghanistan travels—it was the smell of human death, and I'd never smelled it this strong. We both stared at the dark entrance. I made out Mayan glyphs carved into the stone beam above the opening.

Hub covered his mouth and nose with his palms.

I took off my shirt, wadded it up, and jammed it tight to my face as I stood and walked closer to the opening. Stone stairs led down into a dark hole. Even though I knew the smell, I still ventured farther. The stairs circled down.

"What the hell's down there?" asked Hub.

I couldn't answer.

In the darkness, I pulled out my cell phone and touched the light icon. Before me lay a room as big as a semi. It was worse than I expected. Forty or fifty bodies in various stages of decay were heaped on the chiseled stone floor. All were young and most were boys, at least from what I could make out. I shut off the light and raced up the stairs, taking two at a time. At the entrance, I forced my body to keep running into the jungle. I barely heard Hub's footsteps behind.

Seconds later, we stopped and caught our breath. We laid against the trunk of a palm in the black soil. Hub didn't need me to tell him what was there. He knew by my face. Neither of us said a word for some time.

Who were those discarded children? They were piled like driftwood.

Hub seemed to read my thoughts.

Mosquito Sands

"It's unforgivable," said Hub. This cult is all about power. Lady Six Sky's power. She's murdering the ones who don't follow her ridiculous reign."

"It makes the others keep in line," I said. It's been used for centuries throughout the world. But this—this is all about profit. The mine, the farm, the fake Mayan glyphs. Do you think she's smart enough to put all this together?"

Hub wiped tears from his eyes. "Crazy people get other people to follow. Think of Hitler and Jim Jones." Hub's shoulders slumped. "I'm never getting that image out of my mind, am I?"

I shook my head. I had seen too many things like that in the military. They haunt you.

We rested, gulped in fresh air, and tried to slow our heartbeats. Nothing seemed to clean the stench from my nostrils. A half hour passed. Then we started to hike, keeping our thoughts to ourselves.

33

Carson

At the peak of the hill, a clearing in the shape of a T-bone steak spanned a long slope that fanned out in front of us. A black hole lay east of that; workers, trucks, and heavy digging equipment were all involved in removing earth the color of coal. Another blast sent a plume of dust and gravel into the air, shaking the ground. Looking through my binoculars, I saw an open-pit obsidian mine stretched about two football fields across. Trucks were hauling loads of obsidian down a wide dirt road that followed the shoreline of La Vega Lake to the main highway that led out of the city of Teuchitlán, Mexico, in the far distance.

The massive operation was churning money up from the earth. Lady Six Sky used the girls for slaves. They worked her farms, her cattle ranch, her mine, and who knows what else. Ancient Mayan ceremonies may have just been a ploy to hide her real purpose. Back at the pyramid, she seemed sincere or fully engulfed in believing her lie. What about those kids in the hidden Mayan ruin, discarded like empty aluminum cans? She was eviler than I suspected. My mind returned to the dead bodies, and I tried to blink the image away.

"I think I know what you're thinking." Hub pointed to the mine. "Slave labor. I get that, but why the old bald guy? These are all young girls with a few boys. And he's the only man." His eyes penetrated mine.

Another blast, and I turned to watch the puff of debris. "He's the anomaly for sure. There must be more involved. This doesn't happen in a vacuum. The more we learn, the more questions we have than answers." I drew in a long breath of air while thinking. My head swam in circles. "Where's Seronia? We assumed they brought her here."

"Find the older escorts in the escape van," said Hub

"Yep, find the escorts." I nodded.

With our view from the mountain, we saw the whole layout. The

Mosquito Sands

pyramid and surrounding buildings were on a flattened mound overlooking the whole complex. To the northeast stretched a thousand-acre farm whose furrows angled away on a slight slope. Corn was ready for cutting, and the young wheat was probably a second or third crop. To the southeast a full cattle ranch spread for a mile with sturdy fences, outbuildings, calf sheds, and a sizeable pond to the left where hundreds of cattle sipped at brown water. The pit mine consisted of hollowed-out earth and a half-dozen tunnels shooting off the far side like legs of a bug. Machinery and workers moved like the inhabitants of a disturbed hornet's nest. The mine lay about five miles from the pyramid. Other buildings were scattered around the complex. I stopped scanning at the largest one and focused my binoculars.

An expansive adobe house that rivaled any millionaire neighborhood in the United States sat on a wooded hill out from the farm. It had five different levels that crept up the jungled landscape and a guarded rock-and-mortar fence with chunks of broken glass imbedded in the top. The rim of the fence sparkled like Christmas lights in the sun. The wall surrounded the whole building with plenty of open space in between. Guards patrolled both sides of the wall, inside and out, like cattle following tails.

We headed back to the pyramid and housing compound. Both of our faces were scratched from streaming through the thick growth. We took our time going back, stopping for a quick lunch of oranges and tortillas we'd found on the climb out of the ravine. Our water was almost gone. We needed to solve that problem too.

The pyramid area appeared vacant except for a work crew busy painting the outside of the far building. We watched for about twenty minutes, and nothing changed. I noticed a way to get closer.

"Watch the grounds," I told Hub. If anything happens, make a bird noise or something to warn me."

I headed to a short peninsula of trees to the north. A banded tree snake wormed its way across a branch above my head. I ducked as if that might save me from it dropping down my neck. The tail disappeared into the leaves behind me. I crept, trying not to stir up a flock of birds that would warn the painters. The birds didn't help; hundreds dotted the sky as they escaped my entry. Feathers curled down into the treetops. So much for my stealth. At the tip of the tree peninsula, I shot for a grove of apple trees planted in the shape of a big foot that grew fifteen to twenty feet from one of the barracks.

I stopped just inside the heel of the apple grove and waited for alarms to sound. They must feel safe at this compound. The only thing we had encountered was a perimeter fence. There were no cameras or lasers in the forest. And I'd spotted only one camera mounted on each opposing corner of the buildings. I decided fear must act as a deterrent.

I made my way through thick tree trunks and low-hanging branches. A few apples dropped on the ground as my head knocked them off the trees. At the end where the big toe of the grove would be, I surveyed the first building in front of me. It lay on an angle with no visible surveillance cameras. Three small glass windows lined the side about five feet up. I glanced back to the area where I'd left Hub. He was well hidden in the bushes. A hand came out of the green growth and signaled with a curled thumb and forefinger that everything was okay.

I moved out of the small orchard and headed for the closest window. My body flattened against the wood slats. My heart pounded in my chest. I crouched and turned to the window, peering over the sill.

Stacks of money were separated on tables. Some tables held paper pesos; others had overturned bags of American dollars. Young girls were loading banded stacks into boxes. A girl who looked like she was about twenty with a shotgun between her legs sat drinking coffee and watching with disinterest. Another guard with a holster and pistol strapped to her waist leaned against the wall and barked orders to a small girl on her left.

I ducked down. My mind puzzled over what I'd just seen. Leaning against the building, staring at the ground, I heard a squawking like a loose fan belt. I spotted Hub waving a frantic finger. Then I heard the voices. Two people were walking toward me from the front of the building. I sprinted around the back corner. It lay closer than the trees and would give me more cover. I listened without daring to peek around the corner. The soft tone indicated young voices, probably guards, in pleasant conversation. Their boots and chatter faded as they reached the next building and kept walking.

Adrenaline soared through my body like four shots of espresso. I hesitated, questions swirling in my skull. With little preparation, I edged over to the far corner, took a brief glance, and headed to a window at the next building.

Hunched over, I angled my head and slowly rose up. Thirty or thirty-five girls sat cross-legged on a dirt floor. Chips of rock were scattered on the ground. These girls had hammers and chisels. The sound of metal against rock echoed through the building. I lifted both eyes over the wood sill. They were carving fake Mayan glyphs onto two-inch-thick slabs of grey stone. The glyphs looked like the ones I'd seen in the tunnel where I helped those kids escape. These girls had been taught real craftsmanship, though I presumed it hadn't been by choice.

One teen noticed me. Her neck straightened, and her mouth opened. I waited for a scream. It didn't come. I mouthed *"por favor"* to her. She glanced at the guard leaning against the wall. The guard looked half asleep. The teen's foot nudged the girl to her right. She pointed with her eyes. The other girl saw me and gasped. I held my finger to my lips. The two of them smiled. I wanted to tell them I would get them out of this but had no idea how.

My head dropped, I turned, and began running back the way I came. The trees of the foot-shaped grove enveloped me. I twisted and ducked, maneuvering to the heel of the foot. I stopped for a brief second, my throat dry as I gasped for air. My hand plucked four green apples to eat later. A short sprint across open space, and I was hidden in jungle again.

I handed Hub an apple. He grinned his thanks. With my back hunched over and my hands on my knees, I waited until my breathing slowed. It took a couple of minutes. Hub patted me on the back.

"What's in there?" Hub asked.

I took a bite of the apple. It was crisp and watery. "You won't believe this." I paused. "Money and newly created hieroglyphics—actually, Mayan glyphs."

"What?"

"My sentiment exactly. Teenagers who want to do anything but count and stack money are boxing up paper cash, both bills and pesos, in the closer building. Lazy guards are watching." My teeth took another chunk out of the apple. "It may be drug money, but I get the feeling it's something else."

"Why do you think that?"

"We haven't seen any marijuana crops or poppy fields. And if it's meth or cocaine, there would be cooking smoke and ventilation systems. So far, we haven't seen anything like that."

Hub tossed his apple core on the ground. "I've been sucked into a black hole. I'm not getting any shamanistic visuals. A few spurts, but nothing meaningful. And the internet reception is just as fuzzy. A five-hundred-dollar phone and I barely get a quarter of a bar."

Jef Huntsman

I rummaged through my backpack. "I've got a pack of beef jerky, a can of black beans, an orange, and those two apples in my pocket. I think we should trade off on guard duty and watch this place through the night."

Hub groaned. "I'd hoped for a bed with sheets and the obnoxious hum of a window air conditioner. You want to do the Boy Scout thing; I guess I'm in."

I tossed him the can of beans and my Swiss knife with its can opener.

Hub's brow raised. "Yum." He snickered. "Please pass the jerky. Nothing better than dead, dried-out, salty cow."

I took the first shift while the sunset painted the clouds orange and red. Under the canopy of trees, darkness fell quickly. Hub laid on rotting leaves and soon snored in a soft warble.

I checked my watch at nine p.m. Nothing had happened. A few spotlights on the building formed a cone of dull brightness highlighting the shape of the egg. There was no illumination from the pyramid. I chewed in a slow grind on the beef jerky to say awake. The day had been exhausting, and my eyelids fought my perseverance to stay awake. I listened to the chirps of bugs and the drawn-out call of an owl nearby. At two in the morning, my back sore from leaning against rough bark, I had had enough of nothing happening. I tried to wake Hub. He lay curled like a fetus and showed about as much response. A finger to the ribs, and his unfolded arms swung wildly. A few minutes later, he took the watch.

In no time, I fell into deep sleep.

Hub shook my shoulder. The serious expression on his face made me sit up. Leaves dropped from my cheeks. I craned my neck. A group of about twenty people holding red, glowing flashlights loaded into the back of a large, covered truck. A vehicle in front of that took off. The truck followed. I jumped up.

"It's 3:35," said Hub.

"Let's follow." I tore through the trees to the back sides of the rectangular buildings.

"They're in vehicles," Hub said as he ran next to me. "Does that first one have a police insignia?"

I shrugged my shoulders.

We reached the furthest barracks. I watched the lights of the truck and car weaving down a road. A plume of dirt dusted the trees on both

Mosquito Sands

sides. To our right three more trucks waited in the dark. "Let's try those." We shot down onto the gravel parking area. I stopped cold and forced Hub back into the trees. Four guards with flashlights wandered around a truck. One stopped to tie her shoe. Another lit a cigarette.

"We've got to find a way to catch up to those vehicles."

"I didn't tell you," Hub said, "but I saw Lady Six Sky earlier. She must be in the second car."

"Crap. Let's circle around and try to find some form of transportation." We moved in the dark around the guards and followed the road the truck and car had taken. Our eyes were adjusting to the dark. A quarter moon barely shed gray light in front of us. I noticed a motorcycle off to one side. At closer glance, the motor was missing and both tires were flat. Frustration clutched my throat.

"Carson. Look over there."

Ahead of us stood a lean-to outbuilding surrounded by a corral. Several horses slept on their feet on the dirt yard. "No. Not horses." I watched the headlights curl around a corner at the bottom of the hill. "You know I'm no good with horses."

Hub widened his eyes and nodded at the corral.

I shook my head and started toward the horses.

None of the horses had saddles, but there were a dozen wool blankets draped over one of the rails. Hub petted and walked around the horses as if inspecting troops. He came back, grabbed two blankets, and tossed them on a couple of horses he'd picked out.

We watched the rear lights of the trucks stop where the big ranch house was.

"The brown one's yours," he said. "She's about as tame as a house cat."

"Cats scratch the hell out of your face," I stated.

"Tonight, you're a cowboy."

"Then find me a pickup."

I straddled my horse and off we trotted. With a stretch of my back, I inhaled a breath of fake relief. Hub snickered. We rode for some time in the dark.

"You don't ride a horse as if you're straddling a log on a river," he said. "You're going to push your manhood up into your lungs."

I ignored him and spotted flashlights flickering through the trees.

We were above the ancient round pyramids of *Los Guachimones* outside the town of Teuchitlán. In the dim light, we watched Lady Six

Jef Huntsman

Sky climb the steps.

"She didn't go in the truck. Or they dropped her off at *Los Guachimones*."

From where we stood the ancient pyramid looked like gray-green stacks of pancakes in decreasing circumference with a flat top. Lady Six Sky wore the same feathered outfit as before. She held the spear in both hands high above her head. She had girls on each side with long, braided hair wearing turquoise dresses that dragged on the steps behind them. Four others followed them in lime-green blouses and thick-belted skirts. Flashlights darted in all directions, centered on the pyramid.

My jaw hung loose. About two hundred young girls surrounded the pyramid. They had come out of the bushes nearby and dropped down on one knee as before. I peeked at Hub to ask where all these girls came from. We had seen only two vehicles leave the compound. Hub held his hands up and shrugged his shoulders before I could even ask the question.

Lady Six Sky stood on the top of the pyramid with the two turquoise-dressed girls at her side. The bubbling of whispers ceased. Her feathered head glistened in the soft moonglow. Their leader bellowed something in a strange tongue. Hub shook his head. He didn't understand anything she said, and we suspected that none of the others knew what she was saying. Her prolonged words came out loud and poetic like thunder. At the end of each chant she repeated three words, paused, and again started the howl of undecipherable words.

I tapped Hub on the shoulder, and we moved in closer. We hid in the brush about five feet from the circle of young girls. I searched the group for Seronia. The sky was turning a light blue at the crest of the far mountains. I took in deep breaths to slow my racing heart.

From off to the side, two girls forced a thin person toward the pyramid. The girls looked like they were in their early twenties, and they wore the same turquoise dresses. The beam of light shone on the thin figure. It was a boy who looked like he was eighteen or nineteen with a sliver of resistance left in him. He tried to dig his heels in. A smack at his calves from a black baton made him cringe in pain and let out a hollow groan. It took everything I had not to interfere. There were only two of us; there were two hundred plus of them, and those girls were deadly. Their faces had the spirit and intensity of Hitler's youth brigade.

The thin boy was dragged up the stairs. Lady Six Sky muttered a screeching cry from above. The unearthly sound penetrated my body as

Mosquito Sands

if a bullet split my heart. The two servants sat the young boy down on the ledge of the pyramid's plateau. His eyes were black in shadows, then his neck bowed in defeat. A blubbering cry came from the boy. Lady Six Sky continued to wail. The girls remained kneeling at the base of the pyramid.

I felt the pressure of something bad happening. Their leader lifted the spear into the sky. The moon and a crest of early morning highlighted her in a silver glow. I pulled out my gun. Lady Six Sky held a death grip on the spear positioned above the skull of the crying boy. The Berretta was an extension of my arms as they unfolded. I sighted down the barrel at the feathered figure swaying on high. Her voice lowered to a deep chant. I watched her muscles tense, perched above the boy child. My grip tightened on the trigger; her head was the target. Hub moved in closer and accidently bumped my elbow just as the shot rang out.

34

Seronia

The white house was big and had lots of food and cola in it. But the cola was too cold, and Seronia needed to let it sit for so long to get the right temperature. The blue-green stuff on the floor was soft but felt weird to her toes. She had to go outside to feel the dirt press on the balls of her feet.

Outside, there were chickens and a chipmunk that visited her every day. She fed them, petted them, and loved it when they sat next to her on the soft earth. Trees were everywhere. She had never seen so many trees. She had also never seen so many kids her age. They worked the farm and cattle below. She watched them with side glances, but they were too busy to pay attention to her.

Donata had Seronia sit at a big table with stacks of paper and let her draw for hours. Taped all over the wall hung her pictures of the jungle, the kitchen, her favorite chicken, and the landscape down the road. Seronia loved to find a new place to tape her newest drawing. Seronia couldn't believe how many colorful pencils and markers were strewn all over the table like a rainbow with no end. Seronia liked Donata because she let her drink all the cola she wanted.

Luciana scowled from the adjoining room. She spent most of her time cleaning her gun or playing with a long knife she kept at her side. She looked at Seronia and Donata with narrow eyes, like a butcher rolling hung beef to the saw. She complained to Lady Six Sky on the front porch the first night they brought Seronia here. Luciana called Seronia, "a worthless little retard." Lady Six Sky pounded her spear to the ground, and such an evil glow came from her face that Luciana cowered like a possum and hunched away.

Luciana was assigned as Seronia's bodyguard. That's all Luciana did. Her whole being couldn't hide the hate that radiated from her pores.

Seronia missed Toro. Sometimes she could hear him breathing in her dreams, and she woke up giggling into her pillow. Her fingers prodded the white sheets and fluffy pillows of her new room, and her tightened face scrunched up until it almost hurt. She loved waking up with Toro on the dirt by her side where she felt his solidness. He was protection. Seronia had snuck in one of her favorite chickens, but it never felt the same to her. And Luciana chased all pets from the house with the dull end of her spear.

Donata found a black-and-white peppered cat that they named *Gato*, and she persuaded Luciana to allow the cat into the house. Seronia approved, but it wasn't much of a pet in her opinion. *Gato* disliked people, hated indoors, and preferred mice to Meow Mix. Seronia settled for the field rats, chickens, and squirrels.

After a week at the farmhouse, Donata and Luciana took Seronia to a small town half a day's drive away. Donata shook papers and pens in front of Seronia and walked her through part of the town. Donata was horrid at explaining what was expected, but Seronia understood and loved it. She flapped her arms and stormed through the streets like a disinterested bird. After several hours, they arrived at a hotel and took Seronia up to a room.

"She's too stupid to even know what is needed of her," bellowed Luciana.

"I tried," protested Donata. "She wasn't interested in even looking at the damn buildings."

"Lady Six Sky is going to have your hide for this."

"Maybe she doesn't like the town. Maybe our information about her was wrong."

"Maybe you're going to end up back in the fields again." Luciana laughed and motioned with her arms as if digging with a shovel.

"What the . . .?" Donata pointed over to a corner.

Seronia ripped a piece of paper from her sketch pad and flung the finished product across the table. She turned to another and began working on a rendering. Within minutes, a picture of the town's gas station emerged in surprising detail. The gas pumps, a bushy dog that rested on its hindquarters, and the sign and florescent lights on the façade filled her pad. Seronia drew the people they had seen as well as the stones of the road.

This was not something she could be told to do. It was a natural extension of her reaction to the sights of any city. She just drew from deep memories after only brief glances at her surroundings.

Even Luciana was impressed.

After her first trip, she was taken to several cities to draw the inside and outside of banks, offices, and stores. Donata took pictures of each and sent an email back to their computer girl at the main compound by Teuchitlan, Mexico. The detailed drawings were then sent to the *Compradores* to pick up needed items. The *Compradores* were not buyers, but thieves who worked for Lady Six Sky.

No one suspected a young autistic girl of carrying all this information in her head with an ability to put it on paper. This worked perfectly. They had tried drones to gather the information, but the drones had two problems: they were seen and shot down, and they couldn't enter small businesses. Seronia solved both those problems.

35

Carson

A thin moment of silence. Then chaos as one of the turquoise-dressed girls folded to the ground. Blood gushed from a hole where her eye used to be. She rolled down three steps. The good eye stared directly at me. I took in a needed breath. Hub grabbed me by the shoulder. As I began to turn, I watched Lady Six Sky race her way down the back side of the circular pyramid.

The hundreds of young girls at the base were frantically spilling the glow of flashlights into the hill above us. Hub and I ran full speed up the incline. I saw the back of Hub's head illuminated. A raise of screeches followed. Another light caught me, and I turned. An army of teens barreled through the trees not far behind. More lights caught our escape. They were only twenty-five feet behind.

We headed for the horses, the first time I'd ever wanted to ride the thousand-pound beasts. Hub tripped on a fallen tree, I helped him up. The noise behind us was deafening. Hub and I yelled encouragement as we darted through brush and lights. I glanced behind. These girls were fast—eighteen feet behind us and closing in. I gasped for air, my lungs raw and aching as the hill seemed to have no end. Where were those damn horses?

I caught the whinny of a horse in the trees to our right. We both shot in that direction. Minutes passed. We reached the crest of the first hill. The silhouette of the horses in a grove of trees gave me the stamina I needed. I couldn't look back—needed to keep bursting forward. Hub leaped on his horse, untied both from a branch; his mouth opened, and his eyes became full moons. I struggled to mount my horse and finally found a *Y* branch to help me get up and onto the beast.

Fifty or more girls stormed us, grabbing our legs as we kicked. The horses began to move through the crazy mass, but the wild eyed girls held mine back. I fired my revolver into the air. Hub fumbled for his gun. The horses bucked at the sound. I grasped the mane with all my might. The gun dropped into the frantic sea of girls. We began to burst forward as something caught my eye.

Several girls in our path held thick reeds to their mouth. I shot a glance at Hub. A burst of blue shot into his face. His hands let go of the horse's mane, and he tumbled to the side. My mind bounced between running and staying with Hub. One of us needed to escape. It was the only way.

A sigh built up in my throat as I punched the horse with my boots. She began to gallop, pressing through the thick mass of bodies. A tall girl stepped from behind a tree and blew on the pipe in her mouth. The last thing I saw was thick blue dust surrounding my head. My eyes blinded as the powder torched my skin. The heat felt like the skin melted from my face. Pain.

The horse moved forward as I rolled back and dropped like a sack of potatoes on the green ground. My body numbed. My face burned. Everything went black.

I sputtered awake. Dizzy. Unsure. With a push up from soft ground, I raised on one elbow. The inside of my head was as heavy as an anvil. I peered through slits of unhinged eyelids. Colors blurred in front of me. I could smell something metallic on the end of my tongue. My brain throbbed as if it was trying to crawl out of my skull. With everything I had, I lifted myself and sat, my arms wrapped around shaky knees. A desert wind swept my mouth as I tried to speak. Cloudy cognition recalled the fall from the horse. It was surreal and dreamlike.

"Huuuubbb." I heard my voice but wasn't sure if my lips moved. A burn singed the hollows of my throat as if I was exhaling sand. "Hub." This time it came out a little louder. The hazy rainbow of colors faded to lighter hues. I still couldn't see. I felt around. My joints grabbed like rusty gears.

My hand caught leather. I followed the contour. It was a boot. Investigating further, a leg ended at a torso. I leaned forward. Spikes of pain shot through my skull. I found the neck, then the face. With my hands searching the shape of the jaw, the tuft of hair curled around the ear, and the prominent nose, I knew it was Hub. I slapped his face, trying to wake him up. A scream developed deep within sawdust lungs. "Hub!" I waited. Nothing.

My fingertips searched his carotid for a thump. I could feel a soft sputter of life. I smacked his face again and again with an open palm. He gasped. The sound filled my heart. I could feel a lopsided smile snake across my face at my relief. He began coughing, so I rolled him on his side and patted his back. His chest heaved with spurts of vomit.

Slowly, feeling came back to my numb face. "Hub!" My tongue was raw, my eyes still not working, but I enjoyed the happiness that swelled finding my friend alive. "Don't try to sit up."

He raised up on his side.

"I'm not sure what they did to us, but I think the effects will wear off." At least, I was hoping so. I scooted over closer to him and put my arm around him. I realized my eyelids were shut. I opened them to find the colors still dancing in front of me. I shook my head then concentrated on trying to see. My head throbbed. Hub sat still, moaning in a low whisper. The reds and yellows began turning to translucent pink and tan.

I could smell the rich soil around us. My free hand scraped the ground. Fertile earth sifted through my fingers. I wanted to try to survey this place, but holding Hub seemed to be the priority. Where were we?

The last thing I remembered was the cloud of blue dust surrounding my head and doing a back flip off the tail end of the horse. I tried to picture it in my mind. Hundreds of young girls with intense faces were storming us with clawing, brown hands. I felt the fear—a fear I had never experienced before. I had been afraid plenty of times, but this level of fear seemed overwhelming. Young teens brutalized by older, corrupt maniacs had been sent after us; I didn't want to harm even one, but I had.

"My eyes," said Hub in a weak voice, "I see bright blues, reds, florescent yellows, and flecks of lime green. It's like a mist or clouds, thick and impenetrable. And my head feels like it was rammed by a diesel."

I patted him on the back. "It'll fade away. I'm beginning to pick out shapes as the colors fade. There's a dot of light coming from up above us." I lifted my chin. "It seems far away."

My legs were numb, but I rolled to my knees. A throbbing behind my forehead stopped me. As the pain subsided, I tried to stand on rubbery legs. I used Hub's shoulder to boost me up. Pain fired from my lower back into my skull. I stood on two weary legs, bent over as if carrying a bale of hay on my back. The torture eased.

My balance became slightly more solid. I felt my way with

outstretched arms. My legs were unsteady but moving forward. Within a few feet, I hit a wall of dirt. It crumbled and fell from my palms. My hands followed the contour. The sound of loosened soil tapped on my boots. I continued along the wall, searching and feeling my way. The floor was uneven; my head wobbled like a creature caught in a cage, but I kept going. As I crept along the wall, the colors began to disappear. The sides of the dirt wall curved, and I found myself in a cavern. I was in a round shaft dug deep into the ground. Like a drunk with a hangover, I raised my head and peered upward. A spot of dim light formed a two-foot circle above me. Colors danced in the black periphery.

I found Hub kneeling.

"They drugged us," he said. "Something powerful, probably ancient. Even the shrooms with Andrea in Boston wouldn't compare, and that spun my kaleidoscope into high gear."

"Just relax. We're deep in a circular shaft." I could feel shovel marks on the sides where it had been dug out. "There's a light above. I don't think it's daylight. It might be a bulb or torch." My body steadied with the passing time, and the headaches were mild enough for aspirin to ease—if we had any. I shifted my weight back and forth and did some stretches. They helped.

I searched for my backpack. No luck. My gun was gone. I thought I remembered the pistol flying out of my grip when I tumbled off the horse.

"Get some good sleep?" asked a voice from above. A man with a slight Spanish accent spoke with the timbre of two cats in a whinny serenade.

I glared up and spotted the silhouette of a bald head peering over the edge of the hole.

"I'll bet your head is throbbing something horrible. You're standing, which is good. Most can't stand for a day or even more." He chuckled as if pleased by his wit.

Hub tried to look up. His hands grabbed above his ears, and he held on for dear life.

"Where are we?" I asked. I shut my eyes tight for a few seconds. When I opened them, my sight focused on what looked like a bald man in pajamas.

"Does it matter?" *Señor* Bald replied. "Your fate is in the hands of my daughter."

"Lady Six Sky?"

Mosquito Sands

"Well, *Dama Sexto Cielo* is the name that has chosen her." He leaned forward, and dirt cascaded down the wall. "I am Enrique Caldera. I make sure things are civilized."

"Do you know Seronia? She's an autistic child. We are trying to find her."

Enrique Caldera walked away. My eyes focused on the circle of light above. The glow went to total darkness. I heard mumblings from on top. My arm swung in an arc to find the wall again. I bumped into Hub with my knee.

"What the . . ." his back arched. "My head! There's something clanging around inside, and you kick my skull like a football."

"Hub . . . sorry." I grabbed him under his armpit and lifted. "You need to move. It hurts like hell, but it disappears after."

"I can't see. Only rainbows and almond bubbles." Hub tried to push me away. He fell back onto the dirt floor.

I grabbed him by the arm like a misbehaved child. He resisted. My persistence paid off. I finally had him walking the edge of the cavern. Not silently, though. He sounded as I imagined an ex-wife would—all ridicule and complaints.

I broke through his blabbering. "Hub, I think it was the blue dust. Did it burn your face too?"

His peg-leg walking stopped. "My face was on fire. And now, I'm blinded by a collage of brilliant colors." He moved forward again, clinging to the wall on one side and my arm on the other. "Drugged. I don't think it was a normal hallucinogenic. Nothing like acid, or shrooms, or peyote."

"Any idea what it could have been?"

He stumbled then regained himself. "A poison would be my guess. Maybe curare, but that doesn't give the pounding headaches. There are a lot of poisonous creatures and plants out there. Beetles, scorpions, spiders, most varieties of nightshade, foxglove, and even acorns if you eat enough. There are hundreds—maybe thousands."

Hub took in a deep breath. "Carson, where are we?"

Before I could answer I heard chatter from above us—soft female voices in a melody of rapid Spanish. We stopped pacing. The subdued yellow light came on again. I could make out the hole above. Then three faces with long, pulled-back hair peered over the lip of the opening, which I estimated at about fourteen feet above us. I scanned for roots or something I could use to pull myself out. I spotted a few along the upper edge, but nothing that would hold the weight of a hundred and ninety-pound man.

One of the girls above lifted a bag the size of a small pillow and dropped it. I shoved Hub to the wall and faced away in case it was more blue dust or an explosive. It landed solid on the ground. Nothing happened. I turned. Another bag puffed up the dirt as it landed with a thud. The girls stood looking down. They began to walk away.

"La luz," I shouted. *"Por favor."* I hoped they'd leave the light on. I heard the patter of feet on hard dirt. They were gone. But they left the light on.

I eased over to the bags. They were made of thick canvas and had a cold gelatin feel to them. My fingers found a spout; I twisted it and let liquid fall over my open palm. My tongue lapped some up. It was water. I took a hearty drink from the bag. The liquid quenched my dry, burning throat. I took some to Hub. My sight cleared slightly.

Why did they drop the bags to us? Were they helping us, or had they been ordered to give us water?

At least four more hours passed before Hub's migraines eased and his sight returned. With the pain gone, he fell asleep on the dirt floor. I wandered the walls of the cavern, trying in vain to find handholds or a hidden passage. The anxiety didn't help my gurgling stomach. I guessed at time but had no way to verify how long we'd been down here. A day? I sat next to Hub. My eyes became droopy; my mind sailed down that river, fighting unconscious blackness.

We were left alone for days, or so I thought. Once we woke to watermelons split and spread in chunks across the floor. Dust-riddled melon had never tasted so wonderful. That same day we found oranges smashed like hockey pucks on the ground. We feasted.

After the food drop, we decided we needed to speak to whomever our benefactor was. We took shifts with sleep. That way we might catch someone who could drop a rope down. After what seemed to be days, I heard the rustling of feet. My eyes focused on the circle above and held steady. A head popped over the edge. It was the bald man, Enrique Caldera.

"You still alive down there?" he asked. A chuckle echoed down into the hole.

"Is that what you're doing? Waiting for us to die?" I spat the words out in disgust. I kept my eyes on *Señor* Caldera and kicked Hub with my boot, trying to wake him.

"No, we just have a lot to do before we can have *your* ceremony. Be patient; my daughter will be back from Guatemala in a day or two. She has plans for the two of you."

Hub stirred and sat up. He rubbed his temples. I was glad we'd hidden the leftover fruit in a crevice in the wall. I didn't want him to go after anyone.

"What plans? Where's Seronia?" In futility, I raised my fist at him. "We let the police know where we were going." It was a lie.

He cackled and held his ample belly. "The police. They would have let us know the minute you called. You're pathetic." He shook his head with a grin. "You think we don't pay every police station from here to Chihuahua?"

He was bragging. It occurred to me that I might be able to use that to get more information. "I saw your mine operation. Puny, but it probably turns a few pesos."

"That's just one of our operations," he retorted. The grin left his face. "We have farms, factories, and silver and copper mines."

"So, why did you need *Mapa Chica?*" Hub asked.

Hub had followed my train of thought. The man was a braggart.

The bald man raised his hands in the air with a booming laugh. His voice echoed through the pit. He dropped his hands to his knees and leaned over the edge. "She is our diamond."

"Diamond? She's just a little autistic girl," I said.

"But her mind sees details even pictures won't capture." A broad grin crossed his face. "She has the shaman gift of her father. That we hadn't realized."

I could tell he was happy with himself.

"She has the gift of sight and artistry. Our Diamond can draw walls, and windows . . . and surveillance cameras as if you're in the building. She draws whole city layouts."

"So, you're going to sell her artwork. That should give you enough for a cup of coffee." I watched his face darken and his cheeks puff out.

"You know nothing of business. She draws banks, and cash exchange offices, and loan companies." He let out a soft snicker. "You are idiots."

That's why they needed Seronia. She filled that barracks I saw with those bundles of cash. She drew the layout. Perfect. Who would give a second glance to a young girl as she walked around a bank? And they had these mesmerized kids probably robbing the places without any connection to Caldera or Lady Six Sky. The young girls were thought to be just runaways.

They must have found something that an autistic girl would want in exchange for the picture-perfect maps. I wished we had thought to ask Juan Diego about what that might be. She loved Toro the pig; I wondered if there was anything else. It might just be the ability to draw. She enjoyed that. But just as with most autistics, she would throw a fit if things didn't go her way. If they used drugs, she wouldn't have the perception for sketching out the buildings. All my attempts to theorize were giving me more questions and fewer answers.

"She wouldn't do anything if you forced her. How do you get her to draw on command?" I asked.

"It is of no concern to you. Life is too short, especially for you two desperados." He laughed.

"We're not the outlaws," said Hub.

Señor Caldera gave a sour grin. "You're the ones in a pit, I'm the one gazing down. Only desperados are put in a pit." He walked away. The light disappeared with the sound of his footsteps.

36

Seronia

The heat rattled the air conditioner. Moisture beaded under Seronia's hairline and matted strands to her wet neck. She had tired of drawing buildings and old architecture. *Gato* peered down at Seronia, as she sat cross-legged on the carpet waving her arms in repetitious strokes.

Donata, a new guard, ran from the kitchen, screeching. She barreled into Luciana, who had just flicked a cigarette as she entered the house. Donata slapped at her pant legs, mouth wide, eyes in dark repose.

"It's in there. It's in there." She danced on one leg while smacking the other.

Seronia hummed and paraded her arms. Her eyelids closed in concentration.

Luciana slapped Donata. "Calm down, whore."

Donata dropped to the floor, yanking her pants down as if attacked by the denim. In her undies, she writhed on the floor searching and swearing in a panic. She tossed her pants across the room. Sweat dripped from her red face in droplets. Luciana stood back with irritation at the noise. *Gato* slipped into a closet.

Luciana picked up Donata's pants with her thumb and forefinger. Her head shook as she gazed in all directions at the cloth. She loosened her hold, and the pants dropped into a heap. Out of the corner of her eye she caught tiny movement and bent to her right. Six legs scampered as a spider no bigger than a peanut made its way from a pant cuff and ran under a couch.

"It's only a tiny spider," Luciana laughed.

Donata searched where the prickling pain centered but couldn't find a thing. Her chest raised and lowered in deep, shuddering breaths. She wiped away tears and glanced up. Seronia stood over her, her neck kinked and her hands drumming on her pantlegs.

Jef Huntsman

Seronia dropped to her knees and bent down close. Like a helicopter scanning the ground, she made several passes over Donata's bare leg with spotlight eyes. She hovered for a moment. Taking one of her hands, fingers playing in the air, she rubbed the side of her thumb along the fine hairs of Donata's thigh. Seronia stopped. With her little finger she dotted a spot. Donata flinched, and a high note of pain spurted from her mouth. Seronia eased up and walked to the kitchen. She returned with a serrated steak knife clutched in her right hand. In her left hand was a cup of water.

"This should be good," said Luciana. "She's going to cure you. I hope she cuts out your heart."

Donata gasped but didn't move. Her teeth clamped tightly to her bottom lip.

The young girl was ready with knife instead of pencils. Her sight followed the corners of the room as she grew nearer. She kneeled again, centering herself by the spot she'd rubbed before. Seronia's girl-like giggle flowed through the room.

Donata's breath stopped. Luciana smirked.

"Maybe it's not so bad. It was just a spider." Donata pulled her leg in closer to her body. A hand grasped her ankle and pulled it back. Sweat dripped. Donata waved her hands and scooted away.

Seronia gave her a look then gazed away into the corner of the room. She set the knife on the floor, stood, and walked into the other room. She returned with pad and pencils. Her trained fingers sketched a brown spider with raised black legs and a mark on its back. She held up the picture.

Donata grimaced. Luciana came forward and nodded.

"Yes, that's the one. That's the spider in her pants."

Seronia shook her head and mouthed a drawn out, soft "*Malo.*"

"*Malo?*" Donata eyes widened from the shock of hearing her speak. Seronia nodded.

"I guess you could let the spider bite kill you. Or *mapa chica*," stated Luciana with a shrug of her shoulders and a snicker.

Donata tilted her head, trying to decide. She finally rolled her leg out straight. Everyone knew by now what Seronia had done for her kidnappers, and some called her a *curando*.

On her knees, Seronia waved her palm slightly above Donata's thigh. There was a pimply rise to Donata's skin. A red spot had appeared with two tiny brown halos around it. Seronia took the knife, and with

Mosquito Sands

surgical precision she made two deep cuts in the shape of an X. Donata screamed and tried to crawl away. Luciana, who fully enjoyed be it all, grabbed Donata in a headlock and held her body down. Donata wailed and her chin trembled, but she kept her leg reasonably still.

With fingertips pressed deep into soft skin, Seronia pushed blood from the capillaries in a slow, kneading fashion. Crimson bubbled up and ran down Donata's leg, pooling on the tongue-and-groove floor. Minutes passed. Seronia pressed out more blood. Then Seronia lifted her fingers and watched patiently. She nodded. She poured the glass of water over the wound and immediately pressed her palm into the wet ooze of the X. She held pressure on Donata's thigh for many minutes, releasing only when she felt sufficient time had passed.

The deep wound appeared to have sealed. A red X marked Donata's leg, and blood diluted with water pooled beneath.

37

Carson

The darkness soured my mood. We were out of food, and we slurped the last of the water bags hours earlier. We had even eaten the hardened peels of the oranges and watermelon.

"This is the first time in my life I actually want someone dead," said Hub. "I'm trying to reason with myself. Am I going crazy?'

My tongue ran over my teeth, trying to loosen the dirt that filled my gums. "Crazy would be to let that bald bastard live."

"How long have we been here?"

I sat down with my head between my knees. I wondered how honest I should be with Hub in his state. We were both hungry, thirsty, and beaten down. He was my best friend, so I used the truth. "I think we've been here four or five days."

I could tell he slumped down against the dirt wall without seeing it. A frustrated puff of air came from his direction.

"Hub, we'll be okay. I've been in worse situations than this." Silence filled the musty cavern. I tried to remember when. Nothing came.

"You've been captured by female teenagers, held by a crazy bald man and a lady that thinks she's the reincarnated queen of the Mayans, and stuck in a hole fifteen feet from the surface in a cave?" Hub paused. "Oh, and without water or food."

"Well, when you put it that way, no—not really."

We both began laughing. Within seconds, we were howling.

I slept well that night. We didn't do shifts; we simply giggled ourselves to sleep.

When we awoke, I brushed damp dirt from the side of my face. It was cooler, which indicated it might be night. I reached in my pocket for my cell. I had forgotten it had been taken with the backpack, guns, and everything else. I let out a sigh.

"I feel the same way," said Hub.

"Do you think it's dinner time or breakfast?" I said.

"Let's say dinner. I usually don't eat a big dinner."

"Probably be better if we called it night and quit relating it to food."

"I've never been afraid of the dark, but this is creepy. No end."

We sat in the blackness with our own thoughts. Hub was humming a Stix tune, and I was thinking about Maria. I should have been on vacation with her. Relaxing on a beach, surf folding ten feet from our toes, sunscreen oiled, and not a care in the world except what fruit-topped drink to order next. Her smile beaming as she read one of her mystery novels. Me, laid back on the soft sand enjoying the sight of her.

The daydream faded. I remembered Seronia's face in the window of the house. Busy sketching felony plans that she had no idea were being used for illegal purposes. She happily worked as Lady Six Sky's puppet

I wondered if she missed Toro and her dad. Autistics have a difficult time forming friendships with people, but they totally relate to animals—even bugs. They focus on things most people ignore.

"Seronia's here," said Hub.

"What?" I blinked.

"You were thinking about Seronia."

Damn, I don't know how he does that. His clairvoyance is unsettling. And as usual, I didn't give him the satisfaction of letting him know he was right. Though I knew he wouldn't care. I stood up and began pacing in the dark.

"All my senses have tuned in on it. Her definitive village-girl smell breaks through all this decay and aged mix of soil. Her happy face as she strolls side by side with Toro lights up the darkness of this earthen shaft. I hear the lullaby rhythm and strange harmony of Seronia's self-understood babble. She's close by." Hub's neck bent back as if staring at the yellow light fifteen feet above us. The light that wasn't there. "She's filled with discomfort and longing. I've used my shamanic powers to tune in to her exact location, but it disappears in wisps of parting clouds. There's an evil force that won't allow me to penetrate."

I patted him on the shoulder. "We'll find her. Juan Diego was assured that we would."

Footsteps on hard ground sounded from above. The light came on. It felt like morning sunshine. Two faces peeked over the edge. One was the same girl I'd seen before. The other stood lean and tall, her hair draping like a shower curtain around her narrow shoulders. They both glanced back behind them. A canvas sack of water dropped on the ground within a foot of Hub.

Hub smiled. *"Gracias. ¿Es de diá o de noche?"*

Another small canvas bag fell onto the dirt floor with a thud.

"El noche. Son las once treinta." She raised her finger to her lips. They disappeared but left the light on.

We both dived for the water bag. Hub drank first then handed it to me. I took a swig, rinsed it around in my mouth, and slurped it down. My stomach boiled at first, then accepted the water with relief. While Hub opened the other bag, I slipped the water into a dark crevice behind a partially raised boulder. The other bag contained stale flour tortillas and oranges. Hub broke a tortilla in half and handed me one with an orange. We savaged it down then hid the rest for later. We had no idea how long we'd be here, but *Señor* Caldera mentioned a couple of days. I thought one had passed, but it seemed like a month. I wasn't sure whether I wanted Lady Six Sky to lift us out of here. I doubted we had a choice.

Another day passed. We slept. We ate sparingly, and we contemplated what we could do. No plans came to mind. We had no idea how she would come at us or what she might do with us. I judged days by when we slept—even though we slept a lot.

"It's almost time for your fate." The voice startled me.

I had just put the water bag behind the rock and had walked around the wall twice to get exercise. I glared up at *Señor* Caldera. He grinned from ear to ear. His silk, purple gown draped from his shoulders to as far as I could see. A golden amulet hung around his neck with shells laced above. He wore a purple cap like a beret on his head. I waited for him to say more.

"Dama Sexto Cielo would like the pleasure of your company tonight. You will have to be bathed, of course. And lose those refugee clothes." He chuckled to himself. "Dinner will be at seven." *Señor* Caldera walked away. I heard him stop then come back.

"Who turned that light on?" he scowled.

We ignored him.

"Won't matter anyway." He scurried away, leaving the light burning.

Mosquito Sands

An hour passed. Hub went over and opened the bag. Only three oranges were left. He tossed me one and reached in for another.

"Ow!" he screamed. He stared at his hand, so I walked over to him. His middle finger had a half-inch diagonal cut on it. I tore off a thin strip from my shirttail and wrapped it up. With his thumb and forefinger, he put pressure on it. I turned the sack over. Crumbs and an orange rolled out along with a short knife. I picked it up. I checked the blade with my thumb. Sharp.

I held up the knife to Hub. My eyes glinted with satisfaction. "It would've been nice if they told us we could peel the oranges."

Hub smiled back. Then his brows lowered. "A single knife against an army of teens. You're tough, Carson, but we need artillery. Remember that MK 153 we read about?"

I nodded.

"That's what I'm talking about."

I tapped the blade on my palm. "A knife's better than no knife."

"Okay." He nodded without enthusiasm.

"I wonder what's for dinner at the Six Sky residence?"

Hub laughed.

Hub and I talked about old times, people, and things we missed at home.

A clacking sound came from above. We leaned back and gazed up. Older girls in camo pants and white shirts peeked over the edge. Eight heads with tight jaws and stern faces stood around the opening. I assumed they were guards or the equivalent of Lady Six Sky's military. I caught the glint of pistols on three of them. They weren't here to fluff our pillows and set out an extra bed mint. They were serious bad asses. I felt the metal of my knife between my boot and my ankle. It reassured me in a worried way. I was a man with a firecracker, while they had their fingers on the trigger of a nuclear weapon. I sighed.

"You're not building confidence, Carson," Hub stated between clamped teeth.

One of the soldiers held a black box with a metal, foot-long spike on top. Her thumb fumbled with something on the box. A high-pitched ticking echoed though the cavern. A ninth head poked over the opening. It was *Señor* Caldera. His grin sickened me.

Jef Huntsman

38

Carson

"Hello boys," *Señor* Caldera stared down at us. His face was shadowed in evil. Several soldiers left his side and moved into the blackness off to his right.

We kept silent. I crossed my arms as if I could care less.

From the dark recesses of the ceiling above the opening something lowered down. The ticking continued. The nine people around the opening stood back a step as a dark, round platform dropped through the opening. A full eclipse formed with a circular halo of light. My pulse raised. I assumed this was our elevator. I watched Hub's muscles tense. His hands clamped together as if cracking walnuts. I didn't have a good feeling about this either. The platform dropped until it was even with my chest; it was shaped like a bowl and held by three, heavily bundled, horsehair ropes. The ropes connected to a metal collar around a massive chain. The plate hit the ground gently. The ticking stopped, but I could hear a motor whirring above.

"Get on the lift, boys," said *Señor* Caldera.

I cranked my neck and tightened my arms into my chest in defiance.

"I could send the girls down to spray you with some more *arenas de mosquito.*" His voice, taunting and hollow, echoed.

"Was that the blue stuff?" Hub asked.

"The blue stuff?" he cackled as he held his abundant tummy. "Yes, mosquito sands, that's the *blue stuff,* as you put it—*mosquito sands.* How would you like to go through that again?

"What was in that crap?" asked Hub.

I could tell *Señor* Caldera enjoyed this. "Sand and a little concoction from the *barba Amarillo.*"

"Yellow chin?" asked Hub. "What's a *yellow chin?*"

Señor Caldera shuffled his feet, kicking dust over the edge. "You Americans would probably know it by *La Fer-De Lance.*"

Mosquito Sands

"The snake?"

I turned to Hub. "What snake?"

"A venomous viper in South America. Kills with one bite."

I wanted to wipe that evil smile off the bald man's face.

"It's an ancient recipe from the Mayan shamans. My daughter came up with the name." He paused. "Mosquitos bite and carry diseases that make you wish you would die; sometimes you do." He waved his hands, trying to hurry things along. "Now, jump on like good little boys, and we'll get ready for dinner."

With the gaiety of his high-pitched voice, my body tensed. I gave Hub a look and shrugged my shoulders. We both stepped on and held tight to the ropes. A shrieking metallic sound began, then the ticking resumed as we were raised out of our earthen jail. My chest tightened. I gripped the rope; my knuckles paled. I'd find an escape. Anything was better than this hole.

Hub began heaving in uncontrolled spates as we lifted. Vomit caught the edge and dripped down. The platform stopped. Hub peeked at me with dark eyes. His mouth hung loose. "The poison." He sputtered. Two girls helped him off first. He clung to them like lost sisters. His feet caught on the dirt edge and he fell dragging them down with him.

I raised my hands in surrender and stepped off. With a grasp on Hub's shirt collar, I pulled him up. The girls came with him. *Señor* Caldera led us down a passageway. Three girls followed him; Hub and I followed with two escorts helping Hub. The three others walked behind us. Two of the girls at our heels had those mosquito sands tubes in their hands. All had pistols strapped to their sides. I thought about grabbing one of the guns but decided it wasn't the time. The knife in my boot fidgeted against my ankle. It would be a futile weapon against eight guns and two wood tubes containing that devil dust. Things were looking bleak.

Sunlight glared from the opening ahead. *Señor* Caldera exited with his three girls. Our procession headed for a ten-foot A-frame to our right. The last hour of sunlight for the day revived my spirits immensely. I glanced back to find that we had come out of a mound of dirt that centered other buildings. We were led between two long barrack-type buildings to the A-frame. *Señor* Caldera stopped and motioned with his hand for us to enter the open door. The two girls led Hub in, I followed. The other young women waited outside the door with mouths like lemonade samplers. The door was shut. A lock clicked.

Jef Huntsman

The room had a steep, angled ceiling with benches around the edge and a long tarp strung on the wall opposite the door. There were no windows. A florescent fixture hung from the main beam, giving off an insurance office glare.

Hub thanked the girls and told them he felt better. They stood still with arms crossed. A frown of impatience with their bad duty filled their faces. One with a scar on her cheek pointed a mangled hand with a missing thumb toward the tarp. I wondered if she had lost her thumb here. The second girl had an eagle tattoo on the side of her neck. Its head faced between folded wings. Its eyes black with a tiny red center.

"I don't think they understand English," I said. "Let's grab their guns and bolt."

In one quick motion, both pulled their revolvers and aimed at our chests.

I smiled. "You know English better than me. Just wanted to make sure. Now, what do you want us to do in here?" I waited.

Hub chuckled, then held one side of his head. His brow wrinkled in pain.

The young women peered at each other. Finally, the girl with one thumb said, "Take a shower. Clothes are in there."

She startled me, and it took a minute to regain my composure. "You have a Boston accent. Where are you from?"

She looked back at the door. "Just use the shower. You don't want to know what'll happen to you if you don't."

Hub and I exchanged glances. He shrugged and walked through a slit in the tan tarp. A minute later, I heard a shower running.

I looked at the other girl. Her bangs parted slightly, and I noticed aother tattoo of a tiny bald eagle on her forehead. "You speak English too?"

She kept a steady stare at me. Her revolver dropped to her side. She shook her head.

"You understand me, but you don't speak English?"

After a long moment, she said, "I speak just fine."

I furrowed my brow. "You two are from America. What the hell are you doing here?"

"Get your shower. This is taking too long," she said, the muscles in her neck tightening.

The one-thumbed Bostonian raised the barrel of the revolver at my heart. "You're going to get us in trouble. Don't make me shoot you. It'll spoil the lady's fun."

I held my eyes steady on hers. Her lip quivered very slightly. It was obvious she'd never fired a weapon. I opened my palm and raised my hands up. "I'm going to help you," I said. "Please don't shoot me, but I usually sing in the shower."

Both gave a fleeting smirk then tightened their lips against their teeth.

Behind the tarp stretched a long, black pipe about six feet off the floor. Fifteen branches extended down to a valve on one side with a garden spray nozzle that came out from the wall. The sprayer sat five feet from the ground. A dip in the concrete floor allowed the water to funnel to a drain at one end. The shower revived us both.

Hub pulled on a maroon gown. His head popped out the top, and he sat on a locker-room bench. A rabbit-fur collar circled his neck. A row of shells was sewn in three concentric half circles down the front. He peeked over at me with a grin.

His hands gripped two spots on his robe, and he stretched it out proudly. "Check out the duds."

"You look like Liberace the buzzard."

Hub patted a stack of maroon cloth next to him. "You're next."

"They're not going to kill us. They're going to embarrass us to death." It felt good to relieve myself of dusty, sweat-soaked clothes.

"Hurry up," said the Bostonian, her voice frantic.

In a few minutes, the two party girls opened the curtain. I caught a grin from our guards as they eyed hairy legs between black laced boots and our maroon gowns. These robes were meant for much shorter people.

Outside, they marched us between the buildings like purple penguins on parade. The barracks to our sides were sleeping quarters. I could see the beds stacked three high. A warm breeze sifted between the two walls.

Eagle Tat and One Thumb grabbed our gowns and stopped us from entering the courtyard. One Thumb walked around in front of us. She seemed to be searching for someone. A girl about ten came up and shook her head. Eagle Tat turned and said, *Esperar.* Her eyes caught my bewilderment. She leaned closer. "Wait."

Several young girls bustled around the courtyard. Each had an armload of small river rocks that she laid out in three overlapping circles. The circles formed a chain. Others used wooden rakes to smooth the area around the loops. I noticed *Señor* Caldera giving orders from the hill just below where we had watched the Lady Six Sky parade. He kept pointing up to the pyramid.

My heart pounded against sore ribs. "What time are our reservations?" I said, trying to lighten the mood. Hub gave a sick smile. The girls ignored me. "How is their lobster?"

"You're going to get us in trouble," said Eagle Tat in a whisper. She stared straight ahead.

"What's going on here?" I muttered between teeth.

I watched sweat drip from her bangs. Both girls held their hands together tightly enough to pop a vein. Their fear didn't help Hub or me. I peeked at Hub. I could hear the air sucking into his open lips. He stood frozen.

"Hub, it'll be all right." My voice quivered with the unknown.

Eagle Tat bit into her lip and muttered, "We're from USC. They grabbed us on spring break a year ago."

Hub's neck suddenly craned. His eyes widened.

"Stare ahead," she said. "If you don't, you'll kill us all."

"We'll get you out of here, like I said before," I whispered. I wondered how many other girls might be tourists.

She dropped her head in despair. "The only way out is dead," she whispered.

A line of people walked up the hill maybe two hundred feet away. The leader carried a yellow-painted palm leaf. I couldn't make out the others winding their way in slow procession. The setting sun gave an apricot lining to the few scythes of clouds that dangled above us. The thickness of the jungle stretched close enough it pulled me to run for it. I knew I'd never make it. I gazed around at all the guns strapped to young workers and grim guards. A few had the wooden reeds hooked into their belts. I didn't want to go through the withdrawal of mosquito sands again. Hub shuddered as if thinking the same thing.

I felt for the knife that I had tucked in my boxers under the purple robe. My eyes scanned the open area. The rock circles were finished, and more girls strolled aimlessly around as if waiting for something. Tables were laid out across the flat bite in the hill where *Señor* Caldera stood. Workers were putting up wooden folding chairs around each table. I counted eight tables. That was clearly not enough for the whole group. Red orchids were lined up in the center of each table.

I glanced the other way. The row of people had crossed over the first

Mosquito Sands

hump of the trail and were getting nearer. I cleared my throat to get Hub's attention. "Eight of those are boys," I said. "Check out the shirtless ones in the middle. They're daisy-chained with a rope." I watched one stumble. A thin female guard three steps behind ran up and kicked him. The boys on both sides helped him up, barely breaking stride. He hunched over and clung to the rope for support. By then, they were about seventy yards away.

I wondered where Lady Six Sky was. *She'll make a grand entrance*, I thought. My eyes searched to figure out where she might appear. No clue.

"They'll kill us after the feast," I said to Boston and Eagle Tat. It was not a question.

"No."

Both girls turned sharply around. Something like fear melted across their faces. They turned back.

I glanced at Hub. "What?"

"We will get out of this," he said. "I feel the sunsets yet to come. There's a peace, and we sit with Juan Diego and his precious Seronia at their humble home. She sketches while we laugh." Hub stared at the ground. His arms hung slack at his sides. The tight cords in his neck had melted.

"Okay, think positive. I like that." All my muscles felt like twisted rubber bands. I realized how irritated I'd become seeing him loose and flaccid.

"Quiet," Boston said.

"I see Seronia in Lady Six Sky's compound. Her minions are trying to dress her up. She keeps ripping the clothes." Hub grinned. "She's a rebel. There's someone else with her. She almost looks like her older sister." Hub's eyes tightened, and he rolled his back forward. "Ha! I should have known. Seronia has help from a great spirit. It's Selena Quintanilla. She's trying to calm her down."

"From the movie?" muttered Boston.

"You've lost me," I said.

"Selena. The one that got shot by her fan," said Hub.

I shook my head. "A dead rock star." I let out a heavy breath. I tapped my knuckles against Hub's.

Hub startled and glared up.

"We need a plan." I pointed to the two guns strapped to Boston and Eagle Tat.

Hub shook his head with an emphatic no. "Give me a minute. Serena was trying to tell me something."

"Yes, she was." I pointed at the guns and with a head jerk and signaled that we needed to run back behind us. I thought we could make it.

"Your friend talks to dead people?" Boston whispered in disbelief.

"He thinks he's a shaman."

"He's a shaman?" asked Eagle Tat. "That's so cool. *Dama Sexto Cielo* thinks she's a reincarnated queen, but I think she's just crazy."

"Watch yourself," muttered Boston.

"She'll let us know when the time is right," said Hub.

"Who?"

"Serena, of course."

"Uh, yeah, I'll wait for her call," I said, my voice laced with sarcasm. "Keep your eyes peeled to *actually* see her."

The boys were getting closer. I could see the look of defeat in their faces. Their bodies slumped as if few bones held them together. Slack mouths and hollow eyes moved in procession. The guards had that Hitleresque attitude—straightened spines and raised chins.

A tear rolled down Hub's face.

Somewhere to the south a stretched note carried on the breeze from a horn, perhaps a trumpet. I searched the hillside and spotted a glint of yellow metal in the trees. Boston nodded to let me know it was time. Young girls came out from everywhere. They crowded around in front of the buildings. Soon, they all dropped to one knee the same as before. The boys were led to a horse corral. They were tied to the rails and forced to kneel. After they were positioned, the guards went to one knee also. Another long blast of the horn. Eagle Tat grabbed my wrist and signaled for me to get down as she did, the same as the others. With irritation, I genuflected with her. Hub had done the same. I shook my head in disgust. Tension filled the air.

Mosquito Sands

39

Carson

A warm breeze created an opposite response and chilled my spine. Shadows of clouds rolled over us like engulfing doom. Murmured chatter clenched my teeth until my jaw ached. The wait.

The parade began. Eighteen girls in puffy, mauve tops and white, flowing dresses led the ritual. They each spun wisps of silver cloth on a foot-long stick. A base drum thumped in rhythm to their walk.

Twenty feet later, Lady Six Sky made her appearance in the same colorful skirt and feathered fan billowing behind her head. She carried her lethal spear in one hand. Her other arm flowed outstretched as if stirring a cauldron of warm liquid with her fingers. Her expressionless face, with red lips and coal-black eyes, stared forward. I leaned in to get a better view, and Boston elbowed my chest.

This time, Lady Six Sky had a whole gaggle of females following her. Their heavy seashell necklaces clacked as they walked. Black feathers surrounded their blood-red skirts. More feathers jutted from their bound hair.

We stood inconsequential to the imposing ritual. Hub looked fascinated, grinning his approval. He loves the pomp of all ceremonies. He makes it to every wedding and ridiculous gold-shovel-of-dirt event. He arrived four hours early for the governor's inauguration last year, even though he hated the man politically. I love Hub, but my muscles tightened, fists clenched; I wanted to wipe the smile off his face. This was probably our death party.

Lady Six Sky and her procession snaked up a curled path onto a dugout embankment on the hill above. Her table had been set with two golden centerpieces of orchids on a deep purple tablecloth. Chairs curved around the back like those in paintings of the Last Supper. Everyone stood waiting with the crazy queen in the center. She stood a head taller than all the others.

Jef Huntsman

I hadn't seen *Señor* Caldera for some time. He seemed to be the one who set these types of things up. I wondered why he wasn't at the ceremony.

The boys were led from the corral. They were marched through the kneeling rows of girls and were seated on a long wooden bench below the dinner tables. Tears rolled down their cheeks as their fingers fidgeted on bony knees. Their defeated bodies curled forward, heads down. The material binding them was cut, and the four guards stood watch behind them. One of the boys glanced up toward Lady Six Sky with deep hatred. The heel of a boot slammed into his spine, tossing him forward into the raked dirt. He was quickly picked up and shoved back onto the bench. The boys stared at a patch of earth before them.

Boston and Eagle Tat grabbed me and Hub and shoved us forward. My eyes darted between escape possibilities and our guards' guns. I could snatch that revolver in seconds, but a hundred-plus weapons would be on me in the same instant. They guided us by the opening in the pyramid that we'd examined before. My eyes scanned inside and stopped on a row of guards holding wooden reeds of mosquito sand. My heart slammed into my ribs as if trying to break through.

Seronia! Elation rose in my chest.

Inside the pyramid, between rows of thick candles, stood five girls. One was Seronia. Unhappiness coated her face. Her body squirmed as if bed lice crawled on her skin. She kept yanking at her emerald cloth dress. With a scowl and both hands on a necklace of lime-colored beads and white feathers, her arms burst forth. Beads rolled out of the pyramid, and feathers floated like snowflakes to the ground. The other girls tried to placate her, to no avail. An unearthly noise bellowed from her lips. All eyes turned to the sound. Soon the dress was in shreds, and streams of emerald-green cloth barely clung to her shoulders. Underneath, I could see a pair of cotton sweat shorts and a Goo Goo Dolls T-shirt.

Lady Six Sky scowled. Her head motioned to the guards at her right. Three of them headed toward the pyramid entrance.

Seronia folded her arms in front of her, triumph in her stance. She calmed as the other girls raced around her with bulging eyes and pursed lips. She smiled.

I kept my eyes on Seronia even though our guards forced us forward. Our progress through the rows of serious-faced girls had slowed with my impudence. Mutterings resounded through the kneeling captors. Lady Six Sky's neck stretched with cords so tight I wondered if her head

228

Mosquito Sands

might sail into the heavens.

Hub blurted, "Seronia."

Seronia showed recognition. Her autism kept her from racing to him, but she seemed distantly glad to see Hub. The other girls stood in front of her in case she stormed forward. She simply stood proudly in her tattered dress.

Two of the guards grabbed Seronia by the arms while the other shoved her keepers out of the way. They hauled her into the pyramid opening. A glass-shattering screech billowed from the shaded entrance.

I peered around. She had disturbed the flow of the ceremony. By the looks of the girls around the Last Supper setup, I could tell it was bad. The crowd hushed. We stopped. Eyes chased between us and where Seronia's mad yelps dwindled into a faint hum. Lady Six Sky raised her spear and thumped it on the ground. Like cattle to the slaughter, we were led forward.

They stood us at one of the tables that was below the queen's platform but raised high enough to see everything. Our backs were to the Lady. My eyes met Hub's. I scanned my lavender sleeve. I wanted to rip this absurd garment off like Seronia had torn her dress to pieces but decided to wait for the right moment.

My eyes caught the glint of Boston's knife on her left leg. I'd have to drop down and reach around her to steal her knife. It would be too clumsy to even attempt. She had a leather sheaf around her shoulder and back that I thought might hold one of the wooden tubes filled with mosquito sand. That would be the easiest to get to, but I wasn't sure about its use. Her revolver was the best bet.

Hundreds of girls faced us, still down on one knee. Many had on Camo pants and white t-shirts with brown-and-yellow cloth belts around the waist, strapped across a revolver on one side and a blow tube on the other. I assumed these girls were the army or guards. Others wore white dresses with purple belts without weapons. I decided they must be *la trabadors*—the workers. It was a fifty-fifty split between the two, and they all knelt side by side waiting for something to happen. It was the *something* that I worried about.

I could hear Hub breathing in long, even strokes as if trying to calm himself. His skin pulled tight against his underlying skull, and his knuckles stretched and pale. Hub has always been a whatever-happens-happens kind of guy. He showed a new side that day as harsh fear and the aura of death seemed to come over him.

Jef Huntsman

Lady Six Sky pounded her spear on the hard ground three times, and several of the guards began moving. They pulled up a boy that was seated on the bench and led him forward. Sweat glistened from his chestnut skin, catching the sunlight on cheeks and chest.

He was a boy with an unsure, frightened face of about fifteen. He began screaming in terror. A knotted tree limb stripped of its bark clacked across his jaw, and he tumbled to the earth. The guard held a satisfied grin as she shoved the other boy back to the bench.

Two guards yanked him back up. He stood loosely while a stream of crimson flowed down the path of sweat from his now misshapen cheek. Blood flowed from his lip, and he spat out a tooth. Tears mixed with the blood and sweat. A low growl echoed across the compound. His legs wobbled like those of a newly hatched bird. The guards dragged him, and his angled toes furrowed a path behind limp legs.

A chubby-faced guard with coal-black hair streaming behind and curling over her ample buttocks clacked the boy on the shoulder. He let out a whelp like a disciplined dog. Harsh words were exchanged from muttered, childlike voices that resembled a schoolyard argument. He stood up. and grimaced.

They walked him over to a grassy spot lined with a worn center. Black-and-white, spotted rocks were stacked in perfect pyramids to either side of the grass circle. A worker, unsure and pained, lifted a perfectly round rock from one of the stacks. Her thin frame strained to lift the ball. With veins raised, she handed it to the boy. He cupped it in both hands. His eyes lifted to Lady Six Sky without raising his head. The queen nodded, and the two guards backed away.

The boy took the melon sized ball and rolled it around until he found a comfortable way to hold it in his palm. I could tell he had had some training, probably under force judging by the knowledgeable apprehension in his face. He heaved it up to his shoulder with his elbow out as if holding a shot put. He glanced quickly toward Lady Six Sky, and his lips tightened.

Lady Six Sky held his gaze. Superiority washed across her face. A stillness settled over the makeshift pyramid.

This was a test of skill and strength. A donut-carved boulder was centered down a worn path. It was like the ancient Mayan ball game but with only one player.

The boy twisted his back with one arm pointing out in front of him and his opposite shoulder dipping behind. His young muscles strained in that position for a second then with lighting speed he unfurled the stone ball forward in an arc. The ball headed toward the massive stone with the hole carved through it. It crested and began its forward descent. I was sure it would drop through the hole with ease. His calculations were slightly off, and the stone clipped the edge with a solid clack. The ball dropped to the earth in defeat.

Hub whispered to me, "That was close. He should get it the next time."

I wondered if there were second chances. I glanced over at Lady Six Sky and her two matrons. They seemed distant yet pleased at the boy's failure.

The hole in the stone appeared about an inch bigger than the ball. Standing where he tossed the round rock, the boy was fifteen feet from the stone. His head canted to the side as he stared at the ground, his injured jaw offset, but tight as a clamp.

I had an awful feeling about what might happen next.

"This is voodoo creepy," said Hub. "I'm picking up true demon vibes from this . . . game? That's what it is, right? A revised Mayan game?"

I shrugged my shoulders. My breath raised my chest in strong gasps. Blood surged through my veins in both an unknown fear and a madness I rarely achieved.

The chubby-faced guard and her companion grabbed the boy by the arms and walked him away. Blood dripped from his battered face.

Two more guards, one with dyed yellow hair and another with a prominent nose and broad shoulders, pulled another young boy forward. He had small eyes and high cheekbones and a chest thinner than his boyish hips. He strained against their arms.

Suddenly he broke loose from Yellow Hair and shoved into Wide Nose. He tripped over his own ankles and fell on top of her. In a swift, terrified motion he rolled up with Wide Nose's revolver in his hand. In the blink of an eye, he fired a shot from the small-caliber weapon.

I watched the astonished look on Wide Nose as a blot of crimson blood trickled from a tiny hole above her left eye. He turned toward Yellow Hair, whose previously pompous mouth had turned into a perfect circle that matched her eyes. He aimed and pulled the trigger. Nothing happened. He pulled the trigger again and again. Each time the clicking sound of an empty cylinder sounded through the stunned group. Like a cornered animal, the boy circled around, the gun held in his outstretched arms as if by a miracle another bullet would appear in the chamber.

I peered around for an escape with Hub. The time was now or never. Some of the followers had parted to our left as they swept around to contain the young boy. His feral eyes burned as he kept his turning motion. I nudged Hub with my elbow and gave him a head shift to let him know what I was thinking. We might be able to make it to the trees and disappear into the thick brush. A slim chance. I gazed at the hundreds of young followers and my determination waivered slightly.

Lady Six Sky stood with a tight grasp on her fancy spear. Light danced off the feathers of her collar. Her superiority never faded from her eyes for a split second. She watched the young boy like a cat watching a mouse.

I tapped Hub and signaled with two fingers to let him know we were running in two seconds.

A chilling scream bore into me. I turned around. A six-foot wooden spear poked out of the skinny boy's chest, streaked with blood along its sharp tip. Deadly. A guard in her twenties gripped the wooden rod tight with outstretched arms, a determined madness set on her face.

A caw like that of a strangled bird sounded from above to my right. I glimpsed the horror in Hub's deep eyes and open mouth as I turned. My sight found the source. Atop the pyramid, the boy who missed the target in their ball game knelt below the two guards who had taken him away. His neck was craned skyward; both of his bound wrists drooped over the top of his sweat-soaked hair.

The chubby-faced guard raised a crescent-moon-shaped blade of a powerful ax above him. Her top teeth bit into her bottom lip, and her eye sockets darkened to hollow orbs. The other guard stood shocked in fear.

I dropped my gaze downward as I heard the whoosh of speeding metal through the air. The shuffle of bare feet on soft earth gave a quiet rumble as the abducted girls backed up in horror. An open path formed. The boy's severed head rolled across the pathway and stopped several feet from where the other boy lay sideways, impaled with the thick wooden spear.

Many of the girls let out high-pitched cries despite Lady Six Sky thudding the nonlethal side of her spear into a flat granite stone. A whimpering, soft thunder crept through the crowd. Sobs and tears stuttered in the heavy air.

Hub embraced me and began sobbing. I patted his back, unsure of what to do.

Mosquito Sands

Another clack from the queen's spear brought us back to reality. Everyone was watching the sight as the soft soil darkened and absorbed the two crimson pools.

Three of the boys on the bench panicked and sprinted through the murmuring crowd. They barreled forward, knocking down girls as if running for a touchdown at a football game. Most of the young girls were so upset by the blood-spattered carnage in front of the queen they barely noticed the three runners. The boys crested the hill and began a downward plunge toward the open space below. One tripped then righted himself after several end-over-end rolls. The other two surged ahead.

They were almost to a stand of trees and the freedom of cover when several successive shots rang out. One by one they dropped into the dusty soil of the rim of the road just feet from the thick forest.

I scanned the grounds through the high-pitched rumbling of confusion. A lone sniper, tall and lean with braided hair that tumbled down her spine, stood in the bed of a Ford pickup with her Smith and Wesson M&P15T with its crimson trace laser. A stream of smoke rose from the barrel and dissipated into the mountain breeze.

In a pickpocket maneuver, I slipped my hand over and around Eagle Tat and grabbed her gun in a swift, breezy motion. She was too involved with the murmur and the grotesque sights to even notice.

With instinctual stealth, I grabbed Hub by the elbow and motioned him sideways in a slow, careful escape. We weaved through the shocked stares of young girls. Some had dropped to their knees at the sight of the boys; others held a pompous, unfeeling glare; still others stood proud and lifted their heads high. We moved five feet, then ten. At twenty, I could almost feel our escape being possible. My eyes focused on a worn path that threaded its way into thick jungle. Hub followed like a lost child as he clung to the gown, they had given me.

I noticed a few of the captured girls were speeding into the brush on the other side of the hill. One turned and glanced back with fear then dove into the bushes. I saw five scurrying through a small clearing and darting into the jungle on the far side.

Other girls stood in shock around the horrid scene. A few seemed to relish the sight. The eyes of the two boys left on the bench leaned forward, scared to death to move from the bench, even though they undoubtedly wished for strength to run.

"We'll need to come back for Seronia," I whispered to Hub. He didn't seem to even notice I had spoken. Sweat poured from our brows. Hub glanced back. His eyes widened.

234

40

Carson

Hub turned back, shook his head, and continued to hurry. His widened eyes scanned the guns, spears, and reeds attached to the guards' belts.

I nodded toward the safety of the forest. "We can't help her if we're dead," I said in a breathy whisper. His slight hesitation told me that he wanted to run back for her.

"I know she's close." Hub pointed to a tiny, stone building to our left just down the hill. Vines clung for life to the ancient stones. The building sat at the crest of the hill where the forest had been hacked away in a crescent cutout around the structure. "Carson, the feeling is strong." His palm patted his chest.

The melee of screams and thumping feet rose behind us. This disorganization couldn't last forever. The guards were so busy they hadn't noticed us. Yet. Against my better judgment, I followed Hub down a deep ravine toward the disregarded building.

We came around a moss-green corner. On a wooden porch, a girl sat with her back to us flinging a string into the air and laughing. She sat alone. The string was tied to her finger and undulated in the air as she flicked her wrist. The string flung out, giggles ensued, and she clapped her hands against her belly. The bulbous cheeks and deep-set happy eyes were unmistakable. It was Seronia. Alone. Her guards had forgotten about her and had joined in the inquisitive sight of murder—the type one doesn't want to see but can't help themselves.

She had wandered off.

My hand clasped around Hub's bicep, and I stopped cold. "Seronia."

We walked to her side. Threads of the emerald-green dress snaked in patches across her Goo Goo Dolls T-shirt. She didn't look up. The string whipped in front of her accompanied by her chortled glee.

Jef Huntsman

Hub wrapped his arms around Seronia and lifted her up. He danced in a circle with her legs flung out into the air. Her string roped around them. Her lips were tight as a jar lid. Her eyes narrowed, and a crease deepened on her forehead. Hub kept repeating her name as he twirled in pure joy.

"She doesn't like that," I stated.

Hub slowed and came to a stop. Seronia pulled away from him, her face red with anger. Within a second, she sat down and began flinging the string again. Her cheeks puffed as a smile spread. She began humming a playful tune. Noise and confusion circled all around.

Hub sat down in front of Seronia. "Do you remember me? I'm your father's friend." He let out a loud breath. "I stayed with Juan Diego for nine months a few years ago."

With the mention of her father's name, she began flipping the string harder. Her smile disappeared. She watched the string with intent as her hand movements quickened.

"I want to take you back to see Toro, *el puerco.*"

She stopped flinging the string. Her chin dropped to her chest. She made a long, guttural sound. With her chin still on her chest, she rotated her body. Her eyes sparkled slightly.

"She thinks Toro is here." Hub shot a look at me then back to Seronia. "No, no; Toro is back at the village." He made a hopping motion with his hand.

We waited. I could hear hurried voices from behind the building up by the pyramids and the shuffle of hysteria. It sounded as if all hell was breaking loose. Two shots rang out. A guard stood at the edge and pointed down at us.

"We need to go," I urged.

Hub held out a flat hand to me. His gaze never left Seronia. "Toro, " he said.

"Hub, we need to move." I began to walk around him to pick up Seronia, maybe throw her over my shoulder if need be, and run as far and as fast as I could.

Hub held out his arm in front of me. Adrenaline surged through my veins. My muscles were as tight as twisted rope.

"Toro." Hub's soft voice came out in compassion and trust. Hub put out his long arm to her, his hand cupped.

Seronia glanced over at Hub's feet. She grasped his hand with her fingertips. The string on one finger hung loose at her side.

Mosquito Sands

From my periphery, I caught the sight of camo and the brown and yellow belt of a guard just yards away, hidden behind a carved stone. The barrel of a gun glistened between the branches. Her arm signaled behind her as Hub stood up with Seronia.

I lurched toward the figure. My one hand reached for my pistol; the other outstretched hand went for a thin, auburn neck. I heard the click of a trigger as my grip tightened around the pistol. My movements were too slow, but my momentum surged forward. The click sounded off—a misfire. A miracle.

At that second, my curled knuckles struck the neck of the guard. A crunch. She tumbled backward, dropping the gun. I grabbed for her throat. The gasping sound of her searching for breath squealed from a crushed trachea. I didn't wait to see if I could help her. I motioned Hub, and the three of us sped for the shelter of the trees and brush.

Within seconds, bullets buzzed around us like a dislodged hive of bees. The thick vegetation was our cover. Bullets thumped into tree trunks by our side.

41

Carson

Seronia and Hub took the lead. She was a fast runner. They made it to cover seconds before me.

I jumped over firehose vines at the edge of the small clearing. I turned and heard the chatter of leaves and branches being flung back about twenty feet behind. I caught glimpses of them as we headed deeper into the thick vegetation. My lungs burned. We were literally running for our lives.

Seronia had never looked at either of us in the eye as we started our journey up the hill into the jungle. She surged forward in fast, mechanical steps. She had endless energy and a sense of where to go. Her twine wiggled in the air behind her like a loose kite string.

There was a loud, bass thump like a rocket, then a whistle, and a smoke tail that moved over us. From behind, fireworks burst in the sky like lit flowers leaving trails of amber, red, and green. We stopped. Another thump and more fireworks came from the opposite side. I motioned to Hub to keep moving. My vision scanned the animal trail we had found and followed.

Out of the brush about twenty-five yards up the slope stepped Maria. My Maria that was supposed to be back home.

I stopped, blinked hard, and looked again. For a second, I thought I was seeing things. I wanted to yell to her but knew better with our tail close behind.

A double-barrel camo shotgun was tightly gripped in Maria's hands. Little Jim poked his disheveled head of hair over his perch on a gray boulder and waved with what appeared to be a 30:30 rifle. Maria's smile lit my heart then torrential fear poured through me. *What is she doing here? I can't let her get hurt*. My cheeks flushed as I watched Hub and Seronia getting closer to Maria. I climbed the hill twenty yards behind them. In heightened chivalry, I turned to verify any trouble that boiled

Mosquito Sands

behind us. They were coming like ants up a disturbed mound. The sounds of crunched twigs and voices rattled the warm breeze.

They weren't quick, but they were persistent. The soldiers wearing camo pants and white T-shirts were forcing the movement of their labor force from horseback like driving cattle. My heart thudded. They were using the workers for foot soldiers—as the first killed.

A streamer whistled then fire exploded in the sky. I suddenly figured out where it was coming from. Harold Sims's goofy smile posed on another hill to Maria's left. He lit another rocket, and it sailed into the sky.

The approaching hundreds below slowed with their faces to the sky. Horses reared. Some soldiers fell backward. Through the trees, I watched their eyes widen then shift from girl to girl with mouths open, legs twisting as they tried to decide whether to go on or run back to safety. The guards on horseback yelled at them.

With a flap of my hands, I yelled for Maria and Little Jim to run. She smiled with a shake of her weapon above her head. Shit! She thought she was John Wayne. Her mouth formed "Hurry!" as another rocket boomed above.

Harold set off more rockets then waved to me like a friendly neighbor over a white picket fence.

Hub and Seronia reached Maria, and they hugged briefly. For once Maria appeared happy to see Hub. I paced up the hill about thirty yards away and to the left of the group, trying to lead the mass away from them. My lungs burned, and my breathing came in hurried draws. My ears caught *"Vamanos"* from my rear. The girls slowed with the onset of more fireworks showering above the trees. I knew without turning that they kept pace with my heels. Close enough for bullets.

My foot caught a loose rock, and I tumbled to my knees. I grasped the earth with my fingers. The ground crumbled, my feet slid on the soft, fertile earth, and I lost any forward momentum. With a glance back, I spotted a solid bush and braced my sliding foot against it. Powered by adrenaline, I plunged forward toward Maria.

Orders were barked from behind scared screams as rattled brush seemed to closed in.

Maria stepped down the slope toward me. Eight feet away she reached with an outstretched hand, her mouth wide open, her brow raised in deep furrows. I shook my head.

Someone grabbed my foot from behind. Maria's face twisted in horror. My chin plummeted into the steep ground. Air grunted from my lungs. Hands clutched my ankles. My nostrils sucked in the smell of unwashed females, gunpowder, and black soil. My face scraped on the earth. My hands clawed at loose soil

I heard more voices approach. I dug one boot heel into the soft ground and kicked with the other. I connected. A wail echoed behind me. The grip loosened from my right foot. Hands wrapped around my left and shimmied up to my knee. Immediately, someone's fingers dug into my right leg just above the boot. I tried to twist and grab my pistol from the cloth belt on my purple robe.

At this point, I didn't care if I killed a young girl or two. My anger swelled at this whole mob. They were rabid. A fight-or-flight response soured through my lizard brain. The branch I had clung to loosened and released. I clasped the leaves and spongy bark in my hand as I dropped, scrapping my cheek across a half-embedded root.

42

Carson

A shot rang out. Pellets sang above me like bees from a hive. Their grips loosened. Dirt clods crumbled, rolled, and trailed down the path in the background. I felt a trickle of blood curl down my neck.

"Girls. *Chicas* . . . Stop. *Detienen ahora*!" boomed Maria.

I shook the dirt from my face and with one eye spotted Maria. Her shotgun was raised in the air. I had seen that look before. It was the one that made me slump into the couch and wait until the storm settled. She could be a force.

In her mad Spanish voice of total command, Maria thundered, "Girls, we are here to set you free. Who wants that? Lady Six Sky is nothing. She is not a sorceress. Think of her cruelty. She's not even Mayan. She's not a queen. She has no power." She paused and raised her rifle. "You have the power, the power of numbers."

I gazed back over all the girls spread across the open grassy hill and the ones who from the thick stands of green jungle. Jaws relaxed, mouths open, long slow glances were exchanged. They paused.

"Let us get you to your homes and families and loved ones. You are not work horses. You are not an ass in the fields for this cruel bitch," she blared in both Spanish and English.

A thick murmur crept up the hill.

Lady Six Sky's guards poised on their horses at the jungles edge. Their rifles stretched over the saddles. Their faces were unsure. A stern-faced young soldier in white t-shirt and camo pants began shouting orders to capture the intruders. Another yelled, "Their talk is poison." Other soldiers joined in—not all, but most. They moved their steeds forward. They screamed at the farm and ranch girls to pick up their weapons. Shots were fired into the air.

Discontented yet scared looks washed over the working girls' faces. They murmured to each other in a roar that increased in volume. They stopped on the rise below. I saw groups of workers in the clearing behind the guards. Unintelligible shouts came from the thick trees.

A rocket soared from where Harold lit it and landed in front of one of the groups of horses. Sparks flared. Several of the horses reared up, dumping soldiers onto the ground. Other horses shuffled backward then bucked in fear.

The sound of the workers swelled like rolling thunder.

Maria pulled the trigger and the blast of her shotgun rang into the sky. In Spanish she boomed, "We are hundreds. They are few." She stared at the soldiers. A flock of chattering geese flew overhead. "I count thirty-three guards down there. That's what keeps you here! You're hundreds. Break free."

I dug my way up the hill toward Maria.

A shot rang out. I heard it buzz past me, and reached for Maria, trying to get to her before more bullets could. I heard the sound as a volley embedded into the ground just a yard from her feet. I was hopeful. Then I saw that blood soaked her arm.

Another gun fired, this time from above me. It was Little Jim. With his well-aimed long rifle, he put a bullet square into the forehead of the soldier who fired at Maria. That jolted me. I had no idea he was a sharpshooter—either that, or he had more luck than anyone possibly could. I'd heard Little Jim was ex-military. The soldier dipped for a few seconds then fell from her horse in slow motion.

Several of the guards retreated on their horses down the path toward the complex. A few took a stand and lifted their rifles. Little Jim picked two of them off with precise shots. The girls began stampeding toward the guards on horseback. They carried pitchforks, hoes, long sticks, and knives. Some had pistols. The remaining twenty guards followed the first group retreating down the hill, meeting more who were coming from behind.

I watched the trees shuffle and listened as grunts and groans echoed through the dense part of the jungle.

Maria had moved toward me. I could smell her sweet perfume before I turned around. My breath caught as I watched her long, black hair silhouetted by the sun. We embraced. A warm flush paraded through my body, the one I get when I haven't seen her for a while. My eyes raised up the slope over her shoulder. I spotted Little Jim, twenty yards away, with his rifle angled across his chest. Harold stood on the far hill as he eyed the mountainside with a sweeping rifle.

Mosquito Sands

I gave Maria a loving kiss on the neck and we separated. "Where's Hub?" I asked. My hand tightened on the pistol I held. "Where's Seronia?" my throat became dry and constricted. Maria's lips dropped their puffy smile as she turned with crescent-moon eyes.

Little Jim turkey-necked in every direction. His face darkened in shades of red. "He was right there." Little Jim climbed up on a black stone that jutted out from the ground like a single devil's horn. At the top, he released his binoculars from around his collar. As if spitting at the earth, he said, "Seronia was with him."

Maria and I raced up game trails through the jungle incline.

"I see Seronia," he yelled. "She's broken through the jungle where the trails intersect to the right of the large pyramid."

I pulled out my binoculars. She was headed for a barn about three hundred yards away and down a dirt trail. A group of farmworkers were beating on a-t-shirted guard at the open door. The guard's arms and legs flayed as she tried to get away. Seronia quick-stepped in a happy jaunt down the trail. She was off to see the wizard in skipping flight. I scanned behind her into the forest and noticed a ripple of trees and birds taking flight.

Seconds later, Hub exited the thick green brush that lined the perimeter of the forest. He stopped. His body swiveled from his waist. From his vantage point he couldn't see Seronia. I watched him do a shaman thing he had done many times before. He knelt on one knee and tented his arms above his head. I knew from past experience that his eyes were closed. He told me once it was his way to tune in on others' thoughts. His spiritual compass. If his vibes (his word, not mine) were positive, he would find a higher level of understanding to decipher than if those thoughts came to him from peril, loss, or anxiety. I had asked him why he would mentally search for someone who was content and happy. He stated the purpose is to read them and hopefully hear their soulful cries. I left it at that.

Seronia was halfway down the trail now. A few of the ranch girls were following her like ducks after their mother.

When I spotted Hub again, he was racing south to the trail fork Seronia had taken. His shamanism blew me away at times.

"Keep an eye on Seronia and Hub; I'm headed after them," I yelled to Little Jim. I barreled down the hill.

"I'm with you," Maria shouted, barely behind me.

Maria and I slowed down a bit as we left the open area and headed into the jungle. Some workers lingered on the hillside. Others raced after guards. Branches swatted at my elbows. Vines grabbed my feet, and I almost lost my balance. We ran through shades of emerald, teal, and lime, thick and seemingly never ending.

We finally found a trail that made movement faster. It opened up under a grove of trees with thick vines climbing up octopus-like trunks. Two of the workers stood and drew knives as we barreled through. When they realized we weren't guards, they smiled and sat back down.

Maria darted ahead as we came out of the thick growth and ran through a carpet of high grass. I tripped and tumbled forward, landing on my shoulder where a bullet had pierced years earlier. I grimaced and grunted between clamped teeth. Maria kept up her pace.

She yelled back with a hint of sarcasm and truth, "Pick up the pace."

I flipped myself up and ran again with one hand rubbing my shoulder and the other grasped my pistol. I could feel the grin on her face as she raced further ahead. She really thought this was some contest? I groaned.

Maria slowed and held out her palms to the sky. She peeked over her shoulder at me.

I caught up and pointed to the east over an embankment of wild, yellow flowers. Within a short time, we arrived on the path I was pretty sure Seronia had taken. I couldn't see any sign of her or Hub. I peered up the hill at Little Jim. With his fingers raised, he signaled the universal sign for okay. Taking a deep breath to ease my raw lungs, I took off. Maria had left seconds before. She was a good eight strides ahead with her shogun pointing the way.

We were on a gentle downhill slope that rivered between stands of trees. I spotted a few of the workers off to the side. The girls' faces were worn and lost. They almost seemed to be waiting for the next order. As we rounded a bend, the trail opened, and the thick group of trees ended. I could see the barn. Two beat up soldiers lay on the dirt to our right. There was a hive of activity in front of us where the farm workers were in a frenzy, darting everywhere, without any purpose that I could ascertain.

We stopped and gazed back. We could see no sign of Little Jim or Harold. I couldn't spot the black outcropping Little Jim had been on. There hadn't been any fireworks for some time. I decided to worry about Seronia first.

As we got closer, we watched more groups of workers with

distraught, lost faces. Some ran wild looking for guards; others sat inanimate, their bodies swaying in the breeze like the trees they huddled behind.

Maria asked several of the wandering workers if they'd seen *Mapa Chica*—Seronia. They all pointed in different directions and said the Spanish equivalent of "maybe over there." Maria pursed her lips and let out a long breath. Her eyes dug for relief in mine.

I tried to look optimistic, but by her facial response I figured I just looked like I had indigestion.

I headed for the barn. Maria side-stepped over to the corral next to it, signaling with a nod of her head.

A horn bellowed from the pyramid above.

"You check the stables for Seronia; I'll head up to the pyramids in case she's there."

I shook my head at Maria, but she'd already sprinted up the trail.

43

Carson

A slice of light cascaded onto the barn floor from a loading window high on the west side. The rest of the interior was all shadows, empty stalls, and stacked bales of hay, everything infused with the acidic smell of dung. I closed my lids to help my sight adjust to the dark. My feet inched along the inside perimeter. Two girls peered over the bales and screeched as I approached. They ducked down, and it sounded like they were muffling their cries with their hands. Their fear twisted at my heart. Slowing my approach, I put the pistol in my belt and raised my palms in front of me.

In a gentle whisper, I said, *"Chicas,* it's okay. *No problema."* I stopped. *"Yo soy amigo."* I needed Maria here. My mind soared back to *Señora* Ramirez, my high school Spanish teacher, the one with the vaporizing scowl and a growth on her thin nose that would be the envy of most witches. I needed to find the right words for these girls, and *Señora* Ramirez's face kept popping up and fueling my nausea. Ahhh, *ayudar* something. *"Quiero ayudarte,"* I said with a passable accent. "I'm here to help," I repeated in English in case I'd blown the Spanish.

After what seemed like an eternity of seconds, one of the girls raised her nose over the top of the bale. Her eyes went from untrusting to maybe. Tears shone in the dull light. Her shoulder nudged the hidden girl. Soon, two half-faces peeked over the stack. One mumbled something in Spanish. I had no idea what she said.

"Amigo." I patted my chest.

Two heads turned. Eyes searched, first each other, then at the tall mangy guy in the absurd purple robe with his hands spread before him. Brows lifted under thick strands of coal-black hair.

"Amigo." That seemed to work, so I tried it again.

They slowly stood up. One was pear-shaped, the other rounded like an egg. The egg-shaped girl questioned, *"¿Amigo?"* Her mouth was tight, her stance apprehensive. Her knuckles bulged, and her tightly clamped hands held a pitchfork, tines pointed in my direction.

"*¿Mapa Chica? ¿Busco Seronia?*" I held out my arm, hand flat, to indicate Seronia's height.

Shrugged shoulders.

"She was kidnapped *por Dama Seis Cielo.*" I marched my arms back and forth as if running. "She came this way. I'm trying to find her."

My English confused the girls. Their faces went from puzzled to exasperated.

"*¿Seronia tomado?* Taken?" I tried again.

Their necks craned, and they glanced at each other as if sharing a secret they would never tell. Their shadowed faces grimaced, and it looked like thoughts were rolling over them. In a conspiratorial whisper, they both smiled and said, "*¿Mapa Chica?*"

The two girls smiled. It was a tight grin, as if they were swearing at their parents.

"Yes, *Mapa Chica.*"

"*Por las puercos.*" The egg-shaped one pointed in a circle around the barn.

"By the pigs? *¿Puercos?*"

Elation got the better of me, and I stepped forward to hug them. The pitchfork came up. My euphoria sunk like a popped balloon, and I backed away. With a nod and a smile, I exited the barn. The pitchfork, still held in a firm grip, poked the air.

Maria went this way—maybe she found Seronia, I thought, looking around for a pig pen. I found only two lone colts, one nestled on straw at the far side, the other erect as he poked his head through the wooden timbers. I couldn't find Seronia or Maria. I stood on the second rung of the corral fence and tried to get a better view.

Cirrus clouds covered the sky in a veil of muted light. I saw riders on horseback racing off miles away. Groups of teens, under the rush of escape, held garden tools high in the air and cheered. Ten or so workers had stopped a black vehicle, and several were bouncing on the hood or trying to break the glass with farm tools. Fires raged through a section of tan wheat.

My eyes focused on a gray wooded pen just below the corral that was surrounded by scrub oak. Sudden movement in the pen caught my attention. I hopped over the top rail of the corral and headed in a straight line toward the gate on other side. The two colts bolted for the far corner. With haste, I yanked the latch on the gate and sailed through. I sprinted to the grey wooded pen, which was about twenty-five yards down a slight hill. My peripheral vision caught a glimpse of fluttering blue and gold cloth. I turned to see Lady Six Sky hurry up a trail and disappear behind a building. I considered chasing her but decided instead to check the most logical place for Seronia. Thoughts of her being safe in the pen were clouded by fears of her being hauled away in another car to who knew where.

A dozen pigs filled the pen; some had their own stalls. A wooden roof with gaps between each board provided shade from the southern sun. The pen was laid out in a sizeable rectangle with water troughs. Scattered throughout were leftover cornstalks, carrots tops, and overripe apples. The rebellion must have broken out right after the pigs were fed.

A piece of torn cloth fluttered from a nail head just outside a separate pen I hadn't noticed. A giggle floated on the air from inside the pen, its high pitch breaking through the snorts and rumblings of the larger pigs. I peered between the roof and the top rail of the separate pen and saw two bare feet. As I angled my head, I saw three tiny piglets gathered on Seronia's lap. Her muddy smile was a gift to my pounding heart.

"Seronia." A lightness rose in my chest.

She was too busy and happy with her little pets to even glance up. I watched her for several seconds.

Out of nowhere, I heard the boom of a rifle and then a scream. *Maria?* My chest tightened. I made a quick decision.

I turned to Seronia. My hands motioned for her to stay. "Seronia, do not move. I'll be back." I turned and ran.

Like a rodeo bull blasting out of a chute, I rammed the gate with my shoulder. Screws popped out of the latch, and I headed in the direction of the shot. I could hear a snorting pig following me in my pursuit. Two more shots rang out through the high bushes to my right. I stumbled into a farm girl laying across the trail. A puddle of blood pooled from her chest. I checked for a pulse, but her vacant eyes told me everything. I slowly laid her flaccid head to the ground. More shots rang out.

With my pistol in front of me, swaying like a windshield wiper, I headed up the meandering trail that cut its way through stands of bushes, trees, and unused buildings. I came to a *Y* where the trail widened and leveled out. A crowd of young worker girls huddled around two bodies. Tears flowed. A chorus whined, filling the air with abandoned sadness.

One young girl was dead; another had lost some blood, but as I examined her, it looked like she'd be okay. Luckily the bullet to her gut had exited straight out without bouncing off bones. One of the girls handed me a skirt; I ripped some strips from it and hastily wrapped them around her middle. I showed a sobbing girl where to put pressure on the wound. She wiped her eyes and did as she was told. Thoughts of Maria surged through my mind. *Was she Okay? Who shot these girls?*

"Get her to a doctor—*Medico*," I said.

"*¿Mapa Chica?*" said one.

"She's fine. Just get your friend to a doctor."

"*Mapa Chica es doctor*," she said.

I had no idea what she meant, but I had to find Maria. "Who is shooting?"

The girl that found the skirt said, *"No pello de padre de Seis Cielo."*

"*¿No pello?*" My mind funneled through my limited Spanish. "Bald. Oh, the father of Lady Six Sky."

"*Si, pello. Señor* Caldera," she tapped her head.

Three more shots echoed down the hill.

I sprinted up the trail. *So, that crazy Señor Caldera is the shooter.*

I turned into an open space where vehicles and horses had trampled small shoots of grass. I could barely make out the bald, tanned head of *Señor* Caldera in the crowd. A dozen girls pummeled him with kicks as he curled himself on the ground. His gun sat twenty feet away. His hand reaching for it without hope.

The body of one girl was spread face down a few feet to my left. I flipped her over. Her lifeless eyes stared into the heavens above.

I glanced up to see the gang of teens dragging *Señor* Caldera along a path toward a dark-gray, octagon building. Mayan writing was along the wide facia, and carved black panthers with red eyes stood ready to pounce from each of the eight corners of the roof. Two sculpted birds with massive beaks graced the sides of the entrance.

I recognized the place now. I remembered the birds from when Hub and I were walked into the sunlight from the pit where we had been imprisoned.

The girls entered the dark opening with *Señor* Caldera. He was being dragged by his shirt collar screaming. His one free foot kicked at the dusty earth.

"Wait!" I yelled. The girls didn't even slow down. Maybe they didn't hear me, or maybe they didn't care—I'm not sure which. I needed to interrogate him. He knew of other places where young slaves were kept, and I wanted all of them to be released. Then I wanted to break his neck.

My eyes searched for Maria. Everything was chaos. Sounds and screams everywhere. It was hard to make a decision.

44

Carson

I finally ran to the opening of the panther building. From my periphery I spotted something move in the bushes. My gun was already out as I dropped and rolled. I saw the glint of a gun, a rifle that seemed to be aimed at me. I crawled through the tall grass off the path. Ahead sat an island of forest not much bigger than a neighborhood park. I eased my eyes upward and caught the sun's reflection off a long barrel. The air smelled of gunpowder and jungle.

Suddenly I heard a drawn-out giggle about ten feet away. It was Seronia's laughter, but she wasn't alone.

How did she get here so quickly? I spotted a thin trail that ran straight from the barn. My mind raced. Was someone holding her hostage in the brush?

I waited in silence. A twig snapped to my left. Summoning all the strength in my legs, I angled up and shot forward. I rammed a white-bloused girl and sent her tumbling backward. Her M-4 carbine flew into the air and landed yards away. I lifted my gun to her temple, straddling her. Seronia, a few yards away with her back against a tree, played with her three piglets. They were no bigger than full-grown hamsters. She was absorbed in her world and paid me no attention. I sighed, relieved she was okay.

The filthy, white-bloused girl screeched at me in Spanish, her words filled with venom. My Spanish was fair at best, and her high-pitched volley of words eluded me. Her arms were pinned under my legs as her hands tried to rip the flesh from my belly.

I grabbed the girl's hands and slammed them to the ground. A soft hand touched my forearm. Seronia had set one of the piglets down and was patting my arm. Her calm face eased my pounding veins. She carefully lifted my wrist with her fingertips and nodded to the girl with a smile. The girl's features went slack.

Jef Huntsman

The girl asked me, *"¿Eres su amigo?"*

Her words startled me. "*Si*, I am her friend." I patted my heart and eased my weight off her.

"¿Eres su amiga?" I asked.

"*Si*, friend."

"¿Como se dice?" I asked.

"Mari. Mari Contango." She replied.

I helped her up and smiled at Seronia then retrieved the gun for them.

"She like *puercos*." Mari pointed at Seronia. "I was trying to get her out of here."

Suddenly my mind changed gears. This was a friend of Seronia. "Stay here. *Por favor, Aqui*. Hide in the bushes. I'll be right back." I stomped my foot on the ground. "I need to check on *Señor* Caldera."

Mari shuddered at the word *Caldera*. *"No pello hombre es muy mal."*

"Yes, he's a bad man. I'll be back. Stay." I motioned with my palm for her to sit down by Seronia. She did. The piglets squealed.

I wondered if *Señor* Caldera was dead by now. I assumed he and Lady Six Sky, or whatever her real name was, were the only ones who knew about all of their complexes. I needed information from one of them. I thought about Maria and gave something I never do—a silent prayer.

I raced through the bird entrance. It was pitch black. I tried to find matches or a torch. Nothing. Finally, I crept along one wall with my hands serving as eyes, hoping the way would lead me to *Señor* Caldera and the girls. I heard a bellowing up ahead; as my hands felt around a corner, I caught a flicker of light down a long corridor. I approached with caution.

A torch lit the wall in front of me. The room opened into the shape of a large donut. No girls, no *Señor* Caldera. I leaned over and searched the pit where Hub and I had been held. My neck tensed at the memories of those days. All was dark. I grabbed one of the torches and held it over the edge, careful not to lean too hard on the flimsy wooden rail.

There at the bottom of the pit was *Señor* Caldera, curled in a ball and speckled with blue mosquito sands. If my memory served me, he would be of no use for a couple of days. Blue dust splattered the pit floor. They must have tossed him into the pit and shot the sand in after him. I wondered if they'd given him too much. Maybe he would never wake

Mosquito Sands

up.

I helped Seronia gather her piglets in her cradled arms. They squirmed and fussed then settled with closed eyes. Mari seemed relieved. We headed toward where I thought Lady Six Sky might be if Maria hadn't found her first. I kept finding and losing people; Hub, Maria, Seronia, not to mention Harold and Little Jim. My stomach twisted. I assured myself that I would eventually find them all.

I knew I'd hate to be an object of Maria's wrath when she was hopping mad at whoever set up Seronia to be kidnapped. Maria had a soft heart for kids, especially young teens like these and the ones she helped every day.

I caught sight of the tip of the pyramid with the wooden post on top. A deep tightening of my gut told me something was up ahead. I didn't want to lead Seronia and her friend Mari into a place I couldn't protect them, and I didn't want to leave them where they would be unprotected.

To our right in the trees stood an adobe hut with vines creeping across its face. Like most autistic children, Seronia hates to be touched, so I signaled with my hands for her to follow. Her eyes scanned her piglets in protection and love, and she followed. The piglets squealed and bounced in her arms as she walked behind. Mari grinned. The piglets seemed to be enjoying the loving attention.

The adobe hut was half as large as a single-car garage. It had a simple wooden door, one window, and a lattice of sticks and palm fronds for a roof. The room was empty except for yellowed paper refuse and hardened bird droppings on a crumbled shell floor.

I told Mari and Seronia to wait there and started to step out. Suddenly, I heard hoofbeats racing in our direction, and I backed myself behind the door. Seconds later, three soldiers in their camo and white uniforms dusted a path on horseback as they sped past us. All had rifles, but they seemed to be running *away* from something. Sure enough, twenty-plus teens armed with rakes, shovels, and determination ran after them. Roles were moving in reverse throughout the complex.

I waited until they all passed and crept out, following the edge of the path. Soon the trail opened, and I could see the pyramid again. On top of it, Maria and Lady Six Sky faced each other. I heard the sturdy clack of the spears as they bashed into each other. Maria was backed against the post in the middle. Lady Six Sky bellowed in an unrecognizable language. Maria's face gritted with determination and a contained madness I'd never seen before. Maria slipped closer to Lady Six Sky and tagged her on the cheek with the dull end of the spear. Lady Six Sky reared back, raising her spear like a weightlifter. An unworldly scream came from her open mouth; her teeth glistened, and her lips parted like a panther on attack. Her hips twisted, and she clipped Maria on the shoulder, the blade cutting Maria's flesh.

I sprinted forward. Within seconds I was at the base of the pyramid, climbing up and over the large stones.

Maria gouged at Lady Six Sky, missing her with most thrusts. Lady Six Sky was in her element. She knew her spear and how to use it. She thrust it downward. Maria screamed in pain. A drizzle of blood reddened her black hair above her ear.

I lost sight of the two. My legs ached as I vaulted and lifted myself up over the large steps of the pyramid. It would have been so much easier going up the other side with the stairstep ramp that shot to the top. My pants under the purple robe were ripped, and blood moistened the frayed edges. I moved with everything I had, but my strength was dwindling. I heard Hub's voice from down below.

"Carson, you're almost there!"

I could hear the terror in his cracking voice. I launched myself up onto another ridge. I couldn't see the end, but I could now hear the rantings of Lady Six Sky. There was no sound from Maria. I knew she was alive. She had to be.

"Carson! Hurry!" Hub howled in a tone filled with so much anxiety I thought my heart would explode.

I peeked over the edge of the last rise and could see Lady Six Sky standing tall. The tip of the spear rolled across the horizon. My chest constricted tight against my ribs. My dry throat gasped at the hot air. I reached for a better hand hold to raise me over the top where Maria lay still. Her spear settled loose across her chest.

Lady Six Sky's eyes met mine. My foot clamped on the edge as I raised myself over. Lady Six Sky moved towards me. Her deadly spear, reddened with Maria's blood, came at me. I rolled to the side, and the spear dug into the hard, earthen top. I fumbled for my gun but couldn't find it. Hub was screaming below. Without missing a beat, the spear tip slide through the air and I knew it was heading my way. I couldn't get out of its path quickly enough. Lady Six Sky's torso twisted. She packed everything into the swing of the blade. Her costume was colorful, her eyes black as evil itself.

Mosquito Sands

A rifle shot rang out. Blood spurt. Lady Six Sky spun backward, and the tip of the spear left a wake of air as it sailed past my face. Another shot and her arms rose to the sky, her feet lifted from the ground. She curled backward, up and over the edge of the pyramid. I watched her feet slip over the edge. I heard a thud, heard her body roll, then heard another hard thud. Then nothing.

A flock of geese in *V* formation flew overhead, their honking breaking the silence.

I raced to Maria. Crimson crawled over her shoulder, ink-blotting her blouse. Her neck was askew, and blood oozed from a gash on her head. Instinctively, my two fingers went to her throat. A faint, perfectly wonderful pulse radiated through my fingertips.

I cradled her in my arms. "Maria, Maria. I'm here. I love you." My voice was shaky, hoarse, and dry. Everything else around me had disappeared. Her chest rose so slightly it was almost unnoticeable. My eyes stared at her beautiful features.

One eye lid opened—black eyelashes fluttered. I gulped in an excited breath. She mumbled something, and I leaned down closer.

"What did you say?" asked Maria.

I smiled in relief. "What? What did I say? When?"

I waited.

The other eye opened, and she raised herself into my arms.

"Stay still. I'm not sure how badly you're injured."

Maria whispered, "That bitch knocked me out." She reached up to her head and rubbed. "Big headache." She gazed back at me. "So, what exactly did you say?"

"What?"

Her face pulled tight and serious. "You said 'I love you' without provocation."

"Well, I did think you might be dead."

She furrowed her brow and squinted her eyes in that playful way. "That's supposed to make me feel better? You only love me when I'm dead?" She reached up and yanked my ear as if trying to tear it off. "This is the first time I haven't had to ask you to say it. This is monumental. And all I had to do was almost die."

"Okay, I love you, I love you. Can you let go of my ear?"

"That's all I asked." She smiled.

Suddenly something occurred to me. *Who shot Lady Six Sky?*

45

Carson

Hub's dirt-speckled face popped over the edge of the pyramid. He was hunched over, his hands fiddling with the neck of his shirt. Behind him was Police Commissioner Jaime Zapata in all his colored-badge glory. Sweat coated Zapata's face in a shiny shellac. As I watched him lean forward to catch his breath, I wondered if I'd need to give him CPR. Four officers trailed him, guns pulled. There was barely enough room for all of us on the plateau of the pyramid.

"How is the lady?" Zapata asked, nodding at Maria.

"Fine. *Bien gracias*." I glanced over the edge at the body of Lady Six Sky. "Someone's a good shot."

Zapata glanced back at his men. "I have always been good with a weapon." He patted his shiny, holstered pistol proudly.

I smiled. I knew it was a rifle that had shot Lady Six Sky not the commissioner's showoff handgun. I glanced at two of the police, who were holding rifles at their sides. Something lodged in my chest— distrust.

"Where is Seronia?" Zapata rubbed his chin.

He *did* know about Seronia. I knew he was lying when he pulled us over outside Copomo. He knew about Lady Six Sky the whole time. I glanced over at Hub. He raised his brow. He knew there was more to this than a happenstance. Hub's eyes pointed to the guards.

Was Hub forced up here? I watched the guards with suspicion. Something was up.

"Thank you," I said. "I'll get Maria taken care of. It's fortunate you arrived." I walked toward the steps that lay just behind the commissioner and his four men. Their eyes followed me like prey.

"I thought you were looking for a young girl. Seronia, wasn't it?" asked Zapata.

Not too clever. He already forgot he'd asked about her. "She wasn't here." I walked between him and his men with Maria in my arms and my pistol concealed below Maria's billowed blouse. Hub followed.

Zapata's voice roared from behind me. "Drop that gun!"

I paused and looked back. All four of his men had their weapons leveled at us. Maria let out a gasp. This wasn't going to turn out well. "Who are you, again?"

"Drop your guns." He nodded at Hub. "You too."

I slipped mine out, held it by the barrel, and dropped it onto a tuft of grass on the first step. Hub did the same with his small .22-caliber.

Zapata peered at Hub's pistol and burst out laughing. He said something to his men, and they all chuckled.

I glanced at Hub.

Hub's lips pinched together. "He asked them if the *Americano* was out hunting canaries with that silly pistol."

Zapata stood with his hands on his hips, elbows out. His uniform strained at the seams. "I am the *Comisario de policia,* and I am the owner of this enterprise." He gestured past the farm to the gigantic ranch house. His chest puffed out. "That is my little home."

I knew he was involved. His expanded ego couldn't keep it in. I wondered who else knew.

"That's not Lady Six Sky's home?" Hub blurted in astonishment.

"She had a room there along with that stupid father of hers." His eyes scanned the countryside.

Guards and workers still hustled about—not working, but wandering like ants in a frenzied, lost search. I saw some huddled in hiding in the trees and behind buildings.

"Where is Enrique Caldera anyway?" Zapata shook his head. "You made me kill my best asset, though Dorthea was becoming a bit of a liability. Her craziness could only go so far. She was out of control. Killing workers with a damn spear. She thought it was nothing to bring in more workers as if they were lining up for the privilege." He peered back over the compound. "Can you believe that bitch? She truly thought she was a reincarnated Mayan queen." His arms crossed his ample belly. "The idea of Lady Six Sky worked for a while, though."

So, Lady Six Sky's real name was Dorthea. It didn't fit. His men probably aimed at Maria. I was glad they were such terrible shots. I let the commissioner ramble as I eased down a couple of steps with Maria in tow. I didn't have a plan, but I knew I needed one. With four guns on us, I wasn't about to try to retrieve my weapon. And I didn't want Maria damaged any more that she already was.

Zapata motioned with his chin to hurry down the pyramid. His officers prodded us with their gun barrels.

I was happy to move on. There was too much open space atop that pyramid; it was too easy to be a target. I stepped further down the stairs. Hub followed, then the two with the rifles, then Zapata, then the other two. I moved a touch faster than the guards to put a bit more distance between us. They didn't seem to notice.

I reached the bottom with Maria in my arms. The guards quickly closed the gap between us. Crap.

"You three are going to take me to Seronia. She has a gift, you know. I'll need that to rebuild." Zapata talked to himself as much as to us.

"What good will she do?" I asked. "Most of the girls have run off." I watched his eyes narrow and detected just a slight nod of his head at the guards.

The butt of a rifle slammed into my skull. My sight blurred. I tried to hold on to Maria, but my arms went limp. Everything turned black.

I woke up to the sun in my eyes. The barrel of a rifle pressed deep into the side of my nose. My thoughts stirred in a miasmic mush. I tried to focus but my vision drifted, and agony pounded like a woodpecker at the back of my head. I took in a shallow breath and felt the bile rise.

After a minute, Maria's voice trotted through my mind. It was fast-paced Spanish being spat out from some distance away. I couldn't make out the words, but I knew the temperament behind them. The barrel slid across my cheek and smacked into my ear.

"Ariba."

I made out the shape of the man who stood over me by his imposing shadow. It was one of Zapata's men—a tall man with a mustache that hid his upper lip. The cords of his thick neck fanned out like the base of a tree trunk. I eased to my elbow and turned my head. Zapata and his other deputies stood at the bottom of the stairs. Hub helped Maria. Her face grimaced with each step. Her legs wobbled, but her mouth worked fine. She yelled at Zapata while pointing one finger. He seemed to ignore her, which was a feat unto itself. I sat up on one of the stone layers of the pyramid.

I stood on unsteady legs. The earth reshaped in my eyes. It took a full minute and two whacks from the gun to my shoulders to clear my head and start to return strength to my legs. With shacky breaths, I robotically moved away from the pyramid.

The sound of a flat hand on skin resounded in the near distance. I glanced up and saw Zapata standing over Maria as fire burned in her eyes and her face reddened from his slap. Propped on one arm, her body was twisted in a stare at him. Hub stood next to her trying to calm her down. Zapata gazed up at me with a smile.

Anger flared, I thought about turning my body in one quick motion and grabbing the gun from the deputy behind me, but I was too dizzy. There was another significant problem: the deputy's finger grasped the trigger, the safety off, and the eye of the barrel was pressed into my skull. It was too high for me to safely yank it without my brains being splattered all over the steps behind. *Maybe I could suddenly slow down and cause him to get bunched up on me.* That way he might raise or lower the weapon. I dismissed the idea; it was too risky, and I was still a touch hazy. *Maybe I could drive my foot back into his kneecap with enough force to make him tumble. That might work.*

The sound of a gunshot clobbered me out of my thoughts. It was a high-powered rifle shot from the jungle above the big house at least a mile away. The reverberated sound was distinct—it was a fifty-caliber gun.

The head of the deputy at Zapata's left exploded. His rifle dropped, and his body followed. Another shot blasted from the distance, and the chest of another deputy burst. Blood and lungs sprayed into the Mexican air behind him. I rolled to the right as his body fell to the ground where I sat coiled.

Zapata crouched down, pistol drawn, hands out in front of him, eyes big as softballs; he scurried like a mouse for cover. The other two guards had sprinted in different directions, hands in the air and chins tucked to their chests.

I heard the zing of the high-powered bullet pass just behind Zapata. It seemed to raise his black, bushy hair. I ran for Maria, who laid on her side. Fear streaked her features. Hub had his arm around her. I helped them up, though they protested. Their heads swiveled in a mantra of *No's.* Their mouths tightened to their teeth.

"It's okay!" I yelled. I knew if whoever was shooting wanted us dead, the deputies wouldn't have been shot first. I glanced in the direction from which the fifty-caliber had come. Monkeys shrieked from the far hill, birds flew to a safer place, and helmeted men with weapons drawn in riot gear were barreling from the underbrush toward the ranch house.

With both of my arms cuddled around my friends, we headed down the trail to where I'd left Seronia and Mari Contango. The whirr of blades caught my attention, and I glanced over my left shoulder. Three black helicopters banked over the hill behind us, *Policia Federal* stenciled behind an open door. The legs of three helmeted men with weapons hung over the edge.

One helicopter dropped in an arc to land on the flat ground west of the pyramid. It bore a star circling an inner shield with the letters *CNR* at the top and *Policia Federal* stenciled in white at the bottom. The other two helicopters separated and swooped over us as if doing surveillance. Over the ground, hundreds of young women and a few boys scattered like a disturbed ant bed. Faces of both fear and hope darted aimlessly. Eight men decked in riot gear and bulletproof vests jumped out of the landed helicopter, rifles in hand.

"They took long enough," said Maria. She was walking mostly on her own now. She brushed back a strand of dark hair that had fallen in a curl around her nose.

"You knew about this?" I pointed at all the black figures rampaging through the camp.

"I called *mi primo*, Daniel, in Mexico City after talking with Harold about where you were headed. And Juan Diego recited his vivid shamanic dream. I had to be here. I was afraid you were headed into something bigger than even you could handle. Daniel is the head of the Mexican Department of Agriculture for President Obrador."

"He's the *Maiz* man? asked Hub.

Maria glared down her nose at Hub. "He plays golf with several top men in the *Policia Federal*. I told him about Seronia and about the two main compounds you described to Harold. He made calls, and here they are." Her chin lifted, and she smiled proudly at me. "I always have to save your ass."

"Yeah, we were a little outgunned," I nodded. My girlfriend came to save me.

Her hand came up, and she pinched my lips together. "Two words. All I'm looking for is two words."

I feigned ignorance.

She began opening and closing my mouth with her delicate fingers. "You can do it. Don't make me reach inside there and yank them out.

Remember, I've been battered."

"Ouch," said Hub.

I took in a dramatic breath. "Thank you, thank you, thank you."

"And you thought you couldn't do it without exploding." Maria limped away happy.

I heard a short squeal of pain. Maria crouched over and stopped. "I could use some help."

In two strides I was at her side with my arm around her, lifting the pressure off her injured leg.

"Thank you."

My eyes widened in fake surprise. An elbow jabbed me in the stomach.

"Shut up." Maria gripped my arm as she felt another shot of pain. Her neck cords tightened. Through gritted teeth she said, "Let's get Seronia."

46

Carson

The door to the adobe hut creaked slightly as I opened it. Light angled over to the corner where Seronia and Mari leaned against each other in a sleeping huddle. One piglet's eye popped open and peeked at us. Then its eye shut, its head dropped, and its pointed ear flopped down across its head.

I peered back at Maria.

"Well, wake them up," Maria said. "They're not staying here."

The compound was overrun by *Federales* from Mexico City. We wandered through the melee of assault-dressed police, dust, and buses loading young worn-out teenagers to be interviewed and sent home. The brainwashed guards were marched to a separate area beneath the fake Mayan pyramid. Some seemed relieved, others stood defiant and smug. They would probably be interrogated in Mexico City.

As the seven of us, including the piglets, walked on the south side of the pyramid, I watched Maria's eyes scroll up the side and rest on the peak. She inhaled deeply then hobbled back in line with us.

Hub strolled over with Eagle Tat and Boston.

"The men in black finished interrogating these two." Hub spread his arms, and his hands rested on their shoulders. "It took some heavy negotiation, but I was able to get them released to me. I'm going to make sure they get back to the states." He slapped his pocket. "If I could find a cell charger, I'd call their parents right now. Can you imagine their surprise?"

"Hub, that's incredibly sweet," said Maria.

Hub's brow lifted. "A compliment?"

"Don't get used to it." Maria smiled.

A row of buses stormed over the road below sending out a serpent of dust and diesel smoke. The squawk of radios cut through the compound, and helicopters searched the hillsides. The place looked like a military invasion—which it was.

Harold and Little Jim came out of the tree line to our left. Harold had the barrel of his long rifle behind Zapata. Little Jim prodded Zapata with a two-foot rocket. The federal police ran over and took the grim commissioner into custody.

Maria held my hand as we waited for our whole group to merge. My eyes met hers.

"Does this count as our vacation?" I asked.

Maria pulled her hand from mine and an elbow struck my sore rib. I gritted my teeth and didn't complain.

A tall, handsome man in a suit and scuffed black shoes wandered over and embraced my girlfriend.

"Daniel!" Maria shouted. She gave him a peck on the cheek.

Maria turned toward me. "Let me introduce you to the . . . love of my life."

"There was a hesitation in that," I said as I shook Daniel's hand. "I understand you are the head honcho of agriculture in Mexico, and you're the reason for all the men in bulletproof vests." I waved my arm over the valley below. "As a token of my appreciation, I give you a farm and a ranch."

He laughed. "I'm sure we can find a use for this land. After we confiscate it."

"Thank you for listening to Maria and sending in the troops."

Daniel nodded. "*Mi primo* Maria is very persuasive."

"What about Zapata and his police force?" asked Hub.

Daniel tented his fingers at his chest and exhaled. "Pandova, the head of the Mexican *Police Federales*, tells me three police departments of three neighboring cities will be disbanded. Some will be prosecuted; others may just lose their badges. Zapata and his brother, Candova, oversaw all this, but he paid off several other police commissioners as well."

"Zapata's brother?" I asked.

"Candova was supposedly on vacation with his wife in Brazil, but the hotel room was empty. The *federales* searched for him everywhere. He's the one with the keys to all the money. We'll find him."

"This operation grows and grows, doesn't it?" I asked.

Daniel nodded.

47

Carson

Poblano chilis and mutton sizzled on the outside grill, and fresh dough was being rolled out and fried for tortillas. The smell of sagebrush and manure swept over us as I helped Juan Diego clean the horse stall and take the dung in a wobbly wheelbarrow to his garden.

I heard Maria's sing-song laughter as she watched Seronia play with the growing piglets while Toro eyed the whole group with discontent.

Seronia selected one piglet and lowered it down on Toro's reclining side. He gave a shake, and the piglet tumbled but was caught in Seronia's quick hand. A snort blew dust into the air. The boar kicked his legs, and six hundred pounds slid a few inches on the dry earth in protest.

Hub yelled over to us that lunch was ready. Perdita slapped his hand when he took a bite out of one of the tortillas he had just cooked. He smiled, and she glared at him with a shake of her head.

We all gathered around a picnic table set up under a lone tree.

Hub held up his can of Pacifico and waited for us to quiet down. "A toast to Seronia, the strongest-willed and happiest young girl on the face of the earth. You've made Juan Diego and Perdita incredibly proud."

Seronia paid little attention to the festivities. She cooed at her three piglets as she fed them from her plate. Her cute giggle had all the villagers watching her from their doorsteps.

I stood. "And to the newest daughter, Mari, who is the best sister Seronia could ever hope for." Mari grinned but kept her eyes focused on her plate.

Mari's parents had been killed while they searched for her. Probably done by some of Lady Six Sky's most ruthless teens. After Mari's complete meltdown at her parents' vacant house, Maria's cousin, Daniel, called and let Maria know of the situation. She mentioned it to Juan

Mosquito Sands

Diego and Perdita. They didn't hesitate to ask if they could take her in. Within the day, she was flown to Balleza and picked up by Juan Diego and Seronia in Andre's truck. Juan Diego had filed paperwork to adopt her, and they were waiting for the bureaucratic wheels to turn.

There was a lot to be happy about. The forced labor camp was out of business. Most of the girls and boys had been returned home, though some faced murder charges. Almost a hundred rewards had been put out for the stolen children during the eight years since the first kidnapping. They had tried to give the reward money to me and Hub; we turned it into an education fund for all the kidnapped teens.

A lot of the guards were held on murder charges, though only a few were being prosecuted. It had been hard to separate the truly evil ones from the forced followers. Several police forces were disbanded; some of the police were taken to jail, others slipped away into Chile and were awaiting extradition. Most of the money from the second building at the complex had come up missing after all the dust settled.

A gunfight in the jungle had seriously wounded Zapata. He was sent to a prison hospital where one doctor takes care of 160 patients. He was convicted and sentenced within two weeks, a record-setting speedy trial ever for Mexico. His brother disappeared without a trace.

The Boston girls flew home to their parents.

A team of various therapists from around the world gave their time to the hundreds of kidnapped victims. Facebook was aflutter about their plight, and donations continued rolling into Go-Fund-Me sites that popped up like convenience stores. The girls and boys from the compound were back attending schools, going to dances, playing ball games, and hugging family.

The DNA of Lady Six Sky was tested, and it turned out that she was one Dorthea Sanchez from Nebraska. She was thirty-two, prone to illusions, and the daughter of two schoolteachers in Pilger, Nebraska. They said she ran away from home when she was thirteen and hadn't been seen since.

Señor Caldera was not her father, but her archaeology professor at an unaccredited college in Arizona. The two had moved in together and disappeared ten years earlier. The news on the internet quoted Dorthea's friend, Sandy, as saying, "She was totally out there crazy."

After a wonderful meal, Juan Diego pulled me to the side and gave me a long hug. "Your life is about to change," he said. His chubby cheeks sparkled in the sun as he smiled. He stared at me with an enormous grin, hands on my shoulders, a slight nod to his head.

"What are you trying to say?" I asked.

He patted me on the back and walked me back to the rest of the group. Confusion rose in my chest. I shrugged it off as I hugged Perdita goodbye, then strolled over to Seronia.

She had tucked herself against a tree below the corral with the three piglets sleeping in her proud arms.

"Seronia, we're leaving now," I said.

Her eyes watched her precious piglets.

"I will miss you," I told her.

Without glancing up, she pulled one of the piglets from her clutch. She held the squirming piglet steady then shoved it against my belly.

"No, no. I can't take this." I backed up. She offered it again to me with a soft sweet whine. Her eyes watched my shadow.

I moved in closer and patted the piglet. I was surprised. The skin was smooth and soft. I understood why she loved squirming little creatures. I smiled and held it for a minute then gave it back to Seronia.

Seronia giggled and put the squealing piglet down on her lap. The piglet nuzzled into the other two and silenced.

Hub rode in the front with Andres to the airport. Maria and I sat in the back, glad for the seatbelts as we tumbled over the desert terrain. Maria squeezed my hand and pressed her lips to my ear. She nibbled for a second.

With her mouth at my ear, Maria whispered. "I have us scheduled for that vacation you promised. We take off in two days."

I sucked in air. "But we only arrive home tomorrow, and you just barely got out of the Mexico City hospital." I pleaded with my eyes. "Doesn't this count as a vacation?"

Maria smacked my arm with her clutched fist. "Yeah, like that's going to count."

Mosquito Sands

ABOUT THE AUTHOR

Jef Huntsman is the award-winning author of several fiction and non-fiction books, short stories, and humorous poetry. He was voted Utah's Writer of the Year for 2017/18.
Jef spends most of his time writing from his loft, swimming, reading, or enjoying the warmth of a raging firepit at his ranch in central Utah.

Check out his website for his newest published works.

Jefhuntsmanauthor.com

Turn the page for an
excerpt from the
next Carson thriller
"Coyote Spill"
coming in December 2020

Jef Huntsman

Coyote Spill

"A CARSON THRILLER"

CHAPTER 1—COYOTE SPILL

Coyotes yipped up a storm just outside my bedroom window. Rough growls of dominance were interspersed with yelps of pain. I scrunched my eyes and snuggled closer to Maria, hoping the racket would move to another location. Minutes later, my teeth grinding in irritation, I curled my neck enough to spot the green illumination from the corner. The digital clock read 2 a.m. I pressed deep into my pillow, my palm crushing it into a foam horseshoe over my ears. The range dogs kept it up.

In frustration, the kind only a sleepless night can create, I released myself from the loving scissor-hold Maria had me in. The tone of her dreamy mumblings said, "Don't wake me up," though she uttered a one-word Spanish expletive. I couldn't believe she could sleep through the ruckus.

My bare feet landed on thick carpet as I sat up and stretched the kinks out of my spine. My eyes still fought against opening. The cool mountain air crawled along my bare skin. Sitting on the edge of the bed, I mentally brushed the dust from my mind. I rose with gravity crushing my every move and pulled back the camo curtains, glancing out the west window. Three coyote pups were fighting over what appeared to be a deer leg. Their high-pitched cries tightened the chords of my neck in irritation. I knocked on the window with my knuckles and shouted, "Shut up!" Maria released a drawn-out grunt. Their young growls buried the sound. Two of the pups latched on with strong jowls and spun in a circle for dominance. The third raced the opposite way with knife-edged teeth bared, waiting for its turn.

With brief thought, I slipped my Beretta out of the top dresser drawer. Living miles away from anything resembling a city, I always kept it loaded. I headed out the front door on the opposite side of my comfortable, small cabin.

I opened one half of my French doors. The night sky was star speckled with a waxing crescent moon on its downhill journey to the west. The canyon breeze rifled through my boxer shorts. Goose bumps prickled my skin. My feet padded down the stairs off the log railed porch and hit the gravel roadway. Walking in grey-blue moonlight as if gingerly stepping across hot coals, I tried to make my body lighter. My teeth bit into my lip with each step. I made it to the corner, wishing I'd grabbed my boots.

Jef Huntsman

The coyotes wailed and hunched their shoulders up. They nipped at each other, trying for control of the bone. I raised the revolver above them and fired. Feathered sparks burst from the barrel and the bullet buzzed over their heads into the field beyond. The coyotes curled their snouts around for an instant, glaring at me in surprise, then bolted into the sagebrush and Russian olive trees. Halfway there, the larger one tripped on a coil of loose barbwire. Its cache flew into the air and landed in front of a knee-high sagebrush. I listened as their barking retreated up the mountain.

What appeared to be a bloodied deer leg lay on the ground fifteen feet from me. I headed to retrieve it, to toss it in the fire pit in case another carnivore came to pick at it. A burr slid between my toes. "Crap!" Standing on one leg, I yanked the miserable thing from my now tender feet. The canyon winds picked up and caught my breath. I stood bare in the morning chill, except for the new pair of heart spotted boxers Maria had given me as a joke for my most recent birthday.

I was about to turn and just go back inside to my warm bed and Maria. An unsettling smell I recognized made my head jerk. I peered closer at the deer leg. My heart stopped. At the end of the leg were four chewed up fingers, attached to a hand. My pulse quickened. It was an arm, a human arm. Bile built up and I urged it down. My ranch turned silent and still as I gazed off into the distance. A slight moan came from my lips. I turned my averted eyes back to the ground.

The hand had been severely gnawed. Fingers hung loosely on bone and tendons. The thumb dangled on a thin band of skin. I stared. The sight took me back to Afghanistan for a few seconds to the sickening discovery of a body blown apart by a crazed martyr. But this . . . this was a child's arm, far away from those extremists.

I headed for the cabin, not even noticing the gravel and wood splinters tearing up my feet. With a shoulder shake, I woke up Maria.

"Where's your cell?" I half-shouted.

Her eyes, slanted open, burned into mine. Her lips puffed as if she had swallowed a lemon. "What the hell time is it?" she squeezed out between clamped teeth.

"Your phone. We have a problem. Mine's out in the Corvair, totally dead." I peered through the window to make sure nothing disturbed the arm.

She rubbed her temples. "In my purse or by the fireplace."

"Get up," I demanded and caught a look from Maria. I watched her brow tighten down over chestnut eyes. A low growl came from tight lips.

Maria hated being ordered to do anything. I ran through the bedroom door into the front room and flipped on the lights. Maria's phone sat on a tree stump we use for a table. I dialed the Sheriff's office in Gunnison, Utah. They were the closest real city, about ten miles away.

A serpentine stream of lights curled around the bends and shifts of the long gravel road from the valley below. It passed over the Sevier river bridge by the swamps. I imagined the sleepy ducks taking to the air in the upheaval. Maria and I sat on my front porch, which was bigger than my bedroom, drinking our second cup of coffee. I had on a blue Henley, Levi's, no socks, and a cap with a canoe stitched along the front. Two hours had passed since I'd made the phone call. I brushed the muffin crumbs from my unshaved chin and stood, watching the approaching vehicles.

"Looks like they're bringing the entire police department from three cities.

Coyote Spill

Probably the Sheriffs from Manti and Nephi, maybe Salina. I'd hate to be the one who woke them up." I leaned over the rail, dumping out the coffee grounds that blackened the bottom of my cup. "Sherriff Gunderson always acts like a stepped-on snake."

"He's always nice to me," she said.

"Different body parts," I replied.

"There's that. But he hasn't touched my shoulder since I bloodied his knuckles with a stapler. That was two years ago." Maria beamed with a satisfied grin, then her face quickly darkened. I'm sure the thought of the arm laying on the other side of the cabin had come back to her.

"I count four pickups and a cruiser."

"I'm not making coffee for the whole lot." Maria stood and came over close to me. Her onyx hair shimmered with the breeze. She had on paisley stretch pants, a man-collared shirt, and my windbreaker. Her head rested on my shoulder.

"When was the last time you even touched the Mr. Coffee here? Or that old pot in my cupboard?" I joked. A white owl with a five-foot wingspan circled the starry sky to our left. I was glad I'd covered the arm with my wheelbarrow.

"That's why they invented Seven-Elevens, stupid."

People tend to busy themselves or try to find humor when they're dealing with horrid situations. We are part of the second group.

I put my arm around her and gave her a loving squeeze. The first truck rattled over the cattle guard and began its swing through the trees that line the deep culvert above my property. The others followed as if tied to it by a long rope. A minute later, the procession roared through my open gate, slid around the pond and stopped to the south of my cabin. Four vehicles bumper to bumper, shut down. But the computers in each gave off an amber glow.

The dust billowed toward my porch. Maria ducked inside, muttering Spanish expletives. I covered my mouth with my shirt until the cloud settled. I wondered if they had even thought about where the arm might be when they barreled in like wild horses.

Sheriff Gomez stepped out first from the passenger side of a white F-250. An older officer exited from the driver's side, whose name I couldn't remember. Sheriff Gunderson from Manti, which lies over the eastern mountains, eased himself out of the next cab. He was followed by Sheriff Stone from Nephi, which is an hour north. The sedan behind them included Dr. Angela Treeton, who acts as the first phase coroner in this area, Deputy Bono, who could tilt a scale against a heifer on the other side, and Deputy Bille who walked like he was a year from retiring, which he was.

Sheriff Gomez scanned the ground in front of his city owned truck as if he alone would spot the arm. The older officer came up the stairs to my cabin and shook my hand. "Deputy Bille," he said. The others fanned out with foot-long flashlights. Deputy Bille pulled out a notepad and pen from his pocket. "So, Mr. Carson . . ."

"It's just Carson," a brittle voice came over my shoulder. I hadn't noticed that Maria had come back out.

Bille glanced at her. He tipped his hat. "Sorry madam. Okay, Carson where did you put the body piece?"

"Madam! Do I look like a madam to you?" Maria glared and crossed her arms tight against her chest.

Jef Huntsman

With a smirk, I grabbed Bille by the arm and began walking him down the stairs. "How about if I show you where it is." Maria is not one who likes to be woken up. She schedules her therapies for DCFS in the afternoons and evenings, just so she doesn't have to be one of those "obnoxious morning people," as she says. She barely tolerates my 7 a.m. rising.

Two more truck lights caught my eyes. They pulled into the sagebrush just outside my gate.

I walked down the graveled road in front of my cabin, the others spoked in toward me. Sheriff Gunderson greeted me with a handshake and a nod. He peeked up at Maria and put his hands deep into his pockets. It seemed he still remembered the stapler.

"Did you find any other signs of the victim?" asked Sheriff Gomez. This was his jurisdiction, but with small police forces they band together if there is a need, or a case that is interesting enough. I think this situation involved the latter, though in small cities the line is diffused.

"I didn't look further." I'd scouted around for a while, but with only a flashlight and a mere scythe of a moon, I hadn't found a thing.

They all eyed me as if I was taking a lie detector test. Sheriff Gomez waited for me to say more. Finally, he broke the silence. "Where's the victim?"

"It's just an arm. The child could still be alive somewhere." I nodded over to the other side of my cabin and moved in that direction.

"Wait!" a voice boomed. "Just point. We'll take it from here."

Gomez was new. The last sheriff had asked for my help several times in the past. Most recently, I'd found drunken Harold passed out in the duck swamp last year, barely alive. The head honcho of the force always pulls out a clean plate, instead of checking to see if there's a slice of apple pie worth considering on the plate in front of him. He would learn.

I had spent years in the marines, tracking and finding bad guys and prisoners in places like Afghanistan and Qatar. My expertise was useful in tracking missing civilians as well, either runaways, the abducted, or the deceased. My "extra-curricular activity" as Maria calls it.

I'm also the head of a company on the New York Stock Exchange that I started to dispense doctor's office posters on organic psychological abnormalities. In English, the posters help diagnose who are going nuts from physical problems. The business had developed into a worldwide on-line service for hospitals, physicians, psychologists and nurses. Other people run the company now, while I sit back on my cowless ranch and soak in the beauty. I still vote at PsychTeck, Inc. board meetings via skype.

"Under the wheelbarrow," I said.

"Where's forensics?" Gomez asked.

I snickered and strolled away. He meant the country doctor, Angela Treeton, and Deputy Bono, who had taken a few on-line courses in forensics. Angela was smart and had done a few autopsies on people who had passed away in their eighties and nineties, but she was mostly a healer. She had sewn me up many times and given good advice, which I rarely followed. A chewed-up arm was out of her league.

I had moved to the second step of the porch when I heard, "Did you shoot the

Coyote Spill

wolf?" I stood silent for a moment.

"Where'd Carson go?" It was Sheriff Gomez with his rough voice.

"I'm about to go back to bed." I stifled a grin. Now, he wanted information from me. The sun back lit the eastern rolling peaks in a welcoming thin glow of gold. Within twenty minutes, the mountains would stretch their stubby fingers across the valley, then roll their shadows back into themselves. It was the time of day that invigorated my decision to live here.

Maria half-smiled down at me, whispering, "You love to rile the authorities, don't you?"

"I told you to stay around in case we needed you." Gomez's voice boomed with irritation from the hidden side of my cabin.

"No, you told me, and I quote: 'We'll take it from here.' That sounded like a dismissal."

The crickets seemed to stop chattering while I waited for his reply. I could see him in my mind, eyeing the other sheriffs and deputies. I heard a door slam and noticed two more deputies getting out of the state-owned vehicles outside my gate. Pretty soon they'd be calling the forest ranger over at Yuba lake.

Gomez came around the side of the house like he could bulldoze gravel. He stopped below me. He is maybe five-foot six and built like an ox. He oozed aggravation as he looked up at my six-foot, tight-corded frame, standing on the steps towering over him by two feet. He spat chew to the side of the stairs. Then his eyes caught Maria's. "Sorry ma'am." He watched his shoes for a few seconds then turned to make sure the others were still around the corner. "Look, I know you assisted Hammond with a few things. I understand you did a lot of good. I don't approve of your tracking methods, probably never will, but we could use your help."

I grabbed the rail and eased down to the hard pack next to him. Hammond was the ex-sheriff. "Tickled to help."

He took one more peek at Maria. She dominated the porch with her arms crossed. "What happened to the wolves?" he asked.

Maria's phone rang, and she picked it up off the post where it laid.

I explained the events of this morning and corrected him about the young coyotes. He was from back east originally and didn't know there was a difference. "Wolves would have chomped that down in two bites. Coyote whelps or pups want to play with their food as much as eat it, unless they're starving. These appeared healthy and well fed. There are a lot of pheasants, rabbits, and quail around here, especially the last couple of years. But it's a cycle. Soon the hunters like bobcats, weasels, and coyotes will outnumber the prey. When food becomes scarce, the hunters will diminish and the prey flourish. The cycle starts over again."

"So, about the arm, any thoughts on that?"

Maria paced with a worried look washing over her face, the phone pressed hard into her cheek.

"Just what you already know. Somewhere, there's a body that was attached."

His face tightened, and he bit into his top lip. "That's what I'm afraid of. Have these coyotes been around before?"

"I hear them yapping and howling most nights, but seldom this close."

I heard my French door slam. Through the window, I could see Maria darting around, collecting things. She barged back through the door, her high heels clacking across the wooden rails.

"Mueve tus coches, idiotas!" Her hands batted in the direction of the police cars.

She always uses Spanish when upset or in a loving mood. The two ends of the spectrum are tightly related. However. even though my Spanish was rusty, her tone said everything this time.

Sheriff Gomez jerked as if having a heart attack. The others ran around my cabin to see what the ruckus was.

She stormed down the stairs. *"Mover movimiento!"*

"What happened?" I asked.

She turned. Her hands clamped in front of her. "Two of my girls from the Stardance Center have disappeared." Worry shadowed her face. "I pray it doesn't have anything to do with, this . . ." She nodded toward the grouping of police. The Stardance Center sounds like a ballet studio, but it hosts young girls whose parents think they are uncontrollable and pay to send them there for "treatment." Most of the girls feel abandoned, though some welcome the ridiculously scheduled vacation.

We parted as Maria jumped into her Rubicon. The engine roared. She honked, yelling Spanish profanities through the closed window. Uniforms sprang to move their vehicles in a panic.

Her Jeep backed up, gears ground as it leaped forward, she spun the wheels past the fire pit. The Jeep went airborne over an embankment, then the screech of branches on paint squealed through the stand of trees. She fishtailed through the ditch, around an open section of barbwire fence, spun around a Russian olive, and then raced through my field of wheat grass. Soon, she turned onto the two-track road. A cloudy tail of dust streamed from behind the Rubicon.

I turned back to the stunned cops with their stance set and mouths open. The trauma of the child was forgotten for a moment in the shadow of a fiery Spanish woman.

Fine clay settled over the wheatgrass and sagebrush, dusting it in shades of redish-brown. Sheriff Gomez tapped me on the shoulder. "Aren't those girls always running away?"

I glanced over his shoulder at the overturned wheelbarrow. My heart chilled as Dr. Treeton gingerly placed the small arm into a clear specimen sack.

Coyote Spill

9 780997 574869